A NIGHT OF ECSTASY

"You're good, very good, mademoiselle. I believe I shall get my money's worth."

She started to protest anew, to insist he had made a mistake; but when his hands moved aside the lace of the chemise that covered her breasts and massaged them, then laved them with his tongue, her fear dissipated and turned into a small flame deep within her. Slowly, so slowly she was barely aware of it, he slid the chemise from her until she lay naked beneath his heated gaze.

Her hair lay on the pillows like golden coins from a pirate's treasure; her lush ivory curves beckoned to him. Though she knew the situation was absurd, this man's touch had stirred her in a way she'd never felt in her whole life. Somehow she sensed he wouldn't hurt her, that the hardness in his eyes was from some horrible suffering, and she understood such pain.

Also by Lynette Vinet:
EMERALD DESIRE
EMERALD ENCHANTMENT

EMERALD ECSTASY

LYNETTE VINET

LEISURE BOOKS ☙ NEW YORK CITY

To
Martin
To
Jason and Jared
To
My Family

A LEISURE BOOK

Published by

Dorchester Publishing Co., Inc.
6 East 39th Street
New York, NY 10016

Printed in the United States of America

Chapter 1

"Ah, that one has the eye for you."

"Whatever are you talking about?" Lianne asked and slipped into the costume for the next scene behind the makeshift stage.

"Him." Paulette Dubois grabbed Lianne by the arm and pushed open the curtain a crack for the young woman to see. The faces of the audience blurred before Lianne for a moment, but his didn't. All through the first half of the performance she had been aware of his eyes upon her, watching her. He drank in every aspect of her beauty like the many glasses of champagne which passed his way. His looks unnerved her, and for a moment she faltered during her solo, able to continue only by gazing above the heads of the audience—beyond one dark head with eyes the color of the ocean on a rainy day.

But Lianne feigned ignorance as Paulette whispered, "The handsome one with dark hair, sitting next to the owners of Flannery Hall, the blond man and his wife."

"*Oui,* I see him," Lianne said and also observed Mr. and Mrs. Flannery seated next to him. It was easy to spot the young couple since this was their home and they were celebrating their fifth wedding anniversary with an operatic performance. Lianne knew Victor Dubois, Paulette's husband and director of the traveling troupe, considered this engagement the high point of his career. Paul and Allison Flannery were well known as lovers of art and music, and he hoped that they and their guests would praise the French troupe of performers so that commissions from others would come their way. It was Victor's dream to perform throughout Ireland for the wealthy and influential landowners who might not object to cheap costumes and scenery, loving opera for its own sake and overlooking the small company's flaws. But if they cared to make a donation . . .

"Perhaps you should make an assignation," Paulette said and stifled a laugh.

Lianne turned away and faced Paulette in a fury. "How dare you suggest such a vile thing! I am Lianne Laguens, Comtesse de la Varre. Not a prostitute for you to make an easy living. I refuse to have my honor violated for your gain."

Paulette's face turned from pasty white to burning scarlet. "You dare to speak to me in such a manner, you no account aristocrat! The other women in the company manage to please wealthy gentlemen and they don't feel their honor has been violated."

"Then the others are whores, as are you. If Victor's health was good, I'd gladly tell him about the men you've seduced, and the women who pay you a percentage of their whore's money. How a man as noble as Victor ever married a creature like yourself is beyond me."

Lianne stared her down with eyes which shot green fire, and when Paulette saw she would get no further with Lianne, she turned on her heels. "I know what it is like to please a man. Unlike you who sleep alone," she shot back and went to help the other cast members assemble for the next act.

Moving toward the stage, Lianne felt tears sting her eyes. Paulette's comment hurt her, wounding her more deeply than the woman could ever imagine. She did sleep alone, hiding her painful memories from everyone, including Victor whom she regarded as a father. Without Victor's support the last four years of her life, she would not have survived.

She remembered the day the rabble crowd stormed the gates of Chateau de la Varre. The peasants swarmed across the estate looting, destroying the expensive furnishings and objets d'art. Her husband André grabbed her hand in panic, and together, they scooped up their infant daughter, Denise. They fled their home for the countryside where he felt they would find safety. They traveled all night with a crying, hungry baby and managed to make it to a little farmhouse on the outskirts of Paris. The home belonged to Victor who had been André's father's best friend in his youth, and he offered them refuge as if they were his own children. Since Lianne's parents had died shortly after her marriage, Victor took the place of father in her heart, and when he suggested that they flee France and join his operatic touring company, she persuaded André to agree.

At first things ran smoothly. Lianne helped Victor with the costumes, the makeup, and André was in charge of the bookings. Soon Victor discovered Lianne had a beautiful voice and promptly trained her to become his lead soprano. André's pride in her and their love for Denise made Lianne feel that life was wonderful and held promise.

However, one night after a performance in an unsavory section of Dublin, a man in the audience approached Lianne and propositioned her. When she refused, he attempted to take liberties with her, but her shrill screams summoned André who was still backstage. He rushed toward the man, never seeing the knife which pierced his heart.

For weeks afterward, Lianne survived in a nightmarish existence, but she had her little girl to live for and pulled herself together for her. But within a year her child succumbed to fever. From that day on, Lianne kept to herself, isolating herself from everyone in the company. Many of the cast members thought her icy, distant and an aristocratic snob. The men branded her the "ice queen." Only Victor knew the full extent of her suffering, and she would have confided more in him, except he had recently married Paulette, a scheming conniver who had once sung with the troupe. When she proved not to have much of a voice, Victor decided she could please him in other ways.

Now as the murmurs of the crowd brought her back to the present, she decided to ignore Paulette and hide the pain which still gripped her. Tossing her hair which was the color of autumn leaves, she walked onto the stage, unaware that the handsome man in the front row had been handed a note by a servant. He gave her a searching look, then stood on unsteady feet and left the drawing room.

For the rest of the performance she sang beautifully, but her heart wasn't in it. The past caught up with her and Lianne doubted if she'd ever feel happy again.

After she took her final bow with the other cast members, she heard a noise and Victor suddenly appeared from the shadows of the stage when the curtains closed. Everyone milled about, eager to join the anniversary festivities to which the Flannerys had invited them, but Victor gently cupped Lianne's chin in his hand.

"Bad memories?"

She marveled at how well Victor understood her, and she rested her head against his chest. "Sometimes I wish to forget but then I'd be unable to recall my André's love or the happy expression on my baby's face. Yet it hurts so dreadfully."

His eyes expressed his sympathy for her, and he hugged her. "What you need is to enjoy yourself. Allow Leon or Maurice to escort you to the party. Have a good time for once, my dear. You must live. Don't bury yourself in your pain forever. André wouldn't have wished you to mourn for so long."

"I can't." She sighed but managed a smile. "I love you, Victor. More than anyone on earth."

Victor led her onto the terrace. He shook his silvery head, a grim expression on his face. "You're too young to care about an old, sick man. There are plenty of young men who would adore just a smile from you, a kiss. Don't throw your affection away on me, *chérie*. But I advise discretion. The company's reputation is important to me, and I won't have women of loose virtue working for me."

Lianne blinked her astonishment. Why would Victor think she might compromise herself and his company by having affairs? After all, she had loved only one man in her whole life and doubted if she'd fall in love again. If he should be suspicious of anyone, it was Paulette. However, Lianne kept her opinions to herself. She knew how easily Paulette swayed Victor into thinking what she wished.

"I'll never give you reason to doubt me," she found herself saying, wondering what had brought about this sudden change in his attitude toward her. On the one hand he wanted her to fall in love. On the other, he cautioned her to be discreet if she did.

At that moment Paulette came by with a half dozen costumes tucked over her arms. "Victor, I must have some help. Everyone has run off and left me to do all the work. These costumes must be packed in the trunks, and I should like to meet our hosts and enjoy myself for once." Her lower lip puffed out for a moment, and then her sly eyes slid to Lianne. "Could you please take these to the summerhouse? Mr. Flannery allowed us the space there for our trunks. I'd appreciate your help."

Lianne realized that Paulette wasn't about to be refused, and since she didn't have any plans to join the party, she agreed and took the costumes. Paulette only laughed and grabbed Victor's arm like a frivolous coquette without a word of thanks to Lianne. She seemed so unusually pleased that Lianne worried for a moment that something was amiss. She watched Victor and Paulette saunter away into the crowd of merrymakers and noted just how thin and sickly Victor had grown of late.

As she left the garden and meandered along the Shannon, the scent of roses and wildflowers drifted over her. Quiet, starry nights always brought memories of lying in André's arms beside the pond of Chateau de la Varre. She remembered tracing his lips, almost able to feel his kiss upon her fingertips, desire welling in her.

No, she mustn't remember! The pain of losing him seemed to have grown more acute, and she was tired of pain. She wanted to live. Live! With a strangled moan, she ran the short distance to the summerhouse where she observed a candle, which must have been lit by Paulette earlier, in the window. As she opened the door, the flickering light illuminated a long, low table which was set with fruits and delicacies to tempt any appetite. Even a bucket containing chilled champagne with two glasses waited on the highly polished mahogany surface. Lianne thought this strange since no one planned to use the small house except for the storage of costumes.

As she set the costumes down on a wooden trunk, she surveyed the rest of the room. Through the illumination of the candle, the blue and white settee, adorned with fluffy pillows, beckoned to her, and the Persian rugs in the same shade of blue cushioned her feet.

She felt such peace, as if a part of her had returned to the Chateau. Such a long time had passed since she had seen such beautiful furnishings. For a brief moment, she longed to recline among the myriad of pillows but knew she must hurry. Though the cast members were enjoying themselves, Victor would soon be rounding them together for travel to Belfast for the next performance.

With a little sigh, she opened one of the trunks and found her own dress and quickly divested herself of the cumbersome costume of Figaro's bride. When she reached for her own gown she heard the creaking of a chair in the far corner of the room.

Lianne turned. Her long hair swung around and covered her pale chemise in a riot of burnished copper curls. A shadowy outline of a man emerged, and she stood in stunned embarrassment, unable to move, barely able to draw breath.

He stepped into the light. The satin of his brown jacket gleamed as did the gray of his eyes. His hair was so dark that not even the soft candlelight highlighted it. He towered over her, and she was dwarfed by the broadness of his chest. As he drew nearer, she recognized him as the handsome man in the audience whose gaze never strayed from her face during the performance.

He bowed in perfect etiquette, but Lianne sensed he mocked her. The pungent odor of whiskey assailed her when he moved closer. Though he seemed steady, he slurred "Mademoiselle," and she knew he was drunk.

"What are you doing here, monsieur? This room is for the company members only. Monsieur Flannery has allowed us its use for our costumes and belongings."

"How magna . . . magnanimous of him. One can always count on Monsieur Paul Flannery to set things right." He took a swig from a bottle of whiskey at his side and motioned for her to sit down.

"I shall stand." Lianne held her dress closer to her, not caring for the glint in his eyes.

"As you wish. Take some fruit, whatever you wish. I had it sent for us." He smiled.

She moved away from him as he drew nearer. He was so close that she even noticed a tiny scar on his chin. "For us? I want no food, monsieur." Lianne felt the inclination to run, to flee before this man touched her because his eyes roamed over her like a hungry lion. "I'd like to dress and hope you will act the gentleman and leave."

The smile he had given her moments earlier turned into an ugly scowl. He set the glass bottle down with a thud on the table next to the settee. "Games! Why must you women play games? I know what you are, mademoiselle, otherwise I'd not be here. Your note offered an invitation as did your secret looks to me during the performance. I demand to sample your offerings."

"I don't understand, please . . ." Her voice trailed away as he threw off his jacket and grabbed her in one motion. His lips came down hard and furious in their assault of her mouth, and the liquor on his breath caused her to swoon against him in weakness. He growled low in his throat, mistaking her faintness for surrender, and picked her up in his arms and placed her on the settee.

Lianne's head cleared when she felt his body against hers, felt the evidence of his arousal against her thigh. Clenching her fists, she pushed at him and tossed her head aside to escape his passionate kisses. "No, please!" she cried and tried to pull her body from beneath his, but it was a futile attempt. His strength overpowered her.

His lips moved over her mouth, her cheekbone and sought the curve of her neck. "You're good, very good, mademoiselle. I believe I shall get my money's worth."

A sob escaped her, because she knew she'd be unable to fight this man off. She was too small, though she had always been taller than other women. However, he dwarfed her and practically smothered her with the strength of his body. What was she to do?

She started to protest anew, to insist he had made a mistake; but when his hands moved aside the lace of the chemise which covered her breasts and massaged them, then laved them with his tongue, her fear dissipated and turned into a small flame deep within her. Slowly, so slowly she was barely aware of it, he slid the chemise from her until she lay naked beneath his heated gaze.

Her hair lay on the pillows like golden coins from a pirate's treasure; her lush ivory curves beckoned to him. Though she knew the situation was absurd, this man's touch had stirred her in a way she'd never felt in her whole life. Somehow she sensed he wouldn't hurt her, that the hardness in his eyes was from some horrible suffering, and she understood such pain.

He watched her for what seemed like hours, but it was no more than a few seconds before he undressed. Though the candlelight was dying and shadows predominated, his powerful physique startled her. He seemed to fill the room with his manliness, and when his fingers touched her, she felt he burned a pathway to ecstasy across her wanton flesh. Never in her life with André had she responded so wildly to lovemaking. This stranger seemed to know her vulnerable spots, giving her the greatest physical pleasure a man could bestow upon a woman. Writhing beneath his hands, his lips, she parted her legs for his entry. The flame which had started earlier with his touch grew until a raging fire consumed her.

He held her buttocks in place and pulled her closer to him. "Hold me tight, *chérie*. Love me, Love me."

And she did. She clung to him as if he were her lifeline and she might lose him in a sea of desire. But with one final thrust, he sent her spiraling into the dark heavens and then joined her ecstasy.

She lay beneath him, panting and drained. A part of her wondered how this could have happened. He lifted his face from her breasts and looked into her eyes. *"Je t'aime, chérie. Toujours en mon coeur."*

Surprise flickered across her face that he spoke French.

She wished to say something, but words seemed

so inadequate. He rolled onto his side, holding her within his arms. Before long, he slept. She watched him, memorizing the arch of his brows, the aristocratic nose, the shape of the sensual mouth. She had shared love with this man, but didn't know his name, and didn't wish to. For one passionate moment, desire and mutual need had brought them together, but now their individual pain tore them apart.

Careful not to wake him, Lianne slipped from beneath his arms. He stirred, mumbling in his sleep. She dressed and headed for the door.

Lianne stepped outside. The cool April night caressed her hot flesh, and she breathed deeply. She must find Victor, flee this place and hide from her own desires. But a hand pressed firmly upon her wrist and looking up, she saw Victor staring at her in loathing. Paulette stood beside her, a victorious gleam in her eyes.

Instantly she knew they had seen her making love with the handsome stranger in the summerhouse, and she flushed so deeply that Victor commented, "Don't bother to be embarrassed now, Lianne, wife of my friend's only son. I asked for discretion and you act like a harlot the moment my back is turned. If Paulette hadn't suggested we see what was taking you so long, I'd never have known the truth about you. You have dishonored my company and me. I cannot forgive you or keep you with the troupe. I am ashamed of you, so ashamed."

His hands shook so badly that he stuck them in the pockets of his coat, then walked away without listening to her explanation. However, Lianne said nothing. She couldn't explain away what had happened, or make Victor forget what he had seen.

Paulette leaned toward her, face glowing in malevolent delight. "Now Lianne Laguens, Comtesse de la Varre, let's see how far your title and pretty voice get you without Victor. And don't worry about who'll replace you. I will be the new soprano after this night.

After all, Victor needs me to mend his broken heart and will do everything I wish." She pranced away to catch up with her husband.

Lianne stood outside the summerhouse, unable to cry, barely able to think, but she wouldn't go inside and beg the stranger to help her. She was a survivor and would take what life offered. The pain started anew in her breast, but not for André, not for her dead child. Now she had tasted real, passionate love, something she had never truly experienced in André's arms. And it was the idea that she'd never feel it again which hurt the most.

She ran into the darkness, along the Shannon and defied the fates which conspired to destroy her.

"I'll find happiness!" she cried over and over.

The fates did smile kindly upon Lianne that night. Within a month she knew she carried the child of the handsome, tormented stranger.

Chapter 2

"The bear's not moving," whispered the small, blond boy with large brown eyes. "I wish he'd wake up. He promised to sketch Mitzie."

"Shh, Douglas," the boy's sister warned. "Momma said we should leave Uncle Daniel alone. We're not supposed to be in the summerhouse. And Uncle Daniel isn't a bear."

Douglas looked at Kathleen who was as dark-haired as he was light, and different from him in every way. He shrugged. "He's as grumpy as one when he first wakes up."

Kathleen knew this to be true. Sometimes their uncle was out of sorts, but he was always kind and gentle with them. Many times he'd prop them beside him on one of their beds in the nursery and do quick sketches of them. Kathleen wanted a drawing of Mitzie, their dashshund, who was as much of a child as they were and just as spoiled, but she would never wake her uncle for such a triviality. Douglas, however, thought nothing of taking a goose feather from the pocket of his breeches as he was doing now, and gently passing it across the tip of his uncle's finely shaped nose.

"Maybe he's dead," Douglas wondered aloud in his nonchalant way.

"Let's leave before he wakes up, Douggie. I don't

want Uncle Daniel to be mad at us.''

The large violet eyes in her heart-shaped face rested for a second on the handsome countenance of her uncle. At that moment he looked quite disheveled as he lay sprawled on the sofa with a quilt thrown across him. His broad, fur-pelted chest and muscular arms were uncovered, and a thin shadow of a new morning's hair growth blanketed his chin. Kathleen smelled the scent of whiskey in the room and associated this aroma with her uncle. More than once, she'd mentioned this to her father, and her father said that Uncle Daniel needed it for medicinal purposes. Though she was past four years of age, as was Douglas who was her twin, and quite intelligent for her years, she thought that Uncle Daniel must be very sick to always require so much whiskey. Yet she loved him, and when his deep voice boomed in the tiny summerhouse, she startled.

''I'm not dead, but if I were, I'm certain that two nameless scamps would soon resurrect me.''

''The bear's coming to life!'' squealed Douglas.

Daniel opened one eye, then the other one, and he slid into a sitting position. ''My head,'' he groaned and put his hands to his forehead.

''Feeling ill?'' came the twins' mother's voice from the open doorway of the summerhouse. Allison Flannery walked lithely into the room. Though she was six months pregnant, she looked extremely lovely to Daniel's red-streaked eyes. She wore a simple morning dress of mauve taffeta with white ruching at the neckline and matching lace at the elbowlength sleeves.

''You can well imagine how I feel this morning.''

''Children, run to the house. Nanny is ready to wash you before lunch.'' Her command was directed to the twins, but her blue-eyed gaze rested sternly upon her brother-in-law who looked as awful as he probably felt. But she decided to feel no mercy for him. Not today.

Though Douglas pleaded and cajoled, he didn't throw his customary temper tantrum. Kathleen followed dutifully behind him, and when they were outside Daniel watched them from the window as they scampered to the house. He smiled despite his headache, but his good humor wasn't returned by Allison. "You and Paul have two hooligans," he commented with a half grin.

"Well, if that's the case, they don't take after my side of the family."

"You mean they have that wild Flannery blood in them. Douglas does, that's for sure. He's the image of my father. Kathleen resembles her grandmother Dera in looks and temperament. Perhaps she'll always be calm and serious like her. But gentle as her mother?"

Allison sighed her impatience. "Don't try to wheedle yourself into my good graces, Daniel. Not after last night." She picked up an empty whiskey bottle, her eyes flashing to the table set for two. "Do you remember anything about last night?"

Without self-consciousness he pulled the edges of the blanket about him when it fell to reveal a powerfully built thigh. "What did I do? Ravish you? That isn't a bad idea."

Though he said this jokingly, that is what he had always wished. He had loved Allison, but the relationship had changed when he realized how much in love she was with his brother, Paul.

He was smart enough to know that she had turned to him years ago out of loneliness, but Paul would always have her heart. He envied his brother the beautiful Allison, the healthy children, and their love. The memory of the kisses they had exchanged in Dublin when she left Paul and ran away with him, stirred something deep within his soul. However, now as he looked at her, and saw the gentle softening of her features, even the tiny smile playing unwittingly about her mouth, he knew he wasn't in love with her. That passion was transformed into a caring, considerate relationship over the years. Allison had never desired him, but still he'd always love her in his way. Seeing her pale beauty brought the image of Amelie to his mind. He didn't wish to think about his wife at the moment or, for that matter, ever again—if he could help it.

"I'm not here to cater to your prurient interests," she said and tried to hide her amusement, but her face grew serious. "It seems you bedded the soprano in Monsieur Dubois' troupe last night. The man was extremely angry. In fact he looked ill, and I feared he'd die on the spot. Paul helped him clear out the trunks in here. Daniel, I think you owe your brother an apology for embarrassing him with your bedroom antics."

"Apologize? Like hell! I won't apologize to him for anything I do! He's my brother, not my keeper."

"I'll have no more profanity from your lips, Daniel Flannery. You were wrong to do what you did, and I hope the whore you bedded knows it, too."

"She wasn't a whore!" he shouted and jumped up from the couch, tucking the quilt about him. "And my name is Daniel Flanders, not Flannery. How often must I remind you and Paul of that?"

She threw up her hands in frustration. "I don't care which name you use or whether you wish to be associated with this family, but please have some sensibilities about whom you bed and where."

Long vertical shafts of sunlight streamed through the windows, haloing Allison's white-gold hair. She looked so much like an angel that he calmed down, sorry for his anger. "I apologize. I shouldn't have embarrassed either one of you, not when you and Paul have been so generous as to offer your hospitality to his prodigal brother."

She threw her arms around his shoulders, not caring that he wasn't fully dressed. "I shouldn't have lost my temper."

Daniel smiled down at her, lost in the loveliness of

her face. They stood in loving camaraderie until they were made aware of Paul hovering near them.

"I believe we played this scene in Dublin once," he said in lieu of a greeting. His massive frame rivaled his younger brother's and the small summerhouse seemed much too tiny for the two of them together. Paul carried a whip and was dressed in dark boots and pants with a tanned shirt. He had just ridden from the tenant farms and his hair was windblown.

Allison giggled and pulled away from Daniel to enter the circle of her husband's arms. "Daniel has apologized for his scandalous behavior."

"I'd think he'd apologize for his scandalous attire."

"How can a person dress with an audience?" Daniel asked, knowing his brother wasn't really bothered by finding Allison in his arms. He didn't think he was a threat to their marriage. In fact Paul never really considered Daniel would take Allison away. Grudgingly Daniel admitted Paul was right. Allison loved only her husband and had eyes for no one else.

Allison blew Daniel a kiss, then kissed Paul soundly on the lips before her departure. Both men watched her cross the lawn to the house. "You're very lucky, Paul."

Paul nodded in agreement. "I nearly lost her once, in fact twice, but never again. She belongs to me."

Daniel grabbed his discarded clothing from the night before and started to dress. Paul poured himself a glass of whiskey and sat on a chair, long legs thrust out in front of him and contemplated his brother. "You really should curb your impulsive nature, Dan. If last night is any indication of things to come, I'd advise laying off the liquor—and the women. You're worse than Father ever was."

Daniel finished buttoning his shirt and turned in fury. "Don't categorize me with him, and don't think you're any better than me! Remember the two of you coveted this damned estate so much that you deceived Allison into marrying you to inherit, and Father was no better. Once he arrived here from Louisiana he couldn't bear to leave his ancestral lands and look where it got him. Six feet under.''

Paul shrugged. ''I've more than made up to Allison for my deception. I love her. She loves me. It's as simple as that. What about you? Why don't you go home to Louisiana, bed your wife? Perhaps then you won't have to tryst with opera singers in summer-houses.''

''You know I can't do that!'' Daniel's voice was strangled and at that moment he wanted to choke Paul. ''Amelie's condition prevents lovemaking.''

Paul swirled the dark liquid in the glass. ''I received a letter from Mother. She thinks Amelie is much improved and suggests that your wife is faking a bit for sympathy.''

Daniel stormed over to the half filled bottle of whiskey and helped himself to a heaping glassful. He didn't bother to reply to Paul. He knew Amelie was more than faking for a ''bit'' of sympathy. She wanted everyone to wait on her, to treat her like a queen, but he knew the seriousness of her paralysis. Amelie's condition was because of him and though Paul would never have guessed, because of Allison, too.

''She's my concern,'' he said at length.

Paul was fond of his brother so he didn't push the issue further. ''Tell me, was your little French pastry a delightful treat?''

''I don't really remember,'' he said and downed the contents of the glass. As he poured another one, he looked at his brother. ''Where was the troupe headed next?''

''Belfast, I think. I hired Dubois in Dublin for the anniversary ball, and he made mention that after the performance here, they'd most probably head in that direction. Why?''

"No special reason. Now if you'll excuse me, I'll go bathe and dress for lunch."

Daniel entered the manor and headed straight for his room where Allison had already ordered a bath. After undressing, he slid into the warm water and watched the shadows on the wall for a long time. He lied to Paul when he told him he didn't remember the woman he had bedded in the summerhouse. Their coupling was more than a bedding. He had made love to her. Love. Something he hadn't felt since Allison rejected him five years ago. And the woman with the pale, porcelain flesh had made love to him. He had been very drunk, but he remembered her with a clarity which startled him. Perhaps he remembered her because she was nothing like Allison or Amelie.

The years melted away and Daniel recalled how devastated he had been when Allison spurned him, how because of his disillusionment with his family, he swore to use the name of Flanders, not Flannery. Flannery was their true name, but his father had escaped from Ireland on false charges of murdering Allison's uncle who was also the first husband of Dera, Daniel and Paul's mother. Quint Flannery took the name of Flanders to hide his identity and then when he met Dera again and married her, they kept using the fake name in their new life together. However, when Paul married Allison and Quint decided the estate was now in the family, they began to use the Flannery name. Everyone except his mother, who still lived in Louisiana and called herself Dera Flanders to avoid confusion. Because Daniel knew how much pain the Flannery name had caused her and hated the double deception of his brother and father against Allison, he vowed he'd never be a true Flannery.

He had kept that promise. After Allison told him she didn't love him, he returned to Louisiana and paid court to Amelie Marchand, who lived at Belle Riviere, the neighboring plantation. Daniel had never been too interested in her before his trip to Ireland, but when he saw her again upon his return, she had bloomed into a beautiful, pale-skinned creature with blonde hair and light blue eyes. He wanted her because she bore a resemblance to Allison, the woman he could never have. Before his mother arrived as a widow from Ireland, he had already married Amelie and was living a tortured existence at Green Meadows.

Even Dera, who was kind and able to get along with everybody, could barely tolerate her. Amelie whined incessantly. When she didn't get her way, she threw the most awful tantrums. Worst of all, her tongue was sharp and she never seemed to know when a person had had enough browbeating. "Why don't you stop painting and spend time with me?" she'd demand of him. "Why do you spend so much time with the slaves? I want a new ball gown. We must go to New Orleans and order satin slippers. Where is that lazy Lallie? She should have been up to do my hair long ago."

She'd go on and on until he thought he'd go mad. His visits to the slave quarters to see his friend Claude, a mulatto, had helped him deal with Amelie. Claude always told him the mistress was just highstrung like a prize filly. She needed soothing and wasn't really as bad as everyone thought. Daniel didn't agree with him. Though he tried to assuage her, he couldn't stand her possessiveness or her temper tantrums.

The accident occurred one night after a particularly violent argument about a new hat she wished to order.

Daniel calmly told Amelie that she had enough clothes. She swore she'd get the funds from her brother if he was too stingy to dress his wife in grand style. Phillipe understood how important beautiful things were to make a lasting impression. Daniel told her that if she asked Phillipe for the money, he'd send her back home with her request. She had just informed him days earlier of her pregnancy, but at that moment he didn't care about her condition. This infuriated

Amelie and she threw a crystal vase at his head, missing him by an inch. This undid Daniel.

He strode across the bedroom floor and grabbed her by the arms and shook her until her curls bobbed free from her upsweep. "Never hurl anything at me again, be it a vase or a word, my wife. If you do, it shall be your last deed on this earth. How could I have married such a woman? You're nothing like Allison. You may look like her, but she's an angel, the only woman I shall ever love. Only a cruel fate could have allowed you to be the mother of my child."

He hadn't expected her stricken look or the terror in her eyes. Never had he wished to wound her so deeply. A part of him did care for her, but she required more of him than he could give. Without warning, she yanked herself free, her howls of desolation rising to the rafters. Amelie ran to the stables and mounted the wildest stallion though Claude tried to prevent her from leaving. She kicked at him and flew fast down the road.

Daniel and Claude rode furiously to catch up with her. Minutes later they found her sprawled and bleeding on the road which led to Belle Riviere. She not only lost the baby, but in the doctor's estimation, she might not walk again.

They began an existence as polite strangers. She never uttered another nasty word in his presence. She just withdrew into a private world which no one could penetrate. He expressed his sorrow, but she said it didn't matter, that he should do whatever he wished. So he did. He packed his bags, kissed his mother farewell and headed for France where he met the artist known as David who was about to take the French nation by storm with his paintings.

David introduced Daniel to Josephine Bonaparte, and he cultivated a circle of friends in high places. Josephine commissioned a miniature portrait of herself to be presented to Napoleon before he left for the Egyptian campaign. This led to many portrait commissions and a proposition from Josephine herself which he charmingly refused. He didn't wish to incur the wrath of Napoleon Bonaparte. But he did incur the wrath of many powerful men by bedding their wives and mistresses.

After a successful showing of his paintings in Paris, he grew weary of the drinking and the whoring. So, he returned to Ireland to visit his brother Paul, his half sister Beth and her husband Patrick. He discovered that Beth and Patrick had moved to Ulster, but Paul and Allison made him more than welcome in their home.

Up until last night, Ireland held no particular interest for him.

Now he found himself intrigued by a beautiful auburn-haired wanton. He didn't know her name, but he wanted her, needed to possess her glorious flesh again. Something had passed between them in the summerhouse, something beautiful and unquenchable. He remembered the sadness in her eyes, could still feel her warm body pressed against his own. The woman was his, the magnificent creature with the emerald eyes.

"I'll find you," he said to the wall before him and saw her face imprinted there. "And when I do, you won't flee me again."

Chapter 3

"This way, señorita."

Lianne followed the tall, tight-lipped servant down the deserted corridors of the palace, the crisp swishing of her green silk gown the only noise. The flickering wall sconces cast ominous shadows on the walls. A feeling of dread washed over her, and she wondered if she should turn around, go home, and forget this interview. But she had heard of Don Raoul de Lovis's reputation as a powerful man in Madrid and knew he wielded much influence with the king, as well as the Spanish nobles. Rumors circulated about how he had crushed promising careers or political aspirations with a shake of his head or a well placed remark to King Charles or Manuel de Godoy, his protégé. No, Lianne decided, it would not be wise to displease Don Raoul when he had sent for her. She had her child to think about now, and she was also curious why he should have singled her out from the other performers.

The servant stopped at an elaborately carved door. When she entered the room, he perfunctorily departed, leaving her to gaze in awe at the furnishings which surrounded her. A highly polished table was set with gilt-edged plates and gold eating utensils. Two brass candles illuminated the sitting area with its high-backed chairs. A few feet away parted drapes framed the door of the bedroom and gave her an unimpeded view of a large four-poster bed with white silk bed covers. Fragrant rose petals rested upon the silken sheets. Lianne averted her eyes, her palms grew clammy. She told herself she was being ridiculous. Don Raoul didn't know her; she'd never seen him. There was no reason the vision of the scattered petals across the sheets and the candlelit table should unnerve her. Don Raoul only wished to speak with her about her career. His message had expressed that thought.

She peered into the gilt-edged mirror. Her mind flew to another night after another performance. Even now in the dim candlelight, she saw the rosy flush creep into her cheeks. How wanton the man must have thought her! What an easy conquest! However, she had no regrets about the short time she spent in the stranger's arms. No matter what pain, humiliation or desire she'd felt after that night when she mentally relived each moment, she would never be sorry for giving herself to him. At that second, her daughter Désirée slept in her little bed with the faithful Maria Alvarez nearby for protection. Lianne couldn't imagine life without Maria's support. She'd been lucky to make the woman's acquaintance when she arrived in Madrid, six months pregnant and out of money.

Maria's humble lodges seemed like a palace. The room Lianne rented was small and in a rough section of the city, but it was clean and Maria, who took an instant liking to her, saw that she ate properly and got enough rest. Maria knew she had no money, and she waived the rent until after the baby's birth. When Lianne was physically able, she obtained a position with the local opera company. She wasn't the lead soprano, and only sang small parts, but she was happy and grateful to Maria who watched the baby while she performed.

A part of her still ached at the harsh parting words from Victor, but she decided things wouldn't have worked out anyway, not with Paulette spoiling things for her. She surmised Paulette had sent the note to the man in the summerhouse. Later, Lianne had been angry enough to murder her, but now realized Paulette had done her a good turn. If she hadn't sent the note to the stranger, her daughter would never have been conceived, and she loved her baby, who to her eyes was the most precious and beautiful five-month-old child in the world.

Désirée's hair was raven black, and her eyes were the color of a stormy sky. Like the stranger's. Lianne believed her eyes would stay that same translucent gray as a reminder of the man who had fathered her. A small smile curved upward on the finely chiseled beauty of Lianne's mouth at the thought of her child, but then she sighed. What did Don Raoul wish of her?

She walked away from the mirror and gazed out of the long window which faced the street. She drew her cape closer. Though she couldn't feel the night's cold sting through the glass, she shivered. She wondered what she was doing here and how long she should wait before Don Raoul put in an appearance. Shortly after the command performance that evening in the throne room, she had been handed the note in de Lovis's bold scrawl.

Until that moment she'd been excited to perform for the king and his queen, Maria Luisa, but felt a little like a voyeur to witness the queen's apparent fondness for Manuel de Godoy. Poor Charles sat like a small toad on a lily pad, away from his queen and protégé. Instantly Lianne knew the rumors about the queen and de Godoy were true. They carried on right under his long nose, and he never lifted an eyebrow.

The evening had been exciting until the servant handed her the note. De Lovis requested her presence in his private apartments, and she should be there promptly at midnight. Well, she was here, and he wasn't. Was he playing her for a fool? Why should

such a powerful man care about her operatic career?
Her part in the performance was minor—no cause to
claim the interest of him. In fact she didn't even know
what he looked like or if she had seen him during the
performance. Apparently he had seen her.

She glanced from the window as a shadow loomed
large near the bedroom door. Her eyes met the dark,
piercing stare of Raoul de Lovis as he emerged and
quietly made his way toward her. She'd had no idea
anyone was in the next room, and she felt violated
somehow, wondering if he had been observing her
unawares.

"Señora Laguens." He bowed and took her
hand, placing a whisper-soft kiss in its palm. "How
wonderful to meet you at last."

She curtsied and quickly withdrew her hand. He
raised an eyebrow in seeming amusement. "I hope you
haven't waited long for me."

"No, Don Raoul, not long at all."

A tall man with a finely made face, his nostrils
flared, and his full lips looked as if they had kissed a
great variety of women. His thin mustache was well-
groomed, and his skin was a deep shade of nutmeg,
but he seemed forbidding dressed in a black jacket
with matching breeches and boots. Except for the
white lace shirt which made a startling contrast against
his person, Lianne would have thought he resembled
the devil himself.

"Is all to your liking?" Raoul de Lovis gestured
around the room.

"Everything is quite lovely, though I'm at a loss
as to why you invited me."

"Are you?"

Lianne nodded.

Raoul grasped her elbow and steered her to one of
the high-backed chairs beside the table. After she sat,
and he took his place, his dark eyes swept across her
face then down to the cape tied at her neck. He
reached out and startled her when he untied the

strings. The cape fell from her shoulders. "Now you shall be more comfortable. The room is stuffy."

Lianne didn't believe that was the reason as he appraised her again, starting from her hairline and traveling to the creamy whiteness of her shoulders and hotly lingered at the globular fullness of her breasts. She felt as if he were a shopkeeper taking inventory of his wares. She resented his blatant perusal, but she remained quiet and waited for him to speak.

He rested his back against the chair, much pleased, and formed his fingers into a tent. "I had hoped you would come, Lianne. My note, it piqued your interest, si?"

"I could not refuse."

He laughed and showed even white teeth. "You're direct, and I value that. Of course, you're correct in your subtle way. No one refuses Raoul de Lovis. Wine?" He lifted a bottle to pour into her glass, but she refused.

"I should like you to state your purpose. I must be home soon."

"Very well." He placed the bottle on the table, sat back and observed her for a moment before speaking. "I've seen you perform many times at the opera. Tonight, however, was the culmination of my admiration for you. You realize, of course, that the company is very small and it was only through my doing that the performance was given in the palace at all tonight." He leaned in closer. "In fact, the company isn't very good. You are the main attraction."

"How kind of you, Don Raoul. However, I sing only a short aria."

"Soon all will change. As of this night, you are under my protection. You've heard of my power, my connections. I can make you the most sought-after diva in Spain, and with my assistance, the whole of Europe will kiss your lovely feet. I know you, Lianne Laguens. Perhaps better than you know yourself."

Lianne fidgeted. If any man other than Raoul de Lovis sat across from her, she'd disregard such outrageous talk as mere prattle. But de Lovis wasn't any other man. He was one of the wealthiest men in Spain, a commanding figure used to having his way. And he thought he knew her.

"I fear, sir, that you don't know me at all."

"But I do, *querida*. I know you're an orphan who married her childhood sweetheart, that you bore your husband a child who later died after your husband's murder. Before this, you and your husband escaped the terror in France and were taken under the wing of your erstwhile mentor Victor Dubois. You left his troupe in disgrace, arriving pregnant and homeless in Madrid nearly a year ago. Since then you've been living at the lodges of Señora Maria Alvarez . . . Need I continue?"

Lianne's face turned white with shock then grew red with anger. "How dare you check up on me!"

He stood up, took her arm and hauled her from the chair in one motion. "I'm an entrepreneur, *querida*. I know everything about the people I wish to possess. And I shall not only make you the greatest soprano in Europe but you will also become my mistress. As of this night."

"No!"

She struggled, but he held her tightly. "You need some inducement, *mi amor*."

He brought her to a closet and threw open the door. Inside were clothes of the finest silks and velvets, capes lined with mink, chinchilla. There was an assortment of shoes, hats, stockings to match, and he pulled a wooden box from a shelf. He yanked it open and spilled the contents onto the floor. Emeralds, diamonds, sapphires in an array of necklaces, earbobs, pendants, lay sparkling at her feet.

"This is what I offer you, Lianne. Not only the continent, but its wealth."

Nothing had ever shocked her to such an extent

that she could barely speak. She looked into the Don's handsome face and knew that she'd be crazy not to let him have his way with her. No matter how long the affair lasted, she would still be better off than she was now. But she couldn't give herself to him. For all the desire burning in his eyes, she feared him and knew he could destroy her. Yet she wanted love, the same love she'd found for a few moments of stolen ecstasy with the stranger.

Her voice shook when she finally spoke, and she hoped he would realize she meant her words. "You may know facts about me, but you don't know me. I refuse your offer."

A self-satisfied smirk played about his mouth. "I thought you would, but, *querida,* you have a child. You'd not want your beautiful baby to starve because of your foolish pride. You shall never sing again in Spain or in Europe for that matter. I doubt if you can find a position to pay as well as what I've offered you, and I doubt seriously if you'd sell yourself on the streets when I'd provide for you . . . if you willingly give me your body. I've hungered for you from the first moment I saw you on stage, *querida,* and I will have you."

She froze, staring wordlessly at him, and her heart pounding in her ears nearly deafened her. From the cruel twist of his mouth to the panther-like readiness in his eyes, she knew he'd not let her leave unless she submitted to him. He meant every word he uttered and her baby would suffer if she refused. But there must be another way.

He evidently saw the shock on her face give way to acquiescence. His hold loosened. His smile was breathtakingly white. "I knew you'd see the sense of my proposition, Lianne. It pains me to have to force you to the same point of view, but in the end, you'll thank me." He pointed to the glittering jewels on the floor. "These are nothing in comparison to what I shall give you."

Lianne found her voice. "Are you so generous to all your paramours?"

"Just the incredibly beautiful ones, and you are the most lovely of any woman I've ever known." He fingered a loose curl.

She cringed when his fingertip brushed her cheek. "You shall soon be used to my touch, lovely Lianne, and you'll beg for it."

Words to sting his ego died on her tongue. She realized it wouldn't help her predicament. Perhaps if she played along with him and let him believe she found him and his wealth enticing . . .

"You're a persuasive man, Don Raoul."

He pulled her tighter against him. "And a man filled with desire." His lips met hers in a brutal kiss which took her breath away. Before she realized it, he had swept her into his arms and carried her to the rose-strewn sheets. His mouth never left her lips. He placed her in the center of the bed, and his hands imprisoned her arms against the softness of the mattress. She broke away to catch her breath.

"Please, you're moving too fast for me, Don Raoul."

"Raoul. Call me Raoul," he growled and nibbled her earlobe.

"Raoul."

For a brief moment she turned her head and spotted a doorway. She wondered where it led. To the hallway, perhaps? But his hands moved her head and forced her gaze to his. "I always get what I want, Lianne. This you should know from the start. You see, I realize your baby isn't your husband's child. I won't ask who the father is, but I'll kill any man who touches you. Understand?"

She nodded; the instinct to flee grew stronger. The fire in his eyes burned brighter. From the way he pulled at her bodice and brought it low over her breast, and from the feel of his swelling manhood against her thigh, Lianne knew it would be only a matter of minutes before he completely undressed her and made her his. She also realized that he would take her whether she was willing or not.

His teeth tugged at her nipples. She had to get away but must be careful.

Pushing suggestively against him, she said, "Raoul, I'm not prepared for this. I'd like to attend to personal matters first."

His head shot up, and anger flared in his obsidian eyes. However, to her surprise, he sat up and leaned across the bed to a table for a cigar. Standing up, he lit it and inhaled deeply.

"Let me know when you're finished," he said and withdrew to the sitting room.

No sooner had he departed than Lianne shot bullet-like from the bed. She didn't run toward the beckoning doorway, however, but inched her way to the knob and prayed the door hinges wouldn't squeak.

The huge door was very old, but the thought struck her that it might be locked. Her prayers began anew. But when she grasped the golden knob and pulled, the door opened a crack.

She waited a second.

A heady sense of relief filled her. Now to make it out of the palace before Raoul realized she had fled. As quietly as possible she opened the door further, her eyes darting to the doorway which separated the sitting room. The unmistakable scent of the cigar filled the apartment and smelled much closer than the next room.

Lianne turned to exit through the door, but stopped still in her tracks to see Raoul leaning lazily against the doorjamb, the lighted cigar held casually in his hand. "Taking a midnight stroll, my little French tart?"

The blood had so completely drained from her that she felt weak and almost fainted. He threw down the cigar on the marbled floor and pushed her wobbly body into the room where she sank onto the carpeted floor.

"I told you I knew you well. It's a pity that you couldn't give yourself to me without going through this foolishness." He bent down and grabbed a handful of hair which escaped from the pins. "You've a beautiful body, Lianne, but I must teach you who your master is. Believe me, I do hate to mar such unblemished perfection." His right hand came up and slapped her harshly across the face. The stinging sensation brought back her survival instinct, and she realized how cowed she must seem as he towered above her. She decided that Raoul de Lovis wouldn't have her without a fight.

His hand loomed forward to strike her again, she seized it, and with a quickness which surprised her, she sank her teeth into his flesh. Instantly Raoul drew back. She rolled away from him, ignoring his cry of pain and the curses he heaped upon her. Running to the sitting room, Lianne pulled at the drapes. They fell forward and landed on Raoul just as he leaped toward her, like a tiger after a gazelle.

"*Puta!*" he hissed and tried to disentangle himself from the mass of material.

At that moment she didn't care if he branded her a whore. She wanted to survive, to flee him, but she knew he'd follow her once he freed himself of the drapes. Noticing the wine bottle on the table, she picked it up and swung at the side of his face as he blindly headed for her.

Lianne blinked when the bottle cracked and shattered in green slivered fragments upon the floor. Wine splattered across the walls and over the white draperies. In fascinated horror, she watched as Raoul staggered toward her. In a panic she searched for another weapon when he fell, landing inches from her feet.

His shrouded figure lay quietly before her. The crimson color which stained the drapes she assumed to be wine, but when she cautiously bent down and touched the stickiness oozing from the fibers of the thin silk, she knew it was blood.

"Don Raoul," she whispered urgently. "Don Raoul."

No answer.

She had killed him!

Standing up, Lianne backed away and grabbed for her cape. As she threw it over her shoulders, she kept her eyes on the still figure. Moving toward the door, she pulled it open and stood for a moment in the drafty hallway. She took deep breaths in an attempt to calm herself.

Raoul's servant knew her identity but assumed she was spending the night with his master. That meant he wouldn't bother de Lovis until morning. She had at least six hours to get home, pack her belongings and take Désirée away with her. She had to leave Spain. She had killed a nobleman and would be hunted like an animal until found. No one would believe he had tried to rape her.

The horror of the situation struck her. Staying within the shadows of the corridors, she slipped from the palace and onto the street. When she was out of view, she ran home.

Lianne had no idea what she should do. She had to escape. But where?

Then the memory emerged through the tangled yarn of her thoughts. As a child her mother told her about her godmother, a woman who lived in Louisiana . . . a woman she could turn to if she ever needed help. Lianne didn't remember the woman. She knew only that when she was a small girl, she and her parents had lived in Louisiana.

Her mother and this woman had been as close as sisters. For a second, Lianne dismissed the absurdity of contacting the woman, but she was her only hope and she grasped it.

Running to the comfort of Maria and her baby, her mind was on her godmother. A woman named Dera.

Chapter 4

Señora Maria Alvarez immediately understood Lianne's plight and took quick action as soon as Lianne arrived home, out of breath and barely coherent. Just the mention of Raoul de Lovis' name was enough to cause Maria to make the sign of the cross. "Madre de Dios," she groaned and sent for her nephew Pedro.

"Not to worry," Maria said, as she calmly packed the baby's clothing in a small valise. "All will soon be well."

Lianne had learned not to question Maria when her forehead puckered as it did when she scooped up a sleeping Désirée and held her tightly against her ample bosom. The baby stirred and whimpered, but immediately fell asleep when Maria handed her to Lianne. "I'll pack your things," she volunteered. Lianne watched her leave the room. Her large hips swayed beneath a simple black gown, widow's weeds, which she had worn ever since the death of her husband Fernando, some five years earlier. Lianne knew many people were intimidated by Maria's iron-faced look and austere hairstyle, a tightly coiled black chignon at the back of her head. However, Lianne felt Maria took the place of mother in her heart and knew her to be incredibly kind and generous and also practical. She'd never allow anyone to take advantage of her or harm those she loved. This protectiveness now inspired Maria to calmly gather Lianne and the baby. She helped them into Pedro's cart upon his return and climbed into the seat beside Lianne with her own valise in hand. "I'm going with you," she said before Lianne had a chance to question her. "Pedro will look after the house and tenants until I can return. You don't really think Maria would allow you and the little one to leave Madrid alone?"

"But Don Raoul is dead, surely, you can't mean to go with us. What will become of you if you're caught?"

Maria laughed, her large bosom shaking. "Maria takes care of herself. What would happen to you and the baby if you're caught? No, I go with you. My brother has a ship in Cadiz. You tell him where you want to go. He'll take you."

Lianne's eyes filled with tears. Her fondness for Maria so overwhelmed her that she threw her arms around her. The baby, jostled by the sudden movement, whimpered. Then they were off, flying down the side streets of old Madrid until they reached the open countryside.

After four months, the *Cristobel* finally docked in New Orleans. The Spanish town had once belonged to the French, but little evidence of that nation remained in the new architectural style of iron lace balconies which clung to the sides of peach and white houses and gateways with matching grillwork which enclosed the courtyards and shielded the inhabitants from the curious gazes of the passersby. Yet a French flavor revealed itself when Lianne caught the lyrical accents of her native tongue. She suddenly felt as if she were in Paris and Madrid at once.

Maria stayed protectively near as they hunted for a place to stay. Night was falling, and they were tired, the baby cranky. Many times Lianne suspected she'd have trouble with the landlords if Maria hadn't stood stoically by her side, glaring at them when they ogled her young friend. None of the rooms were satisfactory. If children were allowed, the rooms were too small.

They turned onto a side street and noticed a house with a room to let. Because it was growing darker by the minute and both Lianne and Maria felt they couldn't take another step, they rang the bell.

The landlady grudgingly showed the room to them and immediately they took it because it was clean and an escape from the sudden rainstorm which pounded upon the roof. When they were settled and Désirée had fallen asleep across Lianne's shoulder and Maria had long since begun snoring, Lianne decided they would move once she obtained a position with the opera company. The walls were cracked, and she swore she heard the scurrying sounds of mice within them.

A feeling of hopelessness swept over her. Maria's money was almost gone, and she was the reason the woman had used it. For the time being, they had escaped de Lovis's men whom she felt sure would scour the world to find her and bring her to justice.

She wanted more for her child than just survival or escape. She needed the love of her mother's friend, and she must find her. While she gazed at her child's angelic face, she realized she needed some connection to her family, her past, something which had been denied her since the day the peasants stormed the gates of Chateau de la Varre.

Three days later with Lianne holding the baby and Maria in tow, the Flanders butler helped them from their rented carriage. Lianne hoped she looked her best and purposely chose a gown of pale golden silk for her meeting with her godmother. The color highlighted her hair and set off her cat-like eyes.

She surveyed Green Meadows in long, appreciative glances. In many ways the elegant white house, supported by stone columns, reminded her of Chateau de la Varre, which was gone forever. How she envied her godmother and her family! Surely they must love sitting on the upstairs balcony on warm, summer nights and listening to the locusts hidden in the tall grasses or the slow movement of the river nearby.

A sense of peace filled her. If only she could share such serenity with one man. The stranger's face rose unbidden to her mind, and she smiled a too bright smile when the front door was thrown open.

Lianne handed the baby to Maria and was barely up the steps before a woman who smelled like spring flowers on a rainy afternoon embraced her.

"Lianne, let me look at you," Dera Flanders said and held her goddaughter at arm's length. "You resemble your mother, but you kept your papa's hair color. What a lovable tyrant that Michel Chevalier was!"

Lianne laughed and dimpled. She liked Dera immediately. Instead of the overweight matron with gray hair she had expected, she found Dera to be slender, full-bosomed and tiny-waisted. Her hair was still dark but streaked with gray in places, and her eyes reminded Lianne of the wild purple blooms which grew on the mountainsides of France. For a woman near fifty, Dera was still incredibly beautiful.

"I was stunned to receive your note announcing your visit," Dera continued in her lilting Irish accent which Lianne found charming. "I still haven't recovered, but I am so happy to see you again! I've paced the room all morning." Dera put her arm around Lianne's waist and led her into the house then took the baby from Maria and played with her before Désirée grew fussy. When Maria and her charge were escorted to rooms upstairs by a servant, Dera smiled apologetically.

"Green Meadows has no facilities for a baby. My son Daniel and his wife lost a child three years ago. Life hasn't been the same since."

Lianne patted Dera's arm in sympathy. "I'm certain they shall have children someday."

Dera shook her head. "Amelie suffered a fall and can no longer walk." She changed the subject. "What brings you to Louisiana?"

Absently stirring her tea, Lianne's face paled. She couldn't tell her godmother the truth, that she ran away because she had killed one of the most powerful men in Spain. So, she quickly hedged on the truth. "I wanted to see my parents' home, the plantation they sold before the move to France."

"Ah, yes, Belle Riviere. It's a beautiful plantation. My Quint was always jealous of your father's ability to turn a quick profit, but no sooner had Michel bought the best farm land in the Louisiana valley than he sold it for an exorbitant amount. I think your father would have been quite pleased if he had seen Belle Riviere even five years ago." Dera sipped her tea.

"You sound as if it isn't prime property any longer."

Dera sighed and laid down her teacup on the table beside the couch. "Not now, and it hasn't been since Phillipe Marchand inherited it from his father." She lowered her voice. "He is a terrible planter and businessman, but I shouldn't criticize him. Phillipe is my daughter-in-law's brother. Poor Amelie received none of the land in the will. Her father hoped that by bestowing the plantation upon Phillipe, it would make a man of him. It hasn't. He squanders the money like river water flowing through his fingers. But as the Mississippi is full, I'm afraid Phillipe's river will soon run dry."

"*C'est dommage,*" Lianne said.

At that moment heavy footsteps sounded in the hallway, and then a large man, the color of light brown velvet, entered the room. He carried an extremely fragile woman whose blonde hair framed a tiny face, set off by light blue eyes. He placed her in a cushioned chair as if she were a china doll and immediately lifted her legs to rest upon an ottoman. Then he moved silently away to stand in the corner of the room.

"Amelie," Dera smiled and addressed the woman, "this is my goddaughter, Comtesse Lianne Laguens. And, Lianne, this is my son Daniel's wife."

Lianne spoke a courteous greeting to Amelie, but the hard stare the woman bestowed upon her momentarily startled her. Never had anyone unknown to her looked at her with such hatred. "You're the mother of the baby I heard crying."

"Oui. Désirée is my daughter. I hope she didn't disturb you."

Amelie shrugged as Dera poured her a cup of tea. "I'm not overly fond of children," she said softly, but her face stayed hard.

Lianne remembered Dera's remark about the loss of her son's child, and pity filled her. "I shall inform Maria to see Désirée remains quiet."

"Nonsense!" Dera's eyes flew to Amelie, and she frowned. "It's impossible to keep children quiet all the time. They were meant to play, to scream their lungs out. Remember, I raised two rowdy boys, and I know that for a fact." She gave Lianne a smile. "Don't give the crying another thought."

Amelie sniffed, not seeming to care for Dera's affinity for Lianne and her child. "I suppose children have their place in life, however, I shall never have to worry about them." Her icy sapphire gaze settled on Lianne. "As you can see, I'll never have children in my condition. However, even if I were well and walking, my husband is never around. So, I doubt there would be bawling brats to keep Dera occupied. She wants grandchildren, you know."

"I have two grandchildren already. By my son Paul." She looked at Lianne, but her comment was directed to Amelie.

"How could I forget?" Amelie asked so sweetly

that Dera winced. "The issue of your oldest son and the beautiful, wonderful, virtuous Allison. Mentioning Allison stirs up memories of Daniel. Have you heard from him, Dera? Any idea when he'll come home and honor us with his presence after taking the Parisian art world by storm?"

Lianne noticed Dera ground her teeth. Even the most unobservant person would realize that Dera and Amelie didn't get on well. She wondered at the strangeness of the situation concerning Daniel Flanders. Why would his wife have to ask her mother-in-law if she knew when he would return from abroad?

"I received a letter just this morning. I meant to tell you about it. Daniel said he'd be home after the new year."

"What wonderful news, Dera! The prodigal husband returns."

"Amelie, I believe you're doing your best to be trying."

"Am I? Then perhaps the petulant cripple should retire to the four walls of her room. Claude." She motioned to the man who waited in the corner like a shadow. "Please take me upstairs." He sprang forward like an obedient puppy and scooped her up into his arms. Her fair skin looked fairer against the dusky darkness of his. "Thank you both for an entertaining chat," she said before he carried her from the parlor.

Dera shook her head in dismay. "I shouldn't have reprimanded her, but Amelie is such a trial. I know it's hard for her, not being able to walk, but sometimes I believe she could if she wanted to badly enough. The doctor said after the fall from the horse that there wasn't any permanent damage, but Amelia insists she can't or won't walk. Sometimes I don't think she wants to live either." She heaved a sigh. "As you can guess, everything isn't right with my son's marriage. He shouldn't have married her, but . . ." She threw up her hands in despair.

Lianne hugged Dera around the shoulders. "I feel sorry for her, and I have the feeling that she wants children very much."

Dera wished to say more, to confide in Lianne about the real state of affairs between Amelie and Daniel. They didn't share a bedroom when Daniel was home, so there wouldn't be any children at Green Meadows to love and spoil as she had been unable to do with the twins who lived in far off Ireland. "Don't take offense at Amelie," she said instead.

"I won't." Lianne smiled. "I really am very glad I'm here. I hope you won't grow tired of me, but I needed to feel family around me. Soon I shall perform in the opera in town, but until then I should like to belong to your family."

Kissing Lianne's cheek, Dera leaned back and studied her beautiful oval face, the green eyes which tilted at an angle and her coral lips. What an enchanting creature she was! Too bad she had never met Daniel. She felt Lianne would be perfect for him. But a match between her son and goddaughter was impossible now. Poor Amelie was in the way.

"You are already part of my family," Dera assured her. "For as long as you wish."

Chapter 5

Boring! Boring! Amelie tossed aside her book, not caring that it careened off the white eyelet bedcovers to land in a corner.

She folded her arms in an exasperated huff across her small bosom and wondered if it was too late to ring for Claude. Perhaps she could interest him in a game of cards . . . But then she thought better of it. Even though he slept in the small room next to hers and no one thought the worst of it, she didn't wish to intrude upon his privacy. And Claude was a private person. She never had an inkling concerning his thoughts.

Amelie only knew that Claude made her comfortable and was more of a husband to her than Daniel had ever been. Each morning Claude carried her downstairs after his mother, Lallie, helped her dress, so she could sit on the veranda and watch the horses graze in the meadow. Claude never spoke unless directly addressed but waited like a sentinel until she motioned to go inside.

She knew Dera trusted Claude, as did Daniel who had been his childhood friend. Amelie remembered Daniel telling her he had been a sickly child, and Claude had entertained him with stories about his life in Santo Domingo.

Amelie sniffed. Well, Daniel certainly wasn't sickly now. During his absence while he cavorted across Europe and painted portraits, some of nude women no doubt, Claude had taken care of her. Daniel had placed his own wife in a slave's care. But as Amelie propped the pillows and settled back, she knew she didn't mind.

She didn't see Claude as an ordinary slave. Perhaps it was his looks. She admitted he was terribly attractive with his dusky skin which was much lighter than his mother's, but darker than her uncle who was a Spaniard. His hair was dark brown but riddled in places with streaks of a lighter shade, and his eyes were a deep chestnut in color.

Amelie had heard rumors that Lallie had been the mistress of a white planter in Santo Domingo and Claude was the result of that union. This information made Claude even more fascinating to her.

A lonely, neglected wife with long hours in which to while away the time, Amelie shocked herself by having incredible visions of being held in Claude's strong arms and growing weak with desire from his kisses. At times she wondered if she might be perverted. Decent white women didn't have such fantasies about their male slaves, or that was what she told herself. She knew white men did dally with the female ones and no one thought the worse of them. Her own father had had a negro mistress on Belle Riviere, and she knew her brother had a quadroon mistress in New Orleans. But since Amelie was brought up to believe that decent women didn't have such thoughts or do such things, she wondered if she might indeed be depraved. Yet, the thought of being kissed by Claude still excited her.

"Mon Dieu!" she exclaimed and punched the pillow. What good did it do to dwell on such thoughts anyway? Even if Daniel returned home and wanted to be a husband in the physical sense, nothing would quell the strange sensations coursing through her lower body. She couldn't walk.

Staring at the tester above the bed, she tried to

remember how long ago some feeling returned to her limbs. Three months? Four? She wasn't certain, because it happened a little over a period of time. She hadn't told anyone and and she didn't want to. Her paralysis was the only way to make Daniel feel guilty for what he had done to her.

A sad smile formed and hovered on her face. She knew now she shouldn't have married Daniel when he returned from Ireland. His pursuit, the courtship, had happened so swiftly. He completely turned her head with his ardor. She wondered why he hadn't seemed interested in her before the trip to visit his brother in Ireland. They had known each other for years, and not once had he given an indication that he thought of her as a potential wife. However, when he saw her again while riding across Belle Riviere one day, everything changed. He wanted her badly.

And she wanted him. The fever in her body whenever he kissed her led her to believe she was truly in love with him, and she would have thrown her scruples to the wind and let him make love to her before the wedding. Daniel protested, so they waited until the priest pronounced them man and wife. She thought the nights they laid together in each other's arms after making love to be lacking in passion. She was basically innocent; however, she realized that Daniel wasn't as eager for her as she was for him. Granted he was a considerate lover, she never felt truly desired in his arms.

She didn't know what to think until Dera arrived from Ireland, a widow. Much concerned about her mother-in-law, she had sought to comfort her, but overheard a conversation between Dera and Daniel in the parlor. Amelie waited outside the door, her temples pounding as Dera's words crushed her heart. "You married Amelie because she resembles Allison. You must get over Allison. She is your brother's wife."

Amelie couldn't see his response, but she heard

the passion in his voice, something he had shown very little of to her.

"I shall always be in love with Allison. Amelie is a poor substitute, but I'm afraid I'm stuck with her."

She felt a part of her die at that moment. "Amelie is a poor substitute." The words rolled around her head for days, and she wished to return home, but she knew Phillipe would never allow her to. "Think of the scandal," she could almost hear his voice in her mind.

Her personality underwent a drastic change. All of her life she'd been rather docile, deferring to her parents, then to her brother after their deaths, and then to Daniel whom she loved. However, once she knew her husband loved another woman, that he wedded and bedded her to ease an ache for his sister-in-law, she decided to get some attention for herself. She demanded his time, ordered expensive fabrics from Paris. She knew quite well she grated on Dera's nerves and had Daniel climbing the walls, but she didn't care. She wanted revenge.

And she got it in a way she hadn't bargained for. The memory of the argument washed over her, and she hid her face in her pillow. Only days earlier she had told Daniel she carried his child. The realization that she was pregnant filled her with a bittersweet pain. She wanted children, but Daniel didn't love her. How could she share her joy with a man who loved another woman?

Knowing this, she threw a huge tantrum about a stupid hat she wished to order. She didn't want it, but it pleased her immensely to see how riled he became. She enjoyed seeing his sad gray eyes light with anger when she taunted him, and to know that she had caused him to feel something for her. Any emotion from him, she felt, was better than apathy. However, things took a nasty turn when she insisted that she'd ask Phillipe for the funds if he was too stingy to dress her in grand style.

She'd always remember the fierce grip he coiled

around her arm, the look of pure hatred in his eyes for her and himself after she hurled the vase at his head. And never would she forget his declaration of love for Allison or the intense pain which ripped through her when he asked how such a woman as herself could ever be the mother of his child. At that moment she wished to flee, never to return to Green Meadows and never to see his cruel, handsome face again.

She barely remembered running toward the stables and mounting the stallion. She'd never ridden Bayrum before, always fearing his wildness, but now she didn't think, didn't care.

Claude tugged at her skirt in an attempt to pull her from the horse, but she kicked at him and rode into the night like a cyclone.

Instinctively she turned the horse in the direction of Belle Riviere, hoping against hope that Phillipe would allow her to come home, and would somehow extricate her from this horrendous marriage she had made. The tears streamed down her cheeks until she couldn't see. The night was dark. There was no moon, no lighting of the road which led home. Then Bayrum spooked. She didn't know what happened. The stallion reared up and she fell, unable to stop herself.

Her next memory was of intense pain everywhere in her body, everywhere but in her legs. She had lost her child, lost the ability to walk. And all because her husband didn't love her. Oh, he was penitent enough. "I'll make it up to you, I promise, Amelie," he had said. But she grew tired of Daniel's false concern. Granted she realized he was sorry, but that wouldn't bring back their child or the love she once felt for him. So, when he expressed an interest in sailing to France, she didn't stop him. After all, there was nothing for him at home anyway.

Now she heaved a huge trembling sigh and reached for the water pitcher on the nightstand beside the bed. The slippery handle slithered from her grasp and crashed to the floor. Small slivers of crystal gleamed on the floor. She felt helpless because she couldn't clean up the mess.

A sob tore from her throat. At that moment a shaft of light spilled from the adjoining room into hers. "Are you all right, Madam Amelie?" came Claude's voice.

"I carelessly broke the water pitcher," she said, sounding almost like a little girl who is about to be chastised.

He moved from the shadowy light, approaching her bed. "I shall clean it up."

A sound of surprise escaped her to see the gleam of his bare chest in the candlelight. Her eyes feasted on the rippling muscles of his back as he bent down and picked up the broken glass. The urge to touch him was so great she felt almost ill, wondering how the texture of his dusky skin would feel on her fingertips, how his muscled arms would hold her. Why, he's so strong he could break me in half, she thought to herself. When he stood up, their eyes met, and she suddenly came to her senses, hoping he couldn't see the naked passion on her face.

He looked like a god standing before her, naked except for his pants. "Claude." Her voice was strangled.

"Madam?" he asked in a toneless voice.

She shook her head, her long hair cascaded across her shoulders and covered the bodice of her lace night-dress. Having no idea what she wished to say, she just smiled and said, "Thank you, Claude."

He nodded and walked from the room without a backward glance. She took a deep breath, hoping to quell the tremors coursing through her body, and thanked God she had the good sense not to touch him when clearly she seemed to be the only one affected. Claude was such a loyal person that she felt he'd never harbor lewd thoughts about his best friend's wife. After all, he was a slave, and she was his mistress, and a cripple. She must never forget that.

Lying back down, she closed her eyes and made her mind a blank. She must stop having such ludicrous thoughts and pray that the desire would eventually cease. Claude didn't even know she existed. He was just helping to care for his friend's wife. She convinced herself of this and fell asleep.

But in the next room, Claude sat on his bed and gazed at the closed doorway, almost seeing Amelie's beautiful face wreathed in slumber. He knew another sleepless night was at hand.

Chapter 6

In the morning after Lianne fed the baby, Maria ordered her to enjoy herself. "Find something to do. Take a walk, speak with Señora Flanders, but relax. Soon the baby shall nap. I do take good care of her, *sí*?"

Lianne agreed readily. "Then make peace with yourself," Maria continued. "Soon the opera company will start and you shall sing again, but you must put the horrible thoughts from your mind about that black devil de Lovis. You're safe here, so forget the past."

Maria's austere face softened, and she took the baby from Lianne and placed her on her shoulder. Désirée's dark head turned inquiringly around, and she seemed completely content. So, Lianne changed into a soft peach-colored riding habit she had bought in Ireland then went downstairs to find Dera at the dining table in conversation with a gray-haired gentleman she introduced as Amelie's physician, Doctor Thaddeus Markham.

"Tad, I mean Doctor Markham, is here to examine Amelie this morning."

"I hope nothing serious," Lianne commented and noticed the high spot of color on Dera's cheeks and the vibrant purple of her eyes as she poured Doctor Markham another cup of tea.

"No, just her monthly examination."

Thaddeus grinned charmingly, his face lighting with pleasure as he took the proffered cup from Dera. "I think you must be tired of my visits by now," he said to Dera, then spoke to Lianne. "Mrs. Flanders pretends to enjoy our chats before I go up to see Amelie, but I know she must breathe a sigh of relief when I leave. I do love to talk."

"Heavens no! Where do you get such a preposterous idea? I look forward to our conversations."

Lianne thought Dera protested much too quickly and when she saw the quick rush of color on Dera's face, she knew the truth. Dera and Doctor Markham were in love with one another and neither one wished the other to know. Not understanding why they didn't tell each other, but sensing they wished to be alone, she excused herself and walked to the stables.

Though it was November, a mugginess clung to the air. Large fleecy clouds hung like cotton balls overhead, and when she reached the stables, she noticed the slave who had carried Amelie into the parlor the night before. He sat hunched in a corner and whittled a piece of wood. The tiny shavings dropped at his feet. Looking up, he saw her and immediately pocketed his knife and the wood. He stood up.

"May I help you, madam?" he asked and Lianne caught the trace of a French accent.

"I'd like to ride, but there doesn't seem to be a stableboy around."

"That Hubert is a lazy boy. Probably chasing after a woman or asleep somewhere. I'll get a horse for you."

He turned and walked towards a stall which had a name written on a piece of wood and nailed to a post. BAYRUM. Taking a beautiful filly from its confines, he stopped the horse before Lianne. The horse was the deepest shade of brown she'd ever seen, and when it gently nudged her, she immediately fell in love with the animal.

"Ah, *chérie,* what a sweetheart you are!"

Claude watched as she tenderly stroked the animal, a slight smile touching his usually solemn face. Only one other person had been as gentle with the horses. Now, she no longer rode.

Lianne smiled at Claude and noticed how handsome he looked. He is human, she thought to herself, having wondered if he was always so carefully restrained. "Is her name Bayrum?" she asked and nodded toward the sign.

The smile disappeared from his face, and he walked the horse into the yard. "No, madam. Her name is L'Amour Impossible, but I call her Amie."

Impossible Love. What a strange name for a horse, Lianne thought. "Where's Bayrum?" she asked, wondering why someone would go to the trouble of placing a sign above the stall.

"Bayrum belonged to Monsieur Quint when he was alive, then when the master didn't return from Ireland, young Monsieur Daniel rode him. But Bayrum was destroyed after Madam Amelie's accident."

"I see." So Bayrum was the horse which had thrown Amelie, resulting in her paralysis. Had she imagined it, or had Claude's face softened at Amelie's name?

"Claude!"

Both of them turned in the direction of the sound. A man came toward them. He wore a tattered hat, pulled low across his forehead, and a roughly sewn blue shirt and pants which had seen better days. Layers of dried mud covered the dark boots that hadn't been polished since the day he pulled them from the feet of a man he had killed at a New Orleans waterfront tavern.

Bruno Haus was a big man, a few inches over six feet, but Claude was taller. When Haus stepped between Lianne and Claude, the slave reared himself up to his full height and looked penetratingly into

Bruno's face. "Yes, Monsieur Haus?" Claude asked in a toneless voice.

"Is this nigger bothering you, fraulein? If so, I'll just use the whip on him." To prove his point, he flicked the long, thin tail of his whip, just missing Claude by an inch. If his object was to frighten Claude, it didn't. He stood just as immovable as a statue. "I'm the overseer on Green Meadows, and my slaves keep their places."

Lianne disliked Bruno Haus from his leering brown eyes to the tips of his dirty boots. She guessed he could be very formidable and frightening at times. She shuddered, but managed a polite smile. "Claude was about to help me mount."

"I can do that. You go about your business, Claude. You're not supposed to be hanging around the stables anyway. I just saw Doctor Markham leave, so your mistress will be wanting you." He emphasized the word mistress, and Lianne saw Claude roll his fists into balls, and his glance filled with hatred. To her surprise, Claude bowed low, turned and walked toward the house.

"I hate for a darkie to get uppity ideas about himself. Sometimes I wonder just what he and mistress Amelie do when alone."

"Monsieur Haus!"

Lianne's shocked tone caused Bruno to look sheepish. "Sorry, fraulein." He helped her onto the horse. Lianne felt his hand lingered too long at her leg when the material rose a bit between her boot and the skirt, baring a bit of ivory flesh to his gaze.

"Good day," she said and kicked harshly, pleased that his fingers had gotten in the way of her boot. She left him in the yard, sucking on his sore fingers.

The incident with Haus soon forgotten, she sauntered across the fields, awash with wild flowers and chirping birds in the tall trees. She reined in the horse and looked toward the house, all gleaming white in the early morning sunlight. To her surprise, she realized that the house wasn't as large or as grand as she had first thought. Balconies on the first and second floors ringed all four sides of the house. Large white columns supported the weight, but the home actually was small. Inside, however, it seemed larger because Dera and Quint had designed each room with unusually high ceilings to cool the house in the unrelenting summer heat of Louisiana. Though Green Meadows was not as large as her childhood home in France or Chateau de la Varre, Lianne felt drawn to it and envied the family who lived within its walls.

The property ended at a small dirt road which ran alongside a wooded area. As Lianne cantered along the road, she passed onto Belle Riviere. Dera had told her that Amelie's brother didn't take much interest in the property and Lianne realized she was right. Whereas, Green Meadows didn't have as much land, the fields were well-tended and the slaves seemed to be happy and well-fed despite their station in life. On Belle Riviere she found the fields to be overgrown with weeds, and the slaves working the cultivated land looked surly and downright thin. But it was the house she wished to see, the house in which she was born. She continued riding until she passed a thicket of trees. Then the house rose before her.

Belle Riviere stood like a pink flamingo in the midday sun. Dormered windows peered at her from the upstairs and a balcony enclosed the back side of the house on the first floor. Though Belle Riviere was much larger than Green Meadows, it wasn't as impressive. At least not now. She remembered her mother telling her how beautiful the house had been when it was first built, that it was perfect for balls and parties. However, since it was too far in the country for the leading New Orleans citizenry to travel, they entertained the Flanders family, including the two sons who ran through the house like twin tornadoes, and their other neighbors. However, most of the people in the area were poor German farmers, so there really wasn't much reason to entertain. After a few years Lianne's parents sold Belle Riviere and the family set sail for France and a new life. Though Lianne knew she was only two when they left, and had no real memories of the house, she did remember a young boy with dark hair who played ball with her on the grass in back of the house. She surmised he must have been one of Dera's sons. But even as she thought about the incident, the stranger in Ireland came to her mind. No, she decided. Now was not the time to think about him.

Just as she was about to turn Amie in the direction of Green Meadows, a man appeared from the French doors which led onto the back porch. She heard his voice call, *Bonjour,* Comtesse! Come here!''

He waved, and she rode toward him. He left the porch and met her halfway. She looked down into his pleasant face, a face somewhat like Amelie's, except the chin was rather weak and his eyes a bit too excited. Making a bow, he lifted his blonde head and smiled disarmingly. "I am Phillipe Marchand, Amelie's brother. You must be Dera's goddaughter, Lianne. Amelie mentioned to me yesterday when I saw her that you would be arriving. Please have tea with me, Comtesse.''

"Madam," she said and slipped from the horse with his help. "I am a widow and have little use for such a title now."

"C'est dommage!" he intoned, but Lianne didn't think he was the least bit sorry about her marital state. Phillipe took her hand and kissed it, then held it possessively against his chest. "Please come inside with me, Madame Laguens. I promise to be the gentleman and not act the notorious heartbreaker, which I am.''

She laughed, warming to the mischievous twinkle in his eyes. They were soon in the parlor, sipping tea, and she surveyed it with the eye of a detached observer. She didn't remember anything about the house, but she knew that the room had been hastily opened. It still smelled musty despite the open windows which looked onto the weedy front lawn, and Phillipe told her the furnishings had belonged to the former owners.

"My parents built this house," she told him. "This was their furniture."

He appeared surprised. "What a coincidence, Lianne. May I call you by your name? Madam seems so impersonal." When she nodded her agreement, he smiled as if he had won a great victory. "You may call me Phillipe."

While they sipped their tea, he watched her in fascination. Never had he seen such a gorgeous woman. Her hair shone like reflections in amber wine, her eyes resembled summer leaves, and her figure took his breath away. The thin material of the riding jacket clearly emphasized her rounded breasts, tiny waist. Ah, yes, he decided then and there, this woman would soon warm his bed and bear his sons. He wanted her as his wife. But he realized she wasn't a woman to be rushed. A sense of independence clung to her. Well, that was fine for now. But once she married him, she'd do his bidding in every way, would content herself only with him, unlike another woman he once wished to marry.

"I'm afraid Belle Riviere is in poor condition," Phillipe said. "I spend a great deal of time in New Orleans where I own a vacant town house. Most of my entertaining is done in rooms I rent on the Esplanade. I have no excuse for the condition of Belle Riviere except for my absence. Soon I hope to have reason to change my situation. I hope to spend more time here in the future. Will you be at Green Meadows long?"

"A few weeks more. I return to New Orleans and hope to win a position with the opera company."

Phillipe nearly crowed with excitement. What a perfect way to ingratiate himself with the beautiful

Comtesse! He wished for her to fall under his spell but realized she didn't seem duly impressed by him. Most women fell in love with him immediately. With his blond good looks and money, he could choose any woman he wanted, and he wanted Lianne Laguens. But why another opera singer?''

"I know the manager," he stated matter of factly. "I'll speak to him about you. Never worry, Lianne, you shall sing like a nightingale."

Her face glowed with animation. "Really? Phillipe, would you do that for me? I'd be indebted to you. I have a child to support."

A child? He didn't know that. Well, that didn't matter. In fact, if he took an interest in the child, then she'd love him all the more. Reaching out, he touched her hand, then lifted it to his lips. A tiny kiss was pressed within the palm. "I think," he said at last, when a color to match the riding outfit rose from her neck to her hairline, "that we shall be very good friends."

Chapter 7

De Lovis was his last hope. Daniel didn't wish to see
him again, never having liked him from the first time
he met Amelie's uncle when he made an unexpected
visit to Belle Riviere shortly after their marriage. He
found Raoul to be arrogant, pompous, and a bit cruel.
But then any number of people could say that about
himself. Amelie would. Raoul made no bones about
the fact that he didn't think he was suitable for his
niece, but the damage had been done. Yet Daniel
suspected the match did please him because of Green
Meadows. It was a prosperous plantation in its way, and
if one thing impressed Raoul de Lovis, it was wealth
and all that it entailed.

Well, Daniel was wealthy and influential in his
own right. His paintings were the rage in Europe right
now, and in Spain he rivaled Goya. Didn't all the rich
matrons and their daughters wish to pose for him, to
lure him into their beds? And he had been luring a
number of them these days. He found Madrid, as well
as Paris, offered a feast for the senses.

Sitting up in bed, his eyes roamed the half-clad
body of Dona Isabelle Hidalgo, wife of a close friend of
the king. He had finished the painting that afternoon
of the beautiful Isabelle, dressed properly in the latest
court fashion. Daniel knew her illustrious husband
would be well pleased with the demure image she

projected on canvas. However, Daniel wondered the man's reaction if he knew that two-thirds of the painting had been executed while the voluptuous Isabelle posed lounging on the bed, her naked body waiting for him, enticing him to take her. What would his reaction be if he knew that this wasn't the first time Isabelle had joined her wanton flesh to his?

Daniel's body was satiated but his soul wasn't. Since leaving Ireland some months ago, he had traced Victor Dubois to a small Irish town where he found the man in failing health and deserted by his young wife. He discovered the name of the woman he fell in love with, a name deeply ingrained in his memory. Lianne Laguens, Comtesse de la Varre. The widow of the son of Dubois' friend. Needless to say that Dubois wasn't glad to see him and blamed him for Lianne's running away that night. He hadn't seen her since and told Daniel he was lucky to be alive, that the whole incident had virtually destroyed his fragile health. He advised Daniel to give up the search, that women were faithless, as he had discovered.

Daniel pitied the old man, but didn't stop searching for Lianne. He picked up on any clue he could find, even engaged people to search for her. Thus, the lead in Madrid. A woman by that name had performed for a small opera company and then disappeared. After questioning a few of the players, he learned they knew practically nothing about her, but that she did perform at the palace the last time they saw her.

It was very little to go on, but Daniel remembered that de Lovis was an influential man in Madrid and very much involved in the arts. So, he decided that as soon as he finished his commission with Isabelle Hidalgo, he'd seek out de Lovis who was away in the country, secluded for some months.

Isabelle stirred and opened large, brown eyes. *"Mi amor,* how long have I slept? I must get home to Franco or he'll suspect something," She quickly sat up

and pulled the sheet about her, but Daniel stilled her.
His mouth came slowly down upon hers, causing her
breath to quicken.

"You have plenty of time, my Spanish rose. The
sun is still high in the sky."

"Oh, Daniel," she said, wrapping them together
in the sheet. *"Sí,* let the old goat wait."

The next day Daniel waited for Raoul on the
terrace of his country home. The peace and serenity of
the Spanish countryside filled him, and he felt he was
getting closer to Lianne, hoped that she was still in
Spain. Perhaps de Lovis was familiar with her name,
her face. Anything. He had to find her.

"Señor Flanders." A servant motioned him to
follow and Daniel walked behind him into the house
and down a long hallway, stopping before Raoul's
office. The servant opened the door, and Daniel
entered the room which was encased in darkness.
Except for a slight crack where the material met,
massive drapes barred the sun's rays. In the darkness,
Daniel heard Raoul's voice,

"Find your way to a chair."

Groping his way to the sound of Raoul's voice, he
found a chair and sat, anger and puzzlement building
in him that he should be treated so shabbily by his
wife's relative.

"How are you, Raoul?" he asked in a restrained
tone.

He heard the creak of Raoul's chair. "Fine, my
nephew. What can I do for you?"

You can pull the damn drapes he started to say,
but stopped himself. He didn't wish to get into an
argument with de Lovis. He only wanted any information the man had, and then he'd be on his way.

Daniel explained the reason for his visit, ending
with, "If you can find this woman, I'd be more than
grateful."

"I see, my niece's husband. Tell me, are you

involved with this woman?''

"No," Daniel answered truthfully. He wasn't involved with her, but he wanted to be. "It is a personal matter. She was in a French troupe, playing in small Irish towns, then abruptly she left." He cleared his throat, not going into detail. "Someone spotted her here, performing in Madrid. She is very beautiful with auburn hair and green eyes."

For an instant, Daniel heard a deathly quiet invade the room. Raoul's breathing stilled. "What is this woman's name?"

"Lianne Laguens."

After long moments, he heard Raoul draw breath. "I know of no such woman."

"Are you sure?"

"Positive. Now, Daniel, I'm very busy. I'd advise you to forget this woman and to return home to your wife. This woman is not for you."

Daniel sensed the animosity in Raoul's voice and decided that Raoul had figured his interest was more than personal and had offended his niece. He stood up. "Thank you for your time, Don Raoul, but I shall find her. Good day."

Opening the door, Raoul saw Daniel's broad shoulders fill the doorway, then he was gone. Through the curtain crack, he watched Daniel mount his horse and ride toward Madrid. Raoul opened the drapes and allowed the morning sunshine to spill into the well ordered study.

He lit a cheroot and sat behind his desk and blew smoke rings, watching them rise to the rafters. He smiled at the coincidence. Fate had decreed his meeting with the beautiful Comtesse and had pulled her from him. Through Daniel, the philandering husband of his unfortunate niece, he might find her yet.

He realized that Daniel must be the father of Lianne's child. There was no other explanation to the question which had nagged at him for months. He wasn't certain how they had met or what had torn them apart, but he knew Daniel was in love with her and would pursue her until he found her.

When Raoul had tried to discover her whereabouts from the bed to which he had been confined until a month ago, her lodgings in Madrid had turned up nothing. Pedro Alvarez wouldn't tell his men where Lianne Laguens had gone, but Pedro wasn't a problem any longer. His men had unburdened him of his silent tongue.

Raoul laughed bitterly and extinguished the cheroot in an ashtray. He touched the puffy eyelid which had been stitched closed by a court physician after his servant found him, lying in a puddle of his own blood. The doctor assured him the puffiness would clear. The infection had been a particularly serious and persistent one. Only recently had Raoul left his bed. He didn't think he'd ever get used to this abomination. For a man who once was physically perfect in every way now to be so hideous caused him to stop looking in the mirror. He hated his reflection and thought he looked grotesque.

The image of his mother flashed into his mind. Dolores de Lovis had been beautiful and fiery like Lianne Laguens. She had been touted as Spain's most beautiful woman and had completely captivated his father . . . and many other men, he later learned. Her unfaithfulness to his father had injured the young Raoul. Though she told her son she loved him, he never believed her. How could she love him when she besmirched the family honor, his honor also, by falling in love with a man far beneath his father? When she ran away with her lover, she destroyed any love he felt for her. He had loved her, adored her. Her betrayal had caused Raoul to mask his feelings. The cynic in him grew until a bitter and cruel man emerged. But Raoul knew that his mother would have been the only person to accept and love him, no matter how he looked at present.

Opening a desk drawer, he withdrew a black patch. He placed it over the offensive eye and tied the string around his head. The doctor had advised he wear it, but so far, he hadn't had a reason. Now he did.

For the first time since the injury he walked to the mirror and studied his reflection. He found his face to be thinner, and this thinness gave his nose more of an eagle-like quality which he decided wasn't unattractive. His dark hair was bountiful, and with the patch over his right eye, he appeared extremely forbidding. He looked like the type of man who could strike fear in the hearts of little children and bend women to his will.

He imagined Lianne with her flaming hair cascaded on a white pillow, her face, her body, his to take and to pleasure. Or to inflict pain. Whichever he deemed necessary. But he decided she'd be more humiliated if he pleasured her, forced mewling submissive sounds from between her coral lips.

Yes, that was it. He'd allow Daniel Flanders to find her. She owed him for cutting his eye to shreds, for the loss of his sight. She owed him for turning him into a grotesque-looking human being, less than perfect.

He rang for a servant and ordered his clothes packed. Wherever Daniel followed Lianne's trail, he'd follow behind . . . ready to take her when the time came.

Chapter 8

All too soon Lianne's visit was cut short by Phillipe who insisted she return to New Orleans with him. He convinced her that he could arrange a meeting with the director of the opera company, that she didn't have to audition if she didn't wish. His uncle owned an interest in the company, and the director knew Phillipe very well.

Lianne was perfectly happy at Green Meadows but wished to get on with her life. She had to support her child, and though Maria insisted she still had plenty of money, Lianne refused to take another peso from her. Though Lianne suspected Phillipe was a braggart and might not even be that friendly with the director, she took a chance. To her amazement, she actually found herself liking him and looking forward to his visits to Green Meadows, and their intimate suppers together at Belle Riviere. Only once had he been anything but gentlemanly, and when he did have occasion to get a bit out of hand, he apologized for his behavior and was so charming that Lianne immediately forgave him. How could she help but like him when he always was so kind and sweet to her daughter?

However, Dera felt differently. "Watch out for Phillipe," she told her many times. "I don't trust him." Lianne weighed her godmother's words, but couldn't find any good reason not to like him. So, the morning she left Green Meadows, she kissed and hugged Dera warmly.

"I shall miss you, but I'll try to visit soon."

"Don't let Phillipe pull the wool too far over your eyes," she said and hugged her back.

With that warning in her head, Lianne, Maria and her baby were escorted by Phillipe into a carriage he had refurbished. A sadness filled Lianne as she waved again to Dera who stood on the front porch. They drove along the river road toward the city. "I shall miss her," she said sadly.

Phillipe took her hand. Maria, who sat in the corner seat with the baby, sniffed. Lianne knew she didn't think any more of Phillipe Marchand than Dera did. He gently brushed a stray wisp of Lianne's hair from her face. "I know, my love, but you have me to ease the pain. When we arrive in New Orleans, I shall show you your new home. I've already made arrangements for you to move into my town house which has stood empty for a long while. I think you shall be most pleased with it."

"Phillipe, I can't. It isn't proper."

"Why not?" he asked blankly.

She whispered low. "It's almost as if you're keeping me."

He laughed but his eyes were serious. "I wish that were true, my darling, except I want to keep you with me always. You know how much I love you, and want to marry you."

She remembered all the ardent marriage proposals, but she wasn't sure. She was fond of Phillipe, perhaps even loved him a little, but he didn't inflame her passions like the stranger.

She rubbed a thin finger across her forehead and looked at him with clear green eyes. "Let's see what happens, Phillipe. Don't rush me."

He nodded he understood, but he didn't. Were his charms slipping? By now he should already have bedded and wedded her. He wasn't accustomed to a female with a will of iron. Or was there another reason for her hesitancy? He'd discover her secret one day.

Amelie sat on the side veranda, completely obscured from view. She hid her clenched fists in the folds of her gown, wanting to scream about the unfairness of life. She had witnessed the touching farewell between Lianne and Dera. Dera, never overly fond of Amelie, had at least shown her affection—no matter how forced. But since the French woman arrived, she spent most of her time catering to her, playing with the child. No matter how hard Dera's disinterest was to take, Amelie convinced herself that she still had Phillipe. And now he had gone with Lianne. Amelie felt abandoned.

As she swallowed the huge lump which formed in her throat, she sensed Claude's presence behind her chair. "Madam Amelie, shall I take you inside?"

The lump became a painful ache, preventing her reply. He moved toward the front, seeing her beautiful eyes awash with crystal tears. When she realized he watched her, she threw her hands over face.

"Please don't stare pityingly at me, Claude!" Her voice broke, and his heart nearly did too.

Bending down, he slowly withdrew her hands from her face. Never had she expressed her feelings to him, always pretending to be cold. He knew better. Amelie was the warmest person with the softest heart he had ever known. And this is what he loved about her.

"Madam . . . Amelie," he spoke in his soothing voice. "Don't allow others to hurt you so. Sometimes people don't realize they're being cruel."

He held her hands in his, unaware of the picture they made. She as white and beautiful as a Grecian goddess, and he, a dusky brown, as handsome as any man she'd ever seen. Claude's touch, his voice, calmed her. "Everyone has abandoned me," she said.

"I haven't," he wanted to say, but instead he

took a small wood carving from his pocket. He'd carried it with him for weeks, not certain he should give it to her. But now he wanted her to have it, and hoped she'd cherish it as much as he cherished the hours carving it. "For you, madam." He held it out to her.

She took it from him, a thoughtful look on her face. Amelie examined the smooth finish of the oak, the beauty of line and detail and could almost imagine Claude's strong, sure hands whittling every inch of Amie's form. She smiled at him, her tears still wet on her cheeks. "You carved Amie for me?"

He nodded, too overwhelmed by her beauty to speak. Every morning when he situated her on the porch to watch the horses graze, she always fastened her gaze on L'Amour Impossible, or Amie. He knew of her love for horses, how she was the best horsewoman in the area before her accident, and though he'd never tell her this, he held Daniel responsible for making her a cripple. Daniel had once been his friend, but he'd never forgive him for abandoning this rare and fragile flower of a wife. A woman who would never ride again, a woman he had grown to love.

Tenderly she stroked the carving. "No one has ever done such a thing for me. Especially for me. *Merci,* Claude. *Merci.*" She took his hand which rested on her gown and gently brushed her lips against it. This simple, unassuming act brought tears to his eyes and a fire to his blood. If he hadn't spotted Bruno Haus meandering toward the house, he'd have kissed her then and there.

Claude drew himself up, standing stiffly before Amelie. For a moment she blushed, afraid she'd offended him. Then she noticed the overseer.

"Good day, Frau Flanders," he said much too pleasantly. "What have you there?"

"A carving of a horse," she told him and cupped the carving in her hands, to keep it hidden from his leering eyes.

"Ah, one of Claude's pieces, I'm sure. Still whittling your time away, boy? You ought to be working hard like the rest of the niggers instead of holed up here with such a pretty lady." He turned his full attention on Amelie, taking in her delicate beauty and wishing that he could be the one to spend his time with her, not some dark-skinned uppity wood-carving slave. "I'd be wary of this one; I hear the slave girls raving over his prowess as a lover. I hope he doesn't get ideas into his head and attack you, Frau Flanders." He openly licked his lips, his eyes resting on the slight cleavage her gown revealed. "If you have any trouble disciplining him, I'll be more than happy to oblige." He patted his whip.

Amelie felt Claude's anger and saw it on his face, but she calmly gazed into Bruno's face until he was forced to remove his eyes from her bosom. "Thank you for your kind concern, sir, but Claude is an admirable slave. If he does give me trouble, I shall be only too happy *not* to turn him over to you. Now, good morning. Claude, take me inside."

They left a dumbstruck Bruno on the veranda, and when Claude had carried her upstairs and settled her on her bed, his mother came into the room to see if she wished to nap.

"Not now, Lallie. I'm not the least bit tired." She took the woodcarving and placed it on her nightstand. "Thank you, Claude," she said again, her smile so bright he felt blinded.

"It was nothing," he told her and left the room, but shortly after he returned to his own room, his mother entered, unannounced. Lallie had been at Green Meadows since Claude was five years old, and she knew her son as well as she knew everyone in the house. Her dark eyes expressed sad concern because now she knew why her son didn't balk when Monsieur Daniel requested he become a house slave and tend to his wife.

"She is the master's wife," she said, standing in

the doorway, her hands on her wide hips.

"So?"

"Don't pretend with me, Claude. I know what it's like to love a white person. And I know it can bring only misery and tragedy."

Claude went to his mother and held her. "The only tragedy, mama, would be not loving her."

When Phillipe's carriage stopped before a small house, he turned to Lianne. "Here we are, chérie. I hope you like it."

Peering from the window Lianne noticed a small town house whose original sandy color was now faded, but Lianne didn't care. She fell in love with it almost immediately, liking the large front window and the side entrance, but most of all because Phillipe told her it was only a short walk from the opera company.

"The house has been empty for some time," Phillipe explained. "I haven't used it since . . . well, never mind that. Suffice it to say that I'm most pleased you shall be living here." He helped Lianne from the carriage, then Maria and the baby. When they entered the house, a servant waited to see to their belongings and immediately showed Maria and her charge to their room. Phillipe had ordered a speedy departure for Maria, not wishing to put up with her disapproving looks or the whinings of the child. He wanted Lianne to himself, without any interruptions.

Lianne surveyed the room and decided she liked what she saw. The furnishings were in the period of Louis XV and covered in a green and peach print. Two small chairs matched the sofa, and all three pieces surrounded a low mahogany table. Phillipe escorted her into the small dining room which contained a round table with only four chairs. The carpet was dark green, and the drapes were gold. He didn't bother to show her the outside kitchen, telling her she'd never need to enter it. After all, that's what the servants were for.

He passed her quickly through the baby's room which Maria shared, and then threw open the door to Lianne's bedroom. Lianne caught her breath and turned a stunned eye to Phillipe.

"This is so very grand!" Her gaze took in the tall tester bed which was covered in lacy folds of fabric to the floor. A white lace counterpane covered the bed and was embroidered with tiny, gold lilies of the valley. Across the French doors, which led to the courtyard, hung the same lace fabric. The remaining furniture of night stand, dressing table and chair were made from the finest oak and polished to a high sheen.

"It looks like something from a fairy story." Lianne's eyes glowed.

This was the response he had intended. He turned her face, easing her chin into his hand. Her eyes tilted at an angle, almost like a cat's, he decided. "You're a fairy princess, my love. My princess. Everything must be perfect for you."

A slight smile parted her lips. "This is beyond my wildest dreams. I haven't seen anything like this since my room at the chateau. *Merci,* Phillipe." She reached up and kissed him, but immediately knew she shouldn't have. His arms flew around her waist, and his mouth refused to loosen its hold on her lips. He had always acted the gentleman, attending to her every need, but now he seemed like an animal and reminded her of de Lovis. She didn't want Phillipe to take her like this, not because he had arranged a house for her, decorated a room for her, and she should show her gratitude. So, she pushed away, forcing him to break his hold on her mouth.

"Lianne!" His voice was ragged, desire still in his eyes. He made a move to grab her again, but she escaped him, putting the chair between them.

"Don't rush me! It's too soon."

"*Mon Dieu,* I am but a man, and you inflame my senses. What do you want of me? Shall I play your devoted admirer lapping any crumbs of affection you throw to me? You're not a cold woman, Lianne. Don't hold back from me. How long has your husband been dead? At least a year since your child is nearly the same age. You must crave a man's touch by now.''

She hadn't told him that André died nearly three years ago and that her child wasn't his. She allowed everyone to think Désirée was her husband's daughter. How could she tell him that it was too soon for her to forget the touch of a stranger, a man she'd never seen again, the father of her child? At that moment she felt pity for Phillipe and almost wished she could make love to him, but she wouldn't allow him or any man to push her into something she didn't want.

"Give me time, Phillipe. That's all I ask."

He watched her for some seconds, knowing he could force her but that would win him nothing but her hatred. He loved her and wanted her, so he decided he'd play the devoted suitor until she was ready. Originally he had wanted to bed her first, then marry her. Now he felt the marriage should come first. After all, he didn't want to compromise her or have her scorn. He wanted her love, and he'd wait, however long it took.

He sighed and held out his hand to her. "Come here. I promise I won't attack you again."

She believed him, and she inched closer, then took his outstretched hand. He held it tightly. "I love you, Lianne, and I'll do anything to prove that love. I want you for my bride, but I know you're not ready for marriage, that you have dreams of an operatic career. So, to prove to you how much I do love you, I shall take you within the hour to the opera company and let you meet the director. When the new performance begins within the next few weeks, I assure you that you shall perform."

"You intend to buy me a place in the company?"

"No." He read disapproval on her face. "I know that you're good enough to be accepted on your own."

He tickled her chin with his fingertips. "However, it doesn't hurt to have friends in high places."

She relaxed. Her eyes brightened, and she rested her head against his shoulder. "I'm very lucky to have you, Phillipe. Forgive me for my behavior."

"I do. I love you very much, *chérie.*" Those are the words he whispered to her, but he didn't tell her that she wouldn't perform long with the opera company. He wanted her to devote herself exclusively to him and Belle Riviere.

Chapter 9

True to his word, Phillipe introduced Lianne to the opera's director less than an hour later. Although she was nervous and wondered if she'd be able to squeak out a note, she sang beautifully and immediately became a member of the company. Told to report for rehearsals the following day, she kissed Phillipe soundly on the lips once they were outside the building.

"Thank you for coming with me and helping me," she said.

Phillipe laughed, pleased with himself. "If I'd known I'd receive such favors, I'd have dragged you here the first moment we met."

She tucked her arm through his, and since it was such a lovely afternoon, she insisted they walk the distance home. Phillipe agreed but told the driver to follow along. He felt like a king with Lianne on his arm, aware of the admiring glances sent their way. She was more than beautiful in a gown of topaz silk, her shining tresses piled upon her head, and her face turned upward to his. With love? He hoped so. He wanted her more than any woman in his life, and he'd have her.

To Lianne, Phillipe was more than a friend, a would-be lover. In the few weeks they'd known one another he had become as important to her as André when he was alive. She found herself depending upon him, asking his advice and hoping he cared for her daughter. Certainly she knew Phillipe's faults, his indolence for one, but she felt that with time and with the right woman, Phillipe would change. Though she knew he wished to marry her and she seriously considered it, she couldn't rush. Marriage was much too important to her to be entered into lightly.

Just as they neared the house another carriage passed them at a leisurely pace. Lianne glanced at it, taking in the two inhabitants. A woman with skin almost as fair as hers was seated with a small boy of about five. The child, too, was fair-skinned but Lianne noticed the woman wore a brightly colored turban which branded her as a quadroon. The Spanish government had decreed all quadroons cover themselves in a respectable fashion, so the women had respectfully done so, except their headdresses were so elaborate that everyone took notice of them. Huge golden hooped earrings enhanced her appearance and in a bright orange gown which matched the turban, Lianne thought she was the most exotically beautiful woman she'd ever seen. The child beside her resembled her but it was clear to see that his father was white. His hair was a curly black and set off his fair skin and the startling blue color of his eyes.

As the open carriage drew nearer, the woman looked at them and her own beautiful face registered surprise and something else, like hurt. The boy began to point and say something, but his mother quickly whispered into his ear, and he sat in regimented silence. But his eyes sadly lingered on Lianne and Phillipe until the carriage turned the corner.

Phillipe's own face had turned ashen. "Who were they?" Lianne asked.

"Who, my dear?"

"The woman and the little boy. They seemed to know you."

"You're mistaken, Lianne. I haven't any idea

who they are. Just a quadroon and her bastard out for a drive, I suppose."

Did she imagine she felt the pressure of his arm tigthen? She stopped walking. "Phillipe, I'm well aware that many white men have quadroons for mistresses. Is she your mistress?"

"You do come to the point. Yes, I do know them. Her name is Chloe and she is the mistress of a friend of mine."

"Then why didn't you tell me that from the start?"

Phillipe shrugged. "I didn't want to expose you to such things. Decent women aren't to mention the quadroons."

"But surely 'decent' women know of their existence. Somes you baffle me so, Phillipe, by your desire to protect me like a fragile flower. I've been married and have had a child, I do know such women exist and am not the least offended."

"Really?" He looked surprised.

She rearranged his arm in hers and began walking. "You forget that I was brought up in French court life. Mistresses of powerful men came and went like summer rains. Though I'm not shocked, I will tell you that I don't really approve. And if I marry again, my husband shall have no need to seek female companionship elsewhere."

He smiled down at her, color returning to his face. "If a man had you for a wife, *chérie,* he'd have to be blind to want another woman." They walked the remaining distance home, arm in arm like two lovers, and Phillipe departed reluctantly.

Maria was thrilled with her news about the opera, but less than pleased with the picture of Phillipe placing a lingering kiss on Lianne's lips before his departure. "Don't get too friendly with that one," she warned Lianne as she took off her gloves.

Lianne threw the gloves on the chair and poured a cup of hot tea. "You sound exactly like Dera."

"*Sí*. Señora Dera knows him better than you. This Phillipe Marchand is not right for you. He'll cause much misery."

"Perhaps, but he is pleasant company. I can't refuse to see him, Maria. He did arrange for me to meet the director of the opera company. I'm in his debt."

"Ha! Before long you'll be in his bed, my poor little goose. I don't want you hurt again."

Maria's concern touched her, but life looked bright at the moment. "Nothing will hurt me any longer, especially not a man. I must think of my daughter and my career before I give love to another man."

Maria sniffed. "Don't end up like poor Honorine."

"Honorine? Who is she?"

Maria sat on the sofa, her large, dark eyes glowing. "I talked to the housekeeper next door. She told me that a woman named Honorine who sang for the opera lived in this house a few years ago. She loved a man, not wisely I'm told, and the poor wretched thing took poison when the man grew tired of her. She died in this room. The housekeeper says the house is haunted."

"What a terrible story. How unfortunate for Honorine." Lianne shivered. "But you don't believe in ghosts, Maria, do you?"

"No, only the living need be feared," Maria said philosophically. "I tell you this, so you won't become like this Honorine."

Maria then left her in the quiet of the room. The hazy afternoon sun filtered through the lace curtains on the window, but Lianne felt cold. A woman died in this room, a woman who sang for the opera. Why hadn't Phillipe told her this? He must have known about the girl. After all, he owned the place. She finished her tea, then hurried from the parlor as

Désirée's cries drove Honorine from her head.

Damn it to hell! Phillipe swore to himself as his carriage stopped along the rue des Ramparts. Why did Chloe have to leave the little white house he provided for her and Jean Marc? Why did she have to pass just as he walked arm in arm with Lianne? What would have been Lianne's reaction if Jean Marc had called him "Papa"? Thank the Lord that Chloe had some control over their son, otherwise, his romance with the auburn-haired temptress would have ended before it had even begun.

Bounding up the small steps of the house, he took out his key and opened the door to find Chloe sitting on a chair and stitching a shirt of Jean Marc's. The orange turban had been removed, and her dark brown hair cascaded softly around her shoulders, the fading afternoon sun highlighting the delicate bone structure of her face. When she lifted her head to smile sadly at him, her lashes uncovered the loveliest pair of brown eyes Phillipe had ever seen, and he felt lucky she loved him.

"I didn't expect you, chérie," she said in her soft way.

Guilt tore through him. She had seen him with Lianne and he knew she was hurt, but he knew her well enough to know she'd never reproach him, never say anything about the incident. In her accepting way she'd do whatever he wished. It seemed he had always loved Chloe. From the moment his father bought the house for him and encouraged him to attend the quadroon ball where his young eyes lighted upon Chloe, easily the most beautiful girl there, he had lost his heart to her forever.

The memory of her in a flowing white gown which any white woman would envy passed across his mind. He remembered asking his father if Chloe was really a quadroon, her skin was so white, and being told that she was the child of a white man and a mulatto woman.

Most of the young creole men were secretly encouraged by their fathers and male friends to form a relationship with the quadroons. After all, why not have the best of both worlds—a white bride who will give legitimate heirs and a dark mistress who will see to a man's every need. To be the mistress of a white man was the aim of every young quadroon. But the men never considered marriage to these women. It just wasn't done though some of them, like Chloe, had fairer complexions than their white counterparts. For Phillipe, this was always a secret yearning—to marry Chloe. No other woman had ever come close to her beauty, her gentleness. Except Lianne. And he knew the time had come for him to marry. Chloe knew it, too.

She laid aside her sewing and standing up, she held out her hands to his and kissed him tenderly. He couldn't help but notice the tears shimmering in her eyes. His heart nearly broke. He pulled her close, catching the scent of gardenia in her hair. "This is the only place I wish to be, my love."

"Our son is visiting a few houses away and will stay for supper. We have a little time to ourselves before he bombards you with questions."

She turned to lead him to the bedroom, but he stopped her. "Have you no questions?"

She shook her head. A stray tear coursed down her cheek. "No, *chérie*. I knew the time would come when you'd take a true wife. I'm grateful I've had you to myself for so long. Most of my friends haven't been as fortunate."

"How do you know I'll marry her?"

Chloe sighed. "Because I saw the way you looked at her, and I've seen that look on your face for me many times. Besides, she is most beautiful, but she'll never love you like I do."

Phillipe realized she might be right but he kept

that to himself. For some reason he had to marry
Lianne. She was a fire in his blood, or perhaps he
enjoyed the challenge she presented. Chloe was so
predictable. Though Chloe had presented him with a
son, he needed a legitimate heir for Belle Riviere.

"Nothing changes for us," he said, hoping to
mollify her. "I'll still provide for you and Jean-Marc.
And I'll still need you, chérie, for other things." He
stroked her cheek.

She said nothing, but in her heart she knew
Phillipe would always belong to her, in every way it
was possible for a man to belong to a woman. With a
certainty born within her, she knew the beautiful red-
haired woman would not make Phillipe happy. So she
led him to the bedroom where her hands, lips and
heart expressed her love for him.

God, life was frustrating! Daniel couldn't help
but think this as he leaned over the ship's railing. The
landscape of Spain blended into the misty morning
sky, and soon the dazzling brilliance of the court life,
the women, would fade into memory. Just as all the
other places he had been the last few years. Everywhere but the summerhouse in Ireland, that is. He
remembered that night with clarity—the beautiful
auburn-haired woman who had given herself so
passionately to him. Lianne. His mind said her name
over and over until he withdrew his gaze from the
speck on the horizon which was Spain.

He moved from the railing and took out his small
sketch book from the top pocket of his jacket. On the
first page was a line drawing of Kathleen and Douglas.
Also one of the dachsund named Mitzie. He smiled,
suddenly missing the two scamps. How lucky was Paul
to have such beautiful children. All his life it seemed
that Paul had been favored. First by his parents
though not as much by his mother as his father. He
remembered the way his father had doted on his eldest
son because he resembled him so much in looks and

temperament. Of course Daniel knew he was loved as well, but not with the same ferocity. Probably because he had been ill as a child and was more or less tied to the house a great deal. He also resembled his mother which may have branded him as hers in his father's mind.

If it hadn't been for Claude, his childhood and young adulthood would have passed without a ripple. He wondered how Claude was doing with Amelie. Probably the fellow was insane by now. Amelie could be so demanding, and Claude was such an easygoing person. But thoughts of Claude depressed him because he had to remember his wife. Soon he'd be home again. He wondered if she'd be pleased to see him. He doubted if time had healed the wounds. For him, it hadn't. Seeing her again would bring back all the agony of knowing he'd never have the children he so desperately wanted.

Flipping through the notebook, he caught sight of the sketch he had done of Lianne. Of course it had been drawn from memory, a rather hazy recollection at best, but he felt it was exact. His finger traced the lines of her face, the tilted eyes, the perfect mouth. For a second he remembered a scene from his childhood. He saw himself as about seven or eight on the back lawn of Belle Riviere before the Marchands bought the plantation. He remembered playing ball with a small child of about two. Her long auburn hair curled like vines to her shoulders, and she laughed in glee every time she threw the ball back to him.

He started because the child reminded him of Lianne, in fact she'd resemble his drawing when grown. But it was impossible. The tiny girl and the grown woman were oceans apart. Hope faltered in him suddenly. He'd never find her. Like a stupid fool, he'd fallen in love with a phantom, a woman who entered his life for a moment and then vanished like a morning mist. If it hadn't been for Dubois and the singers at the opera in Madrid, he would have doubted her existence.

"Lovesick fool," he muttered under his breath and put his sketch pad away.

At home his wife waited, a woman crippled because of him. For all of Amelie's faults, he wondered if she still loved him. She had loved him once, and he realized he needed someone to care for him, needed a safe harbor from the stormy seas of life, the turbulence of his own soul. He vowed to make things up to Amelie, to become the husband she wanted.

The time had come to start life anew.

Chapter 10

Tingles like pinpricks ran up and down Amelie's legs. The sensations had started earlier that morning, before dawn, and now it was nearly noon, and she still hadn't confided in anyone. She rubbed her hands along the softly rounded calves, stopping at her upper thighs. She could feel them, could actually move her toes! Tears streamed down her cheeks. God, please let me walk again, let me ride! she prayed silently.

She still wore her nightgown, a pale pink creation with soft lace at the neckline and loose sleeves, cuffed at the wrists. Lallie had inquired more than twice as to why she didn't dress today and watch the horses. Even Dera had looked in on her after Lallie told her that she was still abed and for a moment she had been touched by her mother-in-law's concern. But she remembered Dera had never cared for her and only checked on her because she was Daniel's wife. Amelie knew if Dera had her way she'd have been returned to Belle Riviere long ago. So, she said she felt fine but was rather tired and thanked her for caring.

"I do care about you," were Dera's parting words, given with a smile.

Sure, thought Amelie. She cares so much about me she forgets I exist when a long-lost godchild appears on her doorstep. Amelie felt momentarily sorry for herself because Phillipe, her own brother,

hadn't visited her in weeks. Not since riding off to
New Orleans with the French strumpet. But as the life
flowed back into her legs, she forgot her dislike of
Lianne and what she felt were Dera's and Phillipe's
disregard.

Suddenly her legs felt light. The tingles seemed to
lessen, and she didn't know whether to be frightened.
She knew she had to try to move her legs, but it took her
some time to gain her courage. Bracing herself, she
willed the limbs to move, and they did. Little by little
she inched to the side of the bed until her legs hung
over the side. Joyful tears flowed fast, but she wiped
them away and held onto the bed post. Then she
pressed her feet to the floor and eased herself up,
expecting her legs to buckle. They didn't.

Her heart hammered in her ears. She did it! For
the first time in three years she had gotten out of bed
on her own power. She waited a moment before taking
the final test. Could she walk the distance to the
balcony doors?

She swallowed hard. Her legs moved in that
direction a little at a time as her fingers slowly slid
from the bed post. She felt wobbly but she steadied
herself on a nearby table, then the back of a chair, and
she made it. Before too long, her hand was on the
doorknob. She opened it, holding onto the door,
happy tears streaming down her cheeks. She looked
toward the river, a barely perceptible streak of silver in
the afternoon sun. Double rows of oaks reached
toward the brilliant blue sky. For the first time
since her accident she felt peace.

She was so consumed with joy she didn't hear the
creaking of the door leading into Claude's room. Not
until she felt a hand on her shoulder did she realize
Claude's presence. She gazed into Claude's equally
surprised and baffled face.

"Amelie . . . ?" he began uncertainly.

She nodded her head as the tears glimmered in her
eyes. "I walked, Claude. I walked!"

She faltered against him, suddenly weak and tired. He gathered her in his arms, holding her gently at first. "I'm so happy. The Lord has made you well." Her eyes met his, and she was so beautiful that all his pent-up emotions, hidden for so long, spilled forth like an exploding volcano. Holding her tightly against him, he said, "I love you, Amelie. I love you so much." His mouth devoured hers, drinking in the honeyed sweetness of her lips. Beyond thinking, beyond caring that he was a slave and she was his mistress, he wanted her with a burning ache which only her love could quench.

When his lips first made contact with hers, Amelie gasped, but then a hot, liquid sensation overwhelmed her. Though she knew she should protest, she didn't. With no warning, her daydreams of being held in Claude's strong arms, of matching him kiss for kiss, became reality. Never had she responded so strongly to a man, even to Daniel. She wanted Claude to sweep her into his arms, to carry her away. And he did. Before she realized it, he had lifted her from her feet. She clung to him in a daze when he carried her to the bed.

Their bodies met and for the first time, her breasts came in contact with his chest. Moans of delight escaped through her lips as his hands stroked them through the soft material of her gown. All this time his mouth had never left hers, his tongue doing delicious things to hers. She felt his hands pulling the top of her gown down to her waist and then he enfolded a breast in one of his warm hands. His mouth broke away and came to rest on a nipple.

Desire washed over her, forcing guttural sounds to escape from her throat. Her fingers curled in his hair, trailing to the nape of his neck. She wanted him, wanted him badly. Her lower body burned with a blazing hot fire.

"Oh, Claude," she moaned. "Make love to me. Please."

He looked at her, his eyes dark and shining in the

dusky velvet of his face. Amelie traced his jawline with her index finger. Her lower body writhed and urged him to take her. He whispered her name like a prayer, ready to pleasure her and himself, but he saw his dark hand wrapped around the paleness of a breast. With a sudden clearness he knew he couldn't make love to her, that Amelie could never be joined to him. He was a slave, less than human in most white men's eyes, and here he was, ready to make love to a white man's woman. The wife of his childhood friend. He loved Amelie, loved her with a passion he had never felt in his life, but he couldn't make love to her, had to spare her the suffering he knew would come if their flesh merged.

As if a bucket of river water had been thrown over him, he pushed away, and he watched as Amelie sat up. Her long hair flowed around her, her breasts taunting him, but she was unaware of the effect she had on him.

"Claude, what is it?"

"We're wrong. This is wrong."

For a moment she didn't understand. Everything happened so fast. She could walk now and had just been in this man's arms. But she realized what he meant.

"It's wrong because you're a slave. That's it, isn't it? But it doesn't matter to me." Her voice grew low. "I . . . love you, Claude."

He groaned. "Our love can never be, Amelie. Believe that I love you, but it's hopeless."

"No! You mustn't say that. No one need ever know. I have no one, nothing, but you. No one means anything to me but you. I don't care what color you are. I don't!" She began sobbing, holding out her hands to him.

He hated to see her tears. If she hadn't cried, he'd have turned his back on her and left her alone. But he loved her, loved her beyond thinking. He gazed at her face, drowning in her beauty. This beautiful woman loved him, and he loved her. What could be so wrong in holding her, kissing her? He wanted to feel her soft flesh against the hard planes of his body, wanted to take her to heaven and beyond. Our love is right, he told himself as he took her outstretched hands and enfolded her in his arms again. He only wanted to hold her for awhile, to kiss away her tears. As the pale pink of her gown fell to the floor, Claude's resistance broke. His clothes merged with hers, and Amelie and Claude discovered love.

Sylvain was the opera in which Lianne performed. Though she sang a small piece, the director encouraged her talent and felt that she'd soon be ready for more challenging roles. After the performance she felt invigorated. Her cheeks flushed with pleasure in the new life she'd undertaken. When Phillipe met her backstage, he seemed withdrawn, remote, not at all the concerned suitor.

"Have I done anything to displease you?" she asked him later as they sipped glasses of wine in the elegant rooms Phillipe had rented on the Esplanade. She moved closer to him on the couch, but he looked away.

He didn't know how to reply. Her operatic performances displeased him because he felt she should desire him as a husband and forget the stage. He wanted her to himself, wanted her in his bed and at Belle Riviere. However, he couldn't say these things to her. Lianne wasn't the sort of woman who needed a man to fulfill her every wish. However, he had a plan to bring about her response but hoped it wouldn't have to be put into action. He cleared his throat.

"When are you going to marry me?"

Twisting the goblet and gazing at the dark red liquid, she didn't know what to say. After all these weeks with him, she still wasn't sure she wanted to marry him, and she didn't think fondness constituted grounds for marriage. "Is it so important to marry, Phillipe?"

"*Oui,* it is! You dangle me from a string like a puppet, and I dance to your song, but still you never let me do anything more than kiss you . . . and that is barely more than warm. Lianne, why do you torment me so?"

"I'm sorry. I didn't think you felt this way. It's just that you act so frivolous at times that I can't take you seriously."

"You mean because I'm noted for my wildness, the high stakes at cards, the many women of whom I'm sure Dera has kindly informed you."

This was all true. During Lianne's last visit to Green Meadows, Dera had again warned her against him. She noticed Phillipe's anger but didn't know how to appease him. "Allow me more time," was all she said.

He had no other choice at the moment, but she looked so beautiful in a deep emerald satin gown with a rose pinned to her upswept hair that he wanted to carry her to the bedroom and make love to her until she grew exhausted. Restraint was new to Phillipe, but he practiced it for the moment. Soon, however, Lianne would be his wife. Much sooner than she guessed. Taking her into his arms, he kissed her with a gentleness which surprised her after his anger only seconds ago.

"I shall wait, *chérie,* forever."

Then he kissed her again and a warmth flooded through her but nothing like the passion she felt for the man who had fathered Désirée. It would be so easy to allow Phillipe to make love to her. Her body craved a man's touch, but she resisted. Only when her heart responded wildly as it had in the summerhouse would she consider Phillipe's marriage proposal. She drew away. "I think it's time for you to escort me home," she said.

After she was in bed and Phillipe sent on his way, she drifted into sleep. Suddenly she came awake, startled, and felt someone's presence in the room. "Maria?" she whispered and hoped her voice didn't sound as thick with fear as it did to her.

She sat up and listened. She heard breathing, and the skin on the back of her neck prickled. For a second she wondered if the house was haunted by the tragic Honorine. "What do you want?" she asked.

She knew no spirit spoke when the gruff voice said, "You pretty mademoiselle."

Before she could scream, a man flew like a bat from the shadows of the room and pinned her to the bed. His hand muffed her mouth. She thrashed and kicked at him but missed her mark. The man forced his hands into her bodice and squeezed her breasts.

"Pretty ladies shouldn't live alone," he scolded.

Lianne had to escape or she would faint. He cut off her air, and she felt the room sway. Suddenly he changed position and came to rest on top of her. She lifted her knee, pushing it hard into his groin. He groaned and removed his hand from her mouth. Lianne screamed a bloodcurdling scream.

"Quiet!" he yelled and came at her again, but he was thrown from the bed by Phillipe who ran into the room from the French doors.

In the darkness she heard the crack of Phillipe's knuckles making contact with the man's chin. To her surprise he fled through the door into the dark night.

"Lianne, are you all right, *mon amour*?" Phillipe cried and held her shaking body in his arms.

She nodded, too stunned to move when Maria ran into her room. *"Madre de Dios!* What has happened?"

Phillipe explained to her about the intruder. "It was lucky that I returned when I did. I heard Lianne's screams from the street."

"Sí, si, Gracias, Señor Marchand. Whatever would we have done without you?"

This was the first time Maria had expressed any sentiment other than scorn concerning Phillipe. "Two women alone with a child, señor. That is not good." making sure Lianne was all right then went to look in on the baby who had remarkably slept through the whole ordeal.
ordeal.

In the candlelight Lianne's hair matched the flame. She rested in Phillipe's arms until her shaking ceased. He stroked her silken tresses. "Why did you come back?" she asked him after she had calmed down enough to speak.

"Because I worried about you, and I wanted to apologize for what I said earlier. But now I see I was right to pressure you into giving me an answer. If tonight is any indication of what will happen if you live alone with Maria and your child, I dread to think what may occur if this intruder returns." He tilted her chin. "I don't believe he came to rob you. Evidently he has been watching your house and you. Lianne, think of your child if you have no fear for yourself."

She shivered. Phillipe made a great deal of sense. If he hadn't returned, she hated to imagine what harm might have befallen her and Maria, or her child. The incident reminded her of the time the peasants stormed the chateau. Held in fear's thrall, she clutched at Phillipe's shirtfront. "I'll marry you. Take us home to Belle Riviere," she said.

"What about the opera?"

Glimmers of pure fright gleamed in her eyes. Always she had had someone to care for her. André. Victor. Now she was really alone except for Maria. And what good was she if the man returned? She realized that her safety and her child's well-being were more important than an operatic career. "I'll tell the director tomorrow that I'm to be married. Then we leave for Belle Riviere."

"Are you sure?" He tried to keep the pleased note from his voice.

"Oui. Take us home with you. Make me your wife."

He kissed her and held her until she fell asleep. Then he laid her head on the pillow and quietly left the house, headed down the alleyway to the end of the street where a man waited in the shadows. He handed him a pouch of gold coins.

"For a job well done," Phillipe told him.

The man looked at him with a surly expression. "I don't usually attack women, monsieur. I'm just a thief but I do have principles." He pocketed the money and massaged his still stinging jaw.

"Very noble to have scruples, but in this instance you've done a good deed. Now be on your way. Tonight's performance has netted you quite a healthy fee."

The man sniffed and headed into the darkness. Phillipe turned and walked back to Lianne's where he spent the rest of the night on a chair in her room just in case she woke and needed him.

Chapter 11

When Dera learned Lianne had arrived at Belle Riviere with Phillipe, she insisted Lianne reside at Green Meadows until the wedding for propriety's sake. Besides, she wasn't certain Lianne loved Phillipe and wished to put some distance between them to allow the young woman a chance to think. Phillipe wasn't pleased when Lianne accepted Dera's invitation, but he didn't balk. After all, in a very short time, Lianne would become his bride. He didn't wish to ruin things now.

"If you insist upon this wedding," Dera told Lianne one afternoon as they sat on the front porch and gazed at the long row of oaks which led to the river, "then I must insist that your marriage take place here at Green Meadows. I know your mother would have wished it."

"Thank you," Lianne said with a soft smile. "I'd like that very much. However, you still don't trust Phillipe, do you?"

A sigh escaped Dera, and she looked down at her hands. "No. He is wrong for you, but then many people told me my Quint wasn't right for me either. So, who am I to say? Love comes from the heart and only you know what you feel for Phillipe."

Lianne averted her eyes. "I shall be a good wife to him."

Sadness overtook Dera. She clutched Lianne's hand. "Once, many years ago, I said the same thing. I married a man I wasn't in love with. Oh, I was fond of him in the same way I think you care for Phillipe, and for awhile I thought I was happy. But one day I realized I wasn't."

"What happened to make you change your mind?"

"Quint reentered my life and turned it upside down, but we were destined for one another. No man has ever made me feel what I felt for him."

"Do you feel the same thing for Doctor Markham?" Lianne impulsively asked.

A blush like berry juice stained Dera's cheeks and she stammered. "Lianne, dear, I'm getting much too old for romance. Doctor Markham is a dear friend, but no, I'll never marry again."

"I never mentioned marriage. Has he asked you?"

Her face grew redder. "Heavens no! Tad is a gentleman and settled in his ways. I don't think he'd ever consider marriage again. He's a widower from Williamsburg and has a grown daughter."

Lianne baited her good-naturedly. "I think you've been thinking about marriage to the good doctor, Dera."

Dera began to protest but instead she nodded in reluctance. "I care for Tad a great deal. Not in the same way I loved Quint but as someone to live out my days with. However, I don't believe he sees me as a potential wife. He'll return to Williamsburg and his daughter eventually."

"Then you'll just have to change his mind."

Dera laughed. "I'm not a young beautiful girl any longer, Lianne." Her face grew serious. "I wish you and my Daniel could have met. I think then your marriage to Phillipe wouldn't occur, and Amelie wouldn't be forced to live a life of pain. She knows he doesn't love her. It's too bad one must live life dependent upon destiny."

Lianne squeezed her hand. "I'm sure your Daniel is a wonderful man, but I'm quite content to be Phillipe's wife."

Dismay swept through Dera. She knew of Phillipe's dalliances with women, of the quadroon woman he kept on the ramparts, and of the debts he incurred at the gaming halls. She couldn't imagine a happy union between Phillipe and Lianne who was so gentle and loving, but also possessed of an independent streak which would drive Phillipe to distraction. But she didn't tell her about these things. Instead she leaned over and kissed Lianne's cheek. "I hope you can say that in a few months, my dear."

The wedding preparations depressed Amelie. She watched as the servants carried fresh flowers into the house and arranged them in vases until she thought she'd go mad with the smell of roses, jasmine, daisies and bright red holly which wreathed around the doorways, the stair railings. Christmas had passed with a sudden flurry of guests to Green Meadows, courtesy of Phillipe. She realized he wished to show off his fiancée and give people the impression that Amelie and Dera approved of the match. Amelie knew Dera's feelings though she did her best to hide them with a polite smile on her face. But Amelie didn't bother.

She sat mutely in the parlor through all the holiday gatherings with a silent Claude who waited in the corner, while Lianne paraded around in the new silk and velvet gowns Phillipe had ordered for her entrance into society as his fiancée.

She resented the way she had wormed her way into her brother's life and Dera's affections. Oh, why couldn't these two people care for her? Why must she share her brother's love with Lianne and relinquish any crumb of affection Dera had shown her to a woman whom she hadn't seen in almost twenty years? None of it was fair.

Amelie could have shocked all of them by rising from the couch and dancing around the room. She hadn't told Dera or Phillipe she could walk. Not even Lallie knew. Only Claude. Her eyes glanced furtively in his direction. She noticed he watched her with love, with a hunger of which only she was aware.

She flushed despite the slight chill in the air as she thought of the wondrous nights when he crept into her bed, inflaming her with a passion she hadn't known she possessed. She had met his hot kisses with her own and surrendered to his every variation in lovemaking.

Claude had taught her many things, things she'd never done with Daniel, and she wasn't the least bit frightened or repulsed as his lips and hands sought her most private places. With Claude, it seemed natural. She knew then that Daniel had never truly wanted her or loved her. Otherwise, he'd have pleased her in the same way. In fact she no longer cared if Daniel ever returned home. She had Claude, and she belonged to him. Yet she couldn't tell anyone she could walk. She feared that if Dera learned the truth and informed Daniel, he'd insist she leave Green Meadows. And she couldn't. Not now. Not when her brother was ready to take a wife. She'd have no place to go, and there would never be a way for her to take Claude with her, not without risking their love affair. She'd never give him up, just as she'd never relinquish her position as Daniel Flanders' wife.

Phillipe had decided that the wedding should take place late in the afternoon on New Year's Day. Amelie grew restless as the servants dashed in and out of the drawing room, sweeping and dusting for the wedding that afternoon. Finally when she could stand it no longer, she motioned to Claude. "Take me for a ride in the buggy or I'll go insane."

"It's rather chilly outside, Amelie."

"I don't care! If I have to run out of here, I will. I

can't stand hearing that French woman's delighted giggles or the child's crying, Claude. Now, take me outside!'' she snapped, then was sorry to see the hurt on his face. "I'm sorry," she said as he picked her up and grabbed her shawl in one motion.

His lips gently brushed against her cheek when the room was empty of the servants. "Tell everyone you can walk. I'll take you away, Amelie. We could be happy together."

She loved him and wanted the same thing. But where could they live in peace? He was a mulatto slave, she the wife of a white planter. There was nothing to be done but pretend, and she couldn't admit how much she loved the pampered life to him, though she felt he had already guessed that. "Don't make it harder for me, darling." She whispered in his ear. "Take me to our private spot before it's time to dress for the wedding. No one will miss us since Dera's too wrapped up in her goddaughter and your mother is pressing the wedding dress."

Her slender hands unbuttoned the first button on his shirt, reaching in and massaging his chest with the flat of her palm. "I love to touch you," she whispered.

Her touch started a fire deep in his loins. Within minutes he settled her in the buggy and had cantered to their secret place, a place he had found at the edge of the property which bordered on Belle Riviere and was covered by thick undergrowth and tall trees. He stopped the buggy behind a clump of foliage, sure that it was hidden from the view of the house and helped Amelie down. The moment she fell in his arms again, he kissed her, taking her breath.

She wrapped her arms around his neck, pulling him closer. He gazed into her eyes, a hazy blue at that moment and clouded with desire. They reminded him of the river on a warm, summer afternoon. He didn't know what he had done to deserve her love, her passion, but she belonged to him and he'd never give her up. Not even to her husband. She smiled a bewitching smile at him, and they entered the foliage which shielded them like a curtain.

With her shawl he made a cushion against the grass. She shimmied out of her gown, taunting him with her small, rounded breasts. She had on no undergarments and his desire increased as he realized that she must have planned this sojourn into the woods.

She reached out and unbuttoned his shirt, her fingers massaging and kneading the dusty brown flesh. Then her hand slid to the rope at his waist, and his pants fell to his feet. She bent to kiss the hairy expanse of navel and abdomen. Claude groaned as her tongue worked lower.

"Amelie, Amelie," he moaned over and over as her mouth and hands showed him how much she loved him, wanted him. Then when he could stand no more, he bent and pushed her onto the shawl and pleasured her in the same intimate way.

Her whimpers of pleasure echoed through the still morning air. Her breasts trembled as she flexed upward at the deep sensations coursing through her lower body. She pulled his head away from her, unable to stand the intense pleasure, demanding more of him. When he snaked up her body to capture her lips, her legs wrapped around him.

"Do you want more, *chérie*?"

"All of you, Claude."

He wanted her too, and when he entered her, he thought he'd die from the exquisite pleasure of it. She arched against him moaning and writhing. Her nails scratched the skin of his back and excited him to a fever pitch. Then his seed of life rushed into her and she cried his name in ecstatic moans which he muffled with his lips.

Amelie lay gasping, unable to believe anything could be so wonderful. The times she and Claude made love had been filled with passion, fulfillment, but she knew this time was different and would remember it for the rest of her life. Her fingertips stroked the hardness of his chest, and he smiled into her eyes.

"I love you, Amelie. Love you so much."

"Even more than the kitchen wenches you've had? As I understand it from Bruno Haus, you're quite a man with the ladies, known for your prowess."

His hand lightly brushed against her breast, an amused look coming to his eyes. "Are you jealous?"

"Not for the women you've had because evidently you were taught very well. But don't take another woman to your bed, Claude. I couldn't bear it."

"I don't want anyone but you." He grew serious. "What happens when your husband returns? Suppose Daniel demands his rights?"

Her tongue flicked across his lips for a second. "Daniel doesn't know I can walk, so he won't bother me. I'm yours, only yours."

She kissed him deeply. Her hands massaged the hard muscles of his thighs, and he knew he'd take her again. And again. And he did. By the time he finished with her, Amelie was so exhausted that she dressed in a warm, sleepy afterglow. They rode back to the house then, and after he carried her to her bed, she kissed him, and fell asleep for a few hours of rest before the wedding.

Bruno Haus wasn't sleepy. He was wide awake and much aroused after silently witnessing the future mistress of Green Meadows writhing in ecstasy beneath a slave.

He knew he had had the power to intervene and whip the arrogant Claude to an inch of his life and perhaps even take Amelie for his own pleasure. But he didn't. The fact that she could walk was important and the way she made love to the slave might just give him power over her at a future date. He laughed. Claude wasn't the only one who wanted her, and he vowed Claude was't the only man she'd service with that hot body. In time, his own turn would come.

That knowledge didn't quench the fire in his

loins. So, to ease it, he went to the fields where a lone slave girl worked. He knew that she feared him and wouldn't say a word to Mrs. Flanders, so he threw her down and hiked up her skirts, taking her in the middle of the field, but his desire was for Amelie.

Chapter 12

Thaddeus Markham waited by the foot of the stairs as Lianne slowly descended the staircase. In an ivory bridal gown made of the finest satin and strewn with tiny seed pearls she looked more beautiful than any woman Thaddeus had ever seen. Except for Dera. He smiled at Dera who stood a distance away and covered Lianne's outstretched hand with his.

"Thank you for giving me away," Lianne said. "It is most kind of you."

"I'm honored," he whispered as strains of harp music drifted from the parlor. "I hope you and Phillipe shall be happy."

She nodded. A small smile curved upward on her mouth. She hoped for their happiness. For the last few years she had known only pain, except for her baby. Now, she had a chance for happiness and love with Phillipe who would also be a father to Désirée. She felt Phillipe was a logical choice for husband. He was wealthy and handsome. Though she knew of his wastrel life style, she determined to change him, and once she did, she felt she'd be truly happy. If only she could stop the memories of the night in the summerhouse and forget the handsome tormented man.

With a pat on her hand, Thaddeus walked her into the parlor. Amelie barely noticed her, her blue-eyed gaze on the figure of her brother. Phillipe smiled broadly, his eyes only on Lianne. A few of Dera's neighbors and Phillipe's cronies from the gaming hall he frequented clustered around the priest then drew into a circle as Lianne exchanged vows with Phillipe.

When the ceremony ended, Phillipe kissed her with gusto, surprising her and delighting his friends. Dera inched over to her and kissed her cheek. "I wish you every happiness, my dear."

"Thank you," Lianne told her but knew Dera didn't think she'd be happy with her bridegroom. A sense of foreboding filled her. She wished Dera could be pleased for her or at least pretend to be.

Maria brought Désirée to her. "The little one wants to kiss her mama before bedtime."

Taking her child into her arms, Lianne cuddled her and kissed her plump cheek. Désirée looked like an angel in a hand-embroidered white gown Dera had sewn for her. "Mama shall see you soon," she told the child and handed her to Maria. Phillipe barely acknowledged the baby as he turned Lianne's face to his.

"Don't fret about the child, *chérie.* She is in good hands with Dera. After all, tonight, we spend our first night together at Belle Riviere. We don't need a child to spoil our wedding night."

Her eyes clouded with tears, but she managed to smile brightly. "Just the two of us."

Phillipe guided her to Amelie who sat primly in an orchid gown on the couch. "I hope you wish us well," he said to her and kissed the top of her head.

"Best wishes to you both," she said stiffly.

"Ah, is that the best you can do on such a glorious day as this?"

"I've offered my congratulations. What more do you want?"

Phillipe sighed. "Amelie, you're as tiresome as ever. Now, if you'll excuse us, I should like to toast my beautiful bride." He grabbed a glass of champagne from a tray and raised it in the air. "To my wife. The woman whom I desire above anyone else.'' At that moment he did desire Lianne who took his breath away with her beauty and completely forgot Chloe and his son.

Phillipe's friends heard him and gathered round to offer their own toasts.

Dera observed Lianne who stood in the middle of the fracas with a smile on her face, but a sadness in her eyes. She wondered again at the foolhardiness of Lianne's marriage. Phillipe wouldn't make her happy, but she reasoned that Lianne must deal with the implications sooner or later.

The sound of voices in the vestibule drew Dera's attention. John, the house servant, beamed and pointed in excitement to Dera.

"Look who's home, madam."

Dera didn't believe her own eyes. Her son stood not ten feet from her with outstretched arms. The three years away had increased his handsomeness, the broadness of his shoulders. She ran into his embrace, too overcome to do anything but weep.

Daniel stroked her hair. "Mother, please don't cry. I'm home. I don't want your tears."

She broke away from the place where her face rested on his chest. She examined his face and found it to be careworn. Tiny lines fanned out from the corners of his gray eyes. Lines which hadn't been there before he left Green Meadows. "I'm just overcome. Your arrival isn't unexpected, but I hadn't thought you'd be home on this of all days."

His gaze traveled to the people in the parlor.

"Phillipe's marriage," Dera explained.

"I suppose I should offer my congratulations, or should I say condolences, to the blushing bride."

"I'll introduce you."

Daniel followed Dera into the room where the wedding guests were assembled. He spotted Amelie sitting on the couch. When she saw him, surprise flooded her face, then dismay. He intended to speak to her, to give her the obligatory kiss on the cheek. However, at that moment, the guests dispersed and opened the circle which enclosed the groom and the bride.

Daniel's polite expression vanished so fast it was as if a towel wiped it away. In its place came a look of such supreme surprise that Dera immediately noticed. In a dreamlike state he moved forward toward the vision in white, the woman whose pale loveliness drew him like a flare lighting the way on the open sea for a lost ship.

"It's you!" he ground out, unable to conceal the delight on his face which anguish quickly replaced when Phillipe took the woman's arm and turned her in Daniel's direction.

"My wife," came Phillipe's voice through the fog surrounding Daniel's brain.

Lianne drew her gaze from her husband to rest upon Daniel. For the first time she looked at him, not really aware of his presence until he spoke. Her emerald orbs widened. She hadn't seen this man in almost two years, but he hadn't changed. In her dreams he came to her often, and now he stood before her. Or did he? Was she dreaming? She didn't know.

The room rocked. She felt herself sway and leaned on Phillipe's arm for support.

"What is wrong, *chérie*?" Phillipe noticed her ashen color.

"I feel faint." Her voice lowered and Phillipe barely heard her. Dera came to Lianne's side and gently led her from him.

"The festivities are too much for her, I fear. I shall take her upstairs to rest for awhile." She turned to her son. "Speak to your wife," she told him gently, aware that he couldn't take his eyes off Lianne.

"Dera, I really think we should start for Belle Riviere," Phillipe called after her.

"Once Lianne is rested." She ushered her goddaughter from the room.

Daniel waited in bafflement, unable to function.

He had found her! After all his searching, all the inquiries which led to nothing, the woman he loved had shown up in his own parlor. And as Phillipe's bride! He raised an eyebrow at Phillipe, his envy and disappointment not easy to suppress.

"You're a lucky man," he told Phillipe.

Daniel's brother-in-law shrugged. "I've always had good luck with the women. Lianne is the most beautiful of any women I've ever seen. She is my wife."

Daniel didn't miss the warning quality in his voice. He wondered how Phillipe would react if he knew he had made love to his bride. With a polite nod to Daniel, Phillipe went off to seek the companionship of his friends until Lianne felt well enough to travel to Belle Riviere.

Joining Doctor Markham who sat alongside Amelie, Daniel kissed her cheek. "You're looking well, Amelie."

"No thanks to you!" she snapped.

Daniel sighed. Nothing had changed in his absence. Thaddeus Markham cleared his throat and stood up. "I'll leave you children alone," he said and wandered away.

After Daniel settled himself beside her, he surveyed the bright flowers which decorated the parlor and reminded him that he had missed Christmas but had arrived in time to see the woman he loved, married to Phillipe Marchand. He wanted to laugh. Lianne was now a part of his family.

"That was quite a scene," Amelie said softly. "My new sister-in-law practically faints when she first sets eyes on you. What is this strange power you have over women, Daniel? I'm certain that in Europe it served you in good stead."

"Yes, Amelie. It did." Why lie to her? She was smart enough to know he didn't lead a celibate life. He wondered if she suspected that Lianne was one of the women he had loved.

Her face looked strangely calm. The blue of her eyes glittered and a stray tear coursed down her cheek. He had hurt her and was instantly sorry.

"I shouldn't have been so cruel to you," he said.

Amelie looked at him. "Now or in the past? I loved you, you know."

"Both. I cared for you, believe it or not. At least I wanted to love you, but . . ."

She heaved a sigh, glad that everyone had drifted outside to celebrate. Though she felt awkward with Daniel, she wanted to sit quietly with him. "Let's not discuss your reasons for our marriage. Suffice it to say we've both suffered a great deal."

He sensed a change in Amelie. A softness touched her features, causing her to look vulnerable, unlike the shrew he had left in Claude's care. He clasped her hand. "I'm sorry for everything."

She knew he was sorry, but that didn't stop the pain which tore through her still. Daniel had caused the loss of their child with his cruel words, and she'd never forgive him for that. Her eyes hardened into agates. "Words, Daniel. Just words! You'll never be able to atone for what you've done. I shall never forgive you!" She pulled the rope which hung near her and summoned Claude.

Claude bowed with respect when he entered the room. John had already informed the other servants of Daniel's happy return, but Claude felt no pleasure. His manner was distant and politely cool. "I wish to go to my room," Amelie told him.

When Claude bent to lift her, Daniel halted him. "I shall take her upstairs."

"But, Monsieur Daniel . . ."

"I thank you for looking after Amelie while I've been away. Now, however, I should take care of her, too."

"I don't need you. I don't want your help!" Amelie's face boiled red with anger and frustration that Daniel should return and unwittingly pull her away from the man she loved.

Disentangling her arms from Claude's neck, he spoke to her as if she were a child. "I need to do this," was all he said. Daniel lifted her into his arms and smiled at Claude. "I do thank you, my friend." He left the room. Amelie turned her head and her large-eyed glance rested on Claude. As Daniel carried her up the wide staircase, Claude watched.

Lallie came into the vestibule and immediately sized up the situation. "The master's home, son. Madame Amelie is his wife, and Monsieur Daniel is your friend."

Conflicting emotions raged within Claude. He knew Amelie belonged to Daniel, but on a more basic level she was his.

Daniel didn't think anything had changed in the past three years. He still thought they were friends. Claude clenched his fists, and watched the empty staircase when he heard the door close in Amelie's room.

Lallie shook her head in dismay and left him. Pain washed over him, and rage that Daniel would return home as if the past three years never happened. Amelie might decide she preferred her husband to him. But he wouldn't give her up, not even to her own husband.

"You're mine, Amelie," he whispered. "Mine."

"Why don't you tell me what the trouble is?" Dera finished placing the cool rag on Lianne's forehead and sat next to her on the bed.

"I felt faint. That's all."

"Should I ask Tad to take a look at you?"

"I'll be fine. Just a few moments of rest."

Scanning her face, Dera knew Lianne was far from fine. Her face was still pale, and she trembled as she adjusted the cloth. Though Lianne had been nervous before the ceremony, she hadn't looked ill. Now she did. Dera knew exactly when the white strain had appeared on her face.

Dera grasped Lianne's thin hand. Her expression was open and earnest. "Did you meet my son in Europe?"

Lianne's eyes closed for a few seconds, then she opened them, barely able to meet Dera's steady stare. She couldn't lie to Dera about Daniel. There was very little about her life she hadn't told her. Except for the horrible incident with de Lovis and the night of passion with Daniel. Though she hadn't known Dera all that long, she realized Dera could read her well. Lying was out of the question.

"Yes," Lianne said and sighed.

"Do you love him?"

"What we shared was very brief. It doesn't matter. Daniel is married to Amelie and I'm now Phillipe's wife."

"But do you love him?"

"Yes." Lianne's eyes filled with tears. Dera embraced her as if she were a small child and rocked her back and forth.

"Is Désirée my grandchild?" Dera whispered.

Lianne nodded. Dera extinguished a long sigh. "I knew it! She resembles Daniel. You must tell him he has a daughter. It would make such a difference in his life."

"No!"

Lianne's vehemence shocked Dera. "Surely he deserves to know."

Lianne pushed away from her. "Promise me you'll never tell him about her. Everyone, Phillipe included, believes she is the child of André Laguens. I don't want her whispered about or ostracized in any way. Phillipe wouldn't accept her as his child if word reached his ears. He has trouble accepting her as it is. Phillipe isn't overly fond of children."

Dera bit her tongue because she knew about Jean

Marc, Phillipe's child by his quadroon mistress. Instead she said, "I became pregnant with my oldest son and didn't tell Quint. I had my reasons, also, and I thought they were sound ones. But in the end the child brought us together. I wasted years when I could have had the man I wanted, if only I had been honest."

Lianne's sharp gaze fixed Dera to the spot. "I forbid you to tell Daniel about my child."

Dera saw Lianne wasn't about to change her mind, so she admitted defeat. "It won't be easy, but I love you like my own daughter. I won't say a word, just know I'm happy your baby is my grandchild."

A knock on the door interrupted them. Dera rose and answered it. Daniel stood on the threshold.

"I want to see Lianne, mother."

Chapter 13

Indecision reigned on Dera's face, but Lianne's gentle voice summoned Daniel into the room. At once, Dera left.

Daniel closed the door and locked it. For a second he didn't know what to say. Lianne looked lovely and fragile, propped against the pillows. Auburn tresses escaped the pins holding her hair up and tumbled acros her shoulders. The smooth creaminess of her skin tempted him to touch her. But he didn't. He knew if he laid a finger on her, he'd be lost.

"It seems I've found you too late," he said after a few moments of silent perusal. "Why did you run away that night? For over a year I've searched for you, following up the smallest of leads in the hope I'd find you."

Tears threatened to spill onto her cheeks. Her eyes were a watery green. "Why did you bother?"

"I fell in love with you. You've been in my heart since that night."

The tears slipped gently from her eyes. Those were the words she wished to hear. He loved her and thought about her, just as she had thought of him. Now it was too late!

Seeing her pain, he broke his promise to himself and sat on the bed to gather her in his arms. His breath against her ear ruffled the feathery strands of her hair. She smelled sweet like summer roses.

"Do you love Phillipe?"

Her arms wound around his neck and brought him closer to her. Though they had been together only once, a silent communication existed between them which not even the time apart could destroy. This wasn't a moment for lies. "No. I belong only to you."

A shiver of joy rocked through him. His eyes brightened, and he touched her cheek. "I can't believe I've found you. You belong to me, Lianne. Forever."

His lips found hers, drowning her in a sea of tender desire. She clung to him as he pushed her into the mattress, aching for him as she had that night in the summerhouse. His hands moved over her body to caress her breasts, her hips, her thighs. The fact that she still wore her bridal gown and the man loving her wasn't her husband made no difference. She felt wanton and didn't care. She loved Daniel and would go to hell and back to have him.

Her mouth drew away from his and she smiled. "We must tell Phillipe and Amelie. My marriage is unconsummated, and I'm certain Amelie will divorce you. Then we can be married."

Lianne's naiveté stunned him. For all her lush, voluptuous beauty, she possessed an innocence. What sort of dream world had she shared with André Laguens? Hadn't he taught her anything about life beyond the gates of the chateau or that men didn't leave their wives for a pretty face? He loved Lianne, but he owed Amelie a debt he vowed to repay.

His fingers twirled an auburn curl. "I can't desert Amelie," he said matter-of-factly.

Pushing him away, she sat up. Her eyes gleamed like emeralds in her oval face. "Didn't you just pledge yourself to me, tell me you would love me forever? Aren't you going to marry me? I've thought of no one but you for months. Am I to be treated like your harlot?"

"No!" He reached for her but she eluded him and rolled to the other side of the bed. She stood up. Splotches of red fury stained her cheeks. "Lianne, I love you, but you see how Amelie is. I left her once, and I promised myself I'd care for her, make everything up to her after I realized I'd never find you. Please understand."

"I don't understand. What is my position to be in your life?" she asked.

"I want you as my lover." He knew he sounded like a cad, but he loved her, needed her, more than any other woman.

"Your whore, you mean!" Thoughts of de Lovis flickered through her head. "I won't be your mistress. If you can't make me your wife, there is no future for us."

He jumped from the bed and in a single motion ensnared her trembling body in his arms. Her beautiful eyes shot their green fire. He held her against him until she stopped struggling. "I do love you, no matter what you think." He scanned her face for some clue that she felt as he did, but saw nothing. "I want you as my mistress. What man wouldn't? Oh, Lianne," he said with real anguish in his voice, "I must know you love me."

How could she not love him? Daniel Flanders was handsome, masculine, and in love with her. But he wouldn't leave Amelie. She nearly laughed at her situation. Not an hour before she had married Amelie's brother, and if Daniel had told her to pack her bags and leave with him, she would have forgotten poor Phillipe. She remembered she had a child, Daniel's child. She hadn't wanted Dera to tell him about Désirée. Now she felt relief she had extracted the promise from Dera.

Daniel would never be free. She convinced herself she had made a wise decision by marrying Phillipe, providing her child with a father. There was no future with Daniel.

Taking a deep breath, she gazed into the depths of his eyes. "I am Phillipe's wife now, and I shall remain so."

"You're more of a whore by giving yourself in marriage to Phillipe, a man you don't love, than if you belonged to me," he said.

Her hand flew from the folds of her wedding gown and slapped his cheek. "Never call me such a name again! I shall never belong to you now, Daniel!"

A knock on the door pulled them apart. "Are you feeling better, Lianne?" came Phillipe's voice. "We must leave for Belle Riviere." He tried the knob. "Will you let me in, *chérie?*"

"Allow me time to arrange my hair," she called.

"Why bother, *chérie?* In a little while you shall be disarranged." His laugh filtered through the door panel.

Lianne blushed. "Let me go," she whispered to Daniel who still held her arm.

"Kiss me first."

Her eyes widened. "No."

"Kiss me. Prove to me you don't want me, that you want to go with Phillipe, that you choose him over me. Prove to me that you don't belong to me, that you don't desire my touch."

She twisted but he held her tighter. Tears of rage, pain and humiliation sprang to her eyes. Phillipe tapped on the door. Daniel's eyes glittered with challenge, tempting her to prove him right.

Suddenly she threw herself against him. Her lips met his in a fiery collision of thwarted passion, but when his arms would have snaked around her waist, she pushed away.

"I admit I want you, Daniel, but I'm Phillipe's wife. As long as you're married to Amelie, there is no future for us. I won't turn away from my husband this night or in the nights to come. Before you fall asleep tonight, Daniel, think of me in my husband's arms."

She couldn't have hurt him more if she had stuck

a dagger through his heart. He watched as she ran to the door and opened it enough to nimbly squeeze through the opening. He heard her laugh, heard the sound of Phillipe's kiss upon her lips. The sound of their footsteps on the landing drifted away.

He had lost her again.

Amelie fumed in her room. Never one to react silently to aggravation, she threw the bed pillows at the wall and yanked the violet ribbon from her hair. She feared being heard if she stormed about the room, so she sat by the dressing table and pushed the expensive glass perfume bottles onto the floor.

"The nerve of him!" she hissed to herself. How dare Daniel return from his European trollops and act the concerned husband. If he had shown her kindness before he left, she might have been able to forgive him for the loss of their child. Now it was too late, and she'd be damned if she'd pretend affection for him.

Lallie waddled into the room, picked up the bottles and pulled out a nightgown. Age showed on Lallie's face and she moved slowly. Amelie became irritated and snapped, "Do hurry!" The room was drafty as she sat on the stool so Lallie could remove her stockings. She wanted to do it herself, to jump up and put on her own gown, but Amelie was on her guard. She mustn't give away her shared secret with Claude. No one but he would ever know she could walk.

"I'm sorry, Madam Amelie. My old bones ache in this chill."

"Then have Claude light the fireplace."

"Yes, ma'am. I'll do that." Lallie's eyes narrowed. "You and Claude been spending a lot of time together."

"He's my slave."

"Even the nights?"

If Lallie hadn't been Claude's mother, Amelie would have slapped her senseless. "I don't know what you mean, Lallie."

"Hmmph! Yes, you do. My boy's bothered by you. I don't know what you both do alone in here under the blankets, but I don't want him hurt. Your husband is home now, so I guess Claude's visits to you will stop."

Amelie gave a fluty laugh. "Dear Lallie, you do have a vivid imagination and are quite amusing but if I didn't need you to tend to me, I'd advise Daniel to sell you for your nasty tongue."

Amelie swore Lallie's face drained of all color. "You wouldn't do that to me, would you, Madam Amelie?"

The woman's fright was obvious, and Amelie relished it for a moment. However, she wasn't a truly cruel person, so she quickly put Lallie's mind at ease. "No, but don't spread such horrible tales about the house. One day I shall be mistress of Green Meadows, and I might just remember your lies."

"Yes, madam." Lallie fumbled with the hooks on the back of Amelie's gown. When she finished removing the dress and it was replaced by a white, lacy nightgown, Lallie told Amelie she'd order Claude to light the fire.

As Lallie opened the door, Daniel was just about to knock.

"Is my wife ready for bed?" he asked her.

"Yes, Mr. Daniel. Go in."

Daniel waited inside the doorway. He wore a dressing gown of such a deep blue velvet it was almost black. Amelie couldn't help but realize how handsome he looked. She had given him the dressing gown on their first wedding anniversary, choosing the color because she thought it would complement his eyes.

He walked toward her. "You look lovely," he told her and admired her hair which gleamed like golden nuggets in the candlelight. Amelie looked very beautiful and childlike in the pristine gown.

Her eyes narrowed speculatively. "Such pretty

words will make me blush.'' Why was he being so nice to her?

His hand brushed against her cheek. ''You deserve that and more. I've been a beast to you, and I know it.'' He smiled.

''Such a change has come over you, dear husband, that I can't quite realize you're the same man who was once so cruel to me.'' His hand continued to stroke her cheek, and she suppressed a shiver. She didn't like the look in his eyes. If he had looked at her like that before the accident, she'd have melted in his arms. Now, she didn't want him. She wanted Claude. Only Claude.

''Let me carry you to bed,'' Daniel said and picked her up. ''You weigh as little as a feather.'' He placed her in the center of her bed and covered her with the sheet. Sitting beside her, he took her hand. Amelie was lovely. He did want to care for her, to let her know he had changed. But the changes in him had happened because of another woman, a woman who now bedded with her bridegroom. If only . . .

Amelie's voice stirred him from his reverie. ''Why are you being so solicitous, Daniel? As I recall if I so much as touched you, you'd cringe.''

He held her chin in his hand. ''I told you already. I want to make things up to you. I want your forgiveness.''

''If that's all you want, then I'll endeavor to forget the past. But . . .''

''Yes?''

''I'm still a cripple, Daniel. Your sudden ardor is misplaced. I suggest if you have physical needs, you go find a slave girl or ride into New Orleans. I'm certain some tart will satisfy your cravings.''

She spoke with such seriousness that he laughed aloud and came to his senses. By law he could force himself on Amelie while he pleasured himself. She was his wife. Yet, she was doomed to lead a limited life

because of him. Certainly there wouldn't be any
pleasure in the act for her, so in the end, it would mean
less than nothing.

"I see nothing humorous," she said in a huff.

"But I do. You've put everything in perspective."
He bent and kissed her as Claude peered at them from
the doorway, carrying firewood.

"Monsieur Daniel."

Daniel drew away from Amelie, not missing how
she flushed under Claude's steady stare. "What is it,
Claude?"

"Madam wished the fire lit."

"Then madam shall have it." He started to take
the wood from Claude.

"Let Claude do it!" Amelie's panicked tone
caused Daniel to raise an eyebrow.

"As you wish." Daniel made conversation with
Claude as the slave tossed the wood in the fireplace
and lit it. "We should fish and hunt soon, Claude.
Just like we did as boys."

Claude wiped his sweaty palms on his pants when
he stood up. The fire blazed and warmed the room.
"Yes," was his only comment. He withdrew from the
room when Daniel wished him a good night, but
Amelie didn't miss the way a muscle twitched in
Claude's jaw.

"Claude doesn't seem too pleased to see me."
Daniel folded his arms across his chest and leaned
against the mantel. "Do you and Claude get along
well? If not, I'll have someone else take you downstairs in the mornings. In fact, I'll do it."

"No, I want Claude," she said much too quickly.
"I mean," she swallowed hard, not liking his
penetrating gaze, "he knows how to please me."

"Does he?" A suspicious note crept into his tone.
Could Amelie entertain lascivious thoughts about
Claude? Did Claude feel the same? He brushed the
ridiculous thoughts aside. Amelie couldn't walk and
Claude was his boyhood friend. "I think Claude sticks

to himself too much. He needs a wife.''

Amelie paled but managed a smile. What would she do if Claude grew tired of her and married? She'd die. ''He appears quite content. Daniel, I'm really very tired. The wedding was long, and your homecoming has just worn me out. I should like to sleep.''

''Of course. Forgive my thoughtlessness.'' He bent and kissed her again and left the room, closing the door softly behind him.

When she heard the door close to his room, she scampered from the bed and turned the lock on her own door. Then she went to the door which separated her room from Claude's. She found him reclining on the bed, but when she entered he didn't look at her.

''Claude?''

''Your husband is home, Amelie. You must wait for him, do his bidding.''

''I do only yours.'' She lay beside him, her hands and mouth touched and kissed his bare chest.

He groaned and grabbed a handful of her hair, hurting her and exciting her at the same time. Rolling on top of her, he pinned her to the mattress.

''Tell me you love me. Tell me I'm the man you want in your bed.''

''Claude, you know that already.''

''I want to hear it from you.''

She pulled him to her, her hands trailing against the dusty skin. ''I love you and want only you in my bed, Claude.'' She kissed him and instantly he was aroused, unable to restrain his passion. He didn't care if Daniel was down the hall, he'd have taken Amelie in the parlor with the whole household in attendance.

''Let's go back to my room where it's warm,'' she whispered against his lips.

Claude shook his head. ''No, my lovely. I shall make love to you in my bed tonight. My passion shall warm you.''

And it did.

Chapter 14

The ride to Belle Riviere passed more quickly than Lianne would have wished. She needed time to sort through her feelings, but they swirled around her like leaves before a hurricane. She was scarcely able to think. The last few hours had numbed her. All she saw in her mind's eye was Daniel's stricken look when she left the bedroom.

"*Chérie,* your hands are as cold as a winter's frost." Phillipe's voice pulled her mind from the image of Daniel's face. "I hope you shall not become ill." His hands enfolded both of hers and he rubbed them between his palms. "We must keep you well."

She managed a grateful smile. "I'm very lucky you love me."

"I am the one who is fortunate. From the first moment I saw you astride your horse the day we met, I knew I wanted you for my wife."

Her gaze wandered over the features of his face and stopped to rest at his eyes, so blue and warm. "Shall we be happy, Phillipe? Really happy?"

"Certainly. How can we not?"

He smiled down at her and kissed her mouth which at first refused to open, then softened under the urgency of his lips. When he drew away, he sighed. "We shall indeed be happy."

She hoped so. Until Daniel entered her life again,

she had thought Phillipe was the answer to her loneliness and would make her dreams of a perfect love become reality. Now, she was Madame Phillipe Marchand and on her way to her new home, and to her husband's bed. Her dreams had come true. Why didn't she feel the happiness which shone on Phillipe's face?

The carriage wound its way up the drive, and she and Phillipe drank glasses of champagne in the parlor to celebrate their marriage. When Phillipe kissed her again, she shivered not from cold but from dread. How different this night would be from the night with Daniel!

Allowing Phillipe to lead her upstairs to the bedroom, she barely realized she shook.

"Lianne, there is no need for fear," Phillipe told her when they arrived at the door. "After all, you're not a virgin bride, *chérie.*" He nibbled her ear as they entered the room. "You were a widow for some time. Your body must be as hot for fulfillment as mine."

She found the bedsheets were neatly pulled back. Candles flickered on the dressing table, and the sweet smell of night jasmine drifted through the open windows. Fresh fruit and wine waited on a sideboard in case they grew hungry during the night. Everything a bride could desire had been provided. Even her nightdress had been laid out for her earlier by a servant when her trunks had been brought to Belle Riviere before the ceremony.

Absently she fingered the thin material. The gown, like the rest of her trousseau, had been paid for by Phillipe. "It's very beautiful," she said softly.

"Not as lovely as you, Lianne." He took her hands in his. Desire shone in his eyes.

"Forget the gown." He dropped her hands and pulled the buttons through the loops of Lianne's wedding dress. When the dress slid to the floor, he exclaimed, "Lianne, you're a goddess!"

The ache inside him intensified. He thought he

should woo her as a proper bridegroom, but Lianne wasn't a virgin, so there was no reason to go slowly with her. The pulsing ache in his loins leaped to a fire when he released the pins which held her hair. The thick amber tresses fell across her shoulders and reached to her waist, captivating him with their perfume.

He picked her up and carried her to the bed, where she lay waiting for him while he undressed. When he returned he removed the chemise with a hint of impatience. Why hadn't she taken it off already? Didn't she realize he was ready for her? Why must she look like a sick calf? But he didn't ask her these questions. Once his body met the soft peaks of her breasts, he ceased to think. Passion thundered in his ears, and he couldn't restrain himself. He needed her pulsing softness to surround him.

Lianne cried out when Phillipe entered her. She expected he would take his time with her, to coax her into submission. He was right when he said she should want fulfillment, but he wasn't the man she wanted. Tears burned her eyes while Phillipe grunted and found his own pleasure without any thought for hers. André had always been gentle with her, and Daniel had introduced her to sexual ecstasy and to the ultimate pleasure a woman could experience in a man's arms.

She felt nothing now but distaste and a desire to have the act over as quickly as possible.

His voice echoed in her ears. "Lianne, hold me tight!" When she did, he groaned and grew quiet. It seemed years passed before he lifted his head from her breasts. *"Magnifique, chérie."* He rolled away from her and pulled the blanket over their naked bodies. She lay there, waiting for him to hold her, to touch her so she might find her own ecstasy. But all she heard were Phillipe's snores.

A tear trickled down her cheek. So, she thought, this is how it shall be.

Lianne got up and pulled on the nightgown. She went to the window and drew the curtains aside. The night was dark—not a star glittered in the heavens and she felt just as black because the happiness she'd hoped for would never exist in her marriage to Phillipe. She knew that now. He had no idea how to give love, only how to take it.

On the lawn below her, she noticed a tiny bright speck which seemed to hover in the air. Her eyes fastened on it and watched as it grew brighter then disappeared. A firefly, she thought. Turning away from the window, she climbed into the bed beside Phillipe.

Daniel threw down his cheroot in disgust. What was wrong with him? He waited like a lovesick fool on the lawn of Belle Riviere, eyes fastened on the upper windows. What did he hope would happen? His secret hope that Lianne would rush from the bridal chamber into his waiting arms dimmed with each passing minute.

"The little tart!" he hissed under his breath when he realized that she wouldn't leave Phillipe's bed but had firmly ensconced herself as mistress of Belle Riviere. He felt like an idiot. To forget Lianne he had gone to Amelie, only to realize that he didn't want her. He didn't love Amelie, though he wished to set things right between them, to care for her as was her due as his wife. He could only blame his visit to Amelie's bedroom as temporary insanity because of Lianne.

Lianne. In his mind he saw her body entwined with Phillipe's and he felt such intense anguish that he turned his horse in the direction of home and rode hard across the dark fields. Dismounting he slowly made his way up the steps but stopped. A slight movement from the dark shadows of the porch drew his attention.

"Come out, or I'll shoot you down," he growled and reached for his pistol.

"Please, no, Herr Flanders." Bruno Haus withdrew from his hiding place behind a stone column. "It's just me."

Daniel eyed him suspiciously, barely able to see the man in the darkness. "What are you doing here?"

"I had trouble sleeping. Just taking a walk around the place. You know, checking up on things, making sure all is secure."

Daniel couldn't argue with that. Security was part of the overseer's job. "Why were you hiding?"

"I didn't know it was you, sir. Thought it might be a stranger."

That made sense to Daniel, so he didn't question Haus further. He went inside the house, unaware that Bruno had intended to climb up the vines to the upstairs balcony and peer into Amelie's bedroom hoping to get a glimpse of her and Claude. Cursing under his breath, he headed in reluctance to his cabin, aggravated that Daniel had ruined his night.

Though the upstairs hallway was in darkness, light spilled from an open doorway. Sounds of a baby's fussy crying drifted through the quiet house. Looking into the room, Daniel saw a dark-haired, heavyset woman rocking a child. Standing beside the rocker was his mother, dressed in her gown and robe.

"What do you think is wrong with her?" his mother asked the woman.

"I think the *niña* misses her mama."

"May I hold her?" Dera inquired and smiled when Maria handed the baby to her.

Dera held the little girl against her shoulder and patted her tiny back. "It's been so long since I've cared for a little one."

"Désirée is a good baby."

"Yes. A special baby."

Daniel watched from the doorway while his mother crooned an Irish lullaby to the child, a tune he had heard many times as a boy. Dera tenderly stroked the baby's dark head. Whose child was she? he wondered.

When Dera had laid the sleeping baby in her crib and closed the door, Daniel met her in the hallway.

"You scared the life out of me!" Dera scolded when she bumped into him.

"Whose baby is that?" he asked without preliminaries.

"Why, Lianne's."

"I didn't know she had a child. Her husband died." Victor Dubois had mentioned nothing about a baby.

Dera turned her back and walked to her room. "Désirée was born after his death." Dera promised Lianne she wouldn't tell Daniel the truth though it was hard not to. However, she wasn't lying to him either. The child had been born after André's death.

Following her, he sat on a chair as she climbed into bed. "I don't understand," Daniel said and ruffled his hair. "She can't be André's child. If she is then that means Lianne was already pregnant when . . ."

"Yes?"

"Mother, when did Lianne say André died?"

"She never has mentioned it." Dera knew by the obdurate expression on her son's face that he wouldn't let the matter drop. Before too long he would put the pieces together and know the truth. She wouldn't have to tell him after all.

He left the room without a good night and headed downstairs to the parlor. He poured a hefty glass of brandy and swallowed it down. Refilling the glass, he sat on the couch and gazed at the last glowing remnants in the fireplace.

Why hadn't Lianne mentioned the baby to him? Had she forgotten her own child in the flurry of the wedding and his shocking entrance into her life again? If André had died before the baby's birth, then she must have been pregnant when he made love to her in the summerhouse. How long before that night had André died?

Questions revolved around his head like carriage wheels. He didn't know why he should care when André died. Apparently the baby wasn't his own; Lianne would have told him. Wouldn't she? But he realized he knew very little about her. He possessed some facts about her life, but he didn't know her as a person, just as a beautiful, bewitching body. And now it seemed he'd never know her. She belonged to Phillipe. Yet a large question still nagged at him. Was he the father of Lianne's baby?

"No, no!" Lianne called and twisted in her sleep. The evil black eyes impaled her, his hands caressed her flesh. She must escape him, must find Daniel. No matter how much she screamed or tried to yank free, de Lovis held her.

"I'll never let you go, *querida*. Never!"

His mouth came down viciously against hers and she felt herself fighting for air.

"Lianne, wake up!"

Phillipe's voice dispersed the image of de Lovis but not the fear. She came awake quickly and sat up.

"Whatever is the matter?" Phillipe queried. "Were you dreaming?"

"Yes," she whispered. "A horrible nightmare."

"Come here." Phillipe drew her naked body into his arms, and she willingly went. His touch which had so digusted her earlier, she now welcomed. She lay trembling, so overcome by fear that she clung to him.

His voice soothed her a bit. "You're safe, *chérie.*"

But was she? During the months since she killed de Lovis, she had begun to imagine she was truly safe, that no one would find her. Now, she felt such intense fear that she imagined de Lovis would harm her, that he'd reach from the grave and grasp her away from life. Away from Daniel.

She buried her face against Phillipe's chest. She mustn't think about Daniel. Daniel wasn't her husband.

Phillipe lifted her face and kissed her lips softly. This was the first sign of true gentleness he had shown her since the wedding. "No one shall hurt you, Lianne. I will protect you."

"Phillipe!" Her voice gasped his name in a mixture of tenderness for him and denied desire for Daniel. She needed him, needed to feel loved and safe. Somehow she must stop the frightening dreams and cling to the life she had made. No matter how disappointing she found it. She must forget Daniel.

Her hands moved slowly but steadily across Phillipe's body until she had aroused him to such a degree that she positioned herself atop him, taking him into her. Her wanton movements excited him, and because she imagined her lover was Daniel, she found the ecstasy she sought.

Chapter 15

Lianne and Phillipe confined themselves to their bedroom for a week before Lianne decided she had had enough of solitude and lovemaking.

"What are you doing?" Phillipe asked her one morning. He watched in shock as she slipped into a lime green riding outfit.

She shot him a vixenish smile. "Going riding, of course. Care to come?"

"Lianne, what will people think to see you out and about? We've been married only a week and by custom should be confined to the bedchamber for two."

"I don't care what anyone thinks," she said and surveyed herself in the mirror. "Being cooped up in here is worse than a prison sentence."

"I didn't know my company was so offensive."

Phillipe sounded hurt. Lianne turned and walked to the bed and sat beside him. "That's not what I meant, and you know it. I need fresh air, to feel the wind upon my face. Don't be upset with me." She bent over and placed a light kiss on his lips.

His arms encircled her waist. "Wait awhile, *chérie.*"

She grew immediately aware of his amorous intentions, and she didn't want to make love again. Phillipe's appetite for lovemaking was insatiable, and she was tired of always pretending to feel something. But she lowered her eyes in a way which he mistook for coyness because she didn't want him to see her loathing. The thought entered her mind that if Daniel was her husband, she'd never have wished to leave his arms.

"You inflame my senses," he whispered into her ear.

She flashed him a smile which promised more than she intended. "Let me ride first, Phillipe. You've completely worn me out."

He kissed the tip of her nose and released her. "Ah, you're right. In fact I'm still rather sleepy. Go for your ride, *chérie,* but when you return, I shall have mine." He winked and she decided she wouldn't return too soon.

Lianne was in such a rush that she forgot to pin up her hair. She wouldn't go back into the room once she had departed, because Phillipe might wish to appease his appetite sooner.

At the stables, a groom saddled a horse for her and she broke into a brisk gallop and headed for the open fields. The morning was fresh and crisp. The January breeze blew her hair about her face and caressed her cheeks until they glowed a soft pink. Her confinement had depressed her spirit, but now it soared higher than the trees.

Unaware of where she headed, she was startled when she saw the white columns of Green Meadows in the distance. She slowed the horse. She guessed when Phillipe learned she'd visited Dera, he'd be angry. Probably he'd feel everyone would think he wasn't good in bed if she showed up only one week after their wedding. Phillipe had his pride. But she wanted to see her daughter and Dera. Yet it was seeing Daniel again which propelled her onward. Despite the awful scene at their last meeting, she ached to see his face again.

Dera, indeed, was pleased to see her. She didn't even look askance when Lianne appeared at her door.

However, Amelie's brows lifted quite noticeably.

"What are you doing here?" she asked when Lianne was admitted into the parlor.

"Visiting. It's nice to see you, too, Amelie." Lianne placed a kiss on her sister-in-law's cheek.

Amelie laid her embroidery hoop aside. "Does Philipe know about this? I can't believe he'd let you out so soon. Why, it isn't proper."

"Your brother isn't my jailer."

"Or your keeper, I warrant."

"I married a man, not a master."

Amelie sniffed. "Aren't all women trapped in one way or another?"

"Lianne," Dera broke in, not liking the turn of the conversation, "would you like to see your daughter?"

"Yes, I would." Lianne left the room, not caring for the gleam in Amelie's eyes and wondering where Daniel was but not asking. She didn't want anyone to know her heart was breaking because she had made the wrong decision by marrying Phillipe.

Maria was pleased to see her and Désirée snuggled up to Lianne, her eyes following her every move.

"Mama's darling has grown so big. Why you look more beautiful than ever!"

Désirée babbled she understood. Maria left the room to fix the baby's breakfast and Dera was called away by a servant announcing the arrival of Doctor Markham. Lianne was glad for the time alone with her daughter. She sat in the rocking chair with her and talked to her.

"Soon you shall come to Belle Riviere, *chérie*. Mama has a nice room waiting for you. There are lots of pretty toys, and horses to ride when you're older. And when you're a big girl, I shall have many gowns made for you, and you shall be the most beautiful girl in Louisiana."

"More beautiful than her mother?"

Lianne looked toward the doorway which

framed Daniel's powerful physique. Her heart hammered in her ears. She hadn't really expected to see him, though she had wanted to. She managed a slight smile. "I didn't see you standing there."

"I didn't want you to. The two of you together is quite a picture. Perhaps I'll paint one. Would you and Désirée mind posing for me?"

Daniel walked into the room, and for the first time, she noticed he looked rather shabby. His shirt was disheveled and appeared not have been taken off for a few days. The dark hair was tousled and hung over his forehead in a way she found endearing. He also needed a shave. Quite unlike Phillipe who always looked immaculate. However, her blood stirred in a way it never did for Phillipe.

"I've never had my portrait painted."

"Then it's time you did. Nothing tugs at the heartstrings more than the image of mother and child."

He knelt beside the rocker, and Lianne smelled stale liquor. Putting out his hand, Désirée clasped his finger, instantly bringing it to her mouth. "She's teething," he told Lianne.

"How do you know that?" she asked in astonishment.

"Désirée and I are great friends. We visit quite often together."

His face glowed a warm brown, and his gray eyes lighted up as he let the child gnaw on his finger. Lianne felt shaky, as if she were in a rowboat on suddenly rough seas. Perhaps she shouldn't have left Désirée in Dera's care. Being so close to the child, Daniel might learn the truth, if Dera hadn't told him already. Otherwise, why should he take such an interest in the baby?

"Has your mother mentioned anything to you about Désirée?"

"Like what?"

"I don't know, anything," she said lamely, not wishing to say too much.

"Let's see." He paused. "She tells me she is the best baby in the world. She sleeps all night and eats her vegetables and has an easygoing disposition. She thinks she has her mother's nose . . . and her father's eyes."

Lianne's hands shook, and she picked up the baby and put her in her bed. "I, I'd better get back to Belle Riviere. Phillipe will wonder what happened to me."

She made a move to leave the room, but Daniel's hand shot out and grasped her wrist. "Is it true she has her father's eyes?"

God, it was true! A fool would have to be blind not to see that Désirée's eyes were the same shape and color as Daniel's. But she couldn't tell him the truth. Phillipe was Désirée's father now, and Daniel would never be free to show her any true affection as a father should.

"Yes, she has her father's eyes," she said truthfully.

"Who is her father, Lianne?"

She gulped. She wanted to tell him, but she couldn't. Things were confused enough, and she'd never admit she made a mistake by marrying Phillipe. She was soon to take Daniel's child to be reared in another man's house.

"André Laguens, of course."

His grip tightened on her wrist until she winced in pain. "You're hurting me, Daniel."

"Am I? Well, you're hurting me by not admitting the truth. Tell me, I am Désirée's father."

"You're not!" She twisted her arm but he refused to loosen.

"I'm not such a fool that I can't see the child is mine. And I don't believe you were pregnant when we made love that time."

"I was."

"And you let me make love to you while you carried your dead husband's child? What kind of a woman are you?" He didn't know what to think and was suddenly confused. Never had he expected her to continue the lie once he confronted her. Unless, of course, it wasn't a lie.

"You're drunk," she scolded.

Daniel laughed lowly. "Yes. I admit I was quite drunk last night, because I've been wondering who the child's father is and torturing myself in the hope that she might be mine. I've always wanted children, Lianne. And I need a woman who desires me as I desire her. I had the mistaken impression that you might be that woman, however, I was wrong. You're a liar; and because you married a man you don't love, you're worse than a whore."

She slapped him with all the force her left hand could muster. "I detest you, Daniel Flanders!"

He didn't even bother to touch the offended area of his cheek which was a splotchy red. "No, you don't. One day, you might, but now you don't. If I wanted to take you here and now, Lianne, you'd let me. I can almost hear your contented mewls of pleasure, but I'll wait. I'll wait until you beg for me."

He dropped her wrist and turned on his heels and started to leave the room, but he stopped and smiled at her. "Give Phillipe my good wishes."

Then he was gone. She waited beside the baby's crib. Désirée played in contentment, but Lianne felt like a wilted flower, left too long in the sun. When Dera returned, she asked her what was wrong, but Lianne hastily kissed her and the baby goodbye. Then she rushed down the stairs, not even bothering to return Doctor Markham's greeting as he stood in the vestibule.

Tears streamed down her cheeks as she rode to Belle Riviere, her self-imposed prison.

Amelie didn't know how much longer she could keep up the pretense.

Doctor Markham's visit had unnerved her, and as

she sat on the side veranda and sipped warm, soothing tea, she trembled.

"Why won't you allow me to examine you today?" Doctor Markham had inquired earlier when he saw her in the parlor.

"I'm indisposed," she had whispered and lowered her eyes in a becoming manner.

Immediately Thaddeus understood, and because he was a gentleman, he didn't press the matter. "I'll check on you in a few days," he volunteered gallantly.

After his departure, Amelie extinguished a long sigh. At least that problem was over for the moment. But a worse one plagued her, and she could barely speak to Claude when he brought her onto the porch for tea.

Now, her gaze followed him as he walked among the grazing horses in the fields and gave Amie a loving pat. She never tired of looking at him. The simple shirt he wore strained against his chest and his pants molded like sculptor's clay to powerful thighs. She loved Claude and longed to shout her feelings from the rooftop of Green Meadows. However, she'd never do anything to endanger her position as Daniel's wife. But she realized that the time had come when she must rethink that position.

What would happen if someone discovered she could walk? Would her life change so drastically? She felt that soon Thaddeus would ascertain the truth about the paralysis. Yet that didn't bother her so much at the moment and wasn't what caused her fingers to shake and drop the teacup.

"Damn!" she muttered. The crash caused Claude to look toward the veranda. With long strides, he reached her just as a house servant appeared.

"Madam has had an accident," the servant girl named Ella said and bent to pick up the broken pieces of china.

"My dress is ruined!" Amelie wailed.

Dark splotches stained the bright blue silk. Claude dabbed at it with a napkin.

"Please." Ella halted him with a hand lightly place on his wrist, but her dark doe eyes expressed disapproval. "I'll tend to Madam Amelie."

"How clumsy I've become." Amelie was on the verge of tears.

"Tsk, madam. Don't cry. The stains shall come out and your dress shall be good as new."

Claude stood stiffly by. Tenderness shone on his face for Amelie, but a look of keen interest for Ella, who had been recently purchased from a planter in the Felicianas, mingled there, too. He liked the way she took control of the situation with a pleasant detachment.

"I advise, madam, that you change from your soiled dress. I shall see that it is cleaned at once."

Amelie smiled her thanks, and Claude picked her up. He headed into the house, unaware of Ella's eyes on him. When he lowered Amelie to the floor in her room, he turned her in his arms. "Would madam like me to undress her?"

"Claude!" Amelie flushed but would have adored to have him remove her clothes. However, she said, "I'll ring for Lallie."

"Are you all right, Amelie? You don't look well lately."

She twisted away from him. Her eyes held no sparkle. Claude mustn't guess her secret. "Claude, you better leave now. Someone may walk in. Your mother suspects us already."

His mouth tightened. The dark eyes snapped. "So, madam issues the orders and like a loyal dog, the slave obeys!"

She hadn't meant to sound imperious, but his nearness bothered her and caused her heart to ache even more.

"Claude!" she called after him, but he had left the room in a huff.

Throwing herself on the bed to wait for Lallie, she allowed herself the luxury of tears. Her love for Claude was hopeless. She hated keeping her secret to herself but saw no other alternative. But what was she going to do?

She had implied to Thaddeus that she had her monthly, but for over a month she hadn't seen any trace of it. For the past few mornings, nausea greeted her upon waking and her small breasts seemed slightly fuller. The signs were there, and she couldn't ignore them.

Her hands traced the contours of her abdomen. She wondered how long it would be before her condition showed. What would she do then? Daniel would know he wasn't the baby's father and would take great delight in throwing her out.

She nearly laughed despite the burning ache in her throat. At last, she'd be free of him and his precious plantation. But she had nowhere to go, no one to turn to. Except for Claude. Claude, her lover. Claude, the slave.

She needed time to think, time to decide what to do. Though she carried a slave's child, she wouldn't rid herself of it. The child was a tie to Claude, the seed of their love.

Rubbing her tears away with small fists, she wondered if the baby would be light-skinned. After all, Claude wasn't much darker than Daniel, and with her as the mother . . .

Slowly she stopped crying and sat up, a plan forming in her mind. Perhaps there was a way to keep Claude and her child, a way to remain Daniel's wife. Admittedly, it was a gamble, dependent upon fate. But all of life was a gamble, and she must take the chance.

When Lallie finally entered the room, Amelie's eyes glowed brighter than they had for days. With just the right amount of happy surprise and disbelief in her voice, she spoke to the woman.

"Lallie, some feeling has returned to my legs."

Chapter 16

The news of Amelie's miraculous recovery drifted back to Belle Riviere. Phillipe left the marriage chamber earlier than he had intended to visit his sister and took Lianne with him.

"Such wonderful news," he told Amelie and kissed her cheek heartily.

"Yes, it is," she agreed and took a few steps in the parlor to show him just how wonderful it was. Amelie sat down, growing quite pale suddenly, and Phillipe patted her hand.

"Please take it easy at first. Remember you haven't walked in some time."

Amelie could only nod as a wave of nausea swept over her.

"I'm pleased for you, also," Lianne said and sipped a glass of claret a servant presented. Though she smiled at Amelie, her eyes darted now and then to Daniel who lounged in a chair near the fireplace. He looked so huge in the small chair, and she wondered how the fragile piece didn't break under his weight.

"Are you?" Amelie inquired, not missing the secret glances her sister-in-law sent her husband or the openly covetous ones he cast her way. However, Phillipe didn't seem to notice.

Lianne laid her glass of claret on the side table. "Of course," she said and meant it. However, she couldn't help thinking how this new development might change things. Would Daniel leave Amelie now that she could walk? Would he declare his love for her and divorce his wife? She felt guilty for harboring such thoughts, but she couldn't help thinking them.

Amelie answered her questions, however, when she reached out an arm and stroked Daniel's hand. "The past few years have been hard on all of us, but we intend to rectify them. Don't we, dearest?"

Daniel hid his amazement. Amelie hadn't touched him since before the accident. "Yes, we will," he said, his gaze not leaving Lianne's face.

At that moment Lianne knew she had lost him. No matter what, he was determined to make up for the pain he had caused Amelie. Even if it meant giving up any claim to his child. Yet he hadn't spoken to Lianne since the day in the nursery, and though he might strongly suspect Désirée was his daughter, he hadn't questioned her again.

Phillipe stood up to leave. He held out his hand to Lianne. "Come, chérie."

She rose but hesitated. "Phillipe, the baby."

"Baby?" He lifted his brow in puzzlement.

"Désirée. I want to take her home with us."

"Chérie, we're still on our honeymoon. A child will be a bother."

"She is my child. I want her with me."

"But our honeymoon . . ."

"Phillipe, I fear your time with your bride has already ended." Amelie broke into the conversation. "Lianne was here for a visit only a few days ago."

He whitened. The look of defiance he saw creep across his wife's face confirmed his sister's words. He had thought she rode only on Belle Riviere that morning she left the house. To think that she'd visit Green Meadows hadn't occurred to him. Didn't she realize a man had his pride? What must everyone think? That Phillipe Marchand's bride was eager to leave his arms? However, he'd never embarrass her in front of others as she had done to him.

He swallowed and smiled at Amelie and Daniel, who seemed amused. "Lianne was eager to see the child. Yes, my dear, gather your little one's things. We shall take her home with us."

Lianne kissed his cheek. "Thank you, thank you." She rushed from the room and up the stairs.

Phillipe sat down again, a sheepish expression on his face. "So, how long shall it be before you make me an uncle, Amelie?"

Amelie's fingers curled around a fold of her gown. She managed to speak in a steady voice, and purposely looked at Daniel. "Soon, I hope."

Daniel didn't bother to reply. Once again, Amelie had surprised him. How unlike her to be so loving, so full of warmth. And children? What was she up to?

When Lianne arrived downstairs with the baby in her arms, Dera and Maria following, Daniel wrenched his hand away from Amelie's and followed Phillipe and the chattering women onto the porch to bid the Marchands goodbye. He felt a part of him dying, because he knew the little girl was his own. He silently cursed Lianne for her stubbornness, but in a way he was glad. He had nothing to offer the child. Lianne was another man's wife, and he already was married. There was too much to untangle if he claimed paternity. He also knew he had hurt Lianne with his cruel words, but he wanted her to realize how deeply she had hurt him by refusing him as her lover.

When Phillipe helped Maria into the carriage, Daniel moved toward Lianne and the baby. "I hope you've made the right choice."

If she hadn't seen the pain in his eyes, she'd have thought he meant to be sarcastic. "I have," she said.

"I'm here if you ever need help."

Tears sprang to her eyes, and she mouthed his name. She watched as he bent down and gently kissed

Désirée's cheek. That was too much for her to bear. She turned quickly and hurried down the steps and into the carriage just as the tears spilled forth.

"Why the tears, Lianne?" Phillipe asked, not bothering to hide the anger in his voice, now that they were on their way home. He still hadn't forgiven her for leaving their marriage bed to ride to Green Meadows. He felt humiliated.

"I'm overcome with emotion. That's all, Phillipe."

"Hmmph!" He sneered. "You'll be overcome by more than that if you ever humiliate me again! Understand?"

She cowered, practically becoming one with the cushion. "I'm sorry."

He ignored her and the baby during the ride home. Maria stared stonily ahead. Lianne controlled her tears, but her heart cried for the man left standing on the porch at Green Meadows.

The last remnants of the brandy slid easily down Daniel's throat. Flickering flames leaped in the fireplace, but he felt no warmth. He kept seeing Lianne in Phillipe's bed, his daughter in an adjacent room of Belle Riviere. In his whole life he'd never felt so alone.

A knock sounded on his door. "Come in," he grunted and tossed the empty bottle onto the floor. He settled himself against the pillows, not even bothering to see who had entered.

"Daniel."

Opening his eyes in disbelief, he beheld his wife. She stood poised in the doorway, her figure clearly outlined against the darkness of the hallway behind her.

"May I come in?"

"Certainly."

She closed the door and entered into the dancing shadows of the room. Amelie wore a thin nightdress which was low and barely covered her breasts. Her golden hair swirled around her shoulders. A sweet smell like lilacs clung to the air.

Daniel had never seen her look more lovely or more desirable. What was the little tease up to?

"Can't you sleep?" he asked her. "Are you ill?"

"I'm very well, as you can see. I wanted to speak with you."

"About what?"

"I'd like to work out our problems, to start our marriage anew."

"Amelie, I thought you hated me."

"I did," she said slowly. "However, I misjudged you. I realized I wasn't a very good wife, not dutiful at all. I imagine I was quite trying at times. I'd like to right the wrongs I've done you."

He stroked his chin, appraising her. "By coming to my bed?"

She swallowed hard. "If you'll have me."

Being a man, and a man without a woman for a long while, desire swelled in him. Here stood a willing woman, a woman who was his wife. Perhaps she'd even ease the ache in his loins for Lianne. He'd be a fool to refuse.

"Are you well enough for lovemaking?"

"Yes, Daniel."

"Then come to bed."

He opened his arms and she went to him. Their lovemaking at first was tenative. He was distrustful of her and she thought of Claude. But soon they reached a climax which, if not of major intensity, was pleasant.

Later she slept beside him and listened to his gentle snores. "I shall give you a child soon, Daniel. A son to inherit Green Meadows," she whispered to his back in the darkness. Then she left his bed, unable to sleep there. Her mind dwelled on Claude.

She padded quietly down the hallway until she came to her own room and cut across to the door which led to Claude's. She found him standing by the window.

"Darling," she whispered and hugged him around the waist.

He looked down at her. A twisted smile played across his mouth, and the moonlight flooding his small room only enhanced the hardness of his eyes.

"Have you not been satisfied in your husband's bed, madam? Must you seek out your slave for complete satisfaction?"

"Claude, please!"

"Amelie, I know you were with Daniel. I may be only a slave, but I'm not stupid!"

"I never said you were."

His hands disentangled her arms from him, almost as if he hated to touch her. "I loved you, and you betrayed me."

How could she explain to him that she carried his child and loved him but couldn't give up the pampered life of a planter's wife? He couldn't offer her and the baby anything but a life of desolate poverty. But she couldn't tell him any of this. She must put her faith in God that their child would have fair skin. Claude must never know the baby she'd pass off as Daniel's was his.

"You shouldn't have loved me, Claude. But we can still be lovers. Daniel need never know."

"I'll know, Amelie. I can't share you with him. Whether you know it or not, I'm the master over your body. Not Daniel."

She knew that very well. Daniel was a good lover, but Claude was the one who excited her and made her feel alive.

Wildly she threw her arms around his neck. "Make love to me, Claude. Now!"

"Didn't Daniel do an adequate job, madam?"

She hated the way he looked at her with loathing in his eyes, but she wanted him and knew how to incite him to passion. Her hands flew beneath his shirt and massaged the muscles of his chest, then strayed down-

ward to his manhood. As she had guessed, he was
ready for her, and this gave her the hope that her plan
would work. She could have Claude, the child, and
still live as Daniel's wife.

"Take me, Claude." She ripped at his pants until
he was naked, then she tore the shirt from his back.
"You're my slave. Do as I say."

She was in a frenzy to have him, and when he tore
the gown from her body, she was more than eager. He
threw her across the bed and slid into her with such
force she gasped. But the pleasure of his entry
overcame the pain, and she wound her legs around
him. Her nails sunk into the tender flesh of his back,
and in that instant they found satisfaction.

Amelie panted. The sweat poured from Claude's
brow onto her breasts. He lifted his head, and his eyes
impaled her.

"I may be your slave, Amelie, but you're my
whore."

He got up and dressed. She could think of nothing
to say, no words to stop him from leaving. After he
had gone she went to the window and watched as he
made his way to the slave quarters.

Chapter 17

During the second month of Lianne's marriage, Phillipe informed her that he was going to New Orleans to take care of business and that she shouldn't worry herself if he wasn't back right away.

This information didn't bother Lianne at all, and she hoped that Phillipe didn't see how her face lit with relief at the news. "Content yourself with preparations for the Mardi Gras Ball, *chérie*. This will be the first time in years that Belle Riviere has had such an extravagant affair. Powerful people shall attend, and I want you to choose the most dazzling costume imaginable."

"Shouldn't I go into town with you?" she asked and finished pouring her cup of morning tea. "I could visit the dressmaker."

Phillipe waved his hand in a dismissive gesture. "Stay here. I shall send a seamstress. There's no need for you to travel."

"I'd like to go, Phillipe. Things are rather dull here."

"Are they?" His blue eyes hardened a bit. "I suppose you'd like to visit with that motley crew at the opera house to boost your flagging spirits. Well, forget it. You're mistress of my home and as such I demand your presence here. That gypsy life style is behind you. Sometimes I can't believe you're the daughter of nobility and were married to a comte. I think you forget your duties, Lianne.''

He pulled himself to his full height. She felt at a disadvantage to be sitting on the bed, cup in hand. She hated it when his eyes frosted in contempt. Phillipe had changed since she had left their bridal chamber earlier than expected and ridden to Green Meadows. She decided he'd never forgive her for that humiliation, which she thought was absurd. However, she guessed that wasn't the only reason behind his wintry look.

"I didn't intend to visit, though I admit I'd like to see everyone. But my main reason is to engage a seamstress for . . .''

"I told you I'd send one here! Aren't you satisfied with the expensive trousseau I bought for you? It seems you're never happy, Lianne. Or satisfied. And I think you understand my meaning."

Phillipe loomed over her, and her stomach heaved. He'd never struck her, but now she wondered if he was capable of violence. No matter what she did or didn't do, he found fault with her. But she took a deep breath and ordered herself to stand her ground and not be intimidated by him.

"What I meant," she said sweetly and shot him an engaging smile, "was that I need to hire someone to make Désirée new clothes. With each day, she grows and now her things are much too small. I don't need any more frocks, Phillipe. And I am satisfied. No matter what you think.''

His face softened. Lianne had a way of twisting him around her fingers like prayer beads. He desired her even now though he recognized the determined set of her jaw when she wanted her way. However, she would tow the mark with him or suffer for it. Friends of his beat their wives for less. His humiliation at Green Meadows didn't sting so sharply any longer, but frustration of another sort ate away at him. Always considering himself an expert in the bedroom, he now felt the amateur.

Lianne never denied him, but he sensed she didn't wish to be in his arms, didn't enjoy the act. Of course, women shouldn't enjoy lovemaking as much as men. He didn't think that was in their nature. However, he no longer found the intense pleasure he craved. So, the trip to New Orleans and to Chloe's soft, willing body. Under no circumstances would he allow Lianne to accompany him.

"Thank you for your reassurance, *chérie.*" He bent and kissed her cheek. "I'll send Madame Dupré to you. She is by far the best dressmaker in New Orleans, and I'm sure will design a gorgeous costume for the ball, and clothes for the child," he said as an afterthought. He'd never get used to having another man's offspring around.

Lianne knew when she was defeated. Shortly after Phillipe left her, she got out of bed and rang for a servant who helped her dress. After checking on the baby and Maria, she headed downstairs and to Phillipe's library where she found paper and pen and began to sketch designs for her costume.

She knew Phillipe wanted the Mardi Gras Ball to be a success. This was the first ball to be held at Belle Riviere since his parents died, and she knew, also, that he wished to show her off to his wealthy friends from New Orleans. Sometimes she felt like a possession put on display for company. Many times during the past few weeks, friends of Phillipe visited. He only permitted her to pay her respects to them as he basked in their compliments concerning her beauty, then he kissed her with a warm but dismissive kiss.

The nights, however, were worse. She tried to respond to him and knew his surliness at times was because he guessed she didn't love him. And she didn't. She cared about him, but she wasn't in love with her husband. Her thoughts centered on Daniel, a man she loved, a man she needed. But a man who would never be free.

Growing disenchanted with her sketches, she threw them aside just as she heard the clip clop of horse's hooves on the drive. She stood up and looked out of the window to see Daniel dismounting.

With an unconscious gesture, she fluffed out her hair and straightened her shoulders and hoped her smile looked genuinely happy. She'd rather die than let him think she had married the wrong man.

A servant admitted Daniel to the study. His eyes slid over her in an appraising manner. "You're looking well, Lianne."

"So are you," she said and wished her heart would stop beating so hard. Daniel looked better than well. His face appeared less haggard, his eyes a bright gray. The brown of his coat and pants enhanced the tanned complexion but the clothes appeared slightly rumpled, as if he had thrown them on his large masculine frame in haste. Still, he appeared devastatingly handsome to her eyes, and it was his rakish persona which appealed to her.

"How is Phillipe?" he asked.

"How is Amelie?" she countered.

He shrugged. "Amelie is Amelie. But I'm not here to discuss her. I'm here to paint you and Désirée."

"I don't recall commissioning a portrait," she said slowly.

"You didn't. If you recall I told you I was going to paint the two of you."

"What if I don't want you to paint us? Phillipe might object." Phillipe wasn't the reason she demurred. She couldn't bear having Daniel so close to her.

"I'm sure you can make Phillipe do whatever you want him to do, Lianne."

"You overestimate my charms, I fear."

"Do I?" He came closer to her, close enough that

he could smell her distinctive female scent mingled with rose water. He ached for her mouth, and he would have pulled her to him and kissed her except she turned her head.

"Now isn't the right time for a portrait, Daniel. The idea is very nice, but Phillipe isn't home, and I don't think he'd be too pleased."

The mention of Phillipe again cooled his ardor. He backed off a bit. "Let me do a quick sketch of you and the child. It won't take long."

Lianne gazed into his eyes then, and knew she'd allow him his way. Though she knew she should send him home with a polite but firm refusal, she couldn't. She wanted to see him for as long as possible despite his cruel words a month past. Phillipe was gone and would't be home for a few weeks. He'd never have to know Daniel had even been there.

"All right, Daniel," she said and was immediately rewarded with a brilliant smile.

He left the study and retraced his steps to his horse. Then he was back inside with sketch pad and charcoal. "Get the child," he ordered.

Lianne took Désirée from under Maria's watchful gaze. "Monsieur Phillipe won't approve." Maria voiced her concern after Lianne had told her the reason for Daniel's visit.

"It's just a sketch. Phillipe shouldn't mind. After all, Phillipe and Daniel are related."

"And very possessive of you. Remember how nasty Monsieur Phillipe became in the carriage that time. I think it was wrong for me to encourage you to marry him. I'm afraid I misjudged him."

"Maria," Lianne scooped up the baby, and her eyes flashed, "my husband has never done anything to warrant such criticism. You're as bad as Dera lately."

Maria sniffed. "You should have listened to her. She knows him better than you."

As Lianne settled herself and the baby in the appointed place by Daniel, she found it difficult to dismiss Maria's warning. Prickles of fear gathered and raised on her skin. She did wonder at times if Phillipe would harm her, but he loved her. So, she convinced herself he'd never hurt her.

Daniel turned her face and tilted her chin a bit after she had quieted Désirée with a trinket.

"You have the most beautiful face of any woman I've ever seen," he said softly.

An ache started in her throat. "Daniel, please."

His fingers moved gently over her auburn tresses. "Your hair looks like an autumn sunset and smells like spring flowers."

"Stop this nonsense or I must insist you leave!" She didn't mean to sound so harsh, but his caressing eyes, hands, disturbed her. She remembered the night in the summerhouse and trembled.

Daniel blinked and came to his senses. "I forget myself, Madame Marchand. Forgive me." He picked up his sketch pad and sat across from her.

Sudden clouds darkened the parlor, and he ordered a servant to light the candles. Then a winter rainstorm broke from the heavens and besieged the house with gales of rain and wind. The warm glow from the fireplace dispelled the gloom.

Désirée started to fuss, and Lianne knew their posing time was at an end. "She's tired, Daniel."

He looked up from his pad, suddenly aware of his surroundings. "Yes, of course. I got so involved, I didn't realize."

She rang for Maria who took the baby. "It's nearly lunchtime," she said to Daniel.

"Is that an invitation?"

Lianne couldn't turn him out in such a rainstorm, so she nodded and ordered the cook to set two places at the table. "Are you always so involved when you draw?" she asked him over soup a little while later.

"Yes."

"May I see your sketches?"

He considered. "Perhaps later. I make it a habit never to show anyone what I've done until it's finished."

They had their coffee in the parlor. Daniel laced his with whiskey, and he didn't miss the way her nose wrinkled in distaste.

"Don't approve, Lianne?"

"You drink too much. I don't think it's good for you."

Laughing, he shook his head. "I'm beginning to find that nothing pleasurable in life is good for me. However, I still indulge." He offered her a sip which she drank but began to cough as the burning liquid slid down her throat.

"I think you're slightly degenerate to enjoy such a drink," she said after she recovered.

He sat close to her on the sofa. "I am, Lianne. If you knew what was good for you, you'd run upstairs this minute and bolt your door."

She turned to him. Her eyes looked like a mysterious feline's in the fireglow. "I'm not afraid of you."

"You should be," he whispered and twisted a long copper curl around his finger.

"Why?" She could barely breathe, barely speak.

"Because of this."

His lips moved over hers, tasting of their sweetness. She moaned. How wonderful it felt to be kissed by this man, to feel her whole body start to come alive. But this couldn't happen, wouldn't happen. She was married to Phillipe and must remember that.

"No, Daniel." She attempted to push away, but he clasped her wrists. His eyes sparkled with ferocity.

"Don't deny me, Lianne. You know you want me. Want me as much as I want you!"

She couldn't deny this, and when his lips plundered hers in a greedy kiss, she didn't want to. The warmth of love flowed through her veins like a golden liquid which entered every artery and fused her body to his. She matched him kiss for kiss, touch for touch.

His mouth trailed to the valley between her breasts, setting her on fire, and she knew the inevitable would happen. She did want him and she'd have him, if only for a few stolen moments.

"I love you, Lianne. I'll always love you."

Daniel's breath was a husky whisper. She knew he would never leave Amelie, but she didn't care at the moment. She loved him, too.

Bittersweet tears slid down her face. Her slender fingers traced the broadness of his back. "If only things were different."

"Shh, love. Don't think about what might have been or could be. At this second, I don't want to think. I only want to feel your flesh against mine."

He unbuttoned the buttons on the front of her bodice until her breasts spilled forth into his hands. As he laved each one with his tongue, the flame within her spread like shafts of fire. He lifted his head, and if she had wanted to deny him, she couldn't have. The desire on his face was thicker than the pelting rain outside.

Helping him out of his jacket, she then unbuttoned his shirt. Her hands slid across the muscled contours of his chest. "You're such a beautiful man," she said and planted tiny kisses on his flesh.

"You're the beautiful one, my sweet."

He pulled her against him and started to hike her skirts. A part of her knew how disgusting this all was. Here they were in the parlor and she was ready, eager, to be taken on the sofa like some strumpet. But Daniel made her feel things, do things, no other man was capable of. She didn't care about propriety but she did vaguely wonder if she should have locked the door, and she voiced this to Daniel in between earth-shattering kisses.

"The servants won't enter without knocking first, Lianne."

She forgot her fear of discovery as Daniel's hands ran over her breasts and down her thighs. His kisses inflamed her, drugging her beyond caring, and hurling her into a vortex of passion she'd never known.

From the front of the house she heard a door slam and the far-off sound of cursing.

"Damn this infernal weather!"

She tried to push Daniel aside and would have bolted from his arms except he held her in a vise-like grip.

"It's Phillipe!" she cried.

Chapter 18

"Let me go!" Lianne wiggled free from Daniel's restraining arms. Hurriedly she buttoned her bodice and shook out her skirt. She urged Daniel to make himself presentable, but he grinned and drove her mad as he put himself back in order in a lazy fashion, as if he had all the time in the world.

"Hurry!" she ordered.

By the time Phillipe entered the parlor, Lianne and Daniel presented a respectable picture. She sat demurely on the couch and sipped her tea, which had grown quite cold, and he finished another whiskey.

"I wondered whose horse that was outside," Phillipe said and extended his hand to Daniel.

"I decided to pay my respects," Daniel told him and shook his hand, "but Lianne said you weren't home."

Lianne felt amazement at Daniel's calmness. Inside she shook and had to put down the teacup which rattled in her hand. She hoped her dress wasn't wrinkled and that her hair was smooth. Most of all she wondered if her lips looked as swollen as they felt. Was her guilt showing on her face for Phillipe to see?

"I thought you were headed into New Orleans." Lianne folded her hands in her lap.

Phillipe nodded. "The rain washed out the road. I

didn't wish to take a chance with the carriage and horses. Nothing's worse than being stuck in ankle-deep mud. So, I ordered the driver to turn around. You're not unhappy to see me so soon, are you, *chérie*?"

She smiled but evaded his question as she stood up. "I'll go get you a nice warm cup of tea."

"Don't bother. What I really want is a warm bath. I'm chilled to the bone. Come join me, Lianne."

She flushed from her toes to the roots of her hair. Phillipe wasn't asking her but telling her to bathe with him. She knew better than to protest in Daniel's presence.

"We should bid our guest goodbye, Phillipe."

Philippe nodded to Daniel. *"Adieu,* Daniel. Give our regards to Amelie."

Daniel rose from his chair. For an instant Lianne noted a flicker of dislike pass across Daniel's face for Phillipe. But when he spoke, his voice was steady.

"We should dine together soon."

"Of course. That would be most pleasant." Philippe took Lianne's hand and walked her into the foyer, stopping at the staircase. "Now," he said and his eyes lit upon Lianne's body, not bothering to hide his lust, "you can soap my back, *chérie.*"

Before Daniel's glittering gaze, Phillipe practically dragged her up the stairs. For one second her face turned toward Daniel in a glance of hopelessness.

The last he saw of her was the lace hem of her petticoat before she disappeared from view. Impotent rage filled him. He knew with a certainty that Lianne didn't love Phillipe. How was he to have her for his own when fate had conspired to keep them apart? He longed to bound up the stairs and take her from Phillipe. But she was married to the man.

Somehow, someway, Lianne would be his. He vowed this to himself as he wrenched open the front door and slammed it behind him.

Phillipe's hands encircled the globular fullness of Lianne's breasts and pinched each nipple. His breath fanned hot on the back of her neck as his fingers traced the pathway of her abdomen to the spot between her legs and lingered there.

She sat in front of him, their legs drawn up, against the sides of the tub, and felt powerless to stop him from touching her. After being with Daniel, she viewed Phillipe with dread. The constant motion of his hands across her body stirred the bath water. She felt his male hardness against her and knew he was ready for her but wanted a passionate response before he took her. She knew very easily she could fake it, but she was tired of playing games with Phillipe, tired of pretending she desired him.

"What's wrong, *chérie*? Aren't I man enough for you?"

"I'm rather tired."

He sniffed. "You're always tired lately. I've never had trouble pleasuring women before you."

"I'd just like to go to bed."

"Then I shall oblige you."

To her surprise he stood up and yanked her from the water. He stepped out of the tub and picked her up in his arms. "We shall retire together, Lianne. Before this night is over, you shall be tired of having me in you!"

His face looked distorted in the candlelight, and he threw her in the center of the bed, not seeming to care that her wet body shivered from the chill in the air and from fear. He fell on top of her and pinned her hands to the bed.

"You're my wife, and I think it's time you give me my due as your husband. After tonight, you'll never deny me again!"

"I've never done that!" she cried and tried to

twist away from him.

"No? Then why is it you don't care for my kisses, my touch? Why is it that when I find you alone with Daniel Flanders your face is crimson and your eyes so bright they could light up the sky?"

"I don't know what you mean."

His eyes darkened.

"Liar! You want Daniel Flanders to make love to you. Or did you and Daniel make love in the parlor? Was that why you looked so guilty?"

"Phillipe, stop this!"

"I noticed your rumpled gown. I'm not someone you can twist around your fingers, Lianne, someone you can take from but give nothing back in return. I'm more of a man than Daniel can ever hope to be. I'll prove it to you."

Phillipe turned her onto her stomach and pulled her upward. Then he entered her body from behind, nearly tearing her apart. After, she lay beside him, defeated and shaking; he fell asleep.

When the first light of dawn filtered through the curtains, Lianne was still awake. Phillipe woke and dressed and told her he was leaving for New Orleans. Standing over her and peering at her, he said, "Who is more of the man, *chérie*?"

When she didn't answer, he grabbed a handful of hair and jerked her to a sitting position. "Who is the man?"

She gazed at him with pain-filled eyes. "You . . . you are, Phillipe."

Satisfied, he tossed her onto the pillows. "Remember that. Otherwise, I will be forced to rid you of your lover."

After Phillipe's departure, she lay in a stupor. She knew she'd never have a future with Daniel, but she feared Phillipe's rages and what he'd do to her and her child, or Daniel, if provoked. Somehow she must convince Phillipe that she was content in their marriage, play the faithful wife. But she hugged her pillow to her breasts and sobbed Daniel's name into the downy softness.

Chapter 19

A gust of February wind whipped past Lianne's face, but she didn't feel its sting as she urged her horse away from Belle Riviere to the open fields.

Her hair streamed like the sun's rays behind her. Her erect stature in the apricot riding habit branded her the expert horsewoman. When she did halt the horse by the boundary line which separated Belle Riviere from Green Meadows, she looked with longing toward the white house in the distance. An aching sensation filled her. She longed to see Daniel again but knew better than to seek him out.

Phillipe had been gone nearly three days, and a part of her hoped he'd never return. The bruises he had inflicted upon her during the brutal taking of her body hadn't healed yet, and she dreaded what might be in store for her upon his return. But seeing Daniel wasn't the answer to her problem. She must try to appease Phillipe, to make him forget his suspicions about Daniel.

She knew she must forget Daniel, must stop yearning for his touch, his kisses. A future with Daniel wasn't possible, and she didn't want to become his mistress.

Turning the horse for home, she cantered slowly back. When she entered the house a maid informed her she had company.

She began to remove her gloves but stopped as she entered the parlor to find Dera with Daniel. Dera rose from the sofa, a pleasant smile on her face as she kissed Lianne.

"How good to see you, dear. You've become such a stranger to Green Meadows lately that I decided to visit you, and Daniel insisted he come along."

Lianne forced a welcoming smile. They chatted for a few minutes. Lianne barely glanced at Daniel but she felt his penetrating gaze upon her until the sheer intensity of his eyes forced her to look his way. He only stared at her, assessing her. She fiddled with a button on the cuff of her jacket.

"Would you like to see Désirée?" she asked Dera.

"I thought you'd never ask!" Dera immediately left the room.

The silence thickened between Lianne and Daniel.

"You didn't ask me if I wanted to visit your daughter," he said.

"I hadn't realized you would. You may go upstairs."

He shook his head. "I'll see her later. Right now, I'd rather speak to her mother."

The abrasive quality in his voice caused her to jump. "We have nothing to say to one another." Rising from her seat, he jumped up and grabbed her arm before she could make a hasty retreat upstairs.

Turning her to him, his sharp glance cut through her. "Am I mistaken or didn't we nearly make love in this room only a few days ago? I could have sworn the soft, yielding body beneath me belonged to you."

"Daniel, let me go. Please. There can be nothing between us. You should realize that."

He groaned as if she had touched a nerve. "Our child is between us, Lianne. Désirée is a bond which can never be broken. Admit to me she's mine."

"She isn't yours."

Her mouth trembled when he brushed a tan finger across it. "Deny it all you want. I know the truth.

Now, admit it to yourself. Tell me you want to leave Phillipe. I'll take you and our daughter away from here. Just say the word.''

She blinked in disbelief, then refocused her gaze. ''Where would you hide us, Daniel? And even if Phillipe agreed to divorce me, what would become of me? I shall not be your mistress!''

Twisting away, she broke his hold. For a moment he studied her intently, as if memorizing her features. Then he jabbed his hands into the pockets of his pants. ''I can't offer you anything more, Lianne. I have a lot to make up to Amelie.''

She closed her eyes. When she opened them, she took a deep breath and noticed his expression was tight with strain. ''You've made your choice. I have made mine.''

He extinguished a low sigh. ''We're both fools.''

A bittersweet smile touched her lips. ''No, Daniel, but fate has decreed the course of our lives.''

Before he went upstairs, his glacial gaze froze her to the spot. ''Somehow, someway, Lianne, we'll be together. Perhaps not in the way you wish, but it will happen. I'll make it happen.''

His words brought a sob to her lips because she didn't believe him.

The next morning Lianne entered the nursery, dressed in a traveling gown of the finest mauve velvet. A matching bonnet covered her auburn tresses, and as she kissed Désirée in farewell, she was aware of the disapproval on Maria's plump face.

''Don't say anything to try and dissuade me from my visit to New Orleans. Phillipe hasn't sent a dressmaker, and the *bal masque* is barely two weeks away. I must have something presentable to wear.''

''Will you stay with Monsieur Phillipe?''

''He is my husband and has rooms on the Esplanade. I think I shall surprise him.''

Maria sniffed. ''You'll be the one surprised, Lianne. The monsieur told you not to go into town.

Why do you disobey him? You know how awful his temper is.''

Lianne knew very well how Phillipe showed his temper. However, for better or worse, he was her husband. Perhaps if she tried to love him, things might work out. The man had honored her with his name, had turned over the running of Belle Riviere to her, and was kind to her child. She owed him a great deal. Since Daniel could offer her no better, she decided she must try and make the best life she could with Phillipe.

"Phillipe is volatile, that's all," Lianne said to Maria and tried to believe he'd never hurt her again.

"Señora Dera fears for you. She will not tell you this, but she worries that your husband might do you or the child great harm."

Lianne stopped playing with Désirée momentarily. "Did you discuss my personal life with Dera?"

Maria folded a blanket and looked downward.

"Well, did you?" Lianne queried again.

Raising her head, defiance in her eyes, Maria nodded. "I wanted Señora Dera to know about how the monsieur abused you."

"You had no right, Maria, no matter how pure your intentions. I resent your interfering. Now what happens if Dera tells Daniel and . . .''

Maria halted Lianne's words with a hand on her arm. "Daniel Flanders isn't your husband. Why should you care about what he might do?"

Lianne hated the knowing look in the woman's dark eyes. Maria always seemed able to see into her soul.

"Because I don't want Phillipe's wrath to touch him. Phillipe will harm Daniel if he thinks I love him. So, I must pretend to care for my husband. I wouldn't be able to live with the guilt if something happened to Daniel because of me."

"Stay home. Don't go into New Orleans," Maria voiced again.

"I must. I have to prove to Phillipe that I desire him. Maybe everything will be all right if I convince him I wasn't unfaithful."

Lianne turned and left the nursery. In the hall she ordered a servant to take her valise to the waiting carriage, then she rode to New Orleans.

Shortly before dusk, the carriage pulled in front of the elgantly furnished apartments Phillipe rented while in the city. Lianne missed the small house she had lived in before her marriage and knew it stood empty, just waiting for her. But she convinced herself that the lavish rooms were more to Phillipe's taste.

When she knocked on his door, she expected a gasp of surprise but the furious blue eyes which met her caused her to tremble.

"I told you not to leave Belle Riviere! What in the name of heaven are you doing in the city?"

"Visiting you, Phillipe," she managed to say without stuttering.

"Get inside!" he bellowed and yanked her into the foyer. The immaculately polished Italian marble floors, the ornate balcony which led to the equally sumptuous bedroom and the golden sconces with flickering candles, were barely perceived by Lianne. All she concentrated on was the distorted, rage-filled face of her husband.

"Phillipe, I thought you might be pleased to see me, would like some company."

"I'd like it better if you stayed at Belle Riviere where you belong." He strode into the drawing room and poured a hefty glass of bourbon. "Do you enjoy making me angry, Lianne?" he asked after drinking it in one gulp.

"No, Phillipe. I don't mean to upset you."

Something in the childlike way she stood against the wall with saucer-shaped eyes touched a cord in him. He loved Lianne and regretted hurting her, but he didn't want her in the city. Suppose she decided to take up her old life again and sing with the opera? He'd lose her. But worse than that was the thought she might discover his secret family. She'd never accept his quadroon mistress and Jean Marc. He liked to think Lianne desired Daniel to ease his guilt. But he nearly broke out into a cold sweat imagining what might happen if she discovered his darkest secret—Honorine.

Phillipe also wondered how she'd regard him if she knew he was in debt and owed too many creditors to count, plus all the gambling debts. Even now, thinking about his penniless state angered him. If only he could borrow the money from someone. He had one last chance to get out of debt, and though he guessed he'd owe his life in repayment, he had to take the chance. He couldn't lose Belle Riviere or Lianne.

He heard her voice from far off. "I expected the seamstress to arrive at the house, but when she didn't come, I decided to visit the dressmaker and to spend time with you."

"Really?" he asked in disbelief.

"Really," she said, her courage rising. Lianne held out her hands to him in a forgiving gesture.

Phillipe clenched her hands and brought them to his mouth where he kissed her fingers. "I swear I shall never be cruel to you again."

Lianne managed also to bestow a forgiving smile upon him. "You're not an evil man, Phillipe."

"No, only a foolish one. Let's order supper for two and eat in tonight. I want you all to myself."

"Buy anything you desire, *chérie*," Philippe told her the next afternoon as she dressed for her appointment with Madame Dupré. "You're my wife, and I want to show you off at the ball. After all, the Marchands of Belle Riviere have a reputation to uphold."

Lianne noticed Phillipe looked edgey though he gave the impression of naturalness. She tied her bonnet under her chin. "What will you do while I'm gone?"

He shrugged and pulled on a blue coat which matched his eyes. "I have a business meeting."

"I hope it goes well for you."

"I do too," he said, uncertainty in his voice. He didn't know what he'd do if his loan was refused. The banks refused him further credit. What would happen to him and his high life style if his uncle refused him the money? "I'll see you later," he said and left without further word to her.

Near two, Lianne arrived at Madame Dupré's. The woman appeared pleased to see her and asked her to have a seat while she finished a fitting.

Lianne watched the passers-by and the street traffic from the storefront window while Madame Dupré measured a city official's wife. The woman was middle-aged and overweight, and she insisted the dressmaker's measurements were wrong.

"That cannot be accurate, madame. My waist has always been much smaller than that. You'd best check again."

"Of course, Madam LeClerc," the dressmaker said obligingly and rewound the tape measure around the woman's waist. "It's just as you said, madame. You were right."

"I know my figure," Madam LeClerc said, taking offense, but Lianne noticed that the seamstress didn't bother to change the supposedly new measurement on her tablet.

As a handsome carriage pulled by, a prancing black stallion came into view, and from Lianne's seat near the window, she recognized its occupant as the quadroon woman who was the mistress of Phillipe's friend. Instead of wearing the orange turban as she did the last time Lianne saw her, her curly hair was covered by a bright pink one, and her dress was made of the finest rose satin.

"Look at that negress!" Madame LeClerc's shrill voice carried thoughout the shop. "How dare those women cavort around town in their fine carriages and clothes, bought and paid for by white men. It's disgusting. Someone should burn those little cottages on the ramparts where they entertain our men and run those whores out of town."

"Madame, please . . ." Madam Dupré tried to quiet her customer.

"Well, it's true. Just take a look at the whore. Doesn't she think she's something sitting there like a damn queen. I heard her lover recently married, but does that keep him away?"

Lianne had had enough of the woman's loud voice. She stood up and faced Madam LeClerc. "Please be quiet, madame. Perhaps the quadroon knows of no other life and loves the gentleman who keeps her. Have compassion."

Madam LeClerc's mouth gaped open, and for the first time in her life, she was speechless. "Just what is your name, mademoiselle?" she asked Lianne after a few moments. "You have a great deal of nerve telling me to be quiet."

"I am Madame Phillipe Marchand, mistress of Belle Riviere plantation."

"Phillipe Marchand, did you say?" Madam LeClerc's eyes glowed in malevolent delight. She'd put this sassy girl in her place, once and for all. No one embarrassed Annabelle LeClerc without regretting it. "I suggest in future, Madame Phillipe Marchand, that you keep your comments to yourself."

"And why is that?"

"Because the quadroon who just rode away in the expensive carriage is none other than your husband's whore."

"I don't believe you." Lianne felt the blood drain from her.

Madam LeClerc shrugged her shoulders. "Don't then, though it is the truth. If you don't believe me, you'll find the woman known as Chloe in a small white cottage on the ramparts. I'm certain she goes by the name Marchand there.''

Before Lianne could disgrace herself further, she flew from the shop and entered her carriage. She ordered the driver to take her back to the Esplanade.

Her fingers shook badly, and her stomach felt as if it were tied in knots. She was a huge fool. She should have known Chloe was Phillipe's mistress the day he pretended not to know her. Why didn't she realize the truth? She definitely wouldn't have married Philippe if she had but guessed.

She remembered the small boy in the carriage who sat beside Chloe that day. The child was golden-skinned and light-eyed. Could he be Phillipe's son?

She spoke to the driver, and when he looked at her as if she were a crazy woman, she repeated the order.

"Take me to the ramparts."

Chapter 20

"Your tea, madame." Chloe's slender hand extended the fragile china cup to Lianne.

"Merci," Lianne said and took a sip of the warm brew though she could barely swallow it. She wondered how she sat so calmly across from her husband's mistress with Phillipe's son playing in the next room.

Chloe's gentle beauty impressed Lianne, and the surprise she knew the woman must feel at seeing her was hidden behind solemn but beautiful brown eyes. Lianne hadn't known what to expect when she disembarked in this section of town where small cottages housed quadroons and their children as they waited for men like Phillipe to put in an appearance.

She found Chloe's house with little trouble because the expensive carriage was parked alongside the cottage. When Lianne's knock brought Chloe to the door, Lianne could barely speak. But Chloe had smiled and said, "Madame Marchand, how nice to meet you at last."

Though Chloe was Phillipe's mistress and probably still slept with him on his trips into the city, Lianne didn't dislike her. Chloe's tenderness, her sincerity, caused Lianne to wonder why such a sweet, beautiful woman would love Phillipe.

"Your son is a handsome boy," Lianne

commented after Jean Marc put in a brief appearance
to pilfer a sweetmeat from under Chloe's nose, then
swiftly returned to his games in the next room. "He
favors Phillipe a great deal."

This was the first mention of Phillipe's name, and
Chloe suppressed a sigh. "I'm sorry you discovered his
secret family, madame. Phillipe never wished you to
know of us."

"I wonder how many other secrets Phillipe keeps
from me."

"I've known him for many years, madame, and I
don't know all his secrets, but I will tell you this
because I believe you must be aware of the circumstances in which he finds himself. Phillipe incurred
many debts the last few months. Always he overspent
and gambled that which he didn't have. But ever the
winner, he managed to pay his creditors. Now, he is
deeply in debt and may lose Belle Riviere unless he can
borrow the money. Alas, the banks refuse to loan him
any money." Chloe shook her head sadly. "I don't
know what will become of him if he loses the
plantation."

Lianne gasped. Her surprise at this news showed
clearly on her face. So, Phillipe was in debt and he
hadn't informed her that Belle Riviere might be lost.
Yet Chloe knew. It seemed he confided more in his
mistress than in his wife.

"Phillipe is a weak man, madame," said Chloe.

"Why do you stay with him?" Lianne questioned
and asked the same thing of herself.

"I love him." Her answer was given simply, but
Lianne heard the intensity with which she replied. "I
knew from the beginning that marriage could never be,
but I shall always love him. No matter what happens
between us."

"Then I'll make life easier for you and your son."
Lianne placed her cup on the table and rose from her
chair. The late afternoon sun bathed the tiny parlor in

a rosy light which enchanced both women's features. "I shall ask Phillipe for a divorce."

"Madame, you mustn't!" Chloe jumped up and grabbed Lianne's arm in an imploring gesture. "I won't allow my situation to break up your marriage. Phillipe can't marry me, and I accept that."

"You're not to blame for any of this. I accept responsibility for my mistake in becoming Phillipe's wife. I should never have married him. I don't love him."

"Mon Dieu," Chloe whispered and wondered why Lianne didn't love Phillipe when she loved him so very much. "I'm sorry, Madame Marchand."

"Don't be. Soon my mistake shall be rectified." Lianne didn't know what she'd do after accosting Phillipe with the news that she wanted a divorce. Probably return to Belle Riviere for her daughter then move back to New Orleans and sing for the company. She knew Daniel would never leave Amelie and she mustn't expect that, still she wondered at his reaction when he learned she'd soon be free.

Lianne patted Chloe's hand. "Thank you for your kindness and hospitality. It grows late and I must speak with Phillipe."

Chloe said nothing else as she opened the door for Lianne. However, when Lianne saw Phillipe standing on the other side, a sound of surprise and dismay escaped her.

"What in the name of heaven are you doing here?" He pushed her back into the parlor. A vicious scowl darkened his pale face.

"I paid a visit to your mistress, Phillipe. I believe it was time we met." Lianne didn't know where her courage came from, she just knew the time had arrived to end her marriage. She smiled at Chloe. "I find her to be charming and gracious."

Nothing had worked out for Phillipe that day. The business meeting with his uncle hadn't progressed in the way he hoped. Of course he could borrow from his uncle but not the full amount he needed. He couldn't fathom the man's reasons at denying him the whole amount. Something about the trust his parents had set up for him and Amelie which gave his mother's brother the power over how the money was to be doled out. He had felt like a child as he sat before that hard unyielding face, trembling at the austere picture Uncle Raoul presented with the black patch over his eye.

Phillipe had found it difficult to appear charming in the hope that a ready smile might force the necessary funds from his uncle's tight fists. When he inquired as to why he couldn't receive the entire amount, his uncle only said, "In time, Phillipe. When I'm ready, the money shall be turned over to you." But that didn't satisfy Phillipe. He needed the money now. The only thing Raoul seemed to want to discuss was his recent marriage to Lianne Laguens, Comtesse de la Varre.

Weariness after the meeting plagued Phillipe, and he longed to find comfort with Chloe before presenting a happy facade to his wife. Now, even that small comfort was denied him. A sensation of rage washed over him suddenly.

"You've been checking up on me as if I were a stupid schoolboy!" he ranted at Lianne.

"Don't flatter yourself!" Lianne grew angrier by the moment. "If Madam LeClerc hadn't shouted the news to the world in the dress shop, I'd never have known. And as your wife, I think you owed it to me to tell me."

He grabbed Lianne roughly by the arm, missing Chloe's alarmed look. "I owe you nothing, Lianne, nothing."

"I want a divorce, Phillipe. I wish to be free of you."

"Why? Do you think Daniel will want you then? That he'll make an honest woman of you? You'll never be free of me. Not as long as I want you."

"Philippe, please don't cause a scandal. Jean Marc is in the next room, and the neighbors . . ." Chloe began.

"I don't give a damn about them! Take the boy and get out of here. I have business with my wife. Unpleasant business."

Chloe regarded him in fear but didn't argue with him. She called Jean Marc; they left the cottage for a neighbor's house where she sent the husband with a note to the only person she knew who could control Phillipe.

"What do you intend to do to me?" Lianne asked.

Phillipe's eyes shone like crystal blue agates. His mouth twisted into a sneer. "Whatever I do, you'll be getting off easy. I won't abide a willful woman as my wife. One other woman defied me once, and what happened to her wasn't pretty."

Lianne thought Phillipe had lost his sanity, and she wasn't about to stay here with him. She made a futile attempt to push past him, but he dragged her to him and dug his fingers into her arm. "You're not going anywhere," he told her.

Fear shot through her. "Hit me and I'll scream. The law shall be on your head in an instant."

He laughed, but his amusement didn't reach his eyes. "No one will rescue you, Lianne. You forget you're in a quadroon's house, and by law, I own it, and Chloe, just as I own you. In these matters the law won't dare interfere. A man has right to reprimand his wife, and the neighbors are discreet enough to look the other way."

"Let me go." She struggled to break loose, but he refused to loosen his grip. With a violent blow to her face, he sent her hurling onto the sofa. She lay there a second until the dizzy sensation stopped, but before she could gather her wits, he yanked her up and pushed her against a wall. "I'm your husband, and your master, Lianne. I own you and expect your

obedience. After today you'll never think of spying on
me again!'' His face was contorted, and his voice
grated harshly upon her ears. She squirmed to break
free, tried vainly to kick at him. Her struggles
infuriated him more.

He kept hitting at her, hoping to elicit moans of
pain from between her lips, but she wouldn't give him
the satisfaction. ''Scream, Lianne! I want to know
you're submissive to me, that I can do anything I wish
to you and you'll accept it. Scream for me, Lianne!
Scream!''

Hate surged through her and a harsh shriek
spilled from her like the cry of a wounded dove.
''Animal! Animal!''

His face didn't resemble anything human.
''Honorine called me that. No one calls Phillipe
Marchand an animal!''

Stark fear glittered in Lianne's eyes, and for a
brief instant, just before his fist came down upon her
head with a mighty thud, she thought of Daniel.

''Daniel. Daniel.'' Lianne's moans barely penetrated her fogged brain. Pain shot constantly through
her body, and her head felt weighted down, almost as
if an anchor was tied to her neck. She had no
conception of time, no awareness of the solicitous
movements around her, no knowledge that Chloe
bathed her body, or that she forced a soothing broth
down her throat.

At one lucid moment she did open her eyes and
wonder where she was. A strange bed, a soft gown, but
the pain! Then she heard a noise like a squeaking chair
and saw a dark shadow bending over her.

''Daniel.'' Her whisper was barely audible. The
shadow loomed closer. In the candlelight she noticed a
face with an eye covered by a black patch. But the
other eye was dark and glittering.

''I'm not Daniel, *querida.*''

She barely mouthed the name—de Lovis! Was she
dreaming? He couldn't be standing over her. She had

killed him in Madrid. Or had that been a dream? She couldn't think any longer and didn't want to. She slipped into the painless realm of sleep.

When she finally woke to a cold morning, she found the fireplace had been lit. The dancing flames warmed her and glided across the logs in a graceful arabesque. Lianne sat up, her hair tumbled across her shoulders and matched the flames. She groaned, however, because her body was still incredibly sore. But her head hurt more. When she put her hand to her forehead, she found it had been bandaged.

The whole horrible situation with Phillipe came back to her, and for an instant she felt waves of fear lapping over her. Chloe walked into the bedroom with a bright smile and carried a tray which contained a cup of hot tea and a bowl of broth.

"Are you feeling better, Madame Marchand? You've been quite ill the last few days."

Chloe laid the tray on a small table and opened the curtains, allowing the bright sunshine to enter the room.

"Where is Phillipe?" Lianne asked, not hiding her fear.

Chloe shook her head. "Do not worry about him. Phillipe is at Belle Riviere. He shall not come near you. He has his orders."

"Orders? From whom?"

Chloe bit her tongue. "No one, madame. Just know he'll not bother you again."

Lianne watched as Chloe added honey to the tea, then presented it to her. "You must regain your strength."

Taking the cup, Lianne smiled her thanks. "You're the one who has been caring for me, aren't you?"

"*Oui*, madame. Philippe did a terrible thing to you."

"You're very kind to allow me to stay here, to take over your room. Where is your son?"

"Jean Marc stays with my mother while I tend to you. I don't wish him to see the damage his father has done. No matter what Phillipe is, he is still his father and Jean Marc must respect him."

"I will divorce him, Chloe."

"I know that, madame."

"Call me Lianne."

"That is kind of you . . . Lianne."

They sat in silent friendship while Lianne drank the tea and the broth. When she finished, she looked at Chloe.

"Was someone here with me while I was ill?"

"Here? Why would you think that?"

The memory of de Lovis's face, bending over the bed, haunted her. It had seemed so real. "I thought I saw a man I knew in Spain."

Chloe laughed, a bit too shortly. "Oh, Lianne, you must have dreamed him."

"I suppose I did," she said after a few moments. When Chloe began to pick up the tray, Lianne touched her arm. "Could you do me a favor? I'm sure you're familiar with Daniel Flanders, the man who is married to Phillipe's sister. I'd like you to get a message to him. I want to see him."

Chloe's mouth fell open. "I cannot!"

"Please, Chloe, I must see him. I love him." Tears sprang to Lianne's eyes and touched Chloe's heart. Chloe knew she shouldn't do this, that Lianne's request would cause untold misery for all of them. But no one at Belle Riviere need ever know if she was discreet.

Chloe nodded her dark head. "I shall have your Daniel brought to you, Lianne."

Chapter 21

Amelie restlessly paced the length of the veranda, watching the horses graze in the open fields. Despite the cold morning, she wore only a thin shawl. But she didn't feel the cold breeze. All she felt was keen disappointment that Claude no longer slept in the small bedroom next to hers. She hadn't seen him since the last night they made love, the night she had gone to Daniel. Had he abandoned her?

She was so deep in her thoughts she didn't notice the creak of the French doors until she heard Daniel's voice. "Amelie, you'll catch your death out here in that flimsy shawl. Come inside and have breakfast."

Ever the solicitous husband! she thought, but went inside and joined him at the dining room table. However, she barely glanced at the platter of bacon and eggs as a slight wave of nausea assailed her. She watched Daniel and realized how devastatingly handsome he looked despite the clothes he wore. He threw on any shirt or pants that were nearby, not caring if they matched. However, she couldn't doubt his good looks, and sometimes found his probing gray eyes exciting when they lit with passion.

If she didn't love Claude so much, she realized she could very easily love Daniel again. After all, she went to his bed every night, taking her own pleasure in his arms and hoping she gave him some. Without being aware of it, Daniel was doing her a tremendous favor. As soon as she told him about her pregnancy, however, their intimacy would stop. She must convince him the child she carried was his. Most of all she prayed for a light-skinned child. Things were working out well for her.

"You're not eating again?" Daniel's words broke into her reverie. "You've barely eaten at all the last few weeks."

"I'm just not too hungry in the morning," she said and pushed down another wave of nausea.

"Perhaps Doctor Markham should check you."

"Yes. I'll send word for him to visit Green Meadows shortly. I know your mother enjoys seeing him." And he can confirm my pregnancy, she decided.

"I have to check one of the slave cabins this morning. Old Benny complains it leaks when it rains. He should have told Haus about it before now."

Amelie brightened. "May I go with you?"

Daniel leaned back in his chair. A lock of dark hair fell across his forehead, and she felt the probing eyes upon her face. "Whatever for, Amelie?"

"I should learn more about the plantation since I'll be mistress of it one day."

He laughed. "Don't let Mother hear you say that. She isn't ready to retire yet."

"Please may I go with you?"

Amelie looked like such an eager child with her eyes so full of hope that he couldn't refuse her. For the past few weeks she'd acted the perfect wife, and he had a soft spot in his heart for her. Yet each night he stared at the ceiling after they made love, and she wasn't the woman he thought about. His loins ached, his heart cried for Lianne. She was so much like the sun, dazzling and warm. He didn't think Amelie would ever compare to her or make him feel the way he did when he kissed Lianne. He pushed his plate aside and stood up. Perhaps he should let the matter rest and content himself with Amelie. Lianne would never be his.

"Find yourself a warm cloak, and let's go," he told Amelie.

Within minutes Amelie and Daniel sipped tea in Old Benny's cabin, prepared and graciously served by Felice, his wife.

"You see, Master Daniel," Benny pointed to the roof when they finished, "the bad weather comes right through the ceiling. And soon the rainy season will begin. Me and Felice ain't young no more. The chill goes right through our old bones."

"I'll have the roof repaired this afternoon. You should have told Haus about this. Then he could have gotten the repairs done sooner."

"I did tell him, Master Daniel."

"I'll speak to him about this. Now you rest easy, Benny. By tonight you'll be safe and warm."

"Thank you, master."

Daniel went onto the porch, intent upon looking for Haus. As overseer it was his job to repair the cabins for the slaves. Daniel disliked the term "slaves," and so did his mother. He wanted to free all of them and hire them out, but he knew his neighbors wouldn't care for that.

"I'll be back as soon as I speak to Haus," Daniel told Amelie and started to help her into the carriage.

"That's all right. I don't mind standing here with Benny."

He left her there, and when he disappeared behind a row of cabins, she asked Benny, "Have you seen Claude?"

"He be in the barn, missy."

"Thank you," she said and casually sauntered in that direction. Entering the dimly lit barn, the smell of fresh hay assailed her, and she heard the distinct whinnying of the horses. She hadn't been here since the night she ran from Green Meadows and fell from that devil horse Bayrum. She shivered to recall it and to think how different things would have been if Claude had stopped her. She'd probably never have

known him, fallen in love with him. And no matter
how awful the paralysis and loss of her child had been,
she wouldn't have had things any other way. Claude
gave her a reason to live.

A woman's giggle drew her attention. Amelie
moved forward but stopped when she heard it again.
The rustling sound of hay came from inside Bayrum's
stall, and then another giggle. Her heart pounding in
her ears, she inched toward the sound.

Peering into the stall, her heart did stop at what
she saw. And when it started up again, she
extinguished a huge breath. Claude lay naked with the
house wench Ella. His mouth and hands moved in
wanton abandon over the girl's dark flesh, giving Ella
the same pleasures he'd once given her. She stared in
mute shock, not able to fully comprehend the scene
before her.

A strangled sob escaped her. Claude heard it and
glanced up. His dark eyes grew huge, and they stared
in agony at the sight of the pale, lovely Amelie with
hands clutched to her slender throat.

"Amelie!"

"No!" She picked up her skirts and ran from the
barn. Tears of pain, humiliation, streaked her cheeks
and when she bumped into Daniel, she couldn't speak.

"What's wrong?" he cried.

At that instant Claude lumbered out, fastening his
pants with a fearful Ella behind him who hurriedly
buttoned her dress.

"God damn!" Bruno Haus stopped beside
Daniel. "Your wife must have seen that uppity nigger
mating with the girl in the barn." He licked his lips in
excitement. Though he knew Amelie and Claude were
secret lovers, he reasoned that Daniel would have
Claude whipped for offending his wife's sensibilities.
And nothing excited Bruno Haus more than the sound
of the whip swishing through the air to land on tender
flesh.

Daniel took her arm and he escorted Amelie's

shaking form to the carriage. "Come to the house, Claude!"

Daniel lifted Amelie from the carriage and carried her inside.

"What happened?" Dera asked, growing alarmed at Amelie's paleness.

"She's had a shock. Send to New Orleans for Doctor Markham."

"I'm sorry you saw that," he said after Dera's departure from the room. "I can't believe Claude would be so crude."

Amelie looked at Daniel as if she didn't see him. All she saw in her mind's eye was Claude pleasuring Ella in the special ways he reserved for her.

She grew aware when Claude and Ella entered the parlor. Seeming ill at ease, he jostled from one foot to the other, but he watched Amelie through defiant eyes, tinged with pain. Ella, however, glanced at the floor and never lifted her gaze to anyone.

"What have you two to say for yourselves?" Daniel folded his arm across his chest, dismayed at Amelie's distress but secretly approving of Claude's taste in women. Ella was a beautiful negress.

"I can think of no answer, monsieur, other than the truth. Madame Amelie's eyes do not lie. I apologize. Ella isn't to blame, so if anyone is to be punished, punish me. I seduced her."

"Is this true, Ella?"

Ella raised her eyes to Daniel. "I wanted him to, master. Punish me, also."

A sapphire light danced in Daniel's eyes. "Claude, have I been such a cruel master that you think I'll punish you?"

"No, you have not."

"I won't inflict physical punishment upon you, but in years to come you may not thank me. I believe you should make an honest woman of Ella. You must marry her."

"No!"

It was Amelie's voice which objected. She jumped from the sofa, the color suddenly returning to her face. "He can't marry her!"

"Why not?" Daniel asked in suspicion.

She didn't know what to say, only that she'd die if Claude married Ella. Never mind that she was married to Daniel and sleeping with him. She carried Claude's child. He must want only her. Only her forever.

"Marriage isn't punishment for what they did, what I saw them doing. They must be whipped. I demand it!"

"Amelie, I don't whip slaves. Claude and Ella didn't do anything wrong but make love. There's no crime in that."

"You would say such a thing. A man who left countless panting whores across the continent." She pounded her small fists against his chest and wished he were Claude. "I want them punished!"

Daniel didn't mean to, but he'd had enough. He slapped her face and this caused her to stare in stunned shock. "You're overwrought, Amelie. I'll take you upstairs to your room until you can think sensibly."

When he took her arm, she twisted away. "I'll go myself!" Whirling from the room, Amelie ran up the steps and locked herself in her room.

Daniel apologized to Claude. "This is a terrible shock to her. When she calms down, she'll see how ill-advised punishment is." He grinned at Ella. "You may leave now." Soon after the girl departed, Daniel halted Claude in a booming voice. "Not you, Claude."

Claude cocked an eyebrow. "Yes, monsieur?"

"Stop the respectful crap. We've been friends a long time, or rather we were friends, but now I sense a difference in you. As my erstwhile friend, I want an honest answer from you, Claude. Have you and my wife slept together, been lovers during my absence?"

Claude's mouth dried. He eyed Daniel in cold contempt. He hated him for Amelie's suffering yet a part of him still cared about his childhood companion. He didn't know what Daniel would do to him if he confessed, but he no longer cared. Life was over for him now that Daniel had returned and taken Amelie to his bed. But he knew he must lie to protect her. For all of Daniel's kindness, he possessed a temper. Claude didn't want her harmed because of him.

Straightening to his full height, Claude shook his head. "Madame Amelie wasn't my lover. She is a lady, and you should respect her more."

For some reason Daniel sensed Claude lied about his relationship with Amelie. He couldn't prove anything against them, so he decided to take his old friend's word.

"If you say it's so, Claude, then I must believe you."

"Mister Daniel." John the butler came to the open doorway and interrupted them. He motioned to Daniel.

Daniel dismissed Claude and followed John into the foyer. "Sorry to break up your talk, sir, but there's a lady in a carriage outside who insists on speaking with you."

"Tell her to come in."

"She won't, sir. She insists you go outside."

Intrigued, Daniel noticed a small and shabby carriage parked by the steps when he opened the front door. Nearing the carriage, a dark veiled woman motioned for him to enter. After he climbed in and closed the carriage door, she pulled the veil up and offered him a tremulous smile.

"I apologize for the mystery, monsieur, but I don't want to be recognized, so I borrowed a friend's carriage. I am the mistress of Philippe Marchand."

"Ah, yes," Daniel said remembering something he'd heard about a quadroon mistress some years ago. He didn't know Phillipe still kept her. What a lucky devil Phillipe was! A beautiful quadroon mistress and a beautiful wife who happened to be the woman he loved. "What can I do for you?"

"Nothing for me, monsieur, but Madame Marchand is in great need of you."

"Lianne? What's happened to her?"

She placed a finger to her lips. "I shall tell you all on the way to New Orleans, but let's leave now, monsieur. I wish to keep my identity a secret."

Without bothering to inform anyone where he went, Daniel left Green Meadows to be with Lianne.

Chapter 22

Lianne sensed Daniel's presence before she opened her eyes. He knelt beside her bed, his large hands stroking her hair back from her forehead but careful not to touch the bandage. Tears of happiness welled within the emerald depths of her eyes.

He enfolded her in his arms and held her as if he'd never let her go. "What has that animal done to you?" he croaked.

"I'll be all right," she whispered, but she clutched at his shirt front. "I'm worried for my baby. If Phillipe harms her . . ." Her voice drifted off, as fear for her daughter washed over her.

"He won't lay a finger on her. I've sent word back to Green Meadows through one of Chloe's neighbors about the situation. My mother will make certain Désirée is unharmed."

"But he won't let Dera take her to Green Meadows."

"Yes, he will. You don't know how fearsome Mother can be when she's angry, and I know Phillipe will comply because of the scandal. He will pay for this." Daniel emphasized his words.

"No more about Phillipe, Dan. I only want to look at you." Her gaze traveled from the top of his dark head to the angled planes of his face. Her fingers stroked the hardness of his jawline. "Crazy artist."

Her voice held tenderness. "You look worse than I do."

Daniel grinned and shrugged. "I've never cared too much about my clothes."

"I love you, you know."

"I know."

"I want you to kiss me."

His eyes caressed her, moving lingeringly across her face. He gathered her to him in a velvet embrace and drank from the sweetness of her lips. But he moved his head away. "I've wanted to do that for so long, but now isn't the time, Lianne. You need to rest."

"I am rather tired," she whispered sleepily against his chest. "But when I'm well again you better be on guard, Daniel Flanders, because I'm going to show you exactly how much I love you."

"I look forward to that."

He pulled the covers around her as if she were a child, and sat with her until she was asleep. Since evening was coming on, he lit the candles in the parlor and one in Lianne's bedroom. Chloe arrived just past dusk, and smiled at Daniel who sat in a chair beside Lianne's bed. She carried a tray which contained bowls of hot gumbo, a highly seasoned broth made with shrimp and rice, and a jar of cold tea.

"My mother wishes you to have this," she whispered lowly. "When Lianne wakes, she must eat. My neighbor informed me that he gave your mother the message about Lianne and you're not to worry. Here is a note from her."

Daniel took the piece of paper and grasped Chloe's thin fingers in his hand. "Thank you for your care of Lianne. I'm most grateful."

"You love her very much, monsieur, and she loves you. I help her not because I want her out of Phillipe's life, but because your Lianne hasn't had a very happy life. I have, despite what you and she might think. I love Phillipe, though at times, he doesn't deserve it."

Chloe left as quietly as she had come, and Daniel read the note.

> Daniel,
> You're just like your father, running off and not telling a soul. Such wild sons I've raised, but I know Lianne needs you. I'll get Désirée from that beast of a man; and Phillipe will hand her over to me, never fear. Between Maria and myself, the weasel doesn't have a chance.
> With love,
> Your mother.

He nearly laughed aloud to imagine his thin mother and large Maria confronting Phillipe. But he knew the baby would be safe. His child. Whether Lianne admitted it or not, he knew Désirée was his.

When he was drifting off to sleep later, he woke at the sound of Lianne's screams. Rushing to her, he held her shaking body in his arms and soothed her with his voice and hands until she realized she wasn't dreaming.

She quieted after a few moments, clinging to him. It was the same nightmare she'd had since Phillipe's attack. Not only did she dream of his contorted face and the feel of his fist, but once he stopped, he handed her bruised and broken body to Raoul de Lovis who was just as brutal.

"You're safe, sweetheart. I'll take care of you." Daniel looked at her and held her at arm's length. "When I return to Green Meadows, I'm going to ask Amelie for a divorce."

"Daniel, do you mean that?"

"Yes. I want to marry you and claim my daughter."

Lianne extinguished a bitter sigh. "I suppose you hate me because I lied to you about her."

His lips sought the corners of her mouth. "I was hurt, but I love you, Lianne. We'll make a life together. The three of us at Green Meadows." Then his tongue traced the curves of her lips.

She tilted her head for an instant, and the emerald eyes darkened in passion. "I feel much better, Daniel."

"I hoped you would," he groaned into her hair. Daniel yanked off his shirt, then his pants before her passion-starved gaze. He stood before her, majestic as a mountain. The blood stirred and meandered through her veins like the ocean tide. When he came to her, she ran her hands across the hairy expanse of chest, the powerful, broad shoulders.

This was the man she'd dreamed of all those nights she laid in Phillipe's arms. All of the yearning, the dreams of him were about to become a reality. Her voice was soft when she spoke and promised them a joyous existence. "I'll marry you, Daniel. Just as soon as we're both free."

He didn't speak, but she felt his smile upon her, felt the hot passion in his eyes. Slowly he unbuttoned the tiny pearl buttons which ran the length of her nightgown. When he parted the gown to reveal her nakedness, he started. He had seen Phillipe's handiwork upon her face, but now to see the dark bruises which spotted her breasts, torso and legs filled him with such intense fury he wished to leave her and rush to Belle Riviere and kill the dog who had done this to her.

She saw the anguish and anger on his face. "The bruises shall heal."

Her calmness touched him, and the fury fled into the night. Gently he kissed each and every bruise, until her entire body was coated with his kisses. As his mouth trailed to the hollow of her neck, then moved still lower until his exploring tongue captured the rosy tip of a nipple, she moaned. Hot waves of sensation washed over her and made her body grow liquid.

The truth of his love, his hunger for her were

written on his face, and Lianne knew that after this night, they'd never be parted again. Waves of passion flowed through her. His hands rippled over the curves of her body, rousing her to ecstasy, while she explored his body with her lips and fingertips. He moaned at her mouth's possession of him but soon brought her face level with his and kissed her so deeply she thought she'd swoon. His eyes were so bright she saw them gleaming in the candlelight.

"I'll love only you the rest of my life, Lianne."

An intense pleasure ripped through her when he positioned her atop him and entered the warm core of her being.

The flame kindled in her, soared higher than the clouds, lifting her into a swirling vortex, a dimension of agonizing ecstasy of licking flames, of blue fire, which was only extinguished by the ebbing waves of total fulfillment.

They clung to each other as they reached the zenith, then spiraled and whirled in a velvet mist.

She gazed at him as he stroked the satin softness of her skin. Her eyes lightened from a dark, passion-laced green to a color which resembled sea foam.

"I feel like your bride."

He kissed the tip of her nose. "Soon you will be. Do you know that I loved you from the first moment I saw you performing at Paul and Allison's anniversary ball? I think it's fitting that we met at a place filled with so much love."

"I'd love any place if you were there."

For the rest of the night they made love. At dawn, both were weary and drifted into sleep. Lianne had no fear that this time she would dream about Phillipe or de Lovis.

After all, she convinced herself before she fell asleep, nothing could mar her perfect happiness now that she and Daniel had found each other at last.

Chapter 23

"There will be a scandal, you know. Are you both prepared to deal with it?"

"Yes," Daniel answered his mother's question for himself and Lianne. "I'm used to curious glances. Believe me, I've had my share."

"But Lianne hasn't." Dera didn't mean to throw damp water on her son's news about his wish to divorce Amelie and marry Lianne. In fact, she was for the marriage, but she wondered if they knew how much adversity lay ahead. If she knew Amelie as well as she thought she did, she guessed Daniel wouldn't have an easy time of it.

Daniel glanced in the direction of the stairway where Lianne descended from the nursery with Désirée in her arms. Seeing her, he forgot about his mother's concern and smiled at the beautiful picture Lianne made with his daughter. His daughter. Pride burst from him to know that he had a child, a child conceived in love and pain.

"Maria told me she was a good girl." Lianne rewarded him with a smile which was a warm caress and handed him the child who immediately squirmed and wiggled to be put down.

When he placed her on the floor, he couldn't contain his surprise and pleasure. "She's walking!"

"Of course she is," Dera said, playing the proud

grandmother to the hilt. "She's as rowdy as her father and uncle when they were small.

Lianne sat on a chair in the parlor. Her long hair swept across her face and hid the yellowing bruise on her forehead. Had it really been a week since that awful day? She shivered to remember it, but knew she had to face Phillipe shortly and inform him in person that she wished to end the marriage. Dera and Daniel had both tried to persuade her not to see him, fearing for her safety, but she knew he wouldn't harm her with a houseful of guests. Tonight was the Mardi Gras Ball and she thought the perfect time to settle matters. And Daniel could ask Amelie for the divorce since she was spending a few days at Belle Riviere with her brother. They could kill two birds with one stone, so to speak.

Daniel read her thoughts and knelt on one leg beside her chair. Taking her hand, he ran his fingers over the silken softness of her palm.

"Everything will be all right. We'll face Phillipe together." He gave her a smile which set her pulses racing.

"I love you, Daniel."

A tear fell onto her cheek, and he wiped it away with his thumb. "Don't cry, darling. Things will work out."

Lianne wanted to believe that but she got such a feeling of fear in the pit of her stomach sometimes. What if Phillipe protested the divorce or if Amelie put up a fight? But she decided to put on a brave face for Daniel and not allow him to see how unnerved she was now that she was about to confront Phillipe.

"I cry out of happiness, my love," she said and kissed him softly.

Dera cleared her throat. "The ball should be well underway by now. It's after nine, and this little one needs her sleep."

He nodded to his mother, then stood up and still holding Lianne's hand, he helped her from the chair.

They walked arm-in-arm to the front door and into the waiting carriage for the ride to Belle Riviere.

Daniel and Lianne were the only two people at Belle Riviere without masks. Many of the women were either dressed in elaborate costumes representing mythical goddesses, Aphrodite being the most popular, or wore expensive silk gowns, their faces hidden behind tiny black masks. Most of the gentlemen wore their evening clothes with masks, and it wasn't hard for Lianne to pick Phillipe out of the crowd. He was the one in the center of a group of his cronies from the gaming tables of New Orleans.

He saw her immediately.

"So you've returned!" he hissed when he stopped in front of her and behind the mask his face turned bright red. "And you've brought your lover, too," he said scornfully.

Daniel rose to his full height. "We don't wish a scene, Phillipe, but if you wish I can accommodate you. I really don't care. We want to speak to you about your divorce from Lianne."

But Phillipe did care. The way his friends watched him from across the drawing room disturbed him. It would never do for anyone to guess that he and Lianne had separated. And a divorce! Out of the question. The Marchands did not divorce. Why, his friends would wonder if he was able to satisfy his wife in bed, and that would be a blow to his manhood.

An oily smile congealed on his face. "Follow me into my study," he said quietly with contempt in his voice.

As they made their way through the group of merrymakers, Amelie caught a glimpse of Daniel with Lianne hanging onto his arm. Now she understood where he had gone off to and bitter rage boiled in her. Heavens knew she didn't love him any longer, but she'd be damned if she'd allow Lianne to take her place at Green Meadows as mistress. She meandered through the throng and tugged at his coat sleeve like a five-year-old. When he looked at her she said, "Haven't you a kind word for your wife, monsieur?"

Suddenly a group of people converged in the vestibule. Their drunken antics pushed Lianne away from Daniel, and when he went to grab for her, he was pushed away from the study door into which Phillipe had just led her. He made a move to follow her, but Amelie stopped him with a firm hand on his wrist.

"Phillipe is her husband. Leave them alone. I'm your wife," she enunciated the words. "And if you leave me standing here by myself I'll throw the biggest temper tantrum and embarrass you in front of our neighbors."

Daniel shrugged his shoulders and moved toward the study doors, but Amelie blocked his way. "I don't care what you do, Amelie. Move out of my way." He worried for Lianne's safety.

"Such concern for your mistress, but I warrant everyone here would like to know what a big whore she is. If you go in that room, Daniel, I'll tell all of them. I'll shout it until I'm hoarse. Lianne Marchand, wife of my poor cuckolded brother, is a whore!"

"Quiet!" He grabbed her arm and propelled her up the stairs to an empty bedroom. Fire sparked from the gray depths of his eyes, and for a moment he wished to slap her when she smiled slyly at him.

"So, Daniel Flanders, cynic and whoremonger, has fallen in love."

"Yes!" he said so sharply she winced. "I do love Lianne and I want my freedom from you, Amelie. I've never loved you in the way you deserve. We both know that. I'll make you a generous settlement where you'll never want for anything. You can marry again, find someone who'll love you and make you happy. Heaven knows, I can't."

She thought about Claude for an instant but dismissed him from her mind. "Marry me? Who would marry a woman who has been cast aside like day-old bread? What man would want another man's leavings? Except you, of course, Daniel," she remarked. "I'd be no better than second-hand goods. No divorce. No!"

The hardening of the blue eyes convinced him she still hung onto the past and hadn't forgiven him, but he decided to try one last tack with her, the one thing which might touch her heart.

"I knew Lianne in Ireland. Her daughter is my child. I want to raise Désirée."

Amelie blinked in utter astonishment. She'd had no idea. Mentally comparing the little girl's features to Daniel's dark hair and gray eyes, she realized the truth. He'd always wanted children, and now he had one. But she'd be damned if she'd lose her position as Daniel's wife and the chance to raise Claude's child as his because of his bastard daughter!

"Your wish for fatherhood touches my heart, Daniel. You shall have the chance to raise your child, and I shall give it to you, but not in the way you think."

He cocked a wary eyebrow. "What game are you playing, Amelie?"

She took his hand and placed it on the material of her gown, over her abdomen. "The game of life, Daniel. I'm carrying your baby."

He looked as if she had struck him. The blazing gray of his eyes dimmed. "You're lying."

"Ask Doctor Markham. He confirmed my pregnancy."

Moving away and toward the door, she blew him a kiss. "No divorce." Then she left the room, and the smell of her perfume filled his nostrils.

A shudder rocked Daniel's large frame. Anger, dismay, pain, all threatened to inundate him. He knew he couldn't divorce Amelie now. For all intents and purposes she was his wife and the mother of his

unborn child. But Lianne was the woman he loved and
the mother of his living one. What right did an unborn
baby have to take his happiness away? Yet he owed it
to Amelie to stay with her, to be a father to this child
because he was the reason she had lost their first baby
and nearly her life.

He must speak to Lianne, to try to make her see
his dilemma and to let her know that he'd find accommodations for her and Désirée. At the moment he
couldn't offer her the marriage they both wanted, the
security of his name. But he could offer Lianne his
love, and he hoped she'd take it.

"Damn!" he cried and rammed his fist through
the wall.

When Lianne entered the study with Phillipe, he
jerked her to a chair by his desk. He removed his mask
and looked at her long and hard. A cold breeze blew
from the open doorway which led onto the back
porch, but a warm sickening feeling overtook Lianne,
and her face flushed.

"Well, my wife wants to divorce me." Phillipe
shook his head in mock dismay. "No one divorces in
this family. I told you once, Lianne, that you belong to
me. I hope you come to accept that, but if you can't,
then that's your problem."

She tried to control the trembling in her limbs as
she held onto the chair, fearing to sit because it would
give him an advantage over her. "I don't love you. I
love Daniel and always have. We were lovers in
Ireland."

"So? Should I grant your request because of an
indiscretion?"

"Désirée is Daniel's child."

His face didn't betray any emotion. "I'll raise her
as my own."

"How generous of you, Phillipe, but I prefer a
divorce. You hurt me a great deal, and I won't have

my child a witness or victim of your brutality."

"I'd never harm a child!"

"Perhaps not, but I no longer trust you. I want to marry Daniel. I love him!"

Lianne reminded him of Honorine for a moment with defiance shining in her eyes. He couldn't have that, wouldn't allow another woman to betray him. An ugly sneer turned up the corners of his mouth and he would have slapped her except at that moment he noticed a tiny red flicker outside on the porch.

"Who's there?" he called out, incensed that someone would actually eavesdrop on him.

Lianne turned as a shadowy figure emerged from the darkness, holding a lit cheroot between his two fingers.

"Oh, it's you, uncle," Phillipe said in relief.

Time stood still for Lianne. She froze, barely breathing when the man Phillipe addressed as uncle walked into the bright ring of candlelight in the study. A full head of hair, the color of a raven's wing, matched his clothes. The nose, the lips, the shape of the face were the same, but it couldn't be him, Lianne thought wildly. This man wore a dark patch over his eye, yet when he spoke, his voice left no doubt that the man before her was Raoul de Lovis.

"How charming to finally meet my nephew's wife, *querida*."

"But I, I . . ." Lianne could barely speak and knew she sounded like an idiot.

"*Mon Dieu,* Uncle Raoul. Do you have this effect on all the ladies?" Phillipe grew agitated at having been interrupted.

"It seems I do on this one." Raoul bowed low and grabbed Lianne's icy hand. He planted a lingering kiss in her palm, but its warmth didn't thaw her body. He surveyed her in grim amusement. "Perhaps my injury causes your wife to lose her tongue." He touched the patch. "Maybe she pities me and wonders how this happened."

"You never did explain the loss of your eye." Phillipe settled himself in the chair behind his desk.

"Nor shall I tell you." Raoul took the cane he held by his side and nudged Phillipe out of the chair. Phillipe started to protest as his uncle took the seat but decided it would be unwise. For some reason Raoul looked quite forbidding, and he was never at ease in his presence.

"Now, Lianne," Raoul said in smooth tones, "you wish to divorce my nephew. Is that true?"

Lianne still couldn't reply she was in such shock to find Raoul de Lovis alive and to realize that he was Phillipe's uncle. She couldn't believe she hadn't killed him. She had tried so hard not to think about him, prayed she wouldn't dream about him. Here he sat across from her, and all she could do was stare dumbly.

"Is that true?" she heard his voice booming, and she jumped.

"Yes!" she cried.

Phillipe interrupted. "I told her the Marchands don't divorce. Even my mother's family, your family," he reminded his uncle, "never divorced. Why, it's unheard of . . ."

Raoul banged his cane on the desk top. "Quiet, you idiot."

"But Uncle Raoul . . ." Phillipe silenced then because the color of his uncle's good eye grew darker than pitch, and he swore he noticed a red flame burning in the depth of it.

Lianne's knees felt like lead, and at any moment she expected them to give out, but she held onto the back of the chair as if it were an anchor. Raoul watched her, appraised her. She felt as if he were undressing her with the roving glance he sent her from head to toe. She vowed she wouldn't stay married to Phillipe, even if this hateful Spaniard decreed it. She'd find Daniel, and they'd leave Belle Riviere and fight for their freedom together. A bit of courage surged through her. She raised herself erect and proud.

"I'll divorce Phillipe. No one can make me stay here as his wife."

"No one intends to, *querida*. Especially not me." His voice was very low, and she barely heard him.

"Lianne, I won't divorce you!" Phillipe gritted his teeth.

"*Sí*, you will, my nephew. As I recall you owe much money to creditors, and only last week you requested part of your inheritance which I gave to you. Now, I'll turn all your money over to you. You may pay off your debts, squander it any way you choose, but you will give your wife a divorce."

Phillipe stared in astonishment. The money was his, but to obtain it, he must lose Lianne. Well, let his uncle think he had won for now. He thought the whole situation was peculiar and guessed de Lovis had designs on Lianne for himself. He'd let him have her for now. But soon, when Raoul grew tired of her, he'd make certain no man ever touched her again. Just like Honorine.

"Meet me at the bank when it opens tomorrow," Phillipe told him and left the room.

"There," Raoul said. "Wasn't that easy? You will have your divorce."

Lianne didn't trust him. Why would he help her after what she had done to him? "I thought I had killed you."

"You nearly did, *querida*. But I'm a strong, healthy man. I'm not so easy to get rid of, as you shall one day realize."

"What's to be my punishment, de Lovis?"

He appeared confused. "Punishment? Why should I wish you punished? All I wanted was your happiness, my dove, and my pleasure. I could have made you happy, I think, in time. If you had not been so wild.''

He stood up and walked around the desk to where she stood. Reaching out a hand, he touched an auburn curl which brushed against her cheek. She drew back as if he had burned her.

"Really, Lianne. I won't hurt you. I'd not inflict bodily injury upon you like my jackass of a nephew."

She started. "You were in the room with me when I was ill at Chloe's."

"*Sí*. Chloe sent for me. Because of me, Phillipe was confined to Belle Riviere and left you alone, otherwise, he'd have killed you."

She felt baffled, upset to realize that she had been at Raoul's mercy until Daniel arrived.

"Why did you help me after what I did to you?"

Raoul moved away from her but watched her like a hawk before it swoops upon its prey. "Because my nephew is a coward and not man enough for you, though I'm certain he believes he is a lover without equal. And he would have ruined your beauty with his beatings and broken your spirit. A spirit I do admire. But I wish for your love, Lianne. One day you shall be mine alone."

"I'm going to marry Daniel Flanders."

Raoul looked amused. "We shall see," he said.

Lianne didn't see the point of saying more to him. Just knowing he watched her, sensing his passion for her, unnerved her. She ran from the room into the vestibule where the maskers still caroused.

They jostled her about, and she wanted to scream in frustration and terror at the polite conversation with Raoul de Lovis, a man she had blinded. A man who still desired her. But suddenly Daniel was beside her, holding her trembling body against his and kissing her greedily in front of everyone.

She clung to him. Her eyes met his, and she wept huge tears. "Take me to Green Meadows," she whispered. "Take me home."

"Just a moment," Daniel said and walked over to

Phillipe who stood sulkily among his friends. He tapped him on the shoulder. "I believe I owe you this."

With a mighty jab Daniel swung and landed a punch on Phillipe's jaw which caused him to fall amid the merrymakers. The bystanders screamed, but no one dared to attack Daniel whose face was a mask of black anger. They had heard about his Irish temper from Phillipe who now lay in a heap on the floor.

"I'm a man who always pays my debts," he said, smiling at Phillipe's friends. Then he grabbed Lianne's hand and they returned to Green Meadows.

Chapter 24

When Lianne awoke the next morning, she lay snug in Daniel's arms, listening to the beats of his heart. She lifted her head and smiled into his eyes. "Soon I shall waken every morning beside you, in this bed," she said and kissed his lips.

Daniel returned her kiss, but his eyes held anguish, something she had been aware of during their return trip to Green Meadows and even while they made love. But she had been in such an emotional state, she hadn't questioned him. Now she did.

Holding her tight against him, he didn't know how to respond to her, but he had to tell her the truth. "Lianne, when I spoke to Amelie last night she told me she was pregnant with my child. The news came as a complete shock. I didn't want to tell you after you had seen Phillipe. You were so worked up."

Her heart skipped a beat. She heard the torment in his voice. She clutched the bedsheets when he stopped speaking and wondered if he'd continue.

"We can't be married now, Lianne."

She shuddered at how hard he sounded. She wanted to be brave and tell him she understood, but she didn't. She loved him so much that the pain on his face transferred to her and became a physical ache inside her breast.

"You must stay with Amelie. That's what you're saying."

He clutched her naked shoulders with his strong hands. "Hell, if I could divorce her, I would, but God, she's my wife and deserves my consideration . . . at least until the baby's born. By that time perhaps I can make her see reason and obtain a divorce."

Lianne shook her head. "She'll never agree to a divorce, Daniel."

How well he knew that! For the first time in years, he wanted to do the right thing, to accept responsibility for his actions and not run off as he had done after Amelie's accident. He loved Lianne, loved their daughter. Yet he must make up for his past actions where his wife was concerned, now that she carried his child. But he hoped Amelie would grant the divorce once the baby was born.

"I can't give you up, Lianne. I won't." Despite his words, a look of wretchedness spread across his face. Lianne realized how much he loved her, and inwardly she admitted she needed him; even if he belonged to Amelie in name, she belonged to him in spirit.

She wrapped her arms around his neck. "I won't let you, darling. If I have to live on the fringes of your life, I will."

She didn't deserve such a life, but until he was free, if ever, she would wait for him.

That afternoon Amelie arrived home from Belle Riviere with her Uncle Raoul. Just as they entered the house, Daniel and Lianne were leaving. Raoul bowed low and kissed Lianne's hand, seeming to delight in her squeamishness. Immediately she took her hand back to be met by Amelie's sarcastic comment.

"Has my husband's mistress enjoyed her last night at Green Meadows?"

Daniel wished to rip the expensive blue bonnet from her head. Instead he only smiled. "You're truly charming, Amelie." He held Lianne around the waist.

"I just want you to know that I intend to do the right thing by you. I owe you for my past misdeeds, but I won't live life without Lianne." He felt her body trembling under his arm.

Amelie's face reddened in outrage. "I'll be laughed at in New Orleans, once everyone knows about this. How dare you keep this operatic singer as your mistress while I sit here, having your baby!"

"I shall treat you with respect, the highest regard, Amelie. Never doubt that. But I want you and your uncle," he nodded to Raoul, "to realize the situation. My heart belongs to Lianne and I intend to pursue a divorce from you and hope you decide to agree."

"Duels have been fought for less than this, Daniel," came Raoul's cool and mellifluous voice.

Daniel quirked an eyebrow. "If you wish to duel, I have no objection."

Raoul laughed, not so much at Daniel's bravery but at the shocked and worried look which crossed Lianne's beautiful face. He shook his head. "No, I don't think I'll risk it. The family honor has been besmirched enough and killing you wouldn't help it."

Daniel began to move Lianne past Amelie, but Amelie's voice rang out clear and strong in the vestibule, not seeing Dera coming down the stairs with the baby in her arms, followed by Maria. "I'm mistress of Green Meadows, Lianne, something you'll never be."

"How very strange," Dera said when she reached the bottom step. "I thought I was mistress here."

Amelie had the good sense to flush. She turned and ran the length of the vestibule and out of the French doors until she was on the veranda. How everyone infuriated her!

"Amelie."

She heard Claude's voice and watched as he withdrew from behind a stone column. Such gladness filled her that she shook with emotion. He hadn't spoken to her since their last night together, and she hadn't seen him since the day she had found him with Ella. But suddenly she didn't care about those incidents. She threw herself headlong into his arms, not thinking they might be observed.

"Claude, hold me."

Claude hadn't expected this display of affection, and he pulled her toward him and rained kisses across her pretty face. Then he captured the pink softness of her mouth and nearly drowned with desire for her. She pushed slightly away and sighed.

"I've missed you so much," she whispered.

He groaned. Life had been hell for him since that day she found him with Ella in the barn. Amelie's shocked face stayed in his mind and wouldn't leave. She was all he thought of, and he knew she was the only woman he'd ever love. But he knew he must make a life for himself, and this is what he had come to tell her.

"I've forgiven you, Claude. But everything will be all right now. Of course Daniel thinks he wants a divorce, but I won't give it to him. I'm having a baby, you know." She almost bit her tongue as that fact slipped out.

Claude's eyes darkened and the pupils seemed to blend with the white. "Is it my baby?" he asked her.

Amelie knew her pregnancy wouldn't have remained a secret for long anyway, but she hadn't wanted to tell him now out of fear that he might think the child was his. She worried Claude might tell Daniel about their love affair, and out of honor, Daniel would be forced to sell Claude. Then she'd have no one. She hoped she could win Claude back and have him return to her as a lover. Life would be so much simpler when she had Daniel, Claude and their child.

"This child belongs to my husband."

"You're lying."

"I'm not!"

Grabbing her arms, his fingers dug through the

material and hurt her. "I think the baby is mine. Tell me so, Amelie!"

"Whether it is or isn't makes no difference. What can you give me, give our child? You're a slave."

"We can run away to the Caribbean. My father is a wealthy man. He'll help us."

"Stop dreaming! I'd like to think you can accept this situation. I won't give up my position as Daniel's wife, and I can't crawl back to Belle Riviere because Phillipe would kill me before he'd take me and a slave's child into his home. But, Claude, we can be together here. No one need ever learn the truth. The chances of my having a white-skinned baby are very strong. I could still be Daniel's wife and you could still come to me at night. Wouldn't you like that, Claude?"

What's wrong with her? he wondered. She had no idea of how insane the plan was, and he wouldn't go along with it, as much as he ached to. He wouldn't share her with Daniel any longer, and he couldn't make her run away. She was right. He had nothing to offer her. Though he was a slave, he was still a man, a human being with principles. As much as he loved Amelie, he wouldn't allow her to manipulate him any longer.

"You've made your choice. I make mine." He looked into her hopeful eyes. "I will marry Ella. It's time I lived for myself." Her agonized scream of denial barely penetrated as he strode from the veranda back to the slave quarters.

Amelie attempted to run after him, but an unyielding grip clamped her upper arm. "Are you such a fool?" Raoul rasped beside her. "You would spoil everything for the love of a slave?"

She turned wide anguished eyes to him. "I do love him! I do!"

Raoul slapped her and immediately silenced her

except for her small cries of pain. He positioned her in front of him and held her at arm's length. He sneered his disgust.

"You will do as I say, Amelie. From this day forth, you'll stay away from the slave and pretend to be a docile, dutiful wife. You will have Daniel come to care for you. When the child is born, he'll accept it as his own." He worried a moment about the baby's skin color, but he would make certain Amelie presented a white child to Daniel. Even if he had to pay a woman for her newborn child, or steal one. It didn't matter to him as long as the baby was white.

Daniel would be a father to this child and he'd make certain that he didn't obtain a divorce from Amelie. As long as Daniel was married and thought himself to be the father of Amelie's child, he, Raoul, could pursue Lianne. Raoul intended to have Lianne eventually. And no one would thwart his plans. No one. Not even the simpering, half-hysterical woman he claimed as his niece.

"Do you understand me?" he said harshly and shook her until she replied that she did.

"Good." His eyes glittered with satisfaction. "Now let's go inside and secure your position as Daniel's wife."

Amelie walked trance-like into the house. Her body trembled with fear of Raoul and the loss of Claude. When she was finally in her room, she threw herself on the bed and cried. She was so alone, so unloved.

Lianne and Daniel arrived at the one-story house he owned in New Orleans on Saint Anne Street. After he helped Maria and the baby from the carriage and made certain they were settled in their new rooms, he found Lianne on the patio. A full moon shone upon her, and the night jasmine perfumed the air. She appeared so lovely and forlorn in the moonlight—he loved her so much, and this was all he could offer her at the moment. She was finally his mistress, but he felt no happiness in the fact. He wanted her as his wife.

His hands caressed her shoulders. "You'll catch a chill, my love."

She shivered in the cool night air. "I'll be all right, Daniel. I always am."

"I know that." Turning her into his arms, he studied her face. Never in his life had he seen a more beautiful one, but he noticed something in her eyes and he wasn't certain he liked it. "Tell me what's on your mind."

She offered him a small smile. "I've been thinking about us, and though I'll love you always and will be here for you, I can't wait here and be idle until you come for me. I'd be in Chloe's position."

Daniel immediately understood. "You wish to sing at the opera."

Lianne nodded. "I was quite good if I recall."

He tilted her chin and looked deeply into the catlike eyes. "You have other talents, too, my sweet."

A giggle escaped her because she realized he wouldn't object if she performed again.

"Just remember, once you're finished at the opera, you perform for me alone afterward," he said in a silky voice which sent delightful shivers down her spine.

Lifting her into his arms, he carried her inside where he loved her, cherished her as if she were his true wife.

The next day, after Daniel left for Green Meadows, Lianne thanked Monsieur Tabary, the director of the theater, for giving her another chance to perform.

"You won't leave us again so soon as you did the last time?" he asked good-naturedly.

"No, monsieur, I won't. I shall be with your troupe for sometime."

"*Bien.*" He kissed her hand and watched her

walk out of the theater. He shook his head in dismay and grimaced as he entered his office. "The mademoiselle was just here," he told the dark figure who sat behind the desk and blew smoke rings.

"As I knew she would be," de Lovis said and flicked an ash from the cheroot onto the floor, not missing Monsieur Tabary's scowl of disapproval. "The key to all things, my friend, is control. From this day forth I control the life of Lianne Marchand." His laugh rang out and echoed across the empty theater.

Chapter 25

Lianne gently squeezed the bright red tomatoes, smiled at the German farmer and offered her basket to him to be filled. The market on this warm winter's day bustled with activity. Farmers unloaded their produce from carts while customers casually browsed among the assorted fruits and vegetables.

She didn't usually go out so early in the day, especially since she had peformed the previous night; but on this morning she felt invigorated and filled with hope that Amelie would eventually free Daniel. This small hope showed in the sparkling eyes which matched the light emerald gown she wore and enhanced the beauty of her clear complexion. Her russet tresses glowed even brighter in the morning sun. Clearly she was in love.

She turned after securing her basket over her forearm and met the black-eyed gaze of Raoul de Lovis. A gasp of fear escaped her.

"Ah, *querida*, am I such a monster?"

She tried to still her trembling and not show the fear which tore through her. With a confident toss of her head, she looked levelly at him. "You're only human, Raoul."

Icy contempt flashed in his eye and he touched the patch which covered his injured one. "As you're well aware," he said bitterly.

She went weak for a moment as the blood drained from her. "I'm sorry for that."

"Such a feeble apology."

"What do you expect?" she snapped. "You wished to make me your mistress, take me to your bed when I was unwilling. You deserved worse!"

"Such a sassy tongue, *querida*." He smiled and passed a rapier glance over her. "But I've always admired your spirit, your passion." Reaching out, Raoul caressed a stray curl. "However, I've not forgiven you for running. No woman runs from me. I've allowed you to get away with more than any other woman, but soon you shall be like the proverbial bird in the cage. Daniel will never be free of my niece, Lianne, so you'll learn to content yourself with me. And enjoy it," he whispered into her ear.

She thrust the basket between them. Even in the busy market she felt alone and afraid. She wished she had never left the house. "Daniel and I will be married one day, and you won't be able to harm me."

He laughed. "I've no intention of harming you. When I finally love you in my bed, *querida*, you'll moan with ecstasy, never pain."

His breath fanned her face, and she cringed.

"No!" She moved away from him and would have run but he caught up with her and brazenly took her elbow.

"I'll escort you to your love nest. I hear the streets aren't safe for a woman alone."

"I hate you!"

"I know." He laughed lowly. "That's part of your charm for me. You fight and that excites me. I wouldn't want you so badly if you went docilely to my bed. What would be the challenge in that?"

After a silent walk where Raoul didn't relinquish his hold on her, they finally reached the house on Saint Anne. To her surprise he released her at the door and very formally bowed.

"Soon, Lianne. You'll be mine sooner than you imagine."

"You're crazy," she ground out from tight lips.

He shook his head. "Not crazy. Dangerous, *querida*." He started to turn away then stopped. "Does your Señora Alvarez ever hear from her nephew Pedro in Madrid?"

"No."

"A pity. He could use family support, I imagine. The poor fellow lost his tongue one night not long after you and she departed the country. A terrible tragedy. Good day, Lianne."

Walking away, he twirled his cane then stuck it under his arm. Not once did he look back to see her standing on the doorstep, still as a statue.

Daniel stopped coming to Amelie's bedroom at night, and she wouldn't have cared except she feared her uncle so much and remembered his warning at their last conversation. But she knew there was no way she could make Daniel care for her. And she didn't wish to. Her thoughts centered on Claude and the wedding which was to take place in the slave quarters that evening.

Lallie was her only source of information about the activities. She informed Amelie about the pretty dress Ella had sewn for the occasion, and what a handsome couple Claude and Ella made. She would have rebuked Lallie for the triumphant looks the woman gave her, but her heart was so heavy, she didn't say a word and lapped up any scrap of information like a starving puppy.

A few times Dera asked her what was wrong when Amelie played with her food at supper, but she just shrugged off Dera's concern with a comment about not being hungry.

"I'd advise you to eat," Daniel said from the far end of the mahogany dining table.

Amelie threw down her fork. "As if you care! I suppose you're going to visit your whore tonight and leave me alone again while I grow as huge as a pear."

"You're perfectly aware of the circumstances, Amelie."

Jumping up from her chair, blue fire flashed from Amelie's eyes. "I hate all of you, every last one of you Irish bastards, including the noble Allison! But more than that I hate your French tart. I can't even go into New Orleans and hold my head up any longer."

She ran from the room, and Daniel rose to go after her, but Dera called to him. "Leave her be, Daniel. Things are hard for Amelie. Give her time to sort things out. I have faith she'll make the right decision."

Daniel wearily returned to his chair. His face was lined, and any happiness he felt at the prospect of seeing Lianne vanished. "She knows I don't love her, Mother."

Dera raised an eyebrow. "Yes, but she carries your child."

"If it is my child. I have serious doubts about that."

"Daniel!" Dera was shocked.

"I think Amelie hasn't been the most virtuous of wives, but I don't blame her for finding love where she could. We all need someone to care about us. Heaven knows I take responsibility for how she has turned out."

Dera reached out and took her son's hand. Daniel had always been her favorite child because he was the one who turned to her in times of trouble when he was small. Paul had never been in doubt about how he would solve a problem, so he never felt guilty if things turned out badly. However, in the past few years, Daniel had drifted away from her and from his legacy at Green Meadows. Now he must face his future and find happiness.

"If you love Lianne, you must fight for her and

believe that God shall answer your prayers. First, you've got to stop feeling guilty for Amelie and live your life."

"Mother, I haven't prayed in years." He smiled sadly if a trifle indulgently at Dera who clung to faith. "I doubt if the Lord would hear me anyway."

She patted his hand. "He hears any sincere plea. He gave me back your father."

"And took him from you in Ireland." He noticed her wince and was sorry he hurt her. Even after six years, the pain of seeing her husband shot down by English soldiers like a rabid dog wouldn't fade. He kissed her cheek. "Perhaps I'm not meant to be happy like you were with father, and Paul is with Allison."

He got up and left the room, thinking that Amelie had already retired. He began to get ready for his journey to spend the night with Lianne.

The beat of drums from the slave quarters told Amelie that Claude's wedding celebration had started. She stood on the veranda, clenching and unclenching her fists. To think of her Claude married to Ella and sharing a bed with the woman upset her. She couldn't bear it. But she had to see him, had to have one glimpse of him.

Stealing a look around, she made certain no one watched as she silently moved toward the drumbeats. When the small cabins came into view, she quietly ran behind a group of trees to watch the slaves. A comely black wench was engaged in a tribal dance while the others snaked around. Amelie's eyes flew to Claude's broad shoulders and the sensual way his body moved along the line with Ella. She clutched at the small pouch of her abdomen and wished to die. She loved him with an agony that was beyond endurance. "Oh, Claude," she whispered tearfully and placed her hand on her mouth to keep from crying out.

A rustling sound caught her attention. She startled to find Bruno Haus beside her.

"Good evening, Frau Amelie. You're out for a stroll?"

She eyed him in cold contempt. "It's none of your business what I do, Monsieur Haus."

"*Nein,* but I do know what you do and who you do it with."

"What are you talking about?" she asked through pale lips.

He slowly withdrew a long knife from his belt and pointed at Claude. "I've seen you and that nigger wrestling in the bushes and heard the way you pant like a bitch in heat when he takes you." He licked his lips. "I'd like you to show me what he's taught you, Amelie." He pulled her to him and she saw he was actually salivating.

Revulsion and fear washed over her. "Let me go, you filthy animal. I'm Amelie Flanders, the wife of your employer."

"So? What are you going to do? Tell your husband about this. I'll tell him how you part your legs for that black bastard every time he wants you. I'll tell him that you were sleeping with Claude even when you said you weren't able to walk." He laughed, seeing that she paled even more. "I bet you thought I was stupid, but I knew all the time about you and that buck."

"Monsieur Haus," she began and tried to remain calm. "Please release me."

"Aren't you the proper one, but no, I won't let you go. I want you to take off your dress for me. Now."

From the lustful way he eyed her and held her, Amelie knew he wouldn't let her go without a fight, so she tried one more tactic and prayed it would work. The long knife was so close to her she could feel the cold steel against the material of her gown.

"I'm having a child, sir."

"Makes no difference to me. I want you anyway."

"If you harm me, my husband will kill you."

That did amuse Bruno, and he laughed loudly, not worried that he'd be heard over the beating of the drums. "Well, if you don't let me have my way with you, I'll just tell him about you and Claude. Maybe he'd like to wonder for the next few months if that brat you're carrying is really his."

Her hesitation gave him the opening he needed. Bringing his lips down hard upon hers he stuck his tongue into the soft cavity of her mouth. Amelie felt bile rising in her throat and knew she'd be ill. She tried to push away, but Bruno clamped her to him and pushed her protesting body to the ground.

He broke momentarily away and held the knife to her breast. "Now take off your dress."

The steel point glinted in the moonlight, but she could see no way out. Each time she moved the knife followed suit. Barely able to swallow she began to unbutton her gown. Bruno's eyes followed the trail of opened loops until the white of her chemise was visible.

"That's more like it," he stated. One hand massaged her breasts while the other held the knife to her throat.

Only a few feet away the slaves danced and the drumbeats penetrated the quiet night. She couldn't scream because no one would hear her. All she thought of was Claude, so near and unable to help her.

Bruno fiddled with the belt on his pants and hurriedly pushed up her gown. His touch brought her close to hysteria. She was beyond caring about her own physical safety and didn't care if Bruno Haus killed her.

A scream of fury escaped Amelie's throat. She heard Bruno demand she stop, but she couldn't. She was no longer in control of her body, her emotions.

"Stupid bitch!" he yelled when the cries of the men reached him. He knew it would be only seconds before the slaves found him, so he barely had time to pull up his pants. Amelie lay on the ground, screaming hysterically, and he realized he was as good as dead if she told the master what had happened. He had no other alternative.

With a sharp jab he stabbed her, then ran as fast as his brawny legs would carry him.

Within moments the slaves came upon Amelie lying in a pool of blood. One of them saw Bruno running away and cried out his name.

"It's Madam Amelie!" another man screamed. "Someone get the master!"

Claude rushed to her barely conscious form and picked her up in his arms. He carried her to his cabin, not aware that he cried her name the whole distance in agony. Ella, the woman he had just married, was forgotten.

Daniel couldn't believe the blood-soaked horror which awaited him in Claude's cabin. Dera accompanied him when the slave summoned them from the house and assisted the women who had removed Amelie's clothing, trying to stop the bleeding.

"She's gonna lose the little one," Lallie whispered to Dera. "But it won't matter none cause Madam Amelie's dying."

"She won't die!" Claude protested and wouldn't leave her side. He knelt by the bed and held her hand tightly.

Daniel touched him on the shoulder. "Who did this to her?" he asked, suddenly feeling as if Claude was Amelie's husband and he was the intruder.

"Bruno Haus," Claude ground out. "I will find him and kill him."

"Spare yourself the trouble. I'll do it for you." With that remark, Daniel strode from the cabin and went to the house. He found his pistol and soon was on his mount, searching the countryside for Haus. When he found him, he'd shoot him down like the dog he was. This was all he could do for Amelie under the circumstances, and perhaps, this was the only way he would assuage his guilt over her.

After riding for an hour across the length and breadth of Green Meadows, he feared Haus had fled to a neighboring plantation. But as he rode into a thick, vine-covered area, the moonlight illumined the crouched figure of Bruno Haus. Daniel saw him but didn't want the man to know it, so he halted his horse and climbed down and carefully searched the underbrush, pretending he didn't see him only ten feet away. Daniel purposely turned his back and expected Haus to attack him. As soon as he heard him scurry from the bushes, Daniel turned and fired, catching Bruno unaware. A look of total surprise crossed the man's florid face. He held his hand across his chest and slumped to the ground.

From bleary eyes, he looked at Daniel. "She was a no-good whore, your wife. Slept with a nigger."

Daniel shot him again. This time in the face. Bruno slumped forward.

"No, you stupid bastard," Daniel voiced and surveyed Bruno's body. "She was only a woman in love."

For a brief moment, Amelie regained consciousness. The first face she saw was Claude's. She managed a smile, because at this moment she felt no pain. Just a strange peace.

"I love you, Claude," she murmured and he bent low to hear her.

"Amelie . . ."

"Tell me."

He groaned. "I love you, love you."

She gasped, and he gathered her to him. "I'm not sorry for loving you," she whispered and felt the life ebbing from her.

"Amelie, please get well. We'll run away, be together always."

Tears streamed down his cheeks and onto her face, but Amelie had ceased to feel them.

"She's gone, son." Lallie came forward.

Claude gazed at her beautiful, peaceful face and the wide blue eyes which didn't see him any longer. Gently he closed them and stood up. This suddenly cold body wasn't his Amelie. Amelie was somewhere else, waiting for him. He must find her.

Laying her carefully upon his bed, he turned. He didn't see his mother, Dera, the other women who clustered around, or his wife. Ella reached out to him, but he brushed past her and went out into the dark, still night. It was a night meant for death, but Claude felt suddenly alive. Amelie waited for him.

Walking into the barn, he found a rope and strung it across a beam in Amie's stall. The horse nudged him, expecting an apple, but Claude absently patted her. Then he grabbed a stool.

"I'm coming to you, Amelie. I'm coming."

Later that night Daniel discovered the lifeless body of his childhood friend.

Chapter 26

Three days after Amelie's funeral, Daniel and Lianne sat in the parlor of the house in New Orleans and listened to Désirée as she sat upon the floor and made indistinguishable baby sounds. At one point, she did say "Mama," delighting Lianne.

"Soon she'll call you papa," she said to Daniel, hoping to elicit a smile from him.

He sat in contemplative silence, then realized she had spoken. "Oh, sorry, I wasn't paying much attention."

Lianne sighed her understanding. "You've been under a great deal of pressure. I know Amelie's death was hard on you. Have you seen Phillipe since the funeral?"

"No. I'm glad you didn't attend. He looked ready to kill me. He was broken up over Amelie, but he still wants you, Lianne." Daniel would remember the sadness of the funeral all his life because it was a double one. He buried Claude next to Amelie in the family plot. In this way, they'd always be together.

Phillipe didn't bother Lianne as much as Raoul de Lovis, but she didn't tell this to Daniel. She had never told him about her connection to Raoul and she didn't intend to. Raoul represented a dark part of her past, something she'd like to forget. But it was hard not to remember she was the reason he had lost an eye, that she had nearly killed him.

"I have no fear of Phillipe," she said at length and sat Désirée next to them on the couch. She touched a curl on the child's dark head. "Désirée looks like you."

Daniel bent down and kissed the curl plus the slender fingers which held it. "I love you both. As soon as I clear up Amelie's affairs, I'll bring you and our daughter to Green Meadows. We'll be married there."

"I know your mother would like that, but, Daniel, I was married there to Phillipe. I'd rather we were married here in this house which has known only our love. When we return to Green Meadows I'd like to already be your wife."

"That may take a little while, but I'll see about hurrying your divorce along."

They kissed. Love surrounded them in a golden haze. Daniel gazed at the woman he loved and wondered if he'd ever tire of looking at her, of desiring her. He doubted it.

Lianne knew she loved every angled plane of his face, the stormy eyes framed by dark lashes, and even the shock of raven hair which hung low over his forehead. In that moment she memorized every feature. Hints of doubt and fear surfaced. Would they be together? She prayed they would. She loved him with her whole heart. Her doubts vanished when he again claimed her lips.

"My nephew, you're not pleased with the news that Daniel has turned over Amelie's inheritance to you?"

Phillipe eyed the document which Daniel had signed shortly after the funeral in cold contempt. "He thinks he has won," he said to his uncle. "My poor sister rots in her grave, and her husband lusts after my wife. My wife," he reiterated.

"But you were eager to dispose of Lianne and bow to my wishes." Raoul studied Phillipe critically.

"I should never have let you control me. I won't let you control me now!" Amelie's money gave Phillipe a sense of power over his uncle. He didn't have to divorce Lianne now to receive a huge chunk of the money left by his parents. Daniel, for whatever reason, thought he was doing Phillipe a favor by signing over Amelie's share of the money to him. Even Raoul couldn't interfere since the money had been bequeathed to Daniel as Amelie's husband.

"Ah, so you intend to win back your wife," Raoul said.

"Oui, I shall."

"Won't you have to fight for her?"

"I suppose so." Phillipe shrugged. "I won't let Daniel Flanders have her."

Raoul made a pretense of examining his nicely trimmed fingernails. His stupid nephew was falling into his trap. "I believe you must do the honorable thing, Phillipe, or risk others branding you a coward, a man who wouldn't fight for what is his."

Raoul's about-face stunned Phillipe. Only weeks before he had forced him to agree to a divorce. However, Phillipe was filled with such a burning desire to have Lianne as his wife again that he didn't bother to analyze his uncle's words.

"I will win her back, uncle. I swear."

Raoul nodded, pleased. When Phillipe left the apartment on the Esplanade, a huge demonic laugh escaped the Spaniard. He shook his head and wondered how his sister had raised such stupid children. Amelie loved a slave and lost her life.

Amelie was to have been Raoul's pawn in securing Lianne, however, with her demise, nothing prevented Daniel from marrying Lianne. Except for Phillipe. A man easily swayed to think what Raoul wished. And right now he wanted Phillipe to engage Daniel in a duel and kill him. However, Raoul seriously doubted if

Phillipe could best Daniel, but then accidents did
happen away from the dueling fields. Either way both
of them would soon be out of the picture.

Taking a large puff from his cheroot, he watched
the smoke rings rise above his head.

"Soon, Lianne. Very soon."

Daniel waited in the audience that night while
Lianne performed. The beauty of her voice never
ceased to surprise him, and the open adulation the
audience poured forth for her. She was now the lead
soprano, and she had told Daniel that Monsieur
Tabary was very pleased with her. Still she hadn't
expected to sing the lead so quickly.

Lianne caught sight of his broad frame and dark
head while she sang. She felt as if they were in Ireland
at their first meeting and hoped this night would end in
his strong arms, and this time she'd stay in his embrace
and not run away.

She didn't see Phillipe who waited in the back of
the theater or know he carried a pistol beneath his
coat. She had no way of knowing that as he watched
her, he thought of Honorine, the opera singer he had
loved and who betrayed him.

In his mind he ceased to hear his uncle's words
about honor. As he watched Lianne perform, he remembered the night Honorine told him she didn't love
him. He clutched at the butt of the pistol, full of
suppressed rage. While Lianne sang, he didn't see her
on the stage. He saw Honorine, and felt the need to
punish the woman over again for not loving him.

When the performance ended, Phillipe hid behind
a piece of scenery and observed Lianne. He followed
her to the dressing room and knew the time was at
hand.

Sneaking behind her, he clamped his hand over
her mouth and dragged her protesting form from the
back door of the theater into an alleyway. Then he
threw her headlong into his carriage. He didn't worry

about being seen and had no idea that Raoul had observed him as he stood in the back of the theater and charted his every move. However, this wasn't what Raoul had in mind, so he followed his nephew's carriage to the town house.

"Have you gone mad, Phillipe?" Lianne asked, shaken and frightened that he'd beat her again.

"Quiet, Honorine! I don't want that singer you're sleeping with to follow us."

"I'm not Honorine. And just where are we going?"

"Home, *chérie*," he said almost affably.

Home, Lianne discovered was the town house, but she had expected this. A sinking feeling of dread overtook her, because she realized that Daniel had no idea where she had gone. Would he think to look for her here?

When the carriage stopped, Phillipe dragged her into the house. She had expected all to be in darkness, but she found the candles had been lit and the furniture uncovered. Even the windows had been opened to allow the cool night breezes to waft through the rooms.

"All is ready for you," Phillipe said.

Lianne made an aborted attempt to flee, but Phillipe halted her with a bruising hold on her wrist. "No, Honorine. You're mine now."

"I'm not Honorine!" Lianne protested again. She guessed Phillipe was insane, so she tried to use logic. "You can let me go. I won't tell anyone what you've done."

"And what is that? I took my woman, my kept woman," he reminded her.

"I'm your wife! I'm Lianne."

He blinked and stared at her for a second. His brain cleared. Yes, she was Lianne. Not Honorine at all. But she had betrayed him like Honorine and must be punished. Honor, a question of honor. He heard his uncle's voice in his mind.

"Phillipe, am I so much like Honorine that you'd harm me? Why did she kill herself?"

His skin resembled vanilla. "So, you've heard about her."

She swore his voice trembled and this gave her some courage. "Did Honorine kill herself because of Chloe?"

His laugh chilled her. "Honorine accepted Chloe. Honorine was a tramp who sang with the opera. Beautiful, like you, *chérie*. But she was unfaithful to me, also like you. I gave her this house, bought her clothes, jewels. Then one day she told me she didn't love me, that I repulsed her. She was in love with a tenor." He gave a derisive sneer. "The conniving little baggage had everything, but I couldn't live with her betrayal. There was only one thing to do. I poisoned her tea. The tart didn't know what happened to her."

Fear glittered in Lianne's eyes. How could she have ever thought she cared for Phillipe?

"She died in this room." He pointed to the spot by the window on the floor. "That's where she fell." Slowly he withdrew the pistol. "You don't want me either, Lianne, so I shall have to rid myself of you. I did want you back, but now . . . Well, I see it would never work. You look at me with loathing. The way Honorine did. You'll not suffer as long this way. Poison isn't a nice way to die, but I guarantee this shall be painless. Then when you're dead, I'll find Daniel and kill him, too. It a question of honor. You understand, *chérie*?"

Phillipe was mad! She had to get away. Slowly she walked toward him, gauging his expression. If she could reach the door, she'd dash into the darkness and he'd never find her.

Phillipe realized her plan. "Don't run for it, *chérie*. I'm faster than you and have no qualms about shooting you in the back."

"This is crazy. The authorities shall try you for murder."

"But I'll be vindicated, Lianne, when everyone learns of your affair with my sister's husband." He wasn't so crazy that he didn't have a sensible plan in mind.

Lianne knew that if she didn't try to fight him, she was destined to die. So, she took a deep breath as Phillipe advanced toward her and kicked hard at his groin. This brought him down and she managed to get a hold on the pistol, but he was very strong. He yanked up her arm. She managed to keep a grip on the butt. When Phillipe brought his arm down, she pushed violently at him and fell backward. Immediately she released the gun, but as he fell, so did the gun and it discharged into his temple.

The sound deafened her. She saw him, staring glassy-eyed at her and knew he was dead. Huge sobs racked her body. What was she to do? Send for the authorities? Get Daniel? She decided she needed him, and turned to flee from the house when the front door opened. Raoul de Lovis stood there, surveying the situation.

In truth he hadn't expected such a mess, but as he walked into the room, Lianne noticed he didn't seem the least disturbed.

He shook his head in mock dismay. "Such an idiot was Phillipe."

For the first time Lianne felt a sense of relief to see Raoul. He'd help her. "Please send for the authorities and for Daniel."

She stood in the center of the room and he noticed she trembled with fear. A situation which should have dashed all of Raoul's hopes to possess her might be turned to his advantage. Always the businessman, the entrepreneur, he knew a good deal when he saw one.

"Don't fear, Lianne. The proper persons shall be sent for." He walked toward Phillipe's body and picked up the pistol.

"I find such objects of pain not to be as noble as the rapier, but under the circumstances, I think this shall do. Lianne, you shall hate me for this, and I hope you're left unscarred, but sometimes the end justifies the means.''

She looked blank. He stood up and pointed the pistol at her.

"Raoul!" she screamed as the bullet pierced her. She sank into the darkness.

Chapter 27

Dead. Lianne was dead.

Daniel still couldn't believe it. Each morning upon waking he expected to see her, or when he heard Désirée playing in her room, he thought Lianne would be with her. But she wasn't.

Never had he known such emptiness. She had been buried in the Marchand plot in the St. Louis Cemetery in New Orleans a month ago. The authorities had called it a murder-suicide. Phillipe had shot Lianne, then himself. Daniel didn't know how it could have happened. He blamed himself for allowing Lianne out of his sight.

De Lovis had discovered the bodies at Phillipe's town house and called in the authorities. When Daniel learned of the tragedy, he had demanded to see her body, but Raoul had given strict instructions that no one was to see either Phillipe or Lianne. As head of the Marchand family, he had sole power over the proceedings. Right after the funeral, he left for Mexico where he owned a silver mine.

Now as night gave way to morning and the bedroom reeked of whiskey, Daniel worked furiously at the painting of Lianne and Désirée he had started once, but never finished. The urge to complete it was strong. He needed to see Lianne's face again and gaze at the clear emerald eyes.

When his mother entered the bedroom, she sighed. Ever since his return to Green Meadows with his daughter and Maria, Daniel had been driven to paint. He looked a sight in paint-smeared clothes. Daniel had eaten little since Lianne's death, but drank a great deal. This worried Dera. After all he had a child to live for.

She opened the drapes. "Shouldn't you stop now, Daniel, and come down for breakfast? I've asked Doctor Markham to join us today."

"No," he answered abruptly. "I've got to finish this."

"You've been working on it for weeks. Please rest."

"Leave me alone!"

Dera knew better than to press him, so she left him.

After working far into the afternoon, Daniel laid down his brush and took a long swig from the whiskey bottle. The painting was done.

He brought the canvas to the window and examined it. The colors blended together in a lushness which was Lianne. Her beautiful face framed by the russet hair gazed in peace at him, and Désirée's head met with hers in a loving gesture. But the eyes held desire and a promise of love and totally captured him in their green gaze.

This was the way he'd always remember her. Loving, at peace, and his.

As he hung the painting above the fireplace in his room, tears streamed down his cheeks. He had found her and lost her again, but in this place of honor, she was his. Forever.

Chapter 28

The early morning light glowed pure, like a translucent pearl, and slowly filtered into the room. Lianne slipped from her side of the bed, careful not to disturb the other occupant. She padded softly to the covered porch and stopped inside an archway which led to the garden. Even now the brilliant new blooms of the bougainvillea graced the new morning with their red flowers. She contemplated the prismatic sky which hung suspended over the Mexican countryside.

As she watched, the night sky faded and became almost white, then suffused to a dusty copper, shot with the fiery flash of an opal. Never in her life had she seen a sky turn so many colors before the sun finally turned it to a bright blue. To the east, her gaze strayed to the mountains, standing tall and strong against the morning sky. On the western side was tawny green countryside in fold after fold of deep ravines and valleys.

And then what? She didn't know. She'd never seen anything of Mexico other than this panoramic view and possessed very little knowledge of the workings of the hacienda. Around her, the help didn't speak, only nodded respectfully and obeyed her orders. However, once she had gone into the mine but turned away in horror at the pitiful conditions of the men. Many of them were Indians, their bodies so poorly covered in rags, they appeared to wear nothing. And children, no older than twelve, worked there, too, carrying heavy loads on their small shoulders. But she was warned not to question or interfere. And she hadn't.

If only she knew where she was, if only she could escape. She nearly laughed at the impossibility as she stood in the garden, among the lush flowering colors, the twisting vines which converged around the thick pink arches of the hacienda. Trapped. She was trapped in a cage of incredible beauty and she wasn't happy.

She sensed the man behind her before she felt his hands on her shoulders. He pushed her head back onto his chest.

"Enjoying the dawn, *querida*?"

"I have little else to enjoy, Raoul. Have you just awakened or have I been scrutinized by you from the bed like an insect?"

He laughed and turned her to him. In the morning light her hair matched the coppery sky shot through with gold. But the eyes were another matter entirely. So bewitching with their catlike slant and so filled with hatred that he couldn't help but be amused. Lianne hadn't changed since the day he shot her. A sense of remorse momentarily overtook him each time he thought about the terrified green eyes before he pulled the trigger. But she was his now, his to do with as he wished. One year ago he had bribed the coroner to declare her dead, which wasn't a hard feat to accomplish. And her perfect body had suffered no ill effects after the wound to her shoulder. In fact nothing marred her skin except for a tiny scar where the bullet had grazed her.

The hard part had been keeping her drugged until they arrived in Pachuca, their destination. If anyone inquired about her condition, he had told them Lianne was his wife and gravely ill. But it had worked. She didn't know where she was or how she had gotten there. However, he had other interests besides the

silver mine. Mexico City was his home and he was tired
of traversing the distance between it and the countryside, tired of wondering if Lianne would try and
escape him. He had to believe that she wouldn't flee,
even if he gave her her freedom, that she was
frightened enough to think he'd carry out his threat
against her. She still stiffened whenever he touched
her, but soon, very soon, she'd yield herself willingly
to him.

"I always watch you, my dove. Your beauty is a
treat for my senses. But I think it's time to show you
off to the world. Would you like to live in Mexico City
with me?"

Speech eluded Lianne. Was this Raoul de Lovis,
the same man who had shot her and kidnapped her
and kept her sequestered in his hacienda? Was this the
man who declared that if she ran away, he'd find her
and turn her over to the authorities in Louisiana as
Phillipe's murderer? Could he be trying to trick her?
She didn't know, could never tell with Raoul.

"You don't want to go?" he asked her.

Lianne quickly nodded before he had time to
change his mind. "Yes, I do. But I thought you had a
wife and daughter there. How will you introduce me to
society? Won't your wife mind?"

Raoul shrugged his broad shoulders, draped with
a red and gold robe. "Elena has been most accom-
modating about my mistresses. However, I think you
may bother her more than the others."

"Why is that?"

"Because I've never wanted a woman as much or
had a mistress longer than a few months. I tire easily
of women, *querida*. Of you, I shall never tire."

Raoul smiled as he said this, and Lianne knew
that many other women would be honored to be in her
place. She was the mistress, though a reluctant one, of
a very powerful man. But the jewels, the clothes and
furs he heaped upon her did nothing to alleviate her
sorrow or her love for Daniel. There were two things

Raoul could never take from her, her love for Daniel and her memories.

"I'll go to Mexico City with you, Raoul."

"Will you be a good girl?" He turned her face half to his and traced a finger across her jawbone. Other than wounding her in the shoulder, he had never been cruel to her or beaten her as she had expected when the drugs first wore off and she found herself here. Even when he took her to bed and she didn't respond in the way he had hoped, he hadn't harmed her. She knew she could never leave him. There was nowhere to go, and she didn't doubt that he'd arrange her arrest for Phillipe's death though she was innocent. Who would believe her word over the word of Raoul de Lovis?

"I will be good," she said like an obedient child.

"Bueno."

He scooped her up in his arms, the thin material of her gown riding high above her thighs and carried her from the garden and through the arches to the bedroom. He deposited her in the center of the bed and threw off his robe, then his hands tore her gown away.

Lianne's pale porcelain beauty awaited his touch, and he fell upon her. His lips, tongue, and hands moved across her body in a vain attempt to inflame her, to make her feel as he did. She lay like a board beneath him, and this outraged him.

"Puta!" he hissed from between his teeth. His face was red and the patch looked blacker, but she wouldn't respond to him. He could force her to submit to him, but he couldn't make her enjoy his caress, his kiss. She wouldn't. Not as long as she lived and love for Daniel still blossomed in her heart.

"I may be your whore, Raoul, but I'll never love you."

"Then I'll have your body, *querida,* and make do with that." He straddled her and took her with a fierce expression on his face. His strokes were short and violent, and when he shuddered atop her, she felt nothing but a gladness that he had finished.

He looked at her. "I believe that if you allowed yourself to put aside your bitterness, you would enjoy it when I touch you, when I enter you." His finger curled around a strand of hair. "I am a good lover."

"I shall never crave your touch," she spat.

"Ah, never say never, *querida*." He kissed her and laughed, then stood up. "I'll order your bags packed. By afternoon we'll be on our way to Mexico City."

The splendor and beauty of Mexico City awed Lianne. As they neared the plaza, the cathedral came into view and appeared massive in size. They drove past a broad arcade where merchants displayed their wares for the bustling humanity, then Raoul pointed out the Palace of Viceroys.

"We shall dine with Miguel José de Azanza at the palace, *querida*. This shall mark your entrance into society as my official mistress."

"You seem to find a great deal of pleasure in the idea of flaunting me before your friends and the viceroy."

Raoul rested his hands on the top of his cane. "You should have stayed in Pachuca if you prefer seclusion to freedom."

His remark quieted her instantly. Lianne didn't know how much freedom Raoul actually intended for her, but she was hungry for any diversion and she decided she'd not ruin her chances by irritating him. So, she sank against the Chinese flowered silk cushions and the gold upholstery and gave herself up to the delicious, heady sense of freedom.

Soon the silver coach turned onto the Calle del Aguila, one of the finest streets in Mexico City. Brick roofs, ornamented with flowering shrubs, covered the columns and arches of stone-trimmed *galerias* which graced the fronts of many of the houses. Raoul explained that the Calle de Aguila housed many gentlemen of note.

The coach stopped in front of a two-story house where the doorway was carved from grayish pink stone. The house was a warm pink in color and contrasted with the cool, deep shadows of the galeria. Raoul helped her from the coach.

"Where does your wife reside?" Lianne asked.

"Not far away. This house is one of many which I own, but please no more questions about Elena."

Lianne practically rushed into the foyer, eager to get away from the prying eyes she felt sure must watch her from shuttered windows.

The coolness of the interior compensated for the heat of the afternoon. The high white ceilings were graced with shell white chandeliers throughout the dining room and out into the sala, or living room, which overlooked the patio. The walls in the sala were also white and supported an arched ceiling, the color of salmon pink.

Outside, large earthenware jars were filled to overflowing with pink gladiolas and red geraniums. A brick walkway led to a small cupola at the end of the garden where philodendron leaves wandered through the lattice and gave an air of tranquility to the setting.

Lianne was speechless. She had thought the hacienda was lovely, but this was more beautiful than she could have imagined.

"I see by the light in your eyes that you approve of my little home for you."

She turned to Raoul, nearly forgetting his presence beside her. "I didn't expect anything so lush in the city."

His appreciative eye traveled across her body. "Mexico City is filled with beauty, but also with such extreme poverty I can't explain to you. Never venture outside alone. I tell you this for your own safety."

"Really, Raoul, that's a pitiful explanation. You wish only to make a prisoner of me here, also."

He frowned, his brows drew upward. "Believe me, I don't wish harm to come to you, Lianne. There are subversive groups, people who will like nothing better than to see the wealthy dead. Also, there are the *leperos,* the beggars of the street who spread vermin and disease. Of these you must beware. They think nothing of life and will slit your throat for a hair ribbon. Promise me you shall never leave the house unescorted."

"I promise," she said, not truly believing him.

Raoul nodded and summoned a servant to bring him a brandy. "Are you tired, *querida*?"

"Yes, I am."

"A pity." He sighed. "I hoped you'd wish to attend the opera tonight and the party afterward at the palace."

Lianne's eyes widened. "The opera? You'd take me to the opera?"

She looked and sounded so full of disbelief that Raoul laughed. "*Sí.* I wish only for your happiness."

"Then let me return to Green Meadows and my daughter."

"And Daniel? Never, but that is off the subject." He stood up. "I have a maid for you who waits upstairs to dress you like a queen. We haven't much time before the opera begins, so I beg you to hurry." He kissed her cheek. "You see, Lianne, that I'm not the monster you think." With that he left her, but no matter how kind he was to her, she didn't allow her heart to soften toward him.

To Lianne's surprise, she discovered Raoul had hired a middle-aged French woman as her maid. The woman's name was Josephine, and as she helped Lianne after a soothing bath, she chatted about the famous Josephine, wife of Napoleon Bonaparte, whom she claimed to have worked for in Martinque before the family moved to France.

"Mademoiselle Josephine was a beauty, even as a child," she said, and her eyes filled with pride. "I'm so pleased to work for a French lady again." She looked at Lianne and smiled. "My husband was Mexican. Most of the ladies I've worked for have been Spanish, but I miss speaking French."

Lianne detected a suspiciousness in the woman's attitude and didn't entirely trust her. "I'm rather surprised Don Raoul hired me for this position," Josephine continued. "But he insisted on a French maid for his lady during my interview with him. He cares for you very much, mademoiselle."

Lianne blinked at her in astonishment. Would Raoul never cease to amaze her?

Josephine helped her step into a shimmering gown of green and silver which was so transparent that Lianne gasped. "I can't wear this. I feel I should sleep in it, not wear it in public."

Josephine laughed. "The Directoire style is all the rage in Paris, I am told."

Lianne stood transfixed as Josephine tied the dark green sash beneath her full breasts. She couldn't believe decent women wore such clothes in public, but she admitted to herself that the color suited her hair and eyes and saw how the small puffed sleeves and low neckline showed off the porcelain beauty of her skin. With her auburn curls pulled atop her head and held in place by a silver band, Lianne resembled a Grecian goddess.

Desire flared in Raoul's eyes when she floated down the staircase, but he said nothing about how her beauty affected him. He had ordered the gown especially for her. He wanted the first time he presented Lianne to Mexican society to be memorable and thought how envious his friends would be. As he entered the opera house with the dazzling creature on his arm, all eyes turned upon them. The men were blatantly envious, the women definitely jealous and disapproving.

Lianne found herself clinging to his arm for support. She heard whispers of "de Lovis's mistress. Poor Elena," rising around her. After he escorted her to his private box and she took her seat, she glanced up at him through watery eyes. "Why do you choose to humiliate me like this?" she asked.

He smiled wickedly. "I want all of Mexico City to envy me my French treasure and to know you belong to me. As of this night, men shall want you but none shall dare approach you. My mark is upon you, Lianne."

How well she knew that. She wondered at the wisdom of leaving the hacienda. There, only a few people were aware of her shame. Here, everyone would regard her as the mistress of the Mexican silver king.

Raoul had just seated himself when a slight disturbance behind them caused Lianne to turn and see the pale round face of a woman with a young girl beside her. The woman stood inside the doorway of the opera box, apparently uncertain what to do. Her dark eyes wandered quickly over Lianne then stopped on Raoul. She snapped shut her fan, and the dark mantilla on her head fell slightly forward with the motion.

Raoul glanced up and saw her. He rose and placed a kiss on her plump cheek. "Elena, my dear, what a nice surprise. And you've brought Carmen with you." He kissed the frozen girl's cheek, also.

"And who might this person be?" Elena de Lovis's eyes raked over Lianne.

"May I present Lianne Marchand, the wife of my late nephew Phillipe. You remember Phillipe, don't you?" He took Lianne's hand and forced her to rise to greet Elena who was much shorter and certainly more dowdy in a simple black gown, devoid of decoration.

She looked more like the widow than the wife of Raoul de Lovis.

"How nice to meet you," Lianne mouthed, feeling as if she were about to faint.

"And this is my daughter, Carmen," Raoul continued, giving Elena no time to say anything. He dragged the young girl around, and Lianne saw she was a near duplicate of her mother except not as round. Carmen barely mouthed a response, and she looked as if she were about to cry.

"Such a happy group we are," Raoul said. "Will you and Carmen join Lianne and me for the opera?"

Elena's eyes narrowed but moved to the audience beneath them and was aware that everyone watched them. She smiled. "May the devil take you, Raoul de Lovis." She grabbed Carmen by the hand and turned toward the doorway. Instead of slamming shut, the door was softly closed behind her.

"Always the lady," Raoul commented and sat down.

"And I suppose I'm to be the whore." Lianne sank deeper into the seat, feeling less than a worm under everyone's perusal. She trembled so badly that Raoul reached out and clasped her arm.

"Calm yourself, *querida*. Smile brightly for your audience."

"No."

"Do it!"

She managed a fake smile which pleased him. "You must learn as Elena has that I am the master and you are the puppet."

"I hate you," she ground out and this time gave him a broad smile.

"I know." He dropped his hand and turned his attention to the stage as the lights dimmed and the opera began.

For a short while Lianne was so engrossed in the Spanish *zarzuela* called *El Laurel de Apolo,* that she forgot Raoul's presence beside her. The music, the costumes transported her to another world where she was happy, and more than once Daniel's face filled her mind, but she felt no sadness, just a bittersweet loss. When the curtain descended, her spirit plummeted to earth with a thud.

Raoul guided her out of the private box, through the throng of people, many of them acquaintances. The men bowed as he pushed past, lust clearly on many of their faces; the women ignored her or gazed at her with such coldness she shivered. Her reaction amused Raoul.

"Don't take it so personally," he informed her. "Think of yourself as a new toy which shall soon wear thin when the novelty has worn off. And it will, *querida*. Soon no one will care that you sleep with me. But I'll never tire of you."

She found no comfort in his reassurance and wished, how she wished, he'd tire of her and find another woman who appealed to him, a woman who'd be eager and grateful to share the bed of one of Mexico's richest men. It seemed that he wanted her and didn't care if she hated him.

They went on to the Palace of Viceroys where she feared the same treatment awaited her, however, once inside the ornate building, she recognized many of the same men she had seen at the opera and with them were younger, more beautiful women. Different women than the ones who sat next to them at the opera.

"Their mistresses," Raoul explained at her look of disbelief.

"Then I shall fit in here quite well," Lianne snapped.

Raoul appeared nonplused by her observation and introduced her to Miguel José de Azanza, the viceroy, and if Raoul hadn't been beside her she feared the man would have carried her off to a private room. Clearly he didn't believe in disguising his lust. Raoul only shrugged when she mentioned this later.

"I can't fault the man for his taste in women, *querida.*"

Lianne wanted to leave, but Raoul seemed quite content to smoke his cheroots with the other men and ogle each one's mistress or talk dull business. It was at this point that she wandered around the room and stopped on the fringes of a group of chattering women who were dressed in bright clothes with much décolletage, not unlike herself. She paid little attention until one of the women said in a high breathy voice, "Daniel Flanders was the best lover I ever had. And what an artist. The things he couldn't do with his hands!" She laughed and the others all joined in.

Lianne drew closer to the group to get a better glimpse of this woman who declared Daniel had been her lover. The woman was dark-haired and wore a red mantilla which fell onto her nearly bare bosom. The gown she wore was red also and emphasized her pale complexion and ripe beauty. Diamonds glittered at her ears and flashed their fire on her neck and fingers.

"You better be quiet, Isabelle, or Diego may overhear and become very jealous," one of the women cautioned her.

Isabelle snapped her fingers. "Who cares? I have all the money. My late husband Franco left me very wealthy. I don't need Diego except for one thing. And even that he can't do well." The women tittered and moved away.

Lianne stood fixed to the spot. Every part of her ached, and she wished to scream. The past swept over her like the lava from a volcano. The woman's comment had made her feel miserable just when she was beginning not to ache with longing for Daniel, their child, and the life that could have been. Damn Raoul de Lovis!

She felt Raoul beside her. He placed a hand on her elbow and when he glanced at her face, he saw the fire in her green eyes, the hatred which she couldn't disguise.

"Who is the woman in the red dress?" she asked.

He scanned the room until he found the woman in question. "Ah, Isabelle Hidalgo. I haven't seen her since Spain. I understand her old, ailing husband died and left her a wealthy widow. Why does she interest you? Do you wish to meet her? I think you both may have something in common."

"So, you know she slept with Daniel."

"Practically all of Madrid did, except for her stupid fool of a husband who was blinded to her many and varied charms. Daniel painted her portrait."

"He did more than paint her!" The jealousy stained her cheeks a bright red. Raoul's grip tightened on her arm.

"If only you could be this jealous over me, Lianne, instead of Daniel. Daniel never deserved you."

"I love him! You can't make me forget him."

"*Sí*, I will. Or one of us will die in the process." He whirled her around and dragged her from the palace into the carriage.

"Somehow, someway," she heard his voice as it filled the small confines, "I shall make you forget Daniel Flanders."

"You can't!"

His head moved in front of her, and she saw his glittering eye. "I will win in the end. One day you shall come to me with passion and desire, because I always get what I want."

She swallowed a sob which threatened to erupt from her throat and prayed Raoul wouldn't have his way.

Chapter 29

Lianne loved the mornings best after Raoul left the house to attend to business matters. Through breakfast she had to restrain her impatience to have him gone by listening to his monologues about the mines, the banks, how he wished he could divide himself in half to take care of his many enterprises. Lianne felt extreme gladness that Raoul didn't have the power to double himself. One of him was enough for the world to handle, she thought. However, she had learned to paste a fake smile upon her lips. Even to accept the farewell kiss which promised hours of his passion when he returned later in the day.

Empty minutes stretched interminably before her. How was she to fill them? Sometimes she thought she'd go insane with her memories for comfort, so she turned to Josephine who was more than willing to while away the time in frivolous conversation.

On one such morning, Lianne sat in the courtyard and watched the shimmering reflection of the sun in the fountain when a servant announced a visitor. The surprise she felt was obvious on her face as Dona Elena de Lovis joined her. After the social amenities, and while Elena sat sipping the chocolate a servant brought them, Lianne composed herself but wondered what Raoul would think if he returned early and found his wife and mistress together. Probably he'd laugh at the ludicrous picture they made: Lianne, with her mass of red-gold hair flowing around her shoulders, in a bright peasant top and skirt; Elena in a dark brown silk which looked as hot as it probably felt, and her tightly coiled hair hidden beneath the black mantilla.

Elena placed her cup on the wrought iron table before her. Her dark eyes lit up when she smiled at Lianne.

"I don't wish to make you nervous, Señora Marchand, but I think we must talk about Raoul."

"I can't think of what we could say to one another, Dona Elena. You see how things are between Raoul and myself."

"I see you live in great luxury as befits the mistress of Raoul de Lovis. I see that you've lasted longer than his other paramours, and this makes me think he is in love with you. No matter what he has done to me or how he has treated our daughter, I still care for him. Not in a passionate way, you understand. But I remember how I felt when we married. Believe it or not, I was once quite pretty, and not that long ago, Raoul loved me a little." She sighed. "A very little. The marriage was arranged, and my fortune appealed to him more than I did. Not that I blame him. What man wishes to be tied to a pious, plump girl? Not a man like Raoul. Always he thought himself physically perfect and must possess the most beautiful women."

Elena studied the blue of the sky for a moment. "I had nothing unusual to offer him, and perhaps that's why he married me. He could always be certain I'd be waiting at home for him. The whole marriage wasn't a loss. At least not for me. I have our daughter, though Raoul always wished for a son. When he realized I'd not give him any more children, he stopped visiting my bed."

Lianne realized Elena had ceased speaking. "Why are you telling me things of such a personal nature?" Lianne asked her.

"Because I think Raoul will demand you present him with an heir. Because I don't believe you care for Raoul and do not wish to have his children, my dear. I saw the way you shook the night at the opera when he touched you, and I knew it wasn't only from your discomfort at meeting me."

Lianne glanced away and this was all the answer Elena needed. "My visit to you is to beg that you not become pregnant with his child. Not only for my sake but for my daughter's. Carmen must inherit that which is hers by right, and if you give him a son, then Raoul will present the bulk of his assets to his heir and rob my Carmen of her birthright. But I fear for you, señora, if you bear his child. He'll never let you go. You'll belong to him then, body and soul."

"So far I've been lucky not to conceive."

"You will. I have no doubt of that. Raoul is a potent lover. I had one daughter but many miscarriages. You're not as frail as I. Believe me, señora, you shall conceive Raoul's child and condemn yourself to a life of living hell."

"Nothing can be more hellish than the existence I'm living already." Lianne's voice broke, and Elena patted her hand.

"You love someone else."

"Yes, I do," Lianne admitted. To her surprise she found herself telling Elena the whole story, beginning with the night she met Daniel, the time she put out Raoul's eye and ending with Raoul's blackmail of her concerning Phillipe's death.

"Daniel and I would be married now if Raoul hadn't ruined things. I love Daniel so much. I'll always love him!"

Elena handed her one of her best silk handkerchiefs and watched whle Lianne dried her eyes. Her mind raced with plans. Of course everything would take a bit of time to accomplish, but Elena felt sure she could help Lianne and herself in the process. Never would she allow a bastard of Raoul's to disinherit her daughter, and she knew that Raoul would somehow legitimize Lianne's child because she realized how in love he was with her.

Madre de Dios, she prayed silently, don't let this poor creature become pregnant with a child until I carry out my plans. When Lianne handed her back the handkerchief, Elena smiled.

"All shall soon be right for you, Lianne."

Lianne shook her head in denial. "No. Nothing shall ever be right for me again. I miss my own daughter, I miss Daniel. There's no way I can ever be free of Raoul."

Elena left, a mysterious grin on her face which Lianne failed to see. Barely five minutes after her departure, Raoul arrived and demanded her presence in his bed. No, she decided, while Raoul found his pleasure, nothing would ever be right for her again.

"I have a surprise for you," Raoul told her some days later. "Get up and dress."

Lianne practically groaned as she pulled herself to a sitting position among the pillows. She was never certain how to regard Raoul's surprises, but she knew better than to question him. He might believe he was delighting her, but she always knew ulterior motives lurked beneath his gifts. However, after she dressed and joined him in the carriage, his eagerness heightened her own. He grabbed her gloved hand.

"Believe me, *querida,* you shall enjoy this."

The carriage wound its way past Alameda Park where fountains gushed sparkling water and the foliage was a riot of spring colors, then past the square and the dark, massive cathedral flanked by the poorest of the poor, the *leperos,* holding out hands for alms. This sight always depressed Lianne, and she felt guilty for the luxury in which she resided while many people were literally starving. Raoul never glanced in the direction of the hungry faces, or the surly ones. He regarded them as less than human.

Soon the carriage stopped in front of the opera

house, and he didn't speak a word despite her questioning look. Inside he headed straight to the office of Señor Dominguez who was acting as the director and introduced Lianne to him.

Señor Dominguez looked her up and down, his hand on his chin in speculation.

"Quite beautiful, Don Raoul," he said after a few moments, "but can she sing?"

"Like a nightingale."

"I know other men are intimidated by your reputation, and would bow to your terms in an instant. However, the young lady must convince me."

There was a challenge in the man's voice, his stance, and Lianne saw Raoul flinch and stiffen, but he bowed graciously and nodded to Lianne. "Sing for Señor Dominguez."

She would have refused, but suddenly she realized that Raoul was willing to allow her the opportunity to perform, and she must win her position. And she wanted to sing, to perform again. She had missed the stage.

Seconds later she found herself singing the aria she had sung the night she met Daniel. Tears came to her eyes, and when she finished, she noted that Señor Dominguez was deeply moved.

"Bella, bella, he whispered and wiped his eyes. Then he was all business-like. "Report to me tomorrow morning. I think we have a great diva here, eh Don Raoul?"

Raoul agreed and ushered Lianne from the office. When they were in the carriage again, he looked at her, his dark eye glittering. "Have you no thanks for me, Lianne? I just gave you your dream. You may perform with the opera."

"I won my place, Raoul. You had nothing to do with it."

Raoul laughed. "Señor Dominguez is a professional man, *querida,* and plays many games. Among them is the one where he likes to feel in control of the situation. I know this, and I play along. It gives me pleasure to do so, because I always know the outcome. Before I walked into the man's office I knew he'd engage you. After all, if he doesn't do as I wish, no one would attend the performances. I'd make sure of that."

"I can't believe you have that much power, Raoul, to sway mens' opinions."

"Then you still don't know the full extent of my power. But I tell you this, once you walk onto the stage, Mexico City shall kiss your beautiful feet. Your voice shall take the populace by storm, not only because you can carry a pretty tune, but because you're my mistress. Because you sleep with me, your dream of becoming a famous diva shall come true. I know you hate sharing my bed, but think what you've gained by belonging to me."

"How insulting!" Lianne shook her head in denial. "Señor Dominguez offered me the position because of my voice, not for the filthy reason you say."

Raoul contemplated her in amusement for a number of seconds. Then he said, "I think your naiveté is the reason I want you, *querida*. Yet never doubt what I've told you. In a few months, you will capture the heart of Mexico City because you're my woman. Never forget that."

Lianne felt unbridled rage and pain rise within her and she denied his prophecy, but from the moment she sang on the stage, the truth of it couldn't be denied. She had captured the hearts and minds of the people. And not only because she belonged to Raoul de Lovis.

The great amount of freedom Raoul suddenly gave to Lianne surprised her. From the moment he left in the morning to the time he returned in the late afternoon, she was on her own. Rehearsals sometimes ran longer than anticipated, and if she returned home after he did, he didn't question her. He seemed to trust she wouldn't run away, and in that regard, he was right. She had nowhere to go.

One afternoon on impulse as she passed the cathedral she motioned the driver to stop and got out of the carriage. She entered the dark church, much upset by the peasantry outside who grabbed at her as she swished past. But she needed to pray and ask God to bless her child, a child she'd never see again, because this was the date she'd conceived Désirée. Walking outside, dusk had fallen and the carriage was nowhere to be seen.

She found herself the focus of attention of the peasants. Arms and hands, faces, pleaded with her for money, for food. Some of these people she couldn't look at, they were so skeletal and deformed. Fear filtered through her, and she wondered if Raoul were right about people who'd slit her throat for a hair ribbon. She had to get away! They were suffocating her.

Lianne dug into her reticule and threw the few pesos she had at them. They dispersed like ants and she managed to push past them. Where's the driver? she wondered over and over. She fled to the side of the church but made it no further when an arm reached out and yanked her against the stone wall.

The cold tip of a blade grazed her throat. Lianne peered into a face with dark, evil eyes and framed by limp, black hair. The man smelled so vile she thought she'd be sick, and his body was pressed tight against hers.

"Where do you run to, señorita?" he asked through rotten teeth.

"Home. I must go home."

"Have you anything for me?"

"I have no more money." She thought she was going to faint.

"I don't want your money." His hand slid into her bodice and squeezed a breast. "Now come with me, señorita, or I shall have to hurt you."

She knew she should fight, but she was so paralyzed by fear she could barely walk. The man dragged her a short distance, and she wondered if he'd kill her when he finished with her, but suddenly he no longer held her. Someone had pushed her away from her kidnapper. She looked at her rescuer and saw he was barely a boy, about sixteen, and very thin. He wore dark pants which molded to his body like a second skin and his shirt was torn and dirty, but he circled the man like a panther, ready to spring.

"Ah, Felix, you don't wish me to kill you on such a fine day," the man said to the boy.

"I'll kill you, Pepe. You shouldn't have touched the señorita."

"She's the whore of Raoul de Lovis. You should welcome the chance to anger the man. Come, you can have her too, right after I finish with her."

"I know what you'll do to her, Pepe. She'll be dead by then." The boy withdrew a long dagger from the side of his pants. "Show me what a man you are."

In the gathering dusk Lianne watched while the boy called Felix circled the man, Pepe, and with a long leg tripped him. Then with a sudden motion while Pepe lay helpless on the ground, he slit the man's throat.

Bile rushed to Lianne's throat and she would have given into the urge to be sick, except Felix grabbed her arm and rushed her from the scene. She didn't know if she could trust him; perhaps he meant to harm her, but she didn't have time to think. She stumbled blindly after Felix until they were on the other side of the square and down a side street.

"You killed that man," she whispered.

Felix shrugged his shoulders. "He would have killed me, then had his way with you. If I hadn't come along, señorita, you'd be lying dead somewhere this very minute. Anyway, no one will mourn Pepe or care that he's dead. That's just the way it is when you're a *lepero.*"

Lianne's carriage came into view and after tongue-lashing the driver, who apologized that he had rushed away out of fear for his safety, she turned to Felix. "Please return home with me. Don Raoul will be most generous to you for helping me, saving my life."

For a moment she noticed his eyes harden and thought he'd refuse her offer, but he nodded and climbed into the carriage beside her.

"He does owe me something," he said aloud and was careful to sit across from her as not to dirty her with his person.

Raoul was in fact very grateful to Felix for rescuing Lianne. He insisted the boy be washed and given some decent clothes which one of the servants provided, and fed in the kitchen. When he learned about the carriage incident, he immediately dismissed the driver and gave Felix the job. But he also had sharp words for Lianne.

"You shouldn't have gone to church there. Too many beggars. I've warned you about them."

"I know." She hung her head. "I wanted to pray, Raoul. This was the day my daughter was conceived."

A vein throbbed in Raoul's temple. "You mean this is the day you laid with Daniel Flanders like a bitch in heat."

She put her hands over her ears. "Stop it!"

He pulled her hands away. "Will you never cease thinking about him? I want you to forget him."

Tears spilled from her eyes and down her cheeks. How could she forget Daniel? She loved him more now if that was possible, and Raoul knew this. Yanking her to him, his anger seemed to die.

He looked levelly at her. "Since today is such an important day to you, then let it remain so. You conceived your daughter on this date. Now, tonight, *querida,* you will conceive my son. I shall make it so."

Sweeping her into his arms, he carried her to the bedroom, and when he finished with her, Lianne had no doubt that if she didn't conceive, it wasn't from lack of trying.

Chapter 30

What was wrong with Elena? Raoul pondered this question as he and Lianne arrived at the house he once called home. It had been almost five years since he had entered the luxurious structure which housed his wife and daughter. He hadn't missed the two-story dwelling which rivaled its neighbors with its light pink facade where lacelike parapets and balconies surrounded the entire home. However, he smiled, he had done well by Elena over the years. No one, not even she, could fault him.

Still he felt uneasy, and Raoul was never a man to be uncertain of anything. But the invitation from Elena, arriving in her perfect penmanship the week before, gave him cause to think that she was up to something. Something he wouldn't like. Why else would she invite her husband and his mistress, plus the elite of Mexico City, he later learned, to her home? Women just didn't invite their husbands's mistresses to their homes.

Lianne, however, wasn't the least upset by the summons to the house of Dona Elena de Lovis. She didn't fear Elena. In some ways she even liked the prim, plain woman. She'd never mentioned Elena's visit to Raoul, but wondered what Elena would think if she knew that Raoul hoped she would conceive a child soon. A child Lianne prayed would never be conceived.

Not only wasn't she concerned about Elena, but she no longer feared the disapproving glances from the Mexican citizenry. Since performing at the opera, she found she was a person of note. Wherever she went, people clamored for a glance of "La Flamenca" as the populace had dubbed her because her hair reminded them of the bright beauty of a flamingo. Even now as she entered Elena's home on the arm of Raoul, she lived up to her name.

A thin gown of shiny pink silk barely covered her voluptuous curves and wantonly molded to her body with her every movement. Tiny diamonds glittered at her ears, and just that evening Raoul had presented her with an exquisite diamond pendant which now dangled between her breasts. Her red-gold hair had been piled high upon her head by Josephine with wispy tendrils curling in disarray about her face and neck while tiny rosebuds were woven through the one thick curl falling across her shoulder. Lianne had never looked lovelier as she carelessly allowed her pink lace shawl to fall away from the small puffy sleeves of her gown, to reveal long, graceful arms.

Inside the house Lianne found that the furnishings, however beautiful, were austere and more practical than comfortable. The *sala* overlooked a garden and the many people there spilled outside. However, when a servant beckoned them inside from the night illumined by torches attached to the house, all came willingly.

Elena had been bustling among her guests, making certain everyone had enough wine, but no one could get a word from her as to why they had been invited. Not even Raoul. Lianne saw the hard set of his jaw and knew he was much put out with her. Yet Elena seemed not to notice, or if she did, didn't care.

"What is the foolish woman up to?" he whispered to Lianne. She nearly laughed at him and was rather pleased that someone could cause him uneasiness, but she felt much discomfort to notice Isabelle Hidalgo nearby. The woman was indeed beautiful with her dark hair sleeked into a chignon and rubies encircling her neck to match the deep wine red of her gown. Jealousy consumed Lianne as she imagined the woman with Daniel. She had to control herself or risk Raoul's temper if he realized how much Isabelle Hidalgo's presence unnerved her.

"My friends," Elena began as everyone formed a circle around her, and she pushed a reluctant Carmen to the forefront. "This is a happy time for me. Our daughter Carmen," she included Raoul with her look, "reaches the age of fifteen in but a few weeks. Soon she shall enter young womanhood and leave her childish ways behind her. Very soon, if God is good to her, she will marry and make a happy marriage."

Everyone politely clapped and lifted their glasses to the girl who looked as if she wished to disappear.

Elena smiled but continued, "To mark this passing into young womanhood, I've commissioned one of the world's renowned artists to capture my daughter's likeness. Many of you know him already." This time her gaze rested on Lianne, then Raoul on whom she bestowed a cheshire-cat grin. *Señores y Señoras,* welcome into your hearts Señor Daniel Flanders."

From behind a curtain inside the *sala* he seemed to appear from the mists of time. The applause and excited comments of Elena's guests were lost on Lianne. She saw nothing, no one but him. His large manly frame seemed to swallow up everyone, everything. The powerful set of his shoulders expressed his self-confident air, and he stood barely ten feet from her, devilishly handsome in a brown coat and ruffled white shirt, opened at the neck with matching trousers and boots. He watched and drowned her in a sea of churning gray water.

The intense pleasure of seeing him faded as she

realized no welcoming smile touched his lips, or his eyes; nothing but a stormy ocean blue.

What was wrong? Was he not pleased to see her, to know she was alive? Then she thought perhaps the shock of seeing her was too much for him. She must go to him, tell him how much she loved him, yearned for him. But as she made an imperceptible move forward, Raoul's hand crushed her arm.

"Move in Daniel's direction and I will shoot him dead before your eyes."

In surprise her gaze flew to Raoul. She had forgotten his ominous presence looming near her. God, she had forgotten everything in her desire for Daniel! What a fool she was! How was she going to explain to Daniel that the woman he loved and thought dead was very much alive and living as the mistress of Raoul de Lovis?

Her face paled. She knew if she moved a fraction of an inch in Daniel's direction that Raoul would carry out his threat. Even if it meant murdering a man in front of a hundred witnesses.

"Let me go. I won't do anything," she whispered and prayed he'd believe her. Daniel's life was more important at that moment than her love for him.

He seemed satisfied. Removing his hand, he smiled blandly. "Elena shall pay for this. Somehow she learned the truth."

Fear shot through Lianne for Elena. Her loose tongue might cause the woman great pain and all because she had confided in her about her love for Daniel. But she didn't think about Elena for long because Daniel strode toward them, his hands carelessly thrust into the depths of his pockets.

Lianne had nearly forgotten how his dark hair shone with blue-black highlights in the torchlight or how his firm, sensual lips quirked into a half smile when amused or angered. And clearly Daniel was angry now though pretending not to show it. The hurricane-like eyes descended upon her, ignoring Raoul.

He stopped in front of her and took her trembling hand and brought it to his mouth. The contact of his warm but unyielding lips against her flesh sparked something long dormant within her. Lianne felt slightly faint. Was it from desire or from the un-nerving hatred in his eyes for her?

"How lovely you look, Lianne. Quite unlike the corpse I thought was laid to rest."

"Daniel . . ." Her tone was low, and she went mute when Raoul placed a hand on her wrist.

"Lianne owes you no explanations. She had nothing to do with the deception, but alas, she didn't know how to get out of the situation and didn't wish to hurt you. She wanted only to be with me," Raoul said levelly and looked Daniel in the eye.

"Am I supposed to believe that?"

Daniel's gaze slid to Lianne and a part of him expected denial. Lianne felt Raoul's arm tighten around her.

"You must believe what Raoul has said." Lianne's voice was low but steady.

Daniel dropped her hand. "I hope Lianne makes you happy, Raoul. Take it from someone who knows; she's a hot piece in bed."

"Daniel!" She gasped at his crudeness, but Raoul only smiled.

At that moment Isabelle Hidalgo slithered up to Daniel and kissed him soundly on the mouth. "Daniel, *mi amor*. How glad I am to see you again! Come with me now, *querida*. Many people wish to meet you, and you mustn't let Raoul and his woman," she said with derision, "keep you from me much longer."

Without a parting word, Daniel moved into the crowd of people with Isabelle. Lianne felt ill, truly and unspeakably sick. She had to get away from everyone or disgrace herself. She flew from the house and into the night. The carriage waited on the street outside and Raoul was right behind her. Before they reached home, she ordered Felix to stop. Barely making it from the coach to the ditch, she threw up until nothing was left inside her.

She felt faint surprise to realize that Raoul had been steadying her all the time she was ill. When she glanced up at him, she expected to see distaste on his face, or anger at her for her reaction to Daniel. Instead he was smiling, a huge white smile which wreathed his face in a way she'd never seen before.

"Well, Lianne, it seems you do belong to me now."

"What do you mean?" she said, too weak to do anything but lean against him.

"For a woman who has given birth, you seem not to be aware of the signs. But I've noticed the past weeks how your breasts are fuller, the slight roundness of your belly." A long finger snaked across her abdomen. "Now this sickness confirms the fact you carry my child. My son."

"No." She stared in mute horror. It couldn't be so. She couldn't be pregnant with Raoul's child, but of course, he was right. She knew the signs and hadn't wanted to admit to them.

Almost in a state of shock, she allowed Raoul to help her into the carriage. Felix drove them the rest of the way home, but the trip, the remainder of the night while Raoul extinguished his lust on her, were a blur. She thought of Daniel and the hatred shining in his eyes.

And she thought of the child she carried. A child which wasn't Daniel's.

No one guessed Lianne's dismay when Raoul's personal physician Doctor Morales examined her upon Raoul's request and confirmed the fact that she carried Raoul's child. She wished to cry as the doctor beamed and Raoul smiled knowingly, but she managed a weak smile. When Doctor Morales left the bedroom, Raoul stayed.

He sat next to her on the brightly colored counterpane. "I'm pleased you shall present me with a son, Lianne. Though Elena easily conceived, she could never carry for long, and gave me only a daughter."

Lianne sniffed. "Suppose I give you a daughter? After all, I've had two children, both girls. I see nothing wrong with daughters."

"You shall give me the son I've always wanted." He touched a long auburn curl. "If not, we shall make more children together. You were meant to bear children."

She tossed her head. "Will all of them be bastards, Raoul?"

For the first time she noticed he looked shocked, an emotion which was hard to decipher on his face, because he always hid his emotions so very well. He considered her for a moment, then he stood up. She watched as he paced the flagstone floor, resembling a dark eagle in his black attire. Suddenly he halted in mid-step. His head had been bowed, but he lifted it in a leonine gesture.

"My son shall not be a bastard. I will see to it that he isn't." With that remark he departed the room. When she heard the slamming of the front door, she knew he had left and didn't care. The morning sickness had taken its toll upon her, and she felt tired and totally drained. More than that, however, Lianne felt an acute depresion every time she thought of Daniel's face the previous night. She wished to go to him, but knew it would be useless. How could she explain the truth to him when it was so preposterous?

Half an hour later, Josephine entered her room. "Felix would like to speak with you, madame, but I told him I didn't think you were up to it."

Lianne roused herself. "Send him in. I feel a bit

better."

Josephine frowned at Lianne's pallor but motioned for Felix who waited in the hallway.

"Hello, Felix," Lianne said and smiled when he entered the room.

Felix gazed around the elegantly furnished bedroom and the small, pale figure in the bed. He bowed.

"I'm sorry to disturb you," he told her, "but I wish you to dress and come with me on an important matter." He handed her a note to confirm the urgency of his visit.

As soon as Lianne looked at the note, she identified Daniel's handwriting. All it said was, "Go with Felix." There was no signature, but she knew Daniel had written it. Two high spots of color stained her cheeks.

Lianne rose from the bed, oblivious of the thin gown she wore, and of Felix's attempts to keep his wayward eyes downcast.

"The man who gave you this note, was he tall and dark-haired?"

"*Sí*, but he wasn't a Mexican."

"I'll dress and meet you outside."

When Lianne had dressed in a watery green silk which highlighted her eyes, she met Felix outside and found he waited next to a plain enclosed carriage. When she entered it, her eyes widened in surprise to find Daniel inside.

Within seconds she was in his arms and he rained kisses over every inch of her face and neck.

"I'm sorry I was so cruel to you last night," he said, holding her against him as if he were afraid she'd run away from him. "But Elena wrote to me and told me what you had confided in her." His gray eyes glittered and gazed with love into hers. "I didn't believe any of it at first. To think that you were really alive and living as Raoul's mistress." For a second his eyes darkened and frightened her, but then the cloud passed and he smiled down at her. "I love you,

Lianne. I always will. I want you to leave with me and return to Green Meadows.''

"Oh, Daniel," she gasped and grew breathless. This was what she yearned for. She couldn't believe he was really beside her. "I love you too, my darling."

He bent his dark head and branded her lips with a kiss which shook her very soul. She was blissfully unaware that the carriage had finally stopped. When he helped her out, she realized they were in front of the Academy of San Carlos, the renowned school of painting.

"What are we doing here?" she inquired as he led her through a courtyard, surrounded by balustrades made of Biscay iron and ornamented with bronze and between Ionic columns where shafts of warm sunlight slanted and touched their faces.

His eyes blazed into hers, and he flashed a smile, but still he didn't answer. He propelled her along with a firm grip on her elbow. They passed large, well-lit rooms where she noticed young people, Indians sitting among the sons of the wealthy men of Mexico, drawing from live models. Lianne quickly noticed that many of the sketches were superb, but she had no time to observe further. Daniel kept up his pace, and just as they ascended some stairs, Daniel stopped short.

Lianne barely stopped in time to see a man approaching, a very handsome man in his middle thirties who wore a gold suit, embroidered in brown at the cuffs. A red cape was thrown across his shoulders. For all his bright clothing, she couldn't help but notice the dreamy faraway look in his eyes.

"Ah, *amigo*," he said to Daniel. "This is the young lady you spoke to me about this morning."

"This is my friend Manuel Tolsa, the director of the academy," Daniel introduced him to Lianne.

Manuel took Lianne's hand and kissed it warmly. "She is indeed beautiful, Daniel. I hope she'll be safe here with you."

"*Gracias, amigo*. Without your help . . ."

Manuel held up his hand. "Don't thank me, but I advise you to be careful." He smiled and left them on the staircase while he descended the stairs.

"What is all this about?" Lianne asked.

Daniel grinned devilishly. "I'm kidnapping you."

"What?"

"Come along." He led her up more stairs until they were on the top floor. Pigeons cooed right above them, and Lianne heard the rustling of their wings as Daniel stopped beside a door. He opened it and Lianne gasped to see a garret room with large windows which slanted at an angle and gave her an unimpeded view of the blue sky above them. In the corner of the room was a bed and on the other wall was a table with two chairs and a chest with a mirror attached.

"No one will find you here, sweetheart. You won't have to worry about de Lovis. He'd never think of looking for you here." He turned her in his arms and planted a kiss on her surprised face.

"You really have kidnapped me!"

"Yes. You're not going to be silly and flee me, are you now, Lianne?"

He grinned as he said this, and she knew she didn't want to flee him or be without him. She loved him with her whole heart, her whole soul.

"You're crazy, do you know that?"

"Hmm," he said and nibbled on her ear. "I'm crazy about you."

"I've missed you so much!" she said, and if he hadn't known of her love for him before this, he heard it in the intensity of her tone. "Raoul arranged everything, and I couldn't fight him, and I didn't . . ."

He halted her with a gentle kiss. "Let's not talk about him. When the time is right, I'll take you to Green Meadows, but for now I need to know you're safe until I make arrangements. Felix will let me know every move Raoul makes."

"Daniel, I'm frightened. Raoul will kill you if he discovers what you've done."

"I can take care of myself. I didn't always just paint, Lianne. You forget I have wild Irish blood in me and I've fought my share of duels over women I didn't care anything about. But I love you. As of this day, you're free of Raoul de Lovis."

She clung to him and wished to believe that, but she found it hard to think as Daniel did when she carried Raoul's child.

His fingers traced her lips to be replaced by the fire of his mouth. Lianne moaned against him, melting into the realm of ecstasy only Daniel could evoke. She wanted him with a fierce sweet desire, but she drew away in time to remember that she carried another man's child.

"What's wrong?"

His question caused her to jump though she had expected it. She shook her head. "Nothing. I'm overwhelmed."

Daniel laughed and scooped her into the circle of his arms again. Her gaze drifted up to his face, and she greedily drank in the startling gray eyes filled with desire for her, the sensuous mouth which was turned slightly upward and revealed the flash of white teeth against the bronze of his skin. She felt his arms tighten around her, drawing her closer to him than she was already, and she knew that if she didn't put a stop to this soon she'd fall into bed with him. She mentally chastised herself for her weakness. She must be strong and pull away, must play the game Raoul had started. Daniel's safety was more important to her than stolen moments in his arms.

Something in her face caused Daniel's smile to wane. He realized something bothered her, and he hated to ask her, because he feared that de Lovis had taken her from him.

"You can tell me what's on your mind, Lianne. I

won't bite you.''

She shivered in his arms but gently pulled away from him. "Our love can never be, Daniel. I'm pregnant with Raoul's child.''

He stared at her in disbelief. He hadn't expected this and didn't want her to know how the news pained him. But he still loved her and was determined to bring her home with him. ''The child changes nothing. We'll raise the baby with Désirée.''

"A baby changes everything, Daniel! In time when you looked at it, you'd see Raoul. The child will be a constant reminder of him. And how do you think we'll raise his child at Green Meadows? He'd kill both of us to have it back.'' She shook her head. ''Too much is at stake. I can't risk your life, mine or anyone else's. You have no idea how maniacal Raoul can be when provoked.'' She didn't know what to expect from him when the slate gray eyes darkened.

Grabbing her arms, he held her to the spot. ''If you loved me, none of this would matter. You'd come with me. Why don't we go to Raoul now and explain to him that you're leaving him? I know you love me, Lianne. I see it in your eyes.''

"No!" Her shout was higher pitched than she intended. Somehow she must make Daniel see reason and understand that she belonged to Raoul, no matter how unwillingly. She carried the man's baby and had no doubt that if Daniel did as he threatened, he wouldn't live to see the sunset. Though Raoul wouldn't do the deed himself, he'd have someone else end Daniel's life.

There was an alternative and she must appear convincing.

"I love you, Daniel, believe me when I say that, but I won't return home with you and it isn't only out of fear. I belong with Raoul de Lovis. You forget he's a wealthy and powerful man, much richer than you could ever hope to be. He buys me the most expensive clothes, jewels, and has made me into one of Mexico's leading sopranos. I was born into wealth, married into it, and I admit I've missed the luxuries money can buy. Your paintings, your plantation can't give me what Raoul has. How am I to become your wife and stagnate at Green Meadows when Raoul has laid Mexico City at my feet? I must think of the child I carry. You can't offer it what he can."

His face looked blacker than a night sky. She saw he attempted to control himself though a muscle twitched in his jaw. Suddenly he seemed taller and loomed over her like a huge falcon, but the explosion she expected didn't come. "Have you forgotten our child?" he asked in a gravelly voice.

She hadn't forgotten Désirée or the many nights she had cried herself to sleep from loneliness for her daughter. However, to save Daniel she must forfeit the little girl, and she made a quick, silent prayer to heaven that Daniel would believe her lie.

"I don't want to raise Désirée with Raoul's child. She is better off with you and your mother than with me. She'd be a bother because she'd remind me of loving you. And I want to forget I ever loved you, Daniel. There's a very good chance that Raoul will secure a divorce from Elena. I want to be the wife of the richest man in Mexico."

He growled and pushed her away as if she were a plague victim. Was this the same woman who minutes ago had melted into his arms, claiming she loved him? What had happened to change her, or was it all an act? He didn't know, but he knew she didn't wish to stay with him. Raoul had changed Lianne. He saw the flicker of fear in her eyes that he wouldn't allow her to leave, a fear he decided she didn't wish him to see. So, for the moment he intended to play the game and give her peace of mind.

"Felix will drive you home," he said harshly. "Get out of my sight."

She waited a long moment, tears building in her eyes. Then she turned and fled out the door, and she was two floors down before he stopped hearing the click of her heels on the stone floor.

Daniel stood transfixed, staring at the empty doorway. He knew she loved him and that she acted the part of greedy whore to keep him safe. But determination rose within him to free her from Raoul's hold, from the bondage enforced upon her.

"Damn you, Raoul de Lovis!" His voice bellowed and echoed in the attic room.

Chapter 31

"No divorce! No divorce!" Elena mouthed, anger exploding within her. How dare Raoul come to her home and tell her such a thing! By God's law she was his true wife, the mother of his daughter. Never in her wildest imaginings had she been prepared for this. She didn't think Raoul would go so far as to want a divorce to marry his unwilling mistress.

He appeared unconcerned by her outburst, not the least disturbed by the fire in her eyes. Sitting on the straight-backed chair next to the dining table, he casually peeled an orange, popping the juicy sections into his mouth one at a time like a man who expects his wishes to be granted and is waiting for the tirade to cease. The glittering dark eye didn't even watch her. This nonchalant attitude infuriated Elena more.

"You seem to forget that my father was Carlos Mendoza, the richest man in Mexico. I am not one of your women to be bought off. My fortune made you what you are today."

"Indeed I'm grateful to you and your father. Now, I am the richest man in Mexico and you understand what that means. Power, Elena. Vast power. I can make or break anyone I wish. I shall bestow a handsome settlement upon you. Never fear. You'll still be incredibly wealthy; Carmen will be taken care of until she marries."

"Ha! What decent family would accept her? Not the Valenciana family. And you know how I have my heart set on a match between Carmen and Fernando." Elena clasped her hands to her ample bosom. "How am I to be respectable if you divorce me? I will fight you, Raoul."

Raoul stood up. *Bueno.* Then do so, but you'll not win. The Mendozas may have been powerful at one time, but no longer. I have the power now, Elena. Never forget that. Men bow to my wishes."

"The church shall not allow this."

A laugh crinkled his eyes. "Do you think I really care what holy mother church thinks? I want to be free of you."

Elena clutched the edge of the table. "She's pregnant, isn't she? Your mistress is going to have your child."

"Sí."

"But you've had other bastards. Why legitimize this one? Carmen is your true child, conceived in wedlock."

He briefly wondered how Elena could be so dense. Didn't she realize there was no reason to divorce her before Lianne entered his life? Didn't she realize that she had served her purpose when she inherited her father's fortune? He didn't need her any longer and certainly he didn't want Carmen, a girl with no spirit, to inherit his wealth. He needed a son, and he'd have one and see to it that the boy was born within the confines of matrimony.

"Carmen shall be well provided for."

"What a cold, cruel man you are Raoul. Yet I don't fear you the way Lianne does. I shall fight you. I will!"

His eyes narrowed in speculation, and he advanced toward her. "What do you know of Lianne's fears?"

Elena's face visibly paled. Raoul did frighten her,

but a surge of courage flowed through her. "She told me how you faked her death, how you've forced her into submission."

"So, it was you who sent for Daniel, eh."

She nodded. "*Sí.* He needed to know the truth. Lianne doesn't love you, Raoul. She loves him!"

The look of triumph on her face caused him to double his fists, but he took a deep breath and controlled himself. He mustn't hit her, but how he wanted to make her suffer. The meddlesome woman! However, he flashed her a smile as a plan to rid himself of her formulated in his brain. A divorce wouldn't do any longer.

"She thinks she loves him, but soon she'll desire only me. Now I leave you to think over what I've said."

"No divorce."

He shrugged his shoulders in a dismissive gesture and left the house. Have it your way, Elena, he thought to himself. No divorce.

Walking the distance to the alchemist's shop, he was ushered into the back room by the owner, a man known only by the name of Ricardo. After he explained what he wanted, Ricardo offered him a blue vial. "This shall put the sick cat you mentioned, Don Raoul, out of its misery." Ricardo grinned knowingly.

"*Gracias.* Also have you anything to spur a lady's ardor?"

"*Sí.* I have just the thing." The grizzled man left the room and then was back with a red vial which he presented to Raoul. "Just two drops of this potion and the lady in question will be so amorous, she shall wear the señor out."

Raoul thanked the chemist and pocketed both vials. He hoped he wouldn't have to use the red one, but he was certain he'd use the contents in the blue one.

Lianne waited on the patio for Raoul's return. The setting sun bathed the flagstones in an orange hue which she watched until the stones at her feet turned grayish-purple with night. She hoped her eyes were no longer puffy. When she returned home from the Academy of San Carlos she cried as she hadn't cried since the day the drugs wore off and she realized she was at the hacienda, under Raoul's thumb.

The future appeared bleak, even blacker than before Daniel's unexpected arrival. She wished he'd never come to Mexico City. Before seeing him again, she had begun not to miss him so much. Now to be parted from him once more was unbearable, but she had no othe choice. She was carrying Raoul's child and she must protect Daniel.

In the darkness she heard a noise. She looked up, expecting to see Raoul but saw Felix instead.

"I hope I don't disturb you, Señorita Lianne."

"No. What is the matter, Felix?"

He shyly bent his head. "I wished to know if you are well."

Lianne realized he was concerned because of her hysterical outburst inside the carriage which he must have heard. She smiled kindly. "I'll be all right."

"You love the señor very much."

She knew he wasn't referring to Raoul. "Yes, I do."

"Then you must tell him this, go to him."

"There are many things you can't understand, Felix, many reasons to keep me apart from Señor Flanders."

"You mean Don Raoul." Felix sneered as he spoke Raoul's name, and Lianne noted this. "He is less than human, señorita, less than the lowest *lepero*."

"Felix, please be quiet." Lianne rose from the wrought iron chair in which she sat. "Don Raoul will return shortly, and I don't want you punished.''

Felix stood bravely, his chest thrust out, and Lianne saw that regular meals had put flesh on his bones. One day Felix would be a handsome man, but for now he was still very young. ''Could Don Raoul punish me more than fate? Not unless he beats me to death, but I've experienced worse than death. The life of a *lepero* is cruel, much harsher than you could imagine, señorita. I watched my mother starve to death because she fed me the crumbs which should have been hers. I saw my father throw himself in front of a speeding carriage to end his torment. And all this could have been avoided but for Don Raoul.''

She motioned for Felix to come closer and sit beside her. They sat down together. Lianne was perplexed by his narrative, but she realized that Raoul had done something to destroy his family. She urged him to continue but held his hand because the boy shook with emotion.

''When I was small my father was a shoemaker. We always had plenty to eat, clothes to wear, and were much loved. My sister was older and very beautiful, very kind. She taught me to read.'' Felix smiled, remembering her dark, kind eyes and gentleness. ''Don Raoul was a customer of my father's. I remember being much in awe of him when he entered the shop. He was so tall and handsome, always in the finest clothes and bought the finest leather for his boots. Papa was very proud of such distinguished patronage. Señor de Lovis paid him handsomely and this enabled me to attend school. My parents were very proud of me and of my sister.''

Felix took a deep breath and tremors shook him. ''One day Don Raoul entered our shop. He hadn't seen my sister, Inez, for some time since she had been visiting relatives in Vera Cruz. On this day she helped my father with the customers, and before Don Raoul left, he said to my father, ''Your daughter, Señor

Martinez, has grown quite beautiful." Of course my
father agreed, but I was there and saw the look of
worry on my father's face. But Inez was young and
unused to such a compliment from a man like Señor de
Lovis. She smiled in shyness. Shortly after that he
came back to the shop when my parents were away.
My sister and I were alone. It was late at night, and I
was in bed. I heard Inez greet him at the door. Then all
was quiet until my sister screamed. I ran from my
room. A man, who looked like a monkey, also waited
in the hallway and blocked my way into my sister's
room.

"I'll never forget his strength, the evil in his face,
but I was small and quick. I dashed forward and
pushed open the door." Shivers rocked through Felix
at this point, and Lianne asked him if he wished to
continue. Without answering he said, "He held her
down on the bed. She was naked and crying, but she
saw me. 'Go away, Felix,' she sobbed. 'Go away.'
Don Raoul looked at me with such pleasure on his face
that I wished to kill him. I would have run and pulled
him from her, but the servant grabbed me by the collar
of my nightshirt as if I were a puppy and threw me into
my room. He locked the door, and though I tried to
wrench it open, I couldn't. In the morning Inez let me
out. Her beautiful skin was bruised and she held me in
her arms and cried. She made me promise not to tell
our parents. They would never have known about the
attack. By the time they returned home, no bruises
marred Inez. Except she became pregnant with de
Lovis's child."

Felix said this with such bitterness that Lianne
winced. "My sister was only fifteen, señorita. She
didn't want to bear his child and have my parents live
in shame. So, she visited a woman who promised to get
rid of the baby. To pay the old crone, she stole the
money from my father's drawer. I took her to the
woman and waited while . . . while it happened. Then

Inez told me to drive the cart home. Before we got there she started to bleed. I've never seen so much blood! When my mother saw her, she was hysterical and I ran for the doctor. But it was too late. Inez died that night.'' Felix gulped back tears but staunchly continued.

"I told my father about de Lovis and how he had raped Inez. Papa was so quiet. I had expected him to rant with rage, to cry, but he didn't. I went to bed and listened to the sobs of my mother. After Inez's burial, my father left us at the cemetery. I discovered later that he had gone to Don Raoul's house and confronted him. He pulled a knife on him, but the servant grabbed my papa who wasn't a big man and beat him and threw him from the house. A passerby took pity on him and helped him home. We thought that would be the end of it, but the next day a fire broke out in the shop, a mysterious fire. We lost everything, and the bank wouldn't loan my father the money to start a new shoe shop. We knew de Lovis was behind it all. My father was too proud to ask our relations in Vera Cruz for help, so we lived among the *leperos*. They had nothing; we had only the clothes on our backs. I grew tough among them, señorita. I had to be strong, otherwise, I'd be dead now like my mama and papa. And all of this because Raoul de Lovis couldn't control his lust for my sister.''

Lianne sat so still she barely breathed. She knew Raoul was capable of many things. But such a brutal rape? Her heart went out to Felix and his grief.

"I'm sorry, so sorry for you,'' she said and put her arm around his shoulders.

Felix gazed at her, his dark eyes glittering with suppressed violence. "I will kill him, señorita. His blood must cleanse my sister's shame and my parents' deaths. I will see that he dies slowly and painfully.''

Fear for him surfaced. Felix wouldn't be a match for Raoul and any henchman he might hire. "You mustn't do anything. Promise me you won't."

"I cannot." He shook his head. "But I will watch over you, señorita. Raoul de Lovis will not harm you while I am near."

Warmth and love for Felix rose inside her, and without thinking, she planted a kiss on his cheek. "You're very kind."

Suddenly a hard cold hand was clasped on her arm. She looked up to see Raoul standing ominously above her like a dark crow.

"Are you in the habit of kissing your servants?" he inquired. His moustache looked dark against the angry white line of his mouth.

Lianne instantly got up as did Felix. "I was thanking Felix for helping me to my chair," she said and hoped she lied convincingly. "I felt rather faint, and Felix was nearby. Nothing was meant in the kiss but thankfulness."

"Go to the servants' quarters," he said harshly to Felix. "There's no need for you here. Señorita Lianne shall not sing at the opera tonight."

Felix bowed and left them alone. A servant came out then and lit the torches on the patio. In the flickering light she noticed tiny age lines around Raoul's eye, and he looked older than forty. "I hope you don't make a practice out of this," he admonished her. "Felix is almost a man and may misinterpret your friendliness. Plus he is a *lepero,* little better than sheep dung. I hired him as your driver because he protected you when you disobeyed my orders not to travel alone. As easily as I took him in, I can throw him back with his own slimy kind."

Indignation filled her, but she forced it down with a smile and a nod of her head. "Anything you say, Raoul."

He seemed not to notice the loathing in her eyes as they dined later that evening. She kept imagining him as he raped an innocent girl; she shivered in the warm night air which wafted from the courtyard into the open dining room. His concentration was clearly on other matters and she was grateful that he didn't immediately come to bed. Later when he did, he didn't touch her.

Chapter 32

The news of the death of Dona Elena Mendoza de Lovis reached Lianne on a sunny morning in mid-April when Daniel arrived at the door with a weeping Carmen, whom he supported by the arm.

The girl was ushered into a bedroom, nearly in hysterics, by a servant. Lianne couldn't believe how stoically Raoul took the news of Elena's death and how he didn't make an attempt to comfort his daughter. All he asked Daniel was, "How did it happen?"

Daniel told him that he had just finished a sitting with Carmen and had been invited by Elena for chocolate in the *sala* with her and Carmen. He refused the chocolate, preferring tequila. He and Elena had conversed for a few minutes, and she praised the work he had done on Carmen's portrait so far.

Then a servant appeared and refilled Elena's cup with the chocolate which Elena laughed and said was her only real enjoyment. Without warning, Elena dropped her cup after she had taken a few sips, and clutched her chest. "My heart!" she had moaned. She fell to the floor. Daniel had barely risen from his chair to help her when he saw she was dead. Carmen screamed and couldn't seem to stop. It was only when a doctor arrived and had given her a sleeping draught that she settled into a somnambulistic state, but didn't sleep.

As soon as Elena's body had been removed from the *sala,* and Carmen had rested, he brought the girl to her father's house, to inform Raoul about his wife.

Raoul sank into a chair when Daniel finished. He appeared pale and drawn. "She didn't suffer long."

"No. She died instantly. The doctor said her heart gave out."

"Bueno. I never wanted her to suffer." He looked at Daniel who never took his eyes from Lianne. She stood with arms folded across her breasts in the doorway. "Have you completed Carmen's portrait?"

Daniel thought that was an odd question to ask given the circumstances. "It shall be finished shortly."

Raoul stood up and squared his shoulders. He was only an inch shorter than Daniel. "Then I advise you to have it finished by the end of the week and return to Louisiana. There is nothing for you here. Lianne carries my child, and soon I shall marry her. There isn't hope for you, Daniel."

Daniel grinned crookedly, arrogance surrounding him. He rose to his full height, totally disarming Lianne with a smile he quickly flashed in her direction. "There's always hope, de Lovis, as long as I'm alive."

Daniel turned on his heels and left the house without further word to either of them.

Raoul sniffed the air. "Arrogant son of a bitch! If you live much longer!" His vicious black-eyed gaze settled on Lianne, and he grabbed her arm. "You're mine. You'll never belong to Daniel Flanders, so get that look of hope off your face. Now go and tend to that wailing, stupid girl I call my daughter."

Raoul was heartless, but she didn't argue with him. She went to the room where Carmen sat on the bed, not caring for Josephine's ministrations. "I don't want a wet facecloth. I want my mother!" she cried and slapped Josephine who tried to wipe her tears away.

Lianne dismissed Josephine with a slight wave of her hand. She moved closer to the bed, but Carmen lifted her face from the kerchief in her hands and saw her. With a quick movement, she tumbled from the bed and stood in the corner.

"Stay away from me, you vile woman! *Puta!*" she spat.

Hearing the word from Carmen's mouth caused Lianne to blink, but she pretended not to be upset by the girl's hatred and distrust of her.

"I'd like to help you, Carmen."

Carmen shook her head so hard the tiny smooth chignon loosened. "I want my mother!"

"She's gone to heaven. I think she'd want you to think of her love for you, and she did love you very much. She'll never return, but her love will see you through this tragedy."

Carmen laughed hysterically. "*Sí!* And what will happen to me without her to protect me . . . from him?"

"Your father?"

"Who else? The filthy bastard will have me married to Diego Gonzales when my mother wished a match with Fernando Valenciana."

"Perhaps I will speak to your father. Do you love this Fernando?" Lianne asked and inched closer to her.

With suspicious eyes, Carmen shook her head. "No, but at least Fernando is not devious like Diego or cruel. Diego was my father's protégé at one time. He used to look after the de Lovis interests until he married a wealthy woman who died under mysterious circumstances. Exactly like my mother."

Fresh tears assailed Carmen, and Lianne tried to comfort her, but she stayed in the corner and shrugged off Lianne's hand. "*Puta!*" she cried again.

Lianne knew she was defeated. She left Carmen and found Raoul in the *sala*. He lounged lazily in a chair and smoked a cheroot.

"Aren't there plans to be made for Elena's burial?" she asked.

He looked at Lianne, unconcern on his face. He smiled at how lovely she was with her long hair pulled atop her head with a peach ribbon and dressed in a morning gown of the same color. Desire swelled in him, but he decided not to touch her until they married. He feared the loss of the child, and he realized she might think it strange if he made love to her an hour after hearing of his wife's untimely death. Better to leave her alone for the moment. But soon she'd be his wife and he would own her, body and soul. Then Daniel Flanders would cease to be a threat.

"All shall be attended to, Lianne. The bitch was my wife and you're worried about her. She knew I wanted to divorce her and refused me. It was God's will that she died. You were meant to be my wife and bear my children. Our son shall not be a bastard. He'll inherit my wealth, my name."

Lianne looked curiously at him. "What about Carmen? She is your heiress."

"Hmmph! A small replica of Elena. She'll make due with the dowry I give her on her wedding day."

"She's worried you'll marry her to Diego Gonzales when Elena intended for her to marry someone else."

He took another puff of the cheroot. "Carmen should be worried. She will marry Diego."

"You should honor Elena's wishes in this, Raoul."

A raised eyebrow told her she had gone too far. "Don't tell me what I should do, or not do, about that worthless daughter Elena bore me. My women do as I want."

"Your women!" she spat. "You're nothing but a vile, filthy rapist!"

He stood up. His face grew white, and when he threw the cheroot to the flagstone floor and grabbed

her arm until it hurt, she knew she should never have
opened her mouth.

"Consider yourself lucky that you carry my son.
If not I would beat you so long and hard you'd have to
stay in your bed for weeks. Tell me why you say such a
thing to me."

She didn't know how to reply, could barely speak.

"I don't know . . ."

"Who told you this?"

"No one." She suddenly felt very weak and
cowered like a lamb, not sure what he would do to her.
He said he wouldn't beat her, but she had an idea that
Raoul could torment a person, especially a woman,
without physical violence.

One of the servants saved her then when he
announced the arrival of Father Lopez, Elena's
confessor.

Raoul told her to leave them, and she gladly did.
She fled to her room like a frightened mouse and
found herself minutes later crying for Elena and herself.

"Daniel, Daniel," she moaned the name into the
bedspread. "I want to go home."

No sooner had Elena been buried than Raoul
informed Lianne to prepare for their wedding.
Carmen, who sat at the far end of the dining table,
away from her father and Lianne, looked up from her
evening meal of beans, tortillas and hot chocolate.

"Have you no respect for the memory of my
mother?" she burst out, without thinking. "How dare
you marry your whore when my mother is three days
dead!"

Lianne felt a cold, sinking feeling in her stomach
at Carmen's unthinking words. Her own eyes flew to
Raoul whose mouth stiffened into a straight line. She
didn't know if she could protect Carmen from Raoul's
wrath, however, Raoul surprised her and apparently

Carmen, also, when he grinned.

"Your dear mother would have wished for all of us to continue living. As I recall her greatest desire was for you to marry." He paused. "Your own wedding shall be arranged shortly, because I don't wish to deny my only daughter her happiness."

Carmen's expression changed from one of anger to hope. "My mother would have been pleased to see me marry Fernando Valenciana."

Raoul's brow rose inquisitively. "Haven't you heard the news? Fernando has left Mexico City to marry an heiress in Colombia. I hope you didn't have your heart set on such a match, Carmen."

Carmen's face paled. "No," she mouthed and glanced toward Lianne who looked just as shocked.

"Don't be dismayed," Raoul said, gesturing grandly with his cheroot. "A suitable husband has already been found. Tonight Diego Gonzalas shall pay his respects to you. I've spoken to him about your dowry, and the man is eager to marry you. Consider yourself lucky that Diego wants you at all. He has grown quite wealthy since the days he worked for me and is considered quite a catch. In fact I believe he has broken Dona Isabelle Hidalgo's heart." He smiled at Carmen's shocked face.

Lianne could see that Carmen wanted to deny her father, but she suddenly asked to be excused and Raoul nodded.

"You see," he spoke to Lianne after Carmen's departure, "one only has to know how to handle Elena's offspring. The girl is gutless, as was her mother, and will do whatever I wish."

How cocksure he appeared! Lianne had the insane desire to rake her nails across his face, to scar it further.

"You somehow arranged for the Valenciana boy to marry elsewhere."

Raoul shrugged in his familiar way. "Señor Valenciana is in debt to me and needed no great inducement to look elsewhere for a bride for his son. I hear the Colombian heiress is quite pretty. The boy should thank me."

"How noble of you, Raoul."

He laughed at her disapproving look and squeezed her hand. "You'll marry me, Lianne, just as Carmen will wed Diego. Both of you belong to me until I decide otherwise." He stood up and went into his library while Lianne fumed, still sitting at the table.

She hated Raoul! To think of marrying him was unbearable, but no other alternative was open to her. She must marry him because of the baby. If only there wasn't a child.

She started in her seat to remember what had happened to Felix's sister. Perhaps she could find a woman who would help her and not botch the job. But shame overcame her and she put her hands over her face. It was wrong to think such a thing. She could never rid herself of a child. Despite the fact that Raoul was the father, a part of her anticipated motherhood again. Finally she'd have someone to love, a baby to take the place of her little Désirée.

But she sighed. There was no one to take Daniel's place in her heart. She loved him fiercely and many times had to quell the impulse to see him once more, to remind herself that she must protect him from Raoul. She had no doubt that if she saw him again, Raoul would discover it and punish Daniel in a way she didn't care to dwell upon.

Shaking her head to drive the horrible thoughts away, she stood up. She picked up her lace shawl and went down the step which led into the courtyard. The purple sky of evening descended, and she wandered aimlessly toward the cast iron fountain in the courtyard's center. Sitting on the bench beside it, she trailed her hand in the cool water and noted the reflection of the rising moon in its depths. Then the moon was gone and she saw Daniel's face.

"Daniel!" Her look of pure pleasure told him

that she loved him. Without thinking she threw herself
into his arms and felt the steel of his chest beneath her
breasts, and the warmth of his lips on hers. But Lianne
drew quickly away and glanced toward the house.

"You shouldn't be here," she cautioned and purposely pulled him away from the center of the courtyard to an area close to the street, bordered by high
hedges and flowering bougainvillea which matched the
crimson of her lips and permeated the air with their
sweet scent.

"Are you so frightened of Raoul?" Daniel asked
and pulled her toward him once more.

She didn't want to answer him, but her silence
told him what he already knew. "Don't take unnecessary risks on my account, Daniel. We can't be
together. I'm going to marry Raoul in a few days."

"Do you love him?"

"I love only you. I'll always love you."

He smiled down at her and marvelled at the way
her eyes glowed a golden green in the deepening
moonlight. His mouth gently caressed her cheek and
sent shivers through her.

"Then leave the bastard. I'll take your child and
raise it as mine. I'll fight for you, Lianne! I won't let
you go."

For a moment she thought he intended to bound
inside and confront Raoul, so she clutched at him.
"Don't do anything foolish. Not for me."

A soft wind blew a few strands of dark hair about
his forehead. Love filled her for this slightly disheveled
man who smelled of oils and whose shirt front was
streaked with spots of color. Whatever happened in
the future, she had this memory of him to cherish.

"I'd do anything to free you from him, but if you
won't free yourself, I can't. Do you want to be free of
him, Lianne?"

His uncertainty chilled her. Couldn't he tell she
did? But she must convince him she didn't want to
leave, to save him from a love which had been doomed

the moment Raoul de Lovis set eyes upon her in Madrid.

"I've told you already why I won't run away with you. The baby, the money, the clothes . . ."

He stopped her short, grinding out his words. "I don't believe you."

"You must!" She pulled away from him. "Accept that as my answer, Daniel. Please."

"Raoul is only a man, flesh and blood, and can die like any other man."

She didn't care for the black look on his face, or for the way he fingered the rapier at his side. "Don't think such a thing. Raoul has people who will avenge his death. No, don't consider it. Please leave me, Daniel. Return to Green Meadows and our daughter."

"Not without you. I'll never believe you want his money and wish to spend your life as his prisoner, because that is what you are, Lianne."

"Believe it! What must I do to convince you?"

"Lianne!" Raoul's voice boomed from the *sala*.

"I have to go inside. Daniel, go home. Forget me, please. It's the best thing for both our sakes." She moved away but he stilled her and held her lips against his in a kiss which left her drugged and tottering for balance. Then he released her and she practically flew across the courtyard to meet Raoul in the *sala* where Diego Gonzalez sat, sipping mescal.

Upon seeing her, Diego stood up and gallantly bowed. His small dark eyes raked her from head to toe, then rested on the valley of her breasts where the shawl had fallen open. Lianne knew immediately she didn't like him and pulled the shawl around her. She remembered seeing him with Isabelle Hidalgo at Elena's party and pitied Carmen if this man was to be her husband. Though elegant clothes covered his small, wiry frame he reminded her of a small monkey.

She hid her distaste when he kissed her hand and hoped she wouldn't have to stay in the *sala* much longer. She really wanted to go to her room and think about Daniel.

But Raoul summoned Carmen and within seconds the girl stood before her father and her future husband, tears welling in her eyes. She was dressed in a very pretty yellow gown, forgoing the black which Raoul insisted she put away. However, the color did nothing for Carmen but make her look sallow and slightly plump.

If Diego noticed this, he pretended not to. He also took her hand, kissing it quickly. "I haven't seen you for some time," Diego said in politeness.

Carmen could barely speak. "A long time," she muttered at Raoul's glance of impatience.

He sat on the chair beside Raoul's while the women sat on the couch. A servant offered tea, but neither of them touched it. Raoul and Diego drank their mezcal. Then Raoul turned his attention to his daughter.

"Diego has consented to marry you, Carmen. The arrangements are being made for June."

"June? But, Father, June is the hottest month of the year. Couldn't we please postpone the marriage until the fall? You know how the heat affects me."

"Hmmph! Just like your mother. Always an excuse. No, the wedding is set for June."

"I should like to mourn for my mother. I've had no time to mourn."

Carmen's balkiness surprised Lianne, as it did Raoul. "Consider yourself fortunate that I don't send for the priest and have you married tonight!"

At the prospect of marrying Diego that night, Carmen grew quiet, almost sullen.

Diego's eyes barely rested on her. He found her totally not to his liking. He thought she was too small, too plump. and if balkiness was part of her disposition, she'd soon outgrow it when she was his wife. His palms itched. Yes, she'd outgrow it, and he'd have a marvelous time beating it out of her. However, what he'd really like would be to have Raoul's beautiful mistress in his bed and to feel her soft flesh beneath him. He wondered if she'd bleed easily. She was such a pale, golden creature that he felt certain she would. How he envied Raoul! Of course he could still see Isabelle, after he married Carmen. She seemed to enjoy a little torture now and then. But all she could speak about these days was the painter and how no man could compare to him in bed or out. Isabelle wearied him lately. Perhaps Lianne would be amenable if he charmed her. He'd seen evidence of her hot-bloodedness earlier that evening, but doubted if Raoul was aware of what transpired. Maybe he should tell him and wipe that self-satisfied smile from his face.

"I'm certain Señorita Lianne can help you plan the wedding, Carmen," he said but didn't once look at anyone other than Lianne.

Raoul jumped in. "Lianne has other matters to concern her, like giving me a healthy son."

For the next half hour, Lianne and Carmen sat through a boring recitation of how Diego had made his fortune with Raoul's help. Finally when she thought she could stand no more, Raoul decided the hour grew late and that his women needed their rest. This attitude of treating her like a child rankled Lianne, but she gratefully left the *sala* for her bedroom with Carmen following.

"I hate him!" the girl hissed when they were in the hallway, and Lianne wasn't certain which man she meant.

Carmen swished into her room and locked the door, leaving Lianne alone.

Once Lianne was in bed, a huge sob spilled forth and she cried for the hopeless future she had made.

But, in the *sala*, Raoul felt far from hopeless. Everything seemed to be going his way for once. Within days he'd marry Lianne, and then in two months Carmen would marry Diego. At least one last thorn would be out of his hair. Elena was no longer a worry to him. He poured more mezcal and contemplated Diego. Yes, he was a suitable husband for Carmen. He'd keep her in line. Then he could devote all his time to Lianne and their son.

"You appear very happy," Diego noted to Raoul.

"*Sí*, I am. No one and nothing stands in my way. I must thank you for doing an excellent job where Elena was concerned. I trust you were circumspect."

"Of course. Elena's servant did as I asked. A trustworthy type." He grinned at his facetious comment. Of all the spies in Elena's household, Pedro was the least suspect. "No one will ever know I paid him to poison her chocolate."

"Too bad Daniel Flanders couldn't have suffered an early demise, also."

Diego stroked his long chin. "Ah, the painter. I have good reason to dislike him. Isabelle is enamored of him, but he doesn't pay her any attention. It seems he has eyes for only one woman."

Raoul lifted an eyebrow. "And whom might that be?"

"Why, your beautiful mistress, of course. Didn't you know that the woman you share your bed with, the woman who carries your child was in the man's arms earlier this evening? I saw them from the street, behind the hedges in the courtyard, just before I entered the house. Raoul, believe me when I tell you, my friend, you do have something to worry you."

Raoul's eye glittered dangerously. He tightened his grip around the cup of mezcal. Damn the scheming bitch! He had thought he could trust her and had even given her the freedom to come and go as she chose. He must discover the truth about Lianne and Daniel. If she was meeting the man, she'd rue the day she cuckolded Raoul de Lovis.

He turned to Diego, already having composed himself. "Diego, I would like you to keep a watchful eye on Lianne for me."

"Of course," Diego answered too cheerfully,

knowing Raoul meant for him to spy on her. That would give him great pleasure.

"Don't enjoy yourself too much, my friend," Raoul said in a warning tone. "Never approach her. Just tell me where she goes and who she meets. Understand?"

"*Sí*. I do. After all, you can trust me, Raoul. Didn't I help you with the shoemaker's daughter?"

Raoul's face paled. "Never mention the incident to me again! Now leave, but I expect a full report from you within the week."

Diego bowed and left.

Raoul quietly went to the bedroom and watched the sleeping face of the woman who obsessed him. He noticed tears stained her cheeks, and a fury seized him to think she cried for Daniel Flanders, that she had willingly been in the man's arms . . . and all the while he had been in the *sala*. What a cunning little tart she was! But he vowed vegeance on Lianne and Daniel if he discovered her to be unfaithful.

A smile spread across his face as he remembered the red vial he had hidden in his study. He wouldn't have to physically harm Daniel or Lianne. In fact Lianne would derive great pleasure from the contents of the vial, as he would also. The only one who'd be harmed would be Daniel Flanders. And this brought a huge laugh from between his lips.

The next afternoon Carmen ordered the carriage sent around and told Felix she wished to ride to the arcade.

"Without a chaperone, señorita?" he asked.

"You insolent thing!" she practically screeched. "How dare you speak to me! My father's whore may allow you such liberties but never I."

"Señorita Lianne isn't a whore."

Carmen blinked in astonishment that a servant and a *lepero*, a person who had slept in the streets and done God knows what, would take up for Lianne.

Well, what could a decent person expect? She wasn't like her sainted mother who looked the other way at the antics of Raoul de Lovis where other women were concerned. She still thought Lianne was a whore, but something in this boy's rock-hard expression defied her to say anything else. Instead she flounced into the carriage.

A hard rain had saturated the earth the previous night, and after Carmen had made her purchases at the arcade and they were headed for home, the carriage suddenly jolted and she fell to one side.

She peered out. "Whatever is the matter?" she called.

"We're stuck," Felix said and jumped down from his position. "You better get out while I try to get us out of the mud."

"Must I?" Carmen asked and eyed the oozing mud which caked around his boots.

"I'd advise it, señorita."

"But I'll get my gown dirty."

Felix eyed the somber black gown Carmen had worn to spite her father and to mourn her mother. He didn't see what difference it made whether the gown became muddy or not. It was dark enough that a person would barely notice a little mud and ugly enough that its appearance might be improved.

He looked around and spotted a group of shade trees on higher ground. "If you will alow me, I'll carry you and you may wait there while I push the carriage."

Carmen looked to where he pointed then back to him in disbelief. "You wouldn't carry me!"

"Sí, but if you'd rather walk I don't mind."

What was she to do? No man had ever touched her except for the gentlemanly peck on the hand. How could she allow a lepero to touch her? But anything was preferable to waiting in the hot carriage with the April sun beating down upon it, or being jostled while he tried to wrest the carriage from the muck. Luckily the siesta hour was upon them and no one was around.

All the shutters on nearby houses were closed tight. Felix would have had to take this road which was in desperate need of repair!

"All right," she demured and held out her arms to fasten around his neck.

Felix picked her up, and Carmen was a bit surprised that he seemed to have no trouble carrying her. Felix was thin, but he was very strong and this was the impression which stayed with her after he had set her down beneath the shade trees.

She watched in fascination while he moved the horses forward, then inched the wheel upward. The muscles swelled on his upper arms and sweat fell from his forehead, but never in her entire life had Carmen been so aware of another human being's anatomy.

When he finished, he looked up and caught her watching him. He flashed her a dazzling smile and came to join her in the shade.

"Your carriage awaits, señorita," he said. Carmen realized he was panting.

"Please sit and rest a few minutes," she said and surprised herself and she should care if a *lepero,* and her father's servant, was in need of a respite.

"Gracias." Felix threw himself on the ground by her feet. "Would you like to sit, señorita."

"Me? Sit on the ground?"

"No one is around to notice, señorita."

Felix was right, and she was tired of standing, so she plopped alongside him.

"It's very hot today," Carmen said, growing uncomfortable when Felix remained silent. "The heat makes me quite ill."

"You're very frail, señnorita Carmen."

"Do you think so? My mother always told me that. Father never believed her. I've always been a disappointment to him."

"Really? How?" Felix's voice suddenly sounded hard.

"Because I wasn't the son he wanted. He hopes

Lianne gives him a boy to carry on the great name of
de Lovis, while I shall marry Diego Gonzalez.''

"Oh, *sí*. I've seen him when he visits your father.
He is the one who looks like the little monkey.''

Felix said this with a lilt in his voice, but Carmen
noticed his eyes were ice cold. She had thought the
same thing herself but never admitted it out loud.

She found herself laughing. "A monkey. *Sí*, just
like a monkey.'' Then the smile left her lips and she
sighed. "I must marry a monkey.''

Felix turned to her, a challenging look in his eyes.
"Why? Because your father wishes it?''

"Of course. I must obey my father.''

"Even if your life will be miserable and you may
be mistreated by this Diego? He will hurt you,
Carmen.''

She had felt everything Felix said, but hearing the
words from another person's mouth was too much for
her. She hated to face the truth and wanted to pretend
the wedding would never happen. Her dark eyes
snapped, and she transferred all her frustrations to
Felix.

"You're too familiar! *Lepero!* That's all you are
and ever will be. Now carry me back to the carriage. I
wish to go home.''

Carmen looked and sounded so much like Raoul
then that he roughly hauled her from her feet and with
a few striding steps, he reached the carriage and un-
ceremoniously dumped her inside. She nearly landed
on the floor except she balanced herself and sank into
the cushion.

"I suggest you take special care. I am the
daughter of Raoul de Lovis!'' she cried.

He climbed onto his perch and grabbed the reins
in his hands. "If only I could forget that,'' he
mumbled.

Chapter 33

Much to Raoul's relief, Diego reported that Lianne hadn't visited Daniel. Each time she left the house, Diego followed her at a respectful distance, but discovered she accompanied Carmen to the dressmaker's one day and to the outdoor stalls in the plaza the next. This information pleased Raoul so much that he anticipated his wedding day with much eagerness.

However, Lianne had different feelings about her wedding. She didn't wish to marry Raoul, but she felt no other path was open to her. She carried his child and no matter what Daniel promised about loving the baby as his own if she returned to Green Meadows, she didn't believe him. The memory of Raoul would be too strong each time he looked at the child. She also didn't doubt that Raoul would fight for his offspring and might even make good his threat and inform the authorities that she was the one who killed Phillipe.

The morning of her wedding dawned brightly. Outside she heard the chirping of birds and golden sunshine filled her bedroom. She wondered why the day should be so beautiful when clearly she was miserable in spirit and not feeling at all well. She felt a cramping sensation in her abdomen but tried to dismiss it. With each of her two pregnancies as she advanced in size, she had felt the same sensations. However, she wasn't far along, and wondered if she should postpone the wedding but thought better of it. Raoul might think she was trying to trick him.

Josephine bustled into the room and pulled the wedding dress from the wardrobe. The gown was a beautiful pale pink silk with a high ribboned waist. Small eyelet lace graced the front of the square cut bodice and the long, sheer sleeves had lace cuffs. Lianne had chosen tiny pink roses and baby's breath to be attached to each side of the white mantilla at her temples.

"Don Raoul has already dressed, and Carmen is ready, too. Poor girl. She looks so sad all of the time," Josephine commented and pulled Lianne's chemise over her head.

"She looks sad because she is," Lianne said and barely squeezed into the garment. She wondered if she was farther along in her pregnancy than she thought. The slight bulge of her abdomen was noticeable beneath the thin material. At least Raoul was making an honest woman of her before everyone could see she was pregnant. She nearly laughed. No one would wish to see "La Flamenca" perform in this condition, and she was glad she had stopped performing at the opera. This pregnancy seemed to tax her, to sap her energy.

"The girl is hard to reach and even harder to like," Josephine said.

Lianne came to Carmen's rescue. "Please remember that she has recently lost her mother and now lives with a father who is barely civil to her and her father's mistress, whom she detests. Now she must soon marry a man she doesn't like, let alone love. I pity Carmen and understand what it's like to live in a luxurious prison."

Josephine gasped. "You can't mean that! Don Raoul has given you everything a woman could want. I admit he didn't care very much for his late wife and you'd have thought he was burying a stray dog the way he acted when she died, but he loves you, Lianne. He loves your child."

Lianne shivered in the warm morning air. Ever since Elena's death, she had wondered how Raoul could be so calm, so unconcerned. Sometimes she thought he had expected such a tragedy but had quickly put the thought from her mind. Raoul couldn't have murdered her. There was no evidence to think such a thing. But his words when Daniel broke the news haunted her. "I never wanted her to suffer."

A cramp jabbed at her and she caught her breath, all sinister thoughts fleeing. Josephine noticed her sudden pallor.

"You must rest. I'll send for Don Raoul."

Lianne halted her with a hand on her wrist. "No, it will pass. Don't alarm him."

Within seconds she felt better though a slight ache persisted. She managed a smile. "See. Now help me on with my gown."

The drive to the cathedral was silent. Carmen barely glanced at her father or Lianne, and Lianne felt rather weak. Diego had joined them shortly before their departure and he now sat alongside Carmen who huddled near the coach door. Raoul was the only one who seemed in good spirits, while Diego glowered when he realized that Carmen regarded him with insolent eyes. When Felix stopped the carriage in front of the cathedral and opened the door for them, Lianne didn't miss the probing look he threw at Diego or the sneer which twisted his mouth.

Into the church Raoul led her where after this day she truly would belong to him. A man capable of rape. Of murder? She didn't want to think about any of this. Raoul took her elbow and walked her down the aisle to where the priest waited to marry them. Since the ceremony was informal, other people knelt and prayed. Lianne wished they weren't so conspicuous and hoped that no one would be interested in a simple marriage ceremony.

She glanced quickly around the church and stopped dead in her tracks. One of the people in a pew at the opposite end of the church was Daniel! She knew it was him by the broadness of his back, the familiar way his hair curled at the nape of his neck. What was he doing here?

"*Querida*?" Raoul asked, concern on his face. "What is the trouble?"

"Nothing. I'm fine." The thought flickered through her mind that Daniel was there to disrupt the ceremony. He mustn't do that! She had to marry Raoul. If what she had begun to suspect about Elena was true, then Daniel could very well be Raoul's next victim. More than once Raoul had hinted that he'd like to see Daniel dead. She made a silent, hasty prayer to heaven that Daniel not interfere.

As if in a nightmare she finally reached the altar and recognized the priest as Elena's confessor. He didn't appear very pleased over this marriage because his face had a stony appearance, a look of contempt in his eyes.

So far Raoul hadn't spotted Daniel. Out of the corners of her eyes, she watched him, watched in dread as the priest began the short ceremony to unite her to Raoul. She wasn't aware of Carmen or Diego who stood nearby as witnesses. All she could see was the image of Daniel in her mind, praying he wouldn't do anything.

She felt ill, unbearably sick when it was her turn to recite the vows. She clutched at the small bouquet of roses in her hands as the ache in her abdomen grew into a sharp point of fire. The world grew dark, and she barely summoned the energy to say the words which finally united her to Raoul. She felt his eyes upon her, but knew her prayers hadn't been answered when she heard the creaking of a bench behind her. Daniel was getting up! She knew it, could see him advancing toward the altar with a look of utter fury on his face. How was she to stop him? How?

It was only when the sharp point of pain grew so

intense and seemed to rip her apart that she screamed.

Through a haze of pain she heard Daniel's voice from the *sala,* but couldn't make out the angry words.

Lianne grasped Josephine's hand which stroked her hair from her forehead. "He shouldn't be here," she gasped. "Raoul will kill him."

"Sh. You must be quiet and rest. Soon the medicine Doctor Morales gave you shall work and you'll sleep. Pay no attention to anything else."

Despite Josephine's calm manner, Lianne stubbornly refused to be still and tried to get up. "I must warn him. Daniel must leave or Raoul will harm him."

"Lianne!" Josephine's voice grew harsh. "Don Raoul wouldn't hurt anyone. Where do you get such a strange idea? He is a kind and thoughful man. He is now your husband."

Lianne looked in bafflement at Josephine through suddenly sleep-shrouded eyes. Why couldn't the woman see what type of man Raoul was? Did great wealth impress her so much that she refused to see the evil which lurked behind the man? Through a still conscious part of her brain, she decided she better not confide any personal feelings to Josephine. She lay back down and felt the cover being drawn over her, aware she had lost her child and should be saddened, but at the moment she worried more about Daniel in the *sala*. Then sleep overtook her.

In the *sala* Daniel stood with fists ready to pummel Raoul, to beat him senseless for the unnecessary pain he had caused Lianne. He hated the man with the glittering black eye and heartily wished to be the one responsible for causing permanent blindness to Raoul de Lovis.

But Raoul seemed not to care that Daniel didn't hide his hatred. Instead Raoul thought this was all a great game. Doctor Morales had informed him only minutes ago that Lianne had lost their child, and though this upset him, he refused to allow Flanders to know this. Or to think that he had lost Lianne when she miscarried the baby. He knew that Lianne wouldn't leave him as long as she was pregnant and the mother of his child, now he wasn't certain any longer. But this added twist of fate only made the game of winning her more interesting. Raoul loved a challenge, and especially goading Daniel.

He took a long puff of his cheroot, sitting while Daniel stood. The deep shadows of the late afternoon lengthened in the *sala* and a servant lit the candles. When she was gone, he spoke.

"As soon as Lianne recovers we shall make another child. She's a good breeder, is she not?"

Daniel clenched his fists with renewed vigor. He tensed and realized Raoul wished to anger him further. In fact he was surprised that Raoul hadn't ordered Diego Gonzalez, Raoul's lackey, to do the job, when he rushed to her side in the church and carried her to the coach. Raoul's anger had been evident by the dangerous gleam of the eye, the muscle which twitched in his cheek. But he hadn't stopped Daniel from spiriting her from the church or sitting beside her during the return trip home.

Now as he stood in Raoul's house, more than willing to take her away from the man, by force if necessary, he wondered why he suddenly seemed so amenable.

"Perhaps Lianne will refuse to conceive again," Daniel said.

Raoul shrugged. "Then I'll have to make sure she does. I'm not averse to force."

"Bastard!" Daniel rushed forward and hauled Raoul from the chair. He knew Raoul wished to provoke him, but the image of her as a permanent fixture in Raoul's bed undid him.

He shoved Raoul against the wall, knocking a painting from it which in turn fell onto a credenza filled with glass objects. They splintered into sparkling fragments. Daniel's face was even with Raoul's own. The tormented gray eyes warred with the angry black one.

"Believe me, if I find you've harmed her in any way once she's recovered, I'll kill you, de Lovis. With my bare hands. No matter what your brave words say, I know that inside that evil mind of yours, you know she hates you and loves me. When Lianne is better, I'm taking her away from you. You can't keep her a prisoner forever."

Raoul managed a smirk he didn't feel. "Lianne is my wife. I let you accompany us home, so you'd see she is well treated. Now let me go or you'll rip the silk of my coat with your childish rowdiness. You Irishmen simply can't control your tempers."

"You're just lucky I don't bash in your head." Daniel released him and Raoul staggered a bit.

Daniel ached to make Lianne a widow, but she had willingly married Raoul. He knew she had married him because of the baby, but the knowledge didn't make his pain bearable. He still loved her.

Josephine appeared with Diego at her side. "Lianne is asleep, Don Raoul."

"Is she all right?" Daniel asked.

"Of course she is," Josephine replied with a bit of frost in her voice. "She's the wife, monsieur, of Raoul de Lovis."

"That's good reason to fear for her," Daniel said. "I would like to see her."

"I told you she's asleep, monsieur."

"I have to know Lianne is all right. If I have to, I'll fight every one of you."

Raoul sighed. "How tiresome you are, Daniel." He nodded to Josephine. "Let him see her if he must."

Before Josephine could get her bearings Daniel was out of the *sala* and down the hallway. "He's a problem, señor. Lianne was worried about him before she fell asleep."

A vein throbbed in Raoul's temple and he couldn't help but notice the amused look on Diego's monkey-like face. "She didn't ask for me?"

Josephine shook her head sadly. "No, señor. She fancies herself in love with the Irishman."

"Then we shall have to keep them apart." He turned to Diego. "Go to Ricardo, the alchemist. Ask him for the powder in the yellow vial. Tell him it is for me. You should have no trouble, but you may have to pay double the price."

"Raoul . . ." Diego began to protest the extra money.

"You wish to marry my wealthy daughter, do you not, Diego?"

"*Sí*, but . . ."

"Then go." Raoul waved him away and Diego left.

Josephine snickered. "That one is tight with the pesos."

"Not an unattractive quality to have, but I need you to help me with Lianne."

"Anything, señor. You helped me when I came to Mexico City, offered me this job. I shall be forever in your debt."

"*Bueno*. Because if Lianne runs away with her ex-lover, you'll have no job. When Diego returns, take the vial from him. Keep it with you, but don't allow Lianne to see it. When she begins to recover, I suspect Flanders will show up again, or she'll try to find him. I want you to pour a pinch of the powder in her morning juice."

"Every morning, señor?"

Raoul nodded. A quicksilver flash of a smile lit up his face for a moment. "We must keep her calm, very calm."

"Ah." Josephine began to see why the vial was needed. "Trust me, señor. I shall take good care of your lady."

"Wife, Josephine. She is my wife," Raoul corrected.

"*Oui*," the maid said, much pleased. She would have a job for a very long time.

Daniel gazed with love at the woman whose red-gold hair fanned the pillows. He watched the gentle rise and fall of her breasts beneath the cover. A feeling of such love swept over him that he knelt beside her bed and took her slim hand in his. He pressed the fingertips to his mouth. She stirred in her sleep, the coral-tinged lips opened a bit as a breath escaped.

Never in his life had he felt so protective of another human being. This was the woman he loved, the mother of his daughter. He'd be damned if he'd let Raoul de Lovis steal her away from them again, not after he had found her! Lianne belonged at Green Meadows in his bed, not in the bed of a Mexican silver king who reeked of cruelty. Why was Lianne so frightened of Raoul?

"Have courage, my love," he whispered. "You can fight him. Only you can free yourself."

She gave a soft whimper, and he hoped she had heard him. Tenderly he kissed her lips and left her to Josephine's ministrations.

Chapter 34

Lianne fingered the embroidered sunburst on the bed coverlet and watched Josephine as she took the silk and taffeta gowns from the wardrobe and ordered one of the house maids to press them.

"Within the next few days we leave for San Augustin de las Cuevas," Josephine explained and handed the gowns to the waiting maid who soon left the room. "By then you shall be strong enough to make the trip with Don Raoul. He thinks you need time away from Mexico City, and I hear San Augustin is quite exciting this time of year. There are dances, card games until all hours of the night, and I also hear that the ladies change their clothes six times a day! I know you shall be the most beautiful lady there." Josephine shot Lianne a bright smile which Lianne didn't feel strong enough to acknowledge.

One of the maids returned and declared that the Aztec girl who did the ironing had scorched Lianne's best green silk. Instantly Josephine left the bedroom to examine the damage. Lianne sighed and lifted her gaze to the salmon-colored ceiling and watched the sunlight as it filtered through the windows. She attempted to count the tiny specks of dust dancing within the beam. But even this activity was too much for her. She would have turned her attention to the myriad of roses in crystal vases on every table in the room which Raoul had ordered cut from the garden, but was too listless to care.

What's wrong with me? she wondered. She was so tired lately, so unenthusiastic about everything. The miscarriage had occurred over two weeks ago, and she didn't feel any better. When Doctor Morales examined her a few days earlier, he said she'd soon regain her strength, that rest was needed. However, she didn't miss the worried look in his eyes. She hadn't seen the man since. Raoul told her she didn't need a doctor's care any longer, that Josephine could care for her as well as any physician. She must rest and not worry.

Lianne did worry. She worried about Daniel, but could barely summon the strength to even pen a note to him. Once she thought she had heard his voice coming from the hallway one night, but had been too tired to care if he had returned. She only remembered that when the sharp pains struck her in the church, he had been the one to grab her before she slid to the floor. He was the one who carried her to the coach and held her against him until they arrived home. Not Raoul. In her mind's eye she still saw the hatred shining on his dark face for Daniel, and in the warmth of the May morning, she shivered.

Maria returned and with her she held a silver tray. On the tray was Lianne's glass of orange juice.

"Here you are, *ma petite,*" Josephine sang out. "Drink this and you shall have strength."

Lianne wrinkled her nose. "No," she said weakly.

"You must drink. Shall I tell the señor that you don't wish to recover and go to San Augustin with him? He shall be much displeased."

Lianne didn't have the strength to argue with the woman. However, she knew the juice wouldn't make her feel any better, but worse. Every morning for almost two weeks she had drunk the orange juice which tasted bitter instead of sweet. Afterward, she would grow sleepier and more lethargic, but now Josephine insisted and helped raise her to a sitting position.

A knock sounded on the door just as Josephine positioned the glass to Lianne's mouth. "Who is it?" she called.

"Felix. I should like to see Dona Lianne," came the voice from the other side of the door.

Before Josephine could protest, Lianne reached weakly for her sleeve to get her attention. "Let him in."

"But you must drink your juice."

"Let him in," Lianne repeated.

Josephine sighed. "Very well, but not for long." She placed the glass on the table next to the bed and opened the door. Lianne waved her out of the room as Felix entered.

He entered hesitantly and shut the door. "I hope you're well, señora."

Lianne managed a weak smile. "I'll be all right."

Felix didn't think so. He thought she looked terrible, a pale shell of her former vibrant self. Her eyes were lackluster, her lips had no color, and her movements seemed heavy. She looked as his sister had looked after the woman took her baby, but Inez had said it was only the powder the woman had made her swallow for the pain.

She inclined her head a bit, and he understood she meant for him to sit in the chair alongside the bed. Before he sat he withdrew the hand he had hidden behind his back and presented a red rose to her. "I hope this brightens up your room," he said, intimidated by the perfumed beauty wafting from the vases surrounding them.

Lianne took it in her hand. "I shall treasure it, Felix."

"Does Don Raoul treat you well?"

Lianne nodded. "Most kind."

"I noticed Diego Gonzalez is around alot lately. I understand he plans to marry Señorita Carmen. This marriage must not happen."

"Why not?"

"Because Diego Gonzalez is the man who was with Don Raoul the night he raped my sister. Gonzalez is the one who threw me in my room like an animal. Señorita Carmen is not very kind to me, but she doesn't deserve such a fate as the wife of Diego Gonzalez. He'll abuse her."

Tears welled in Lianne's eyes. "I pity her, Felix, but you see how things are. I can't help her. Right now I'm so weak I can barely sit up."

"Forgive me," Felix said at once. His dark shaggy hair fell across his forehead. "I should not have bothered you." He spied the orange juice glass on the table and picked it up. "Drink this, señora. You shall be strong."

"No, Felix. It tastes bitter and never helps anyway."

Felix took a taste and made a face. The juice was bitter, not sweet like oranges at all. His eyes widened. With Lianne looking on, he walked to a potted plant and dumped the juice into the soil.

"Felix!" Lianne admonished him but her eyes sparkled at his daring.

The dark eyes which lighted upon her were serious. "Señora, when Josephine returns, pretend you have drunk the juice. Do not drink any more of this. It was drugged."

Suddenly Lianne understood why she hadn't sufficiently recovered. Josephine had drugged her every day for over two weeks. But why? Then the answer came to her. Raoul must have instigated this as a way of keeping her from Daniel.

"What am I to do?" she asked Felix.

"You must run away from here."

"I can't walk, much less run."

Felix nodded, considering. Then he said, "I shall get someone to help you. I shall find Señor Flanders. He has been here many times the last few days but always he is turned away by Diego or Don Raoul. The back of the house is even watched by extra men, so he can't possibly get past any of them. But never fear. I shall help you and before this day is over, you'll be in the arms of your beloved."

"No," Lianne said. "Please don't risk your safety for me, or Daniel. Raoul is a dangerous man."

"You don't need to tell me that, Dona Lianne. I was there the night he raped my sister and forced a child upon her. I must help you since I was unable to help her. *Adios,* señora. Until tonight."

He left the room just as Josephine returned. "I don't like that boy," she commented drily but smiled to see that Lianne had finished the juice.

Despite the fact that Lianne hadn't drunk the juice that morning, by late afternoon she still felt listless and woke with a start to realize that the sun had set. She stirred and sat up. Her fingers trembled as she righted the quilt over her and wondered how Daniel and Felix would free her from Raoul. Though she wished to leave, a sense of dread filled her. What would happen if Raoul stopped them before she escaped?

Almost as if sensing she thought about him, Raoul entered the bedroom. He approached her bed and smiled at her. The deepening shadows of the evening spilled forth, enclosing the room in gloom, but she saw the flash of his white teeth.

"I'm glad you're awake, *querida*. You sleep a great deal of the time lately."

"Yes, I do," she readily agreed. "I'd prefer not to be confined to this bed."

"I think in a few days you'll be well again," he

said pleasantly.

"Just in time for our trip to San Augustin de las Cuevas." She grit her teeth because she knew he drugged her to keep her under control until it was time to leave the city.

He studied her for a moment, a puzzled expression on his face. Finally he sat beside her on the bed and enfolded her hand in his. "I love you, Lianne. I hope you understand how much. I promise to be a good husband." He hesitated a moment and an emotion flitted across his face, a look of such pain she had never thought to see. In all the time we've been together you've never told me . . . you love me."

She sucked in her breath, unable to believe what she heard. How could such a worldly man as Raoul hope to gain her love, her affections, by kidnapping her from the man she loved, from the child she adored? Was he so unfeeling, or just used to having his way by whatever means? A part of her did feel something for him because, despite the absurd situation in which she found herself, Raoul had provided well for her. Yet she knew he was an evil man, although he could sometimes feel pity or love like other human beings. However, none of these qualities were enough to whitewash the vices . . . especially not the rape of Inez Martinez or the horrible feeling that he was somehow responsible for Elena's early death. But an inner voice warned her to be careful, to tread softly with Raoul. She mustn't unknowingly give away her hope that tonight she'd be free of him. He was a man who loved to play games and come out the winner. She decided for once to play along.

"I care very much for you," she said at last.

"That's not the answer I hoped for, Lianne, but if you had told me you were madly in love with me, I'd not have believed you." He sighed and stood up to light the candles in the room. The flickering light illumined the white of his shirt and emphasized the proud aristocratic profile. "At least you have grown to care for me. I suppose I'm grateful for that. But tell me why you haven't asked about Daniel these past few weeks?"

He turned to face her. The ominous black patch which hid his bad eye did little to ease the trembling that suddenly afflicted her. She hid her hands beneath the covers, not prepared for this question.

"I didn't know you expected me to ask about him, Raoul. To be honest I haven't thought about much at all since I lost our child."

"Do you love Daniel?"

"Shall I tell you the truth or a lie?" she inquired.

Raoul cocked an eyebrow. "The truth, by all means."

"A part of me will always love him. He is my child's father, but our love was doomed from the beginning. My place is here with you. I realize that now."

She scanned his face in the hope that he believed her. She must escape him tonight. She must!

Apparently he found her convincing, because he visibly relaxed. Sitting beside her again, he drew her into his arms and kissed her gently. When he released her lips, he said, "You've made me the happiest of men, *querida.*"

Her heart lurched. Raoul truly loved her and this surprised her. However, she knew she'd never be able to return the emotion. The quiet of the room, the intensity of Raoul's gaze upon her, washed over her but when a knock sounded on the door, she started.

"You're too nervous," Raoul noted and his voice rang out to admit entrance to Josephine. She announced the arrival of Diego for supper.

"Perhaps you should join us," he said to Lianne.

She paled and protested she didn't feel well enough to eat. Raoul frowned and as he left the room with Josephine she heard him say to the woman, "No more juice in the mornings.''

A sigh of satisfaction escaped from between Lianne's lips, and she settled back onto the pillows. So Raoul trusted her now. She almost hated having to betray his confidence in her, but eagerness to be free, to be reunited with Daniel filled her. No matter what Raoul conjured up for them, somehow they'd survive.

She listened to the noises drifting from the garden and heard only the sound of locusts, an occasional bark of a dog. In the dining room she discerned the laughter of Raoul and Diego. She grew nervous, and she had no idea what to expect. Should she dress? But she was still weak and doubted she'd be able to walk the short distance to the wardrobe.

Then she heard the crashing of glass and someone from the east wing of the house scream, ''Fire! Fire!'' Sounds of running feet filled her ears. Dear God, not a fire! she thought wildly and wondered how she'd escape. She heard Raoul's voice calling for water and urging the help to hurry, that the kitchen was in flames.

Lianne attempted to move off the bed. Perhaps if she made it to the open patio doors, she'd be safe outside. At that moment, Daniel bounded into the room. He was dressed in a black shirt, opened at the neck, with matching pants and boots.

''We don't have much time,'' he whispered and folded the blanket about her, then scooped her into his arms. ''The fire was a diversion to keep the guards at the back of the house busy. Felix waits on the street with the carriage. Are you strong enough to hold me around the neck?'' he asked, and she noted he looked worried.

''I'm always strong enough to hold you,'' she said and nipped his earlobe.

Daniel grinned. ''Plenty of time for that later, my love, but for now I'm kidnapping you.''

"How delicious," she mumbled and buried her head against his chest as he hurried from the house to the safety of the carriage.

Chapter 35

The garret room above the Academy of San Carlos was where Daniel brought Lianne. Felix quickly disappeared into the night with the carriage after they were inside the academy. But when Daniel had lit the candles on the table and she sat on the bed, a light tapping on the other side of the door jolted her. He smiled at her in an attempt to allay her fears and opened the door to Manuel Tolsa.

The tall Mexican stepped inside and he bowed to her, but Lianne sensed his tenseness by the hard set of the man's jaw.

"Everything went well, I gather," he said to Daniel.

"You see the results for yourself." Daniel grinned and took Lianne's hand.

Manuel nodded, but his eyes held no pleasure. "I think you must find another place to hide your lady, my friend. You may stay the night, but I can't risk de Lovis finding her here. The man contributes large sums of money to the academy and considers himself a collector of the arts. No matter what he has done, I cannot afford his ill will."

A vein throbbed in Daniel's temple. His face matched the black of his shirt, but he offered Manuel his hand. *"Gracias, amigo.* In the morning we shall be gone."

Manuel bowed and gallantly kissed Lianne's other hand. Then he left the room and they heard his footsteps fade away down the empty hallway.

"Where will we go?" she asked when Daniel didn't say anything.

He rubbed his chin in thought. "I'll find a place for us. Don't worry." His face brightened when he looked at her. With gentleness he touched her chin and brought her lips near his. Then he kissed her with such a tender warmth that she melted against him.

"Oh, Daniel," she breathed his name and wound her arms around his neck. "I can't believe we're together. I've missed you so much!"

"We'd have been together sooner except for that stinking bastard de Lovis! When I think of all he's put you through. And now to drug you." He held her face between his hands. "As soon as you're better, we're leaving Mexico for home."

This was what she wanted more than anything, but her delight was tempered with fear. "Raoul will find us. You have no idea how powerful he is, Daniel, or what he's capable of."

"I can guess," he said bitterly. "But we're not going to sneak away like thieves, Lianne. I took you from him to protect you, to help you recover. But when I know you're all right, we don't run away in the night. We leave in daylight and if the bastard thinks to stop us, I'll kill him or anyone he hires to do his dirty work."

She leaned against him, suddenly feeling drained. She liked the musky scent of him, the hardness of his chest against her soft cheek, the way his chest hairs tickled her soft lips. A pleasant tingling sensation started between her thighs, and when she lifted her eyes to his, she saw desire shadowed in them. But instead of fanning the flame between them, he put her away from him and ordered her to get under the covers.

"I want you fully recovered before we make love again, Lianne."

His concern touched her. She truly loved this man, loved him more than she ever thought it was possible to love another human being. For her, he put his life in jeopardy. Though he seemed not to be aware of this, she knew he had to know Raoul's reputation.

"Would you lie next to me?" she asked like a little girl. "I've missed you, *chérie.*"

The candlelight illumined the flash of a smile. She watched him undress completely, then blow out the candles and join her in bed. The long length of his naked body stretched next to hers which was clad in the thin nightgown. His arms pulled her toward him, holding her in the warmth of his love. Her satiny fingers stroked his naked forearms.

"I'll be well very soon," she whispered.

"I hope so, sweetheart, or we'll have to find a place by a cold mountain stream."

The next morning after an Aztec servant who could be trusted to remain quiet about the inhabitants of the garret room had brought them chocolate and boiled eggs for breakfast. Daniel insisted she stay in bed while he scoured the city for a place for them.

She clutched at his shirt front when he bent to kiss her goodbye. "Be careful. Raoul has spies everywhere."

"I'll take extra care, my love. You mustn't worry. No harm will come to me," he insisted. She had no other recourse but to believe him, and after he left, she grew bored lying in bed.

The bright rays of the sun shone through the high windows, and for the first time since the miscarriage, she felt well and strong enough to get out of bed on her own power. The drug, she realized, must have finally worn off. She shivered in dread to think how obsessed Raoul was with her. To drug her again for God's sake!

She wondered again about Elena. Had he killed the poor woman? Would he kill her, too, because she had left him? She didn't wish to think about him or what might happen if he found her, what he'd do to Daniel. She knew Daniel could hold his own with Raoul, but Raoul was such an insidious man, a person who could smile at his victim while someone like Diego knifed the victim from behind. All she wanted was to be totally free of Raoul de Lovis and return to Green Meadows with Daniel, to live life with their child. Was that so much to ask?

She moved about the room with small steps. On one side of the room she noticed dozens of canvases. Bending down to sort through them, she saw that every one of them was of her. She realized Daniel must have sketched the drawings at Green Meadows then painted them on the canvas later. Tears misted her eyes, because Daniel had painted her as a goddess, a woman of incredible beauty, an inner purity. Was this how he truly saw her? She felt sordid and dirty. Raoul had changed her opinion of herself in the last year, and she guessed that was part of the reason she wanted to protect Daniel. Not only from Raoul, but from the woman he had made her. She didn't feel worthy of Daniel's love, or of the way he steadfastly refused time and again to believe she didn't want him.

She wondered what would happen once they returned to Louisiana. Would Raoul follow and convince the authorities that she had murdered Phillipe and faked her own death? He was powerful enough and rich enough to arrange her execution. She shook her head. "No, I won't think about these things," she told herself and concentrated on the paintings.

She found a sketch book buried beneath an old shirt which Daniel wore while painting. Again, she felt surprise to discover that the sketches were of her and some of Désirée. But a hot flush stained her cheeks at one of them. "How dare he!" she breathed in indignation, but was secretly amused and flattered at a small sketch Daniel had done of her naked. She remembered a time when she and Daniel were together in the French Quarter house. They had just made love and to her aggravation, he began to sketch. She had asked to see what he was drawing, but he refused to show it to her. Now she knew why. What a devil he was!

She heard the rattle of the doorknob, and standing up, she waited with an amused smile on her lips, determined to pretend she was outraged at the sketch. However, when the door opened, Raoul stood in the doorway.

"So this is all your lover can offer you. I'm disappointed, *querida*. To think I have given you jewels, furs, and you prefer a humble artist's garret."

The room spun, and Lianne steadied herself against the table which was still littered with the breakfast dishes. Though Raoul smiled, she could tell he was angry. The black patch stood out against the sudden stark whiteness of his usually dark complexion.

"How did you find me?" she asked in a strong voice which surprised her.

He came into the room, filling it with his glittering black gaze. "Diego is an excellent spy, *querida*. He saw your lover dash into the carriage with you and followed you here. I was much disappointed to realize you didn't care for my hospitality, but I allowed you a night with your lover. See, I'm not such a monster. Am I?"

She suddenly had a mental image of Felix. "What about Felix?" she asked with dread in her voice.

"Ah, the *lepero*." Raoul put his thin forefinger to his lips. "He was in much pain for a while, but he will live. For the rest of his life, he'll work like a slave among the Indians at my silver mine in Pachuca. He was lucky I didn't kill him, but I know how fond you've grown of him.''

"I hate you!" Lianne spat.

Raoul shrugged in a dismissive gesture. "So? I'm used to that by now."

"I won't return with you. You can't force me to go back to the house with you."

"Lianne, you're my wife, and soon I want sons from you."

"And I want to be free of you! I want to marry Daniel. I love him."

He dashed toward her and towered over her like a dark crow. His fingers snaked around her upper arm and bruised her flesh. "I hear your words of love for Daniel in my sleep," he said. "And I am sick to death of them. You love him, well, show me how much you love him. Do you want him to live, Lianne? Do you want your Daniel to raise your child, to die an old man in his bed?"

"What are you saying?" she asked him but feared she knew the answer.

His grip tightened. "If you love him as much as you say, then you'll walk out of here with me. There will be no love notes of farewell, no parting tears. You simply come with me and leave Daniel to think what he likes. Otherwise, if you try to see him again, his life will be ended."

"You'll kill him as you did Elena?"

He raised an eyebrow. "Elena suffered a merciful end in comparison to what will happen to your Daniel. Believe me, Lianne," he hissed. "Your child will never see her father again."

Raoul knew all the right strings to pull. He knew she'd never resist if Daniel's life, her child's welfare, hung in the balance.

When he felt her go slack, he knew he had won. Without a word, he went to the doorway and snapped his fingers. Immediately Josephine appeared with one of Lianne's gowns under her arm. He took it from the woman and threw it at Lianne. The violet silk lay in a crumpled heap at her feet.

"Wear this and hurry about it!" he snapped. "The carriage waits outside for our trip to San Augustin de las Cuevas."

Daniel was wild, filled with an unbridled fury as he threw the contents of the room around, as if by disturbing the bedclothes, the furniture, the paintings, he could find Lianne hiding in a corner somewhere. He expected her to appear at any second. Hadn't he held her in his arms only hours earlier? Now, she was gone, plucked away from him by a monster as if she were a toy.

"I'm sorry, Daniel," Manuel Tolsa said and attempted to calm him with his soothing voice. "I couldn't refuse Don Raoul entrance. The man is too powerful to be turned away."

"You mean you didn't want to lose his patronage or the money which fills the academy's coffers." Daniel's eyes blazed like blue flames.

Manuel sighed and positioned himself in the doorway. "I admit the truth, Daniel. De Lovis contributes much to the academy. I'm as mercenary as anyone else. But the woman you love is the wife of Raoul de Lovis. Admit to yourself you've lost her. She can never belong to you."

Daniel threw a canvas he held against the wall instead of at Manuel whom he felt was responsible for allowing Raoul to saunter into the academy and steal Lianne away. The man had given him his word that Lianne would be safe. He had trusted him, leaving her in his care while he sought a place for them to stay until she recovered her strength. Just an hour ago he had made arrangements to rent a house on the outskirts of the city. But nothing mattered now. Lianne was gone.

"She may be his wife," Daniel told Manuel, his

face contorted in pain, "but she loves me."

"Be that as it may, de Lovis will never set her free. I am your friend, whether you think it or not, and as your friend, I warn you to leave Mexico and forget this woman."

Daniel managed a small smile. Manuel didn't know him at all or recognize the stubborn set of his jaw which clearly indicated his Irish heritage. At that moment he realized he was a lot like his father. He'd never give up his dream of Lianne, as his father had never given up the dream of acquiring the Flannery estates from the English. At that moment he understood his father better, and his brother. Sometimes you had to be like the proverbial dog who fastened his teeth around a bone, he thought.

Daniel raked his hands through the thick blackness of his hair. "Do you know where they went?" he asked Manuel.

"*Sí*, but I don't wish you any harm, Daniel."

"Tell me!" Daniel barked.

"San Augustin de las Cuevas. I heard de Lovis mention this to your lady as I waited in the shadows on the stairs." Manuel pointed to the stairway near the door. "I didn't desert her, as you think. I was watching in case there be need to protect her from bodily harm."

"Thank you for your concern," Daniel said and immediately began to throw some clothes into a valise.

"I gather you are on your way to San Augustin de las Cuevas."

"That's right, my friend. *Adios.*" Daniel buckled the valise and without a further word to Manuel, he pushed past him and was gone.

Chapter 36

The May afternoon was warm. Daniel, however, had ceased to feel the sun's hot rays on his back or even care how demonic he appeared to other travelers on the road out of Mexico City, which led to San Augustin de las Cuevas. He had removed his jacket and rolled up his shirtsleeves. The jacket hung carelessly across his saddle, and as he urged the black stallion toward his destination, he was unaware how his forehead creased into a frown or that his eyes looked blue-black. Rage filled him, and he was determined to take Lianne from Raoul. Even if it meant endangering his life to do it.

He knew all about the unsavory stories which circulated throughout Spain about Raoul. He'd heard them many times while he was in Madrid, but Raoul had never been called to task because he was powerful and capable of silencing his enemies. Then in Louisiana, Raoul received the same treatment. Money, it seemed, could buy anything. Even the authorities' silence about faking Lianne's death. Here, in Mexico, however, Raoul was in his element. He had been born here, and, Daniel knew, was regarded with the same awe as the viceroy. He wondered if there was no end to Raoul's power, to the fear he could strike within people's hearts. But Raoul didn't frighten him and never had. Yet Lianne feared him, or something he was capable of doing. He reasoned that she had never left the garret room willingly with Raoul. She loved him, Daniel, and this was the only reason he rode after her. If there had been any hesitancy on her part after he took her from Raoul's house, he would have left her to him. But he knew differently. She loved him, and soon they'd be together.

Yet he must tread carefully, because Raoul was a man to be reckoned with.

Ahead of him was a carriage, a rather garish-looking black one with gold trim. He paid no attention to it as he rode past. His eyes were on the distant slopes of the two volcanoes Popocatépetl and Iztaccihuatl which rose mistily before him. He knew San Augustin de las Cuevas was not far off.

He rode past a carriage and heard his name—a white, lacy handkerchief beckoned from the carriage window. Then he saw the beautiful face with the black eyes, the full-lipped, sensual red mouth which turned upward in an inviting smile.

"Daniel, Daniel," Isabelle Hidalgo called until he cantered toward the carriage. The driver halted, and when Daniel stopped beside the carriage, Isabelle laughed.

"I'm so happy to see you," she said huskily. "Are you going to San Augustin, too?"

She extended a gloved hand to him through the window. Daniel took it and kissed it.

"Yes, I hear there will be quite a crowd this year. I thought I would play a game of cards or view the cockfighting."

"Ah, *sí*. The cocks. Raoul de Lovis will probably enter one of his. He bets quite heavily, I think. Of course he hasn't entered in years because he was in Madrid, but he will win. Raoul always does."

The casual mention of Raoul by Isabelle grated on him, but he hid his aggravation with a disarming smile.

"Please ride with me, Daniel," Isabelle invited prettily.

Daniel tied his horse to the back of the carriage and got in beside her. The heady fragrance of her perfume filled the small space of the coach. She leaned suggestively toward him and tucked her arm through his. She wore a gown of gold silk with a froth of white lace at the bodice which did nothing to conceal the lushness of her breasts.

"I've been quite upset with you," she said and gave a fake pout. "You haven't seen me in some time."

"I've been busy," he said evenly, aware that her thigh pressed against his.

"With the ladies?"

"Perhaps."

"One lady in particular?"

"You ask too many questions, Isabelle."

"I understand Raoul married his French whore. Could she be the reason you've neglected me?"

His eyes narrowed as he took in her cunning smile. When he didn't reply, she sighed and leaned closer, placing her dark head on his shoulder. "Well, it doesn't matter any longer, Daniel. She is Raoul's wife and belongs to him." Her fingers stroked the hard lines of his muscled arm. "Now you can concentrate on me. You may stay with me if Señor Guerrero has no more rooms."

She smiled up at him, her mouth ready and willing to be kissed. But he resisted. He found Isabelle attractive and knew she wouldn't mind if he made love to her in the carriage. What a pleasant way to spend the remainder of the journey. But he didn't want her. He wanted a woman with red-gold hair and eyes as green as sea foam. He wanted Lianne, and Isabelle just wouldn't do.

He settled back against the cushions and closed his eyes, pretending to nap. He heard Isabelle extinguish a sigh, then her husky whisper. "One day you'll want me, Daniel. You shall want me bad."

* * *

Josephine finished putting Lianne's gowns in the wardrobe and turned to Lianne who sat on a stool near the dressing table.

"Mooning about never helped anything, *chérie*. Put the Irishman from your mind and concentrate on your husband. Now there is a man for you." Josephine winked.

"You would think that!" Lianne said, her head flying upward and the green eyes glinting in the candlelit room. "A person who would willingly drug another in the name of duty to her employer, I care nothing for her comments. And you haven't any idea how Raoul truly treats me. I thought you were my friend. I see I was mistaken."

Josephine stood with arms akimbo before Lianne. "I think you should learn that sometimes a person has no choice but to play the game, or pretend to. I didn't enjoy forcing the juice down your throat each day, but Don Raoul insisted you be kept calm. I'd lose my position, otherwise, and I've gone hungry some in my time. I don't wish to feel the rumbling in my belly again, *chérie*."

Lianne refused to break eye contact with Josephine. "I hold you in as much contempt as Raoul."

"Well," Josephine said, shrugging, "I can't change your opinion, but I won't allow you to hurt Don Raoul after he has treated me with courtesy. He has many faults, but he's the only person to treat me with respect." She picked up a hairbrush. "Now, let's fix your hair for tonight."

"Get out of here! I don't want you to touch me."

"Tsk, tsk. Don Raoul will be much upset. He expects you to join him downstairs with Señor Guerrero and his guests."

"No! Get out!" Lianne, in an unaccustomed gesture, raised her hand to strike Josephine's face, but the woman backed away and threw down the brush on the carpeted floor.

"I shall tell Don Raoul!"

"Do that!"

When the door slammed behind Josephine, Lianne sank onto the carpet. She felt weak, unbearably tired, but her heart ached with such wrenching pain she wished to die. Would she ever see Daniel again? Would he realize that she hadn't left of her own free will, that she left only to save his life? But she knew he couldn't ever know these things. Raoul wouldn't give her the opportunity to tell Daniel.

Again, Raoul had made certain their accommodations were luxurious. Señor Guerrero was a well known banker, a man of great wealth and known for his hospitality. The large house in which she now stayed was his and was the grandest in San Augustin de las Cuevas. From the open doorway on the second floor which led to a small stairway at the back of the house, she smelled the sweet aromas of roses and jasmine in the garden below. She had barely glanced at the view from the French doors, but now she rose and stood within the door frame. In the misty twilight she barely made out the shapes of the mountains of Popocatépetl and Iztacchihuatl. Vaguely she remembered seeing their immense beauty when they neared San Augustin and recalled the silver popular trees which shaded the roads. So much beauty surrounded her. Raoul always saw to that, but the beauty of the area, the jewels, the fine houses, the clothes, couldn't drive away his ugliness of spirit.

She was trapped. Trapped! Would she never be free of him, free to marry Daniel? The baby had been the only reason she married Raoul. Now her baby was gone. Nothing bound her to him, but she knew he'd never release her. Sometimes she felt that there were invisible shackles around her wrists and that Raoul had swallowed the key.

A knock sounded on the door.

"I told you to leave me alone!" Lianne cried.

"It's Carmen," came the small voice on the other

side.

Lianne called to her to enter. Carmen peered cautiously in, then pushed her whole body through the doorway. "I don't wish to disturb you," she said.

Lianne put a hand to her forehead and smiled. "No, you don't disturb me." Lianne realized how pale Carmen looked, how her large, dark eyes seemed bigger in her round face. She wore her dark hair in a braid wrapped around the top of her head, and her dress was a blue taffeta with a white ruffle at the neckline and the wrists. The girl looked charming and very pretty but it was evident to Lianne that she was worried.

"I need to talk to you about . . . something."

"I'm listening." Lianne motioned her to a spot on the bed. Carmen sat and Lianne sat beside her.

Carmen lowered her eyes a moment then lifted them shyly. "If my mother was alive I'd speak to her about this. I could tell her anything, and no matter how stupid she thought me, she never said so. Not like my father. He thinks I'm very stupid, only needed to make a good marriage and to bear children. My marriage to Diego is within a few weeks. I am afraid, Lianne." Carmen swallowed. "Diego is not a patient man, I fear. I sense his cruelty. What will happen to me if . . . if I displease him?"

Lianne's heart went out to the motherless young girl. She understood Carmen's fears, because she had suffered from them every day since Raoul wrenched her from Daniel and her child. She couldn't advise Carmen to pretend indifference to Diego. She feared indifference might do more harm than good. So, she smiled and held the girl's hand, and said, "If I were you I'd not worry about Diego hurting you. He won't. Raoul is your father and though Diego thinks he can control you and do whatever he wishes, he can't. Your father won't allow Diego to lay a hand on you. You must submit because he will be your husband, but Diego won't do any more than what any husband expects as his due. But if Diego does harm, you, come to me. I will see to it that your father is made aware of your treatment.''

''I doubt if Father would even care,'' Carmen said shakily.

Lianne knew this to be true, but she'd never tell the girl this. However, she also knew that she could have Diego punished if he abused Carmen. All she had to do was use her wiles on her husband, to charm him with her beauty. This was something she had never done, but now she saw the advantage. And if she played the game well, she might become the winner in the end.

''He cares a great deal,'' Lianne told her.

Carmen squeezed her hand then released it and stood up but a shadow crossed her face. ''You heard what happened to Felix.''

Lianne remembered he was forced into servitude in Pachuca. ''Yes.''

''He tried to help you escape from my father, Lianne. Felix will spend his life in the mines; he'll die in the mines.''

''Don't remind me, Carmen. I feel badly enough about his fate.''

''I know you do,'' Carmen agreed, ''but don't try to escape again. Next time my father may not be so generous.''

Lianne winced though Carmen didn't say this to be nasty. She was stating a fact. After Carmen left, Lianne stared at her reflection in the mirror. Despite the miscarriage and the drug she had been forced to take each morning, she didn't look any worse for her suffering. The violet dress she wore enhanced her beauty, the color of her hair, the porcelain quality of her skin. She was a desirable woman, a woman Raoul de Lovis had wanted so much that he might have ordered Elena's death to marry her.

For the first time she realized the power she wielded over Raoul. If she went along with him, pretended she was happy, she might deceive him, lull him into a false sense of security. Then she could escape to Daniel and return to Green Meadows.

She turned from the mirror and went to the wardrobe and extracted a gown made from the thinnest of materials. Its ivory sheen glimmered in the flickering light; the gold coronet she pulled from the jewelry box highlighted her shining tresses.

She'd dress and go downstairs, surprise Raoul. Let him wonder what she was up to, let him wonder if she was up to anything.

"Well, *querida,* you are enchanting." Raoul met her at the foot of the stairs leading into the vestibule. He took her hand and smiled a smile which reached the fathomless depths of his eye.

Lianne heard the sweet straining notes of a violin as they drifted from the open patio where Señor Guerrero's guests were assembled. She suppressed a tremor when Raoul touched her, taking her hand and twining it around his arm. "You are tired?" he commented, noting her still pale complexion.

"A bit."

"Tomorrow we shall let the Mexican sun paint your face with its warmth."

Raoul's allusion reminded her of Daniel and she mentally braced herself. Was he sparring with her, trying to get a rise out of her? Well, she wouldn't let him see how much she hated him, and refused to allow him the privilege of reading her thoughts.

"That would be very nice," she said and gave him a dazzling smile. His eyebrow rose a fraction of an inch. He led her onto the patio where flickering lanterns illuminated the bright decorations which hung above their heads like sunbursts. The cream-colored walls and pillars were swathed in garlands of flowers, laced through with red berries.

Couples swayed to the music, but beneath the whining of the violin could be heard the undertone of voices coming from the nearby *sala* where guests

played card games. Señor Guerrero spotted them and
came forward, and kissed Lianne's hand.

"How beautiful you are, Dona Lianne." His
small, fat jovial face beamed. "I'm so very pleased to
have you and your husband as my guests." He waved
a plump hand and gestured about him. "As you see, I
have a great many guests. I love people around me.
Since my Carlotta passed away, life is very lonely.
Perhaps you'd please an old man and sing for my
friends later this evening. I heard you sing in Mexico
City and was so moved by the beauty of your voice,
you brought tears to my eyes."

"My wife no longer performs," Raoul interjected
before Lianne had a chance to respond.

She gritted her teeth. How dare he determine
whether she would sing or not! She liked Señor
Guerrero and realized his compliment was given from
the heart. She would not disappoint him.

"I would be delighted to sing for you, señor," she
said.

"*Gracias,* Dona Lianne. *Gracias.*" He kissed
her hand anew, then left, seemingly much pleased.

Raoul's mouth tightened. "Elena was an obedient
wife. Never would she have disobeyed me, as you have
just done."

"If you were so fond of Elena, Raoul, you should
not have murdered her." Lianne fluttered her fan and
moved on, aware that his eyes shot daggers, but as a
man bedazzled by her beauty, he followed her.

Lianne moved through the seductive swaying of
the dancers, drawn to the voices in the *sala*. A
mahogany card table had been placed in the center of
the room. A crowd of people surrounded it, many of
them men, but some women. Their cigar smoke curled
and drifted upward to the beamed ceiling, and Lianne
felt surprise to observe a large Mexican woman
smoking a cigar. When she drew closer she realized the
woman was the dealer.

Her fat fingers laid out three cards, face downward, on the table. She spoke to a person on the other side of the table whom Lianne couldn't see.

"Señor, take your pick," the woman said, her hands fluttering over the cards. "Choose the red queen."

At that point some people moved away and gave Lianne an unobstructed view of the two people who sat opposite the woman. She stood still, and her mouth fell open. Daniel lounged in a chair, Isabelle Hidalgo sat next to him, or almost on top of him. Their bodies were so close Lianne couldn't determine where the buff-colored jacket he wore began and Isabelle's naked arm ended.

Isabelle's long, thin finger pointed to one of the cards. "Choose that one, Daniel. That is the red queen."

He smiled at her. "Are you sure? I've bet the bank quite a bit of money."

"*Sí*, I am sure," she said and pressed her red silk bodice against his arm.

He nodded at the Mexican woman. "The third card," he said, indicating the one which Isabelle had pointed out to him.

The woman smiled and turned the card upward. It was the red queen. Isabelle shrieked her delight and threw her arms around Daniel. "I've won for you again!"

Daniel laughed and began to collect his winnings, but he glanced up and saw Lianne with a menacing Raoul behind her.

He inclined his head. "Don Raoul and Dona Lianne. What a pleasant surprise." Gallantly Daniel stood and surprised both Raoul and Lianne by reaching for her hand and kissing the palm. His lips seared her flesh, and she wanted to throw herself into his arms, to beg him to take her away with him. But she couldn't. Not now. She must be careful, mustn't move too quickly. However, she vowed she'd tell Daniel what had happened at the academy and warn him to be careful.

Then they'd somehow escape Raoul and find happiness together. They just had to.

Though she thought he should pretend indifference, she saw the glow of love in Daniel's eyes and grew fearful when Raoul moved forward and clutched her arm.

"I didn't think you'd be inclined to visit San Augustin de las Cuevas, Daniel. There's nothing here of interest to you." Raoul scowled and threw Isabelle a black look.

"Raoul, you know I love to gamble, appreciate fine liquor and beautiful women." Daniel reached for Isabelle but his eyes were on Lianne.

She wished he wouldn't look at her like that. A tremor, mixed with fear and desire, ran through her. She felt Raoul stiffen next to her, then he bowed very formally. "We shall retire for the night. Good evening."

"I should like to retire, too, Daniel." Isabelle's hands moved sensuously across the front of Daniel's chest. The woman couldn't have been more obvious in her desire for Daniel, and Lianne silently fumed.

"What an intriguing idea, Isabelle, but we must persuade Don Raoul and his bride to join us in a glass of wine. We must drink to their marriage."

Lianne interpreted this remark as a way of keeping her from Raoul for as long as possible. He did love her and must have an inkling of what had happened.

"I want no toast of congratulations from you!" Raoul's bitter voice echoed across the *sala*. People stopped chatting and looked curiously at him. When he was aware he had drawn attention to himself, he bowed and managed a tight smile. "Some other time."

He started to drag Lianne away, but she caught the eye of Señor Guerrero. Seeing that Raoul was leaving, the man waddled over to them.

"Please, señora, a song to warm my old heart." Lianne felt Raoul's hand tighten on her arm, but she wasn't going to disappoint Señor Guerrero, no matter what Raoul threatened later.

"I would be most happy to sing, señor," she said and managed to disengage herself from her husband. As she walked toward a small stage in the courtyard, Daniel winked at her.

The violins began to play and she sang a folk song in Spanish. It was a song about a hopeless love, but a love which would endure throughout eternity. However, as she sang it, her eyes lighting upon Daniel, she didn't feel hopeless. Love surged through her and she sang for him. It didn't matter that Isabelle hung on to him tighter than a leech. Daniel loved her, and she loved him. Somehow this bond of love, of trust, would bring them together forever.

When she finished, the applause deafened her. Shouts of "La Flamenca" filled the courtyard and the people wouldn't let her leave. She noticed the hardness of Raoul's face but didn't care if he was aggravated. She wanted to sing and realized she had missed this aspect of her life. The only person who mattered at the moment was Daniel, and time seemed suspended as she lifted her voice again in a haunting melody. She imagined she sang only for him, that they were alone. But too quickly the song ended, and she was thrust back to reality.

No sooner had she finished and accepted a small bouquet of roses from Señor Guerrero, than Raoul pressed an iron grip around her wrist and practically pulled her through the crowd, but Daniel halted them.

"Leaving so soon?"

"*Sí*, you slimy snake," Raoul hissed. "I'm taking my wife to our room, our bed. You cannot best me, Daniel, so do not try."

"If that is the case, then why are you so upset?" Daniel asked calmly. "You were the one who took her from my room. You're her husband. Why do you fear me so, Raoul, if you know I can't best you."

"Are you challenging me?"

"Yes. You decide the sport."

"Ah, you think to duel with me, Daniel, and make Lianne a widow. No, that isn't what I have in mind."

"Raoul, please . . ." Lianne broke in, not liking the way Raoul's glance viciously raked across Daniel.

"Quiet!" he ordered, then turned his full attention upon Daniel, not noticing Isabelle beside him. "Tomorrow there is a cockfight. I've entered my prize cock, El Diablo, against El Tigre, who belongs to Señor Guerrero. Let the outcome decide which one of us is the winner."

"What is the stake?" Daniel asked.

Raoul smirked. "My wife, of course."

With that comment, he turned and dragged Lianne from the patio and up the stairs to their room.

"How could you do such an unspeakable thing to me?" she demanded when he released her and slammed the door shut. She massaged her sore wrist.

Raoul looked surprised. "I thought you wanted Daniel, desired him, *querida*. You should be pleased Perhaps he will win." He went to the sideboard and poured himself a glass of tequila. He raised it to her in a toast. "To you, Lianne. A woman who inflames a man's senses, but a woman who'll never attain her heart's desire."

"What do you intend to do to Daniel?"

"Why nothing, *querida*. The cockfight will determine the outcome, but El Tigre won't win. I shall make certain that Señor Guerrero sees to it that his prize cock will lose. Remember how awful you felt after the miscarriage, how nasty your juice tasted. Well, the cock will also be unwell."

"You filthy bastard!" Lianne leapt from her place in the center of the room and clawed at Raoul's face.

He grabbed her hand, wrenching it back. A thin streak of blood ran down his cheek. "How well I remember the hellcat! Madrid should have taught me something about you, Lianne, but I love you, whether you know it or not. Daniel won't win tomorrow even if El Tigre doesn't lose. I own you, body and soul. If you love Daniel, don't force me to take drastic measures against him, because I could have done so by now. Only because you love him, because he is your child's father, have I resisted."

He dropped her arm then went to the door and called for Josephine who stayed in the next room. "See that the señora is put to bed," he instructed her. "Also, she is not to leave the room tonight or tomorrow, not until the cockfight."

"I won't stay locked in here!" she protested. "I'll get away somehow."

Raoul shrugged. "Suit yourself. Only Diego will wait in the garden below. I don't think you'd like to come up against Diego. He can be very nasty."

He left the room with that ominous threat.

"What have you done now?" Josephine asked.

"Be quiet!" Lianne cried and flung herself on the bed.

Chapter 37

Daniel wasn't the least surprised to notice Raoul as he left Señor Guerrero's library. It was as he suspected. Raoul had paid the man a visit, probably to discuss the cockfight the next afternoon. And knowing the working of Raoul's mind as he did by now, this nocturnal visit wasn't unexpected.

Daniel waited in the *sala,* ignored by the servants. He sat in the shadows of the room, his large frame lounging lazily in a highbacked chair until he heard Raoul's confident voice bidding Señor Guerrero a good night. When Raoul's footsteps grew faint, he got up and tapped on the library door.

Señor Guerrero bade him to enter. He closed the door silently behind him as the older man looked up.

"Ah, Señor Flanders. Not an unexpected visit."

"Well?" Daniel asked.

Guerrero nodded and offered Daniel a cigar. "It was as you said, señor. De Lovis has just left. He requested at first that I sell him El Tigre. When I refused, he demanded I bow to his wishes and give the bird a drop of this powder." He picked up a yellow vial and handed it to Daniel.

"What was your answer to him?" Daniel lit and puffed on the cigar.

Guerrero grinned. "I told him I would, but I didn't tell him that I had already sold El Tigre to you.

You're quite an astute young man. Not many people are able to decipher de Lovis' moves."

Daniel grinned in reply. "I'm indebted to you for selling me the bird. I know how fond you are of El Tigre. But I promise you that when the fight is over, I shall return him to you."

Guerrero was surprised. Clearly he hadn't expected the return of his bird. "Señor, that is most kind . . ."

"Think nothing of it. I'll even give you back your money. El Tigre will win the fight, I'm certain."

"*Sí*, El Tigre never loses. But the stakes between you and de Lovis must be very high for you to go to such trouble and expense."

Daniel extinguished the cigar in an ashtray and smiled at Guerrero. "What I do, señor, is done for love. Only love."

"El Tigre will win, never fear. I can't wait to see Raoul's face when he discovers that you now own the cock. He once took liberties with my late wife who was quite young and pretty. I'm only too glad to oblige you, Señor Flanders."

Again, Daniel thanked Señor Guerrero, and when he left the library he was filled with plans. He'd win the cockfight, and he'd win Lianne. No matter what Raoul was, he would keep his word about the bet. It was only the gentlemanly thing to do. However, Daniel suspected that Raoul would attempt to keep Lianne while making it seem that he was freeing her. He must be careful.

When he entered his room, he discovered a luscious Isabelle reclining on his bed. All she wore was a sheet, and her long dark hair cascaded around her shoulders.

She smiled invitingly. "I wondered if you'd ever come to bed tonight, Daniel." Her voice was a purr. He felt an ache in his loins, but he didn't want Isabelle.

"Need I remind you that your room is down the

hall?''

"But this is where I choose to sleep."

He pulled off his jacket and began to undress. "Suit yourself," he said and climbed into the bed.

Isabelle snuggled against him, not sure how to take his last remark. She nibbled at his ear, but Daniel lay there with his eyes closed. What is wrong with him, she wondered. She knew he was all male. In Madrid his sexual prowess had nearly worn her out.

"Daniel?"

"Hmm."

"I want you to make love to me."

Slowly he opened his eyelids until his ocean gray eyes were visible.

"Is that a command?"

Isabelle blanched at the amusement she heard in his voice. Could it be he thought her a foolish woman, a woman who was only good for one thing? Anger boiled in her. She wouldn't allow Daniel Flanders to ignore her.

"*Sí*," she spat. "I want you to love me."

"Isabelle," Daniel said, growing tired of her, "your poor dead Franco may have serviced you upon demand, and I suspect too much of you may have been the cause of his death, but don't think you can order me to perform stud service. I don't want you tonight. Now be a good girl and go back to your room. I'm tired."

"Tired, is it?" Her black eyes snapped. "You'd not be too tired if Raoul's *puta* was beside you. You want her, but let me tell you this, Raoul will not give her up to you. This silly bet you made with him, how stupid. Your Lianne wants to be with him, and you better accept this."

Daniel threw back the covers, and in one swift move, he hoisted Isabelle over his shoulder and got out of bed. He pulled open the door and tossed her casually onto the hall floor. He pointed down the hall.

"Your room is down there. Or perhaps another gentleman will appreciate your company for tonight. Knock on some doors and find out."

Then he shut the door in her shocked face.

Chapter 38

The huge clock in the hallway had just chimed two when Raoul offered Lianne his arm. "Shall we go?" he said, his eyes sweeping over the vision she made in a white skirt with peasant top, embroidered at the neckline and hem with bright flowers. Her long hair was pulled up on one side with a white rose he had plucked from Señor Guerrero's garden that morning. Her green eyes flashed like twin emeralds. A ripple of amusement coursed through him. How she hated him!

"You can't make me watch, Raoul. I refuse to watch those cocks fight. It repulses me as much as this bet you and Daniel made. I'm not a piece of property to be disposed of. I am your wife." She stood apart from him, not giving him her hand. Her hatred of him wasn't easy to conceal and she knew he read it on her face easily.

"You should have remembered that when Daniel took you from our home. As I recall you weren't too eager to return when I arrived to claim you. My wife? Our marriage is a sham. I know you don't love me."

"Then let me go. Divorce me," she said quietly.

He shook his head. "No, *querida*. You belong to me and only death can separate us."

A chill passed over her. How far would Raoul really go to keep her? If she left him would he carry out his threat against Daniel? Of course, he would, she told herself and allowed him to take her hand. He killed Elena. "Then you don't intend to honor the bet if Daniel wins."

"But of course I do, *querida*. I am a man of honor and to renege on a bet is unthinkable." He smiled down into her puzzled face. "However, you mustn't get up your hopes of belonging to Daniel Flanders permanently. I won't allow it."

She didn't understand him, couldn't fathom him at all. Raoul had a plan to destroy any crumbs of happiness fate might throw her way.

When they left their room and walked to the sheltered area which Señor Guerrero had set up as a cockpit away from the main house, Diego hailed him. He sauntered toward them looking more than ever like a small monkey in his dark jacket, but his face was bright.

"Carmen sends her regrets," Raoul told him. "The sun disagrees with her, and her delicate constitution abhors violence."

"Too bad." But Diego didn't look the least upset as his eyes rested on Lianne and the lush picture she made. His gaze drifted slowly back to Raoul and he rubbed his hands together. "El Diablo is in rare form. There shall be much blood this afternoon."

"*Bueno*. The handler has prepared him well."

"You both disgust me!" Lianne cried.

Raoul didn't suppress a laugh. "My dove, you must understand the game. The cocks are bred to fight. If they don't fight, they're killed. A rooster can only service so many hens. A farm can have only so many roosters. The remainder must fight if they wish to live. It is their fate. The birds wish this, otherwise, they'd not attack so viciously." He tipped her chin and looked into her fiery eyes. "Only the strong survive, Lianne."

Raoul made the sport seem so sensible, and when they stopped at the cockpit she felt little shock to see finely dressed gentlemen and their ladies gathered around the small arena where the fight would commence.

Her eyes instinctively moved to Daniel's towering frame. She had expected to see Isabelle Hidalgo at his side, but she noticed the woman was standing next to an elderly man who appeared much taken with her.

Daniel inclined his head and approached them. "Betting fever runs high today," he said smoothly.

Raoul gave him a tight smile. "Certainly. El Diablo is a winner, and the populace loves to win."

"Ah, Raoul, how true. El Diablo is a fine bird. He is strong and proud as his owner. I wonder how he'll feel when El Tigre wins the match."

"El Tigre shall not win, Daniel. El Diablo will be proud, I shall be proud, when his opponent lies dead in the arena."

"So sure of yourself, de Lovis," Daniel said and flashed a grin.

"I am a man who knows the outcome, who has great confidence in El Diablo."

"Good. You'll need it. Here." Daniel reached into his pocket and tossed a small yellow vial to Raoul. "I hope you can still smile after the match. I bought El Tigre from Señor Guerrero. I don't believe I'll have use for this."

"Bastard!" Raoul hissed and gripped the vial with tight fingers.

"You look quite pale," Lianne commented, knowing that whatever was in the vial had somehow been meant to ruin Daniel's chances. She couldn't suppress the smirk which hovered around her lips.

Raoul nodded his head at familiar faces in the crowd, and Lianne felt the tight pressure on her arm increase as they took their places. She couldn't help but notice the contrast between Raoul and Daniel. Raoul looked concerned though he attempted to hide it with a bravado she imagined he didn't feel. Daniel, however, looked quite merry with twinkling gray eyes which warmed her.

The startling contrast between the men was mirrored in their respective birds. The short, fat Mexican with the solemn face who served as El Diablo's handler came forward. One glance told Lianne why the bird was so named. He was a huge, black cock with eyes full of black fire. She shivered because he seemed to resemble Raoul. El Tigre was a russet red with gray spots, not an overlarge bird. In fact he looked rather thin, but she heard someone in the crowd say that El Tigre was very fast despite his build.

The two handlers held their birds against them, and Lianne saw that long steel-pointed gaffs were attached to their natural spurs. The birds seemed eager to be let loose, but it wasn't until Señor Guerrero appeared and motioned to another man who served as the referee to begin the event that they were dropped onto the dirt floor in the middle of the pit.

The moment the birds landed, the refined, well-dressed men in the audience went wild. Their mood changed from civility to murder. Lianne saw the hot, fierce fire in their eyes and heard their voices raised in betting. When El Diablo rushed for El Tigre new bets were made. When El Tigre countered, the bets were in his favor.

There was a wild collision of feathers, beaks and claws. A thin mist of spraying blood streaked the air. Lianne felt sick to her stomach. Some of the women left the pit to escape the blood-drenched atmosphere. She moved to join them, but Raoul halted her with a firm hand on her arm.

"The game isn't over, *querida*. Do you leave because your lover's bird is losing?"

Lianne hadn't realized that El Tigre was losing. In fact she didn't care. The sight of the poor creatures sickened her. All she wanted was to escape this brutal scene.

"I feel sick, Raoul."

"Stay," he said in a demanding tone. "Stay and see your lover in defeat."

Lianne couldn't help but think how strange Raoul was. It didn't matter to her if Daniel won or lost. She'd love him anyway. Apparently winning mattered a great deal to Raoul and to Daniel. She watched as Daniel became as immersed in the event as everyone else, saw the bloodlust in his eyes.

A huge shout went up as El Tigre flew at El Diablo. His gaffs pierced the ebony bird's head before they separated. Blood trickled down the bird's beak and his head tilted to the right. He tripped, almost as if he were drunk, and kicked out, flapping his wings in wild abandon.

"El Diablo has been brained," Lianne heard Diego say worriedly to Raoul.

"The bird won't die if his brain is hit," Raoul said calmly, but he didn't look as confident as he sounded. "El Diablo may not feel the injury for hours."

"But if he is injured again, Raoul, El Diablo will die. You'll lose the match."

Raoul looked hard at Diego. "Raoul de Lovis never loses."

At that moment Lianne's attention was drawn to the ring. She watched in fascinated horror as El Tigre took advantage of his opponent's disorientation. He drove the three inch gaff attached to his left heel straight into the stomach of El Diablo. Blood spewed everywhere. Women screamed and moved out of the way. Daubs of bright crimson stained the front of Lianne's dress. As far as she was concerned the match was over. She didn't care what Raoul thought or said. She picked up her skirts and fled through the arches of the shelter to the bright clear air, away from the wild cheers of the crowd.

Taking deep drafts of air, she calmed herself, but she'd never forget the awful spectacle of two animals as they fought to the death. How barbaric it was! She felt sick because of what she had witnessed but also because of the way Daniel had participated. She'd never known he possessed a dark side, then the thought struck her that perhaps he loved her so much, he'd do anything to have her. But she knew it wouldn't matter that Daniel had won the match. Raoul didn't intend to free her.

"So you think you have won!"

Lianne turned at the venomous sound of Isabelle Hidalgo's voice. The woman glared at her from hard eyes. The bright orange of her dress enhanced the color of her cheeks.

"Go away." Lianne didn't wish to confront the woman. The afternoon had been too much for her, and she guessed her day would worsen once Raoul found her.

"Puta, how dare you tell me to go away! I am Isabelle Hidalgo, wife of one of the wealthiest men in Madrid. You are nothing but an opera singer!"

Lianne nearly laughed. She made it sound so vile. "Your husband is dead. I've heard what a merry chase you gave the poor man."

"Franco loved me." Isabelle actually pouted for a second, then her face twisted in a sneer. "You were Raoul's whore before he married you, and your ways have not changed. You want Daniel now, but you can't have him. He is mine! I'll never give him up."

"What if he doesn't want you?" Lianne said and smiled pityingly. "He's told me more than once that you were only a diversion."

Isabelle screeched, and Lianne would have been the victim of red clawlike fingernails if Daniel hadn't come along and hauled Isabelle from the ground before she reached Lianne.

"From a cockfight to a near cat fight in one afternoon." When Isabelle calmed down he stood her beside him. "Ladies don't behave in such a manner," he scolded but sounded amused.

"She is no lady." Isabelle pointed to Lianne, the fury still in her eyes.

"And you are less than a *lepero*," Lianne said, steadying herself in case Daniel's grip relaxed and Isabelle attacked.

"*Puta!*"

Raoul sauntered over to them. "Such unbecoming talk, Isabelle. Didn't Franco teach you anything after he pulled you from the gutter all those years ago? If I recall you didn't even own a pair of shoes. Now be on your way and don't bother us again."

"Raoul . . ."

"Go," he said softly.

Isabelle broke free of Daniel's restraining arm and swished imperiously away.

Raoul motioned for Lianne and Daniel to follow him into Señor Guerrero's study. When she sat in the highbacked chair, Raoul continued to stand with hands folded behind his back while Daniel leaned against the terrace door. She didn't know what to expect. Everyone was so polite, so civil. Such a change from earlier in the day. She didn't trust Raoul, didn't trust the way he observed her as if she were of no more importance than a noisy mosquito.

"Daniel won the match. According to our bet, he has won you. You're free to go with him, Lianne."

"I don't believe you!" she blurted out and looked in disbelief from one man to the other. It was all so simple. Too simple. Didn't Daniel see this?

"Ah, *querida,* you wound me with your distrust. But it's true. You have your freedom."

She looked at Daniel in stunned disbelief. He nodded. "Raoul has agreed to a divorce." Daniel took a paper from his pocket. "He legalized the bet and had it witnessed. I must admit he is a gracious loser."

"Don't be a fool, Daniel. You don't believe this any more than I do. You can't."

Lianne's breasts heaved with emotion. Raoul

made a move to the door. "I will leave you lovebirds to sort out your problems. I have kept my end of the bet." When he left the room, she got up and ran to Daniel.

"He's lying. He told me only an hour ago that he wouldn't let me go. You mustn't believe him."

Her nearness was like heady wine to Daniel. He had wanted to hold her for so long, and now he did. He pulled her toward him and kissed her lips, drinking of their sweetness, until she wrapped her arms around him. He groaned into her hair. "I don't believe him either, Lianne. Raoul is a devious man, but he won't destroy us this time. I have his word as a gentleman that he'll honor the bet. I just have to keep you with me, be wary of him. He may try something else, but I'll be ready for him."

"Be careful. The day he took me from the academy he promised he'd kill you if I didn't come with him. I'd die if anything happened to you."

He pushed loose strands of auburn hair from her forehead and traced her lips with his fingers. "Nothing will happen to me. I have all I want at this moment. Raoul can't destroy our happiness. Not this time."

Lianne leaned her head against his chest, hearing the steady beat of his heart. She hoped he was right.

Isabelle laughed delightedly up at Raoul. She poured him a glass of amber-colored wine, her eyes shining.

"Your visit has made me feel much better," she said and sat on the divan beside him in her room. "I thought I had lost Daniel. It seems, however, that your little game has only begun."

Raoul swallowed the liquid, relishing the warm feeling as it slid down his throat. His dark eyes glittered. "This night Lianne shall be mine, and you can do whatever you wish with Daniel. He won't want her when I finish with her. He'll never want to see her beautiful face as long as he lives."

Isabelle leaned toward him. "Let me see it again," she begged.

"Such a nag," he teased but took the red vial from his jacket pocket. He hadn't forgotten how Daniel had tossed the yellow vial in his hands earlier in the day. The man had been arrogant to think he had bested him. Well, perhaps momentarily, he silently thought. But now things would turn in his favor and not in a way Daniel Flanders would like, in a way he'd never forget.

"Can it really do all you say?" Isabelle asked and licked her lips like a cat who sees the milk but can't reach the bowl.

"Ah, Isabelle, don't tell me you can't fire a man's ardor with your seductive charms."

"I can, but the possibilities are intriguing. Perhaps you can save me a drop for Daniel."

"What a lusty wench you are!" Raoul was amused by Isabelle. If he weren't so obsessed with Lianne, he'd bed the woman right now. But he must keep his wits about him. The next few hours were too important to be swayed by anything or anyone.

Before the night ended Daniel Flanders would detest the woman he claimed to love, and he, Raoul de Lovis, would hear her ecstatic cries when he possessed her. Her body, her heart and soul would belong to him forever.

Chapter 39

A fog of disbelief still shrouded Lianne as she waited in Daniel's room that night. The evening sky had long since turned from dusky purple to velvet black. Stars twinkled overhead, and the voices of the other guests rose from the courtyard which was bedecked for dancing. Glittering torchlights outlined festive figures in brightly colored clothes.

The party had barely begun when Daniel took her to his room with strict orders not to unlock the door while he spoke to Señor Guerrero in his study. So she barred the door and wondered if she'd ever feel a sense of security as long as Raoul lived. She still couldn't believe he had freed her, that he'd grant her a divorce. Something was wrong, very wrong, but she had no idea what Raoul would do to keep her from leaving with Daniel.

She hadn't changed from the white peasant-style dress with the embroidered flowers. Some red stains still showed on the skirt though she had taken great pains to remove them. She could go to Raoul's room and get other clothes, but she didn't wish to take anything from him now. The break with Raoul must be clean, but she still didn't trust him.

When a knock sounded on the door, she jumped. Collecting herself, she asked who was there.

"It's Josephine, señora. Please let me speak with you."

"No, go away!" She didn't trust Josephine. The woman idolized Raoul and would do whatever he asked.

"Please listen to me," said Josephine in urgent tones. "Señorita Carmen needs you."

Lianne moved closer to the door. "What's wrong with her?" she asked in concern but not wholly trusting Josephine.

"Open the door for me. I can't tell you here in the hallway. Someone may overhear."

The maternal instinct in Lianne couldn't deny Carmen. She had to know what might be wrong. Slowly she withdrew the bolt and opened the door. Josephine smiled at her and forced her way into the room.

"Tell me what's wrong with Carmen," Lianne said, staying on her guard.

"I shouldn't mention this to you, señora, not now that Don Raoul is giving you a divorce. But señorita is very upset that without you she will have to endure much from Diego Gonzalez, once she marries him. She fears no one will aid her if he abuses her. Certainly not Don Raoul. The girl is beside herself and has locked herself in Don Raoul's room."

"Does Raoul know about any of this?"

Josephine shook her head. "No, that is why I've come for you. If he returns and finds her in his room, locked in and hysterical, there's no telling what he'll do to her. The girl hasn't a mother any longer, and for some reason she feels closer to you now then she did. Please talk to her, Señora Lianne."

Lianne knew all Josephine said was the truth. She couldn't desert Carmen, couldn't leave without speaking to her. She remembered the girl's fears of Diego, that she'd have no one to help her. She must see that Carmen felt secure before she left, must let her know she cared for her and would speak to Raoul about Diego.

"I'll come," Lianne said and left the room with Josephine following her.

The walk to Raoul's room was brief, and when Lianne entered the room she found Carmen huddled on the bed. Tears streaked her face, and her eyes were puffy. Lianne went to her immediately and cushioned her in her embrace.

"Carmen, everything will be all right." She stroked the girl's dark hair which tumbled around her shoulders. "You mustn't worry about Diego. I'll speak to your father about him."

Sobs racked Carmen's shoulders, and she glanced at Lianne with wet black eyes. "I'm sorry," she moaned over and over. "So sorry."

"Sorry for what? You've done nothing wrong," Lianne said in a vain attempt at consolation but Carmen wailed all the louder.

"Señorita Carmen needs to return to her own room," Josephine said quickly, "but first I think she should drink some wine to soothe her." She handed a cup of wine to Carmen then offered another one to Lianne.

"For you, señora." Josephine held it out to her and Lianne took it.

"Drink, señorita," Josephine urged Carmen. "You, too, Lianne. The wine is soothing."

Carmen sipped at the wine as did Lianne who still held her around the shoulders. "All will be well," Lianne promised her. At that moment Carmen sobbed and dropped the cup.

"I'm sorry, Lianne. Forgive me! Father made me do it." Carmen jumped from the bed and ran out of the room, her high-pitched wails echoing down the hall to her own room.

"Whatever is wrong with her?" Lianne asked and put down the cup from which she had unwittingly drunk half of the wine.

Josephine smirked. "The girl will be well soon. She has done her job and will be rewarded by her father."

"I don't understand."

"Don't you?" Josephine went to the wardrobe and laid out a flimsy gauze creation of white and gold which Lianne would have worn on her wedding night to Raoul if the miscarriage hadn't occurred.

"You're baffling me, Josephine. I demand to know what's going on."

"In a few moments you won't care about anything but Raoul de Lovis." She stroked the soft folds of the gown. "See how generous the man is to you, señora. He loves you and buys you beautiful clothes and jewels. And you repay him by desiring an artist. Granted a very handsome one, but he can't give you what Don Raoul can. You've been very foolish, Señora Lianne, but after this night, I think you'll see the error of your ways."

Something in Josephine's face, perhaps the glittering eyes, frightened Lianne. What was wrong with her, what was wrong with Carmen, and why did she, herself, feel so strange suddenly?

She tried to move but felt a heaviness of limb. When she finally lifted her hand to cluch at the bedpost, she saw it moving slowly, so slowly. She felt and saw Josephine removing her clothes, but was helpless to protest. She felt so languorous, so dreamy, that she barely registered when Josephine had pulled the thin gown over her body or seemed to care that the woman brushed her hair. She stood by the bed like a zombie.

She registered the fact that Josephine turned down the bedsheets and plumped the pillows. She heard the woman's voice from behind her. "Don Raoul shall have his wish tonight, Lianne. When he comes in, you'll desire him as he desires you. The drug takes a few minutes to work, but soon, your body will come alive with passion, and when Don Raoul fills you, you'll welcome him.''

Still in a trance-like state, Lianne was helped onto the bed by the woman. Then Josephine went to the door which led to the stairs and opened it. The gay music drifted up to Lianne, but she barely heard it. Something was happening to her. She felt so warm, felt every nerve and muscle come to life within her. Yet she found it difficult to move.

She heard Raoul entering the room. "She is prepared, señor," came Josephine's voice, sounding as if it were far away.

Then she saw Raoul gazing at her, saw him take a few puffs of his cheroot before dropping it in the cup of wine she had drunk from earlier. Dimly she noticed he was dressed in his robe, that it was open to the waist. When he removed it, she found herself thinking what a handsome man he was with broad shoulders and a powerful chest. He bent over her and smiled.

"How do you feel, *querida*?"

She couldn't speak and had no idea that her eyes were glazed over with a hot green flame. She began to writhe on the bed, not from agony but from the glorious sensations she felt when his hands moved across her thinly veiled breasts. Lianne moaned as his fingers traced across the flatness of her abdomen to the secret recess between her thighs. Raoul laughed. Desire flickered in his dark eye.

"You're mine, *querida*. Mine!" He tore at the gown, ripping it away from her body, but Lianne didn't care. Suddenly her arms opened for him and he came to her, branding her lips with his as she drank in the ecstasy he promised her.

Her body was on fire, the unquenchable flames rising higher and higher within her. She wanted Raoul de Lovis, and though part of her was shocked at this discovery and ached for Daniel, she couldn't still the rushing tide of desire which washed over her when

Raoul's lips teased her breasts or resist the thrilling sensations as his hands moved hotly across her body.

"Do you want me, my wife?" he rasped into her ear. "Do you wish to belong only to me?"

She moaned, and he positioned her head so she would look into his face. "Tell me. Tell me, Lianne. Beg for me to take you." She felt him begin to enter her and then withdraw. Her body had a mind of its own and lifted to seek his manhood, arching of its own accord.

"Please," she gasped at him.

"Please what?" he taunted and she didn't notice his gaze sliding to the open porch doorway. "What do you wish, *querida*?"

Her mind had begun to clear but her traitorous body still writhed and begged for him. She barely knew the words she had chosen to tell him she wanted him, but Raoul laughed and whispered, "*Puta*," in her ear. Then he entered her and she gasped as the heat of their joining fired the flame higher within her. Her body pushed hard against him as she urged him to end her torture.

"Tell me first that you love me, *querida*. Tell me."

"Raoul . . ." she moaned, knowing he held himself in check. "Say it," he said and nibbled at her breasts.

"I . . . love . . . you." Her breathing was ragged.

This was the answer Raoul wanted. With a mighty shove, he impaled her and her body convulsed with exquisite pleasure as he found deep satisfaction within her.

Lianne lay there with Raoul's head suckling at her breasts, feeling a strange contentment. She knew what had happened was wrong, but she couldn't summon the strength to leave him. In all their times together this was the first time she had begged him to make love to her, and the only time she had allowed herself to enjoy his touch. She wanted to push him from her, but intead of falling asleep, she began to feel her body tingling again, craving this man's hands upon her.

Daniel waited for her, and she knew this, but when Raoul began to stroke the satin softness of her thighs and to part them for his entry again, she didn't resist.

She was so engrossed in lovemaking she didn't see Daniel standing outside on the porch or hear his muttered curse of "Whore!" before he ran down the steps into the throng of dancing people.

Daniel's insides felt twisted. He wound his way through the people in the courtyard, not seeing them. Without realizing it he made his way back to his room where he found Isabelle waiting in his bed.

"Don't you ever give up?" he growled and threw her a look of distaste.

"Mi amor, I never get enough of you. You excite me, Daniel, as no man has ever done before, and I've had many men." Her long polished nails held the sheet below her waist, and her unbound hair covered the round fullness of her beautiful breasts.

A willing woman, a wanton woman. Didn't this woman know that his dreams had been shattered? Couldn't she realize that when he came upstairs and found Lianne gone that he thought Raoul had ensnared her, taken her from him again? What a surprise awaited him when he asked the maid, Josephine, if she'd seen Lianne. "She is upstairs in Señor de Lovis' room," the woman had told him with a hint of a smile. At first he thought he'd have to fight for her, to kill Raoul.

He'd never forget climbing the back porch stairs and hearing the mewls of pleasure coming from the open doorway. He wondered if he had the right room, when looking in he saw Lianne, her legs wrapped around Raoul, whispering filthy words to him, begging to be taken. His first inclination had been to rush in and pull her away from Raoul. But Raoul was still her husband, and from what he saw, Lianne craved him as a lover.

He wondered how he could have been so blind, so stupid all this time? Lianne wanted de Lovis.

Daniel went to the round table near the window and poured himself a huge glass of whiskey. He drank it down like water and filled the glass again.

"You shall become quite drunk, Daniel, and will be of little use to me. I detest a drunken lover. They don't know how to please a woman."

"I'm far from drunk, Isabelle, but I guarantee that you shall be very pleased this night."

To her delight he shrugged out of his clothes and joined her satin body on the bed. He loved Isabelle wildly and passionately until the candles on the dressing table extinguished themselves. Later she slept in his arms, but he didn't sleep. All he thought of was Lianne and the revenge he'd take on her and de Lovis.

A very sweet revenge.

Chapter 40

The bright afternoon sunshine hurt Lianne's eyes. Golden rays streamed through the opened doorway and inundated the bed in its brightness. Slowly she opened her eyes and shielded her face from the glare with her hands.

"Good afternoon, *querida*. I trust you slept well."

She started at Raoul's voice and turned her head in the direction of the sound. He was putting on his dark jacket, a pleased expression on his face as he surveyed her half-naked body.

Heat suffused her and she realized that the covers were twisted around her. A long thigh was uncovered as were her breasts. She stared at him, wondering what she was doing here.

She sat up, but her head felt slightly heavy, as if she had drunk too much. But she didn't remember drinking anything. Or had she? Her gaze slid to the cup on the table beside the bed. Wine. She had drunk wine. Why? Then she remembered coming here and finding a distraught Carmen, then being handed a cup of wine by Josephine.

Her green eyes flew back to Raoul as everything grew clear. "You planned this!" she cried.

"*Sí*, Lianne. I planned all of it. As I recall you didn't protest too much last night." He smiled wickedly, so sure of himself. "You were fantastic, *querida*. We belong together. I think you know that now."

He stood up and finished buttoning his jacket. "Shall I have Josephine send you up a tray?"

"No! I wouldn't eat anything that terrible woman gives me."

"Don't judge her harshly. She only carried out my orders."

"I hate you, Raoul!"

He looked amused. "No, you don't. Look at your reflection in the mirror, my dove. Notice the way your eyes gleam this morning, the flush of love upon your skin. Lianne, we made love all night. Don't tell me you don't remember."

She did remember. That was the problem. He had drugged her to gain a response from her, and responded she had. Just thinking of the wanton way she had taken him into her repulsed and excited her. Dear God, she had enjoyed it! How truly wicked was she?

Looking down at the rumpled sheets, her head shot up. "Daniel. I must speak to Daniel!"

Raoul blocked her way when she rose from the bed.

"You won't stop me!" she cried and angrily pulled the sheet around her.

"I have no intention of stopping you, but I think you should be warned. Daniel is packing his bags and returning to Mexico City with Isabelle Hidalgo. I understand that she is now his mistress."

The blood drained from her face. "You're lying."

Raoul shrugged. "Go and see for yourself."

Before his calm gaze, she dressed in the discarded peasant dress from the previous day and ran barefoot to Daniel's room. He wasn't there. She flew down the staircase, nearly knocking down a maid, and out onto the street.

In front of the house was Isabelle's gaudy carriage, and helping Isabelle into it was Daniel.

She called to him, and when he looked at her, she stopped short. His ocean-gray eyes swept coldy over her. She vaguely wondered why he was doing this to her. He couldn't possibly know she had willingly and wantonly slept with Raoul.

Approaching him, she had no idea she looked as if she had been thoroughly loved the night before. Her hair streamed across her shoulders in a mass of tangled curls. Her coral lips were swollen, and the dress was rumpled, the blood stains from the cockfight still visible. Plus her feet were bare, and because the dress was so thin, he saw she wore no underclothes beneath it.

"Daniel, why are you leaving me like this? Let me explain what happened."

He took her arm and roughly led her near the wrought iron gate of the garden, away from the prying eyes of the passersby. "Don't bother, Lianne. I have eyes and know what happened. Believe me, I saw you and de Lois mating like a stallion and its mare, which is very well and good since you are his wife."

She winced at the nasty way he emphasized wife. She felt like a whore. "Can't you see that Raoul planned all of this, Daniel? He wanted you to see me with him, he drug . . ."

He cut her short. "I knew he was devious and would stop at nothing, but I thought you hated him, detested him." He dropped her arm. "Well, love, if that's how you hate, I've never been the recipient of such hatred, and I feel slighted. Well, one day, my beautiful wanton, you're going to hate me, hate me more than any man you've ever known. Even more than de Lovis. Then maybe I'll let you crawl in my bed and pleasure me in the same way. Until then, *adios,* Lianne."

Daniel turned and walked the short distance to the carriage where Isabelle waited. He climbed into the carriage beside the woman and swept her into his arms, drugging her senses in a long kiss. When the carriage pulled away, Lianne leaned against the gate post, unable to move but feeling the stinging sensation of tears in her eyes.

Why hadn't he listened to her, let her finish explaining what had happened? However, she wondered if the truth would have mattered. She had responded to Raoul and enjoyed his lovemaking. She didn't think Daniel would care whether she had been drugged or not. He was determined to hate her.

She sensed Raoul's presence.

"Come inside and change your clothes," he told her in a surprisingly gentle voice.

She allowed him to lead her to their room where Josephine waited with a warm bath. While she bathed Raoul watched her, but she felt unable to say anything. Her heart had broken. She felt desolate and alone. When she finished bathing, she put on a robe and sat by the dressing table while Josephine attempted to brush her hair.

"Leave me alone!" she managed to say in as harsh a voice as she could muster.

"But señora . . ."

"Go!" Lianne cried.

Raoul waved his hand and Josephine departed.

He came and stood behind her, his hands resting on her shoulders. "You truly belong to me now," he said and watched her reflection in the mirror. "You're the woman, the wife of Raoul de Lovis."

"A great honor, I'm sure," she said bitterly.

"Don't act the shrew, Lianne. You must admit you loved my hands upon you last night. You were insatiable."

"Only because you drugged me, Raoul."

"Be that as it may, you wanted me."

Her eyes met his glittering black one. She had grown so used to the black patch over his other eye that she had ceased to notice it. She turned from the mirror and faced him directly.

"I admit I wanted you. I admit I enjoyed making love to you. You got what you've always wanted from me, Raoul. A passionate response in your arms." She stood up and traced her fingers along his jawline, her breath fanning his chin. "Will you take me now, Raoul? I know you want me." Slowly she undid the tie at her waist and shimmied out of the robe until she waited naked before him. She placed his hands on her hips, writhing as they trailed lower upon her. She wrapped her arms around his neck, pressing her breasts onto the silken front of his jacket.

"Lianne." His voice was a groan of pleasure and he picked her up in his arms and carried her to the bed. His body fell atop hers, covering her face with kisses.

"I love you, *querida*. I am a most happy man. This is the way I've always wanted you, writhing and moaning with ecstasy in my arms."

"Oh, Raoul, is that all? I thought you wanted my love. If I had known you wanted only a response I could have granted your wish long ago."

His hands stopped their wanton travels across her flesh, and he lifted an eyebrow as he looked into her face. Her catlike eyes glinted in the dark, and for the first time in a long time, Raoul shivered.

"What game are you playing?" he asked.

"No games, Raoul. Aren't you pleased with me?"

"No!"

"Why not? Aren't I responsive and willing in your arms? Aren't I the wife you wish me to be?"

"Stop it, Lianne!" He held her face in his hands. "I want you to say you love me. Last night you did."

She laughed a long, fluty laugh like the ring of fine crystal. Then she stopped and her tone was bitter. "I shall never love you, Raoul. You may make love to me, and I will enjoy it from now on. Why not? Last night you broke down my inhibitions. However, no matter how much you want me and make me purr like a little kitten for you, I'll never love you. As long as I live, I shall always love Daniel. And you can't change that.''

"You are a bitch!'' he rasped.

"Perhaps, but you've made me one. You told me I belong to you, so, Raoul, I'm ready for you.''

"No! You're overwrought from all that has happened. I will wait until we're back home in Mexico City. You'll see things differently then and realize I am the man you love.''

He got up, and she sighed. "Of course, my husband. And I was all ready and willing for you.''

Raoul looked in disgust at her, and he left the room with her peals of laughter following him. It was some time later before she collapsed in a heap and cried for the man she'd never have, the man she loved.

Lianne never realized the power of her allure for Raoul until they arrived in Mexico City. She decided that he had ruined her life too many times, had deprived her of the only man she'd ever love. So, she took him to her bed and revelled in their lovemaking. Let him wonder if I love him, she thought. Let him live with the torment she did, knowing now that the man she loved didn't love her.

For all of his power, his wealth, she realized Raoul was as vulnerable as any other man. Until the day Daniel turned away from her, she had been Raoul's victim. Now he was as much a victim of her beauty, her sex, as the fly in the web of a black widow spider. She knew he longed to hear that she loved him, and she tantalized him with love words when they were in bed, but she never told him she loved him. It would be a lie. However, she enjoyed taunting him with her flesh, enjoyed the rapturous look on his face when she responded wildly to him. Each time they made love, she knew she ensnared him more. And this vengeance was all she had to appease her hurt.

So entranced by her, Raoul even relented and allowed her to perform again at the opera. Each night he sat in his box, supported by delicate columns twined with gilded flowers in riotous profusion, while she sang. And each night after a late candlelight supper at home, she knew she was the one who controlled Raoul. With her intervention he was no longer so partial to Diego, and she hoped this would help Carmen when the wedding night arrived.

"My father is much in love with you," Carmen said one afternoon as she and Lianne sat in the courtyard, away from Josephine's prying eyes. Josephine was another matter Lianne was eager to take care of, and she hoped she'd have little or no interference from Raoul.

"Yes, he is," she said with self-assurance.

"I know you don't care for him, Lianne. Why do you stay with him?"

"Because I owe him for many things, Carmen." Lianne thought about the child she'd probably never see again, the loss of Daniel. Yes, she owed Raoul for many things.

Carmen looked down at her hands, and shame suffused her face. "I apologize for what happened in San Augustin de las Cuevas. My father used me to bring you to him. He knew you wouldn't come to him on your own. I am the cause of your unhappiness."

Lianne reached over and hugged the girl in a forgiving embrace. "You're not to blame for your father's actions."

"I fear him so, Lianne. I've always been afraid of him."

"Afraid of Raoul?" She felt suddenly disbelieving to think that Carmen—or she herself—had been frightened of Raoul. Now that she knew how to control him, she wasn't afraid of him any longer.

"He's only a man, Carmen."

Carmen seemed about to cry. "I'm also afraid of Diego. I fear him more than my father, I think."

"I've told you before not to worry about him. If he touches you, I'll have him groveling on his knees for hurting you."

Despite the sadness and fear Lianne saw in Carmen's face, the young girl laughed. "I should like to see that!" Then she sobered. "I think a great deal about Felix sometimes and wonder if he is still alive. Many people perish who work in the mines, but I tell myself that he is very strong."

Lianne looked questioningly at her. "You cared for Felix?"

"Oh, no! Not like that." Carmen put her hands to her face in a gesture of shock. "He was kind to me once."

Lianne nodded she understood, but she guessed that Carmen cared for Felix a bit more deeply than she let on. Sometimes Lianne wondered how Felix was, but tried to put his face from her mind. He had helped her escape Raoul and had paid for it. She never knew Carmen liked Felix, but then it didn't matter. Carmen was destined to marry Diego Gonzalez.

"I saw your Señor Flanders yesterday in the square. He was buying a pretty mantilla for the woman he keeps."

"Isabelle Hidalgo," Lianne said tightly.

"*Sí*, she is very beautiful. He wouldn't be with her if it weren't for me."

Lianne sighed. "I've told you not to blame yourself, Carmen. What happened with Daniel was my fault. If I hadn't been so foolish, I'd have known your father had laid a trap for me. I just didn't imagine he'd go so far as to use you."

"Señorita Carmen!"

They turned at Josephine's voice. "The seamstress is here to fit your wedding gown!"

Carmen visibly paled. She stood up and smiled at

Lianne. "Two more days before I enter a living hell as the wife of Diego Gonzalez. I'd rather enter a convent than marry him."

Lianne felt pity for her, but she patted her hand in comfort. "I shall help you if you need it."

The wedding of Carmen Fortuna de Lovis to Diego Gonzalez was a huge affair. They married in the church which was bedecked with white roses, interlaced with red ones. Carmen made a sweet bride, and when the young couple left for their honeymoon at Diego's house on the other side of town, pity filled Lianne. She looked so young and vulnerable as she rode in the open carriage with Diego. Raoul was happy that, at last, his daughter was married and would no longer bother him with her looks and mannerisms which resembled Elena's.

A few days after the ceremony, an invitation was delivered from the Academy de San Carlos. Don Raoul and Dona Lianne were invited to an exhibit of paintings by Daniel Flanders. This was destined to one of the social events of the year, and Raoul had to attend to keep up appearance and because he contributed a great deal of money to the academy.

"You can stay home," he said to Lianne. "I shall go."

She looked up from arranging freshly cut flowers in a basket. "Are you afraid I'll fall into Daniel's arms, Raoul? I assure you I won't. I doubt if he can stand to think about me. You made certain he detests me."

"Are you still in love with him?" he asked.

She went to him and kissed him. "Don't ask questions if you don't wish to hear the answers." She left the room and headed to the bedroom where she began to dress for the performance that night. She shook so badly as she tried to button the hooks on the back of her dress that she was forced to send for Josephine.

Daniel. Just to think his name disturbed her, and now, she would see him again at the exhibition of his paintings. Oh, she was going all right. No one would keep her away.

Revenge was sweet. Who said that? Daniel wondered as he took another swig from the brandy bottle. He knew he drank too much. Isabelle told him that all the time. But what the hell? The alcohol helped the pain.

The afternoon light was perfect as he observed the painting which was to be the focal point of the exhibit. He had the usual landscapes, portraits of Mexico's leading citizens to show. He knew he'd sell all of them and at high prices. But this painting was special and not for sale to just any buyer. The canvas was ten feet high and five feet in width. The background colors were soft shades of peach, green and gray; the iridiscent blue of the water beside the shoreline was so lifelike that he felt he could dive in and drown in it.

Yet it was the soft colors of the flesh rising from the blue pool which held his attention. With an artist's eye, his gaze traveled upward from the bare calves to the swell of hips and upward to the perfect breasts. His eyes lingered there a moment, remembering. Then his gaze moved to the long graceful neck, then the face which even now on canvas had the power to make him gasp. The incredible green eyes stared at him, inviting him as they would every man in the room. The sensuous quality in their shining depths wasn't lost on him and wouldn't be lost on Raoul de Lovis.

Daniel laughed, quite pleased with himself, even when Manuel Tolsa entered the studio.

Manuel folded his arms in observation. "You shall be called to duel for this, my friend. I shall be lucky if de Lovis doesn't cut off all funds and order me to the dueling fields."

"Ah, Manuel, it will be worth it. I ache to see his face when he sees the nude painting of his wife. All people of note will see it and know what a whore de Lovis is married to. And what makes it all the better is that he will make an offer to buy the painting, and I will refuse." He took another gulp of liquor.

"You love her still, Daniel. The woman is a fever in your blood."

"I hate her, Manuel, yet as you say she is a fever in my blood. Perhaps this humiliation will appease my own pain."

Manuel shook his head. "No, my friend. I think your pain has yet to begin."

Chapter 41

Lianne dressed carefully the night Daniel's paintings were to be exhibited. Though Josephine had laid out a gown of golden taffeta, Lianne chose a gown of thin blue voile, over which she draped a wrap of sheer white tulle with small golden roses embroidered in the material. Before she left with Raoul for the academy she covered her head with the tulle which enhanced the beauty of her red gold hair, but did very little to cover the low bodice of the dress.

"Don Raoul won't approve of this dress," Josephine told Lianne and shook her head in disapproval.

"Of course, you know exactly what pleases my husband, Josephine. Have you his ear in every matter, including his taste in my clothes?" Lianne pulled on her long lacy white gloves and shot the woman a withering glance.

"No, I do not, but he shall think as I do, that you dress to attract the attention of Daniel Flanders."

Lianne laughed. "Don't worry about Daniel. You and Raoul made certain he'd never look at me except with scorn in his eyes. I doubt very much if he'll care I'm in the same room with him. Raoul has his wish. I'm now completely his. Isabelle Hidalgo has Daniel, and from what I've heard, she sees to his every need. Everyone is happy."

"Everyone except you?" Josephine asked with a softness which surprised Lianne.

Grabbing the white beaded reticule from the bed, Lianne turned and said over her shoulder, "Don't pretend concern for my welfare, Josephine. It's so out of character."

When she and Raoul arrived at the Academy, she was aware he didn't seem pleased with her attire. His dark eye had raked over her like a hot coal earlier, and though he didn't say a word about the gown, she knew he was displeased. She thought Mexican men were strange. They didn't mind flaunting their mistresses in skimpy gowns, but their wives should appear in high-necked, long-sleeved dresses. But she also knew that Raoul was so in love with her, he'd allow her to wear whatever pleased her. Yet she wondered if he knew she had purposely chosen this gown because it would cause a stir, and that she had worn it to see if Daniel would notice her.

Lianne still hadn't gotten over him, would never forget the hatred in his eyes for her in San Augustin de las Cuevas. She shivered even now in the hot night air to remember he had seen her in bed with Raoul, that he knew she had enjoyed their lovemaking. No matter what the circumstances, she had welcomed Raoul's touch that night. And the reason why wouldn't matter to Daniel.

Inside the Academy Mexico City's leading citizens were present. The Viceroy sauntered over to them, looking like a peacock in his red and gold embroidered jacket next to the somber suit Raoul wore.

He bowed and kissed her hand. "Dona Lianne, what a lovely treat you are to my eyes. Every man in the room wishes to be in your husband's place."

Lianne smiled but cringed inwardly. The man was actually salivating as his gaze rested on her partially concealed bosom. For once she was glad when Raoul took her elbow and politely steered her in another direction.

They wandered around the room, examining the paintings when he stopped and looked at her. "I hope you're aware that your gown has the attention of every person in this room, especially the men."

"Does it?" she asked innocently. "I remember once you told me you wanted to flaunt me, to show me off to your friends."

"That was before you were my wife."

Lianne sighed. "I can't deny that I am your wife."

Suddenly the black look was displaced by a twisted sneer. He grabbed her arm and spun her around so her gaze would rest on the figure of Daniel with Isabelle Hidalgo hanging onto him like a leech.

"It appears that your ploy for Daniel's attention hasn't worked, *querida*. See, he hasn't looked once in your direction. Isabelle has his black heart now."

Lianne couldn't deny that either. She plainly saw the two were so close they appeared attached. "Why should I deny it, Raoul. I did dress to please him, to see if the flame burns within his eyes."

She surprised herself with her newfound confidence. A month ago she would never have dared utter such a sentiment. Now she didn't care. Raoul no longer frightened her. He had taken everything from her, even her fear of him and his power.

"You're brazen, *querida*. Don't become a slave to your own arrogance."

"I'd never do that, Raoul. I need no other slave but you."

She knew she had gone too far when he whispered harshly, "When we get home we shall see just who is the slave."

Lianne had the good grace to blush. Though she hated Raoul, she admitted to herself that she was entrapped by her own base desires in his arms at night. She needed someone to hold her, and since Raoul was the one who had destroyed her happiness, she took her pleasures from him like a greedy wanton. She let out a long sigh.

"I look forward to it, *chérie*," she said with a frozen smile.

He stiffened, and she knew he would have said more, but Daniel looked in their direction and casually sauntered over to them with Isabelle's arms wrapped around him like an octopus holding its prey.

When the couple stopped before Lianne and Raoul, Lianne immediately smelled whiskey and knew Daniel had been drinking heavily. However, no one would have guessed he was inebriated. He bowed and, with a touch which burned Lianne's flesh, kissed her hand.

The hot light which flared in his eyes was the response she needed to know the gown had worked. Daniel wanted her. He did! Did he still love her? Could he hear the beating of her heart?

Daniel's dark head tilted toward Isabelle, and he flashed them a dazzling smile. "Dona Lianne, you've captured the men with your beauty. I know your husband appreciates such a beautiful wife. I know that for a fact."

Did his voice harden just a bit, or did she imagine it? Was Daniel jealous to remember the night at San Augustin de las Cuevas? If so, then he must love her. Hope rose within her. She managed to smile at Isabelle and knew that if she wanted, she could take Daniel from the dark-haired woman with no trouble.

"I'm grateful to you, Raoul, for putting in an appearance tonight," Daniel said. "I believe you shall be most astonished by my work."

Raoul surveyed the handsome figure Daniel made in a buff-colored satin jacket and breeches which emphasized his tanned good looks. He clutched Lianne's elbow tighter. "I doubt that. In your present state of drunkenness, I'd be surprised if you could sketch a pear correctly."

A low laugh escaped Daniel, and he hugged Isabelle closer. "I'm a man of many talents, Raoul."

His eyes rested on Lianne's beautiful face for a second. "As Lianne can attest."

Lianne's emerald orbs met Daniel's ocean-gray ones. She imagined for a moment she saw pain there, but she was forced to look away when Isabelle turned her face up to Daniel's and kissed his lips. "Daniel is a man of much 'insatiable' talent," she said when she allowed him to draw breath again.

Lianne wanted to scratch the woman's face to shreds, but was prevented by Raoul's restraining grip on her elbow. Manuel Tolsa came forward then and whispered to Daniel that it was time for the showing to begin. Daniel nodded and flashed his smile again. "I believe you both shall be interested in the unveiling of my new work."

Reluctantly Lianne and Raoul followed Daniel and Isabelle into a huge room where a platform was set up. On the platform stood a large painting, covered by a white cloth. Daniel detached Isabelle's arms from him and Lianne watched as he bounded onto the platform.

She stood close to the front and didn't miss Manuel, who stood next to her, mouth to Daniel, "Are you sure?" Nor did she miss Daniel's slow nod or the sidelong glance Manuel shot in her direction.

Manuel sighed and nodded his head. Lianne wondered what was happening, knew somehow that this concerned her. It wasn't until the applause for Daniel diminished in the room after he thanked everyone for coming that a sense of foreboding filled her. During the whole speech Daniel had watched her like a cat who will soon swallow a bird.

She began to tug at Raoul's coat sleeve, to tell him she wanted to leave, but at that instant Daniel turned toward the painting and pulled the cloth from it.

"I call this painting 'The Beautiful Wanton,' " he told the audience.

Large gasps echoed throughout the room as all eyes focused on the canvas. Lianne blinked, unable to believe what she saw. She felt faint when the room swung around her, but she didn't fall. She clutched at Raoul's arm and willed herself to stand tall. No one must know her heart was breaking anew. No one must guess she wished to crawl into the floor and die. She was used to people's eyes on her when she performed, but never in her life had she felt like an insect under a microscope. Snickers and some laughs came to her ears, but she pretended not to hear them.

Her eyes moved slowly from the painting to Daniel. Though she attempted to hide her shock, her face was ashen, her lips pale. She wondered how he could do this to her, how he could freely humiliate her like this. Didn't what she felt for him, and what he had once felt for her, mean anything?

Daniel watched her, unable to take his eyes from her, but whatever he had hoped to see in her face must have been absent. Suddenly he didn't seem as thrilled with himself as he had moments earlier.

Raoul's reaction surprised Lianne. She half-expected him to rush onto the stage and challenge Daniel for this humiliation. She sensed he wanted to by the way he gripped her arm so tightly it hurt. Clearly she saw his jaw tighten, but then as quickly, relax. He appraised the painting with a critical eye.

"Your painting is quite beautiful," Raoul said in a loud clear voice for all to hear. "I'm certain you shall fetch a high price for it."

"Don't you wish to purchase it, Don Raoul?" Daniel asked in a challenging tone.

Raoul shook his head. "I have no need of it. Why should I buy your painting when I have the woman who inspired it as my wife?"

Taking Lianne by the hand, Raoul bowed and they walked through the throng of people. She felt unable to look at any of them, but when Raoul whispered softly, "Smile, *querida,*" she did. It was only after they had left the building and settled in the coach that she gave rein to her emotions.

"How could he have done this to me?" she asked
Raoul in a near-hysterical voice and made no attempt
to still her trembling hands.

Raoul didn't reply, and this unnerved her almost
as much as the unveiling. When they reached the
house, she went to the bedroom. She undressed and
climbed into bed and would have allowed herself the
luxury of tears, but she resisted. Daniel's feelings were
clear to her now. He truly hated her. There was no
hope of winning him back. She wouldn't cry over a
man who cared so little for her feelings that he'd paint
a nude portrait of her for the whole of Mexico City to
see. But without meaning to, she began to sob into her
pillow.

Raoul sat on the patio outside the bedroom
window. He heard Lianne's sobs through the open
doorway and knew she cried because of Daniel
Flanders. Would he ever find peace with Lianne as
long as Daniel was alive? Daniel still loved her. Otherwise, he would not have taken such trouble to humble
her. He rose after a few minutes, unable to stand the
sound of her sobbing, and went to his study. He wrote
a quick note to Diego and ordered a servant to deliver
it. He knew Diego wouldn't be pleased to be disturbed
so late at night. However, Raoul sensed the words on
the paper would ease any discomfort Diego might
initially feel.

Taking a cheroot from the leather case on his
desk, he lit it and sat down. Raoul's pleasure with
himself grew. Soon Lianne would stop pining over
Daniel and grow to love him. After all, she seemed to
like it when he made love to her and was an eager
participant. He chastised himself for not taking the
necessary steps sooner because Daniel was the father
of Lianne's child. Well, he would ease Lianne's pain
when he sent for the little girl. Once Lianne had her
child with her, she would grow to love him. He convinced himself things would work out the way he
planned. If Diego didn't botch things . . .

He wouldn't think about that. Instead he thought about the wonderful news he'd receive within the next few days—the news of Daniel's untimely death.

Soon Lianne would truly belong to him. Soon she'd tell him she loved him.

Chapter 42

The next morning Daniel suffered from the worst headache he had ever had after a night of heavy drinking. He felt sluggish, unable to order his thoughts. However, he was grateful that Isabelle's maid hadn't yet tiptoed into the bedroom to pull the drapes. He didn't know if it was morning or afternoon. He didn't care.

When his brain began to clear and the headache abated, he remembered the exhibition. The memory of the stricken look on Lianne's face hit him like a thunderbolt. Now he knew why he felt so awful. He had consumed a large quantity of mezcal to forget the way she lifted herself to her full height, pretending the painting was unimportant. But he knew she was hurt, more than hurt. Lianne was disillusioned with him. Hell! he thought angrily. She had led him on, declared she loved him. Then he found her in bed with Raoul, responding to the man like the worst whore.

"I love you, Raoul." Lianne's voice echoed in his mind, laced with passion, as he had heard it that night in San Augustin de las Cuevas. For the rest of his life, he'd hear her voice, remember the look of ecstasy on her face for Raoul.

Damn he was a fool!

Isabelle's soft breath fanned his shoulder. Looking down at her dark head pressed against his arm, feeling her voluptuous body against his, he knew he must forget Lianne. Isabelle would help him forget. He had to lose himself within her or go insane.

His hands traced the rounded fullness of her breasts. Isabelle gave a startled moan and opened her eyes.

"Daniel," she said, groggy from sleep, "wasn't last night enough for you?"

"Don't deny me, Isabelle." His voice was harsher than he intended.

She wrapped her arms around him and pushed her body upward so that it rested on top of him. "I never do, *mi amor*."

And she never would. Daniel knew that. All he had to do was touch Isabelle and she melted. He knew she was slightly devious, but she didn't play games with him as Lianne had. He must forget, forget. Positioning her body so that her hips were level, he slipped into her without preliminary but she was ready for him. Within minutes her cry of ecstasy filled his ears and he spent himself within her.

Later, Isabelle got up and pulled open the drapes. "The day is beautiful, Daniel." Her voice drifted to him from the other side of the room. "But the weather is too warm. Perhaps we should take a trip, leave the city for the remainder of the season. I have a house in the mountains, near Pachuca. Would you like to go?"

Pachuca. He remembered Raoul had a silver mine there. Lianne. Would he never stop thinking of her?

"That would be nice, Isabelle. When do you wish to leave?"

"Tomorrow."

"We'll leave tomorrow." He patted the side of the bed next to him, and Isabelle laughed and came to him.

"You don't want me again, *mi amor*."

He pulled her down to him, her dark hair falling across her shoulders. "I want you as often as I can have you."

Isabelle pressed her lush breasts against his chest.

"Then that shall be very, very often," she said.

The deed was done. Raoul smiled to himself while he watched Lianne perform the next night. From his private box in the opera house, he drank in her incredible beauty with an eagerness he hadn't felt in years. To him, she was the only person on the stage. Her lovely, melodic voice drifted to him, mesmerizing him.

Soon the news of Daniel's death would reach them. He must pretend to be shocked, must console her when she learned Daniel was dead. Never must she know he arranged for the carriage to be waylaid on the road to Pachuca. He wasn't certain how Diego intended to kill Daniel Flanders, but he must never let Lianne know he had had a hand in it.

Well, he didn't kill the man, Raoul told himself. Just put the plan into motion. And Diego justified his position as the husband of his daughter. Of course, Raoul realized that Diego enjoyed torture, and he was assured by him that Daniel did indeed suffer before he collapsed. Raoul felt certain the authorities would decide banditti had killed Daniel, the driver and Isabelle.

Isabelle. That was the only part of the plan for which Raoul felt remorse. He never intended to harm her, but alas, she was with Daniel, and to make the job convincing, she had to die. Still, it grieved him in a heart which felt little grief, to think of the beautiful raven-haired Isabelle lying dead on the road in the hot sun. He hoped someone had come upon the bodies soon after Diego, who was dressed like a bandit, and the men who helped him, made their escape.

Raoul sighed about the unpredictability of life and turned his attention to Lianne on the stage.

Word of Isabelle Hidalgo's fate spread like wild-fire throughout Mexico City. Lianne heard the news from Señor Dominguez just as she arrived at the theater two days later.

"A tragic loss," the head of the opera company said and shook his head in dismay. "Señora Hidalgo was a bright spot in my audience. Many nights she came to the opera with the gentleman, the artist."

Lianne blanched at the reference to Daniel. Dominguez continued, unaware he had struck a nerve in her.

"My housekeeper is a friend of Isabelle's maid, Sophia. When Sophia learned the news of her employer's death, she fainted."

"Señora Hidalgo's gentleman, the artist you mentioned, must be taking the news of her death very hard."

Dominguez shook his head. "I can't really say. No one has seen him since he left for Pachuca with Isabelle Hidalgo. It's very strange that her body was found and not his."

He sighed and left Lianne standing in his office when he was called to tend to a matter concerning the scenery. Tremors erupted within her like tiny earthquakes. Daniel had left for Pachuca with Isabelle, but his body hadn't been found. Where was he? Had his attackers taken him away, or had he crawled off somewhere to die?

Lianne couldn't stop trembling as she put her hands over her face. Tears formed in the emerald depths of her eyes. Suppose Daniel was dead? She didn't know if she could face life if he were truly gone. She'd never see his face again. She knew he didn't love her, but just to know he was nearby had helped her to go on with her life. The prospect of never seeing him again tore through her until she fell into a chair and wept for what had been and what would never be.

Stupido! Imbecile!" Raoul ranted and paced the floor of his study like a man possessed.

Diego waited. Sweat beaded on his forehead, and his tiny eyes held true fear. Never had he seen Raoul so enraged and he didn't believe the fact that his wife was Raoul's daughter would save him from whatever punishment Raoul decided to mete out for him. Diego wondered how this had happened. He had thought the artist was dead.

"I thought you told me Flanders was dead when you and those idiots you hired left." Raoul rasped and sounded like the devil himself to Diego.

"He seemed to be dead, Raoul. We stabbed him many times. I know the driver and Isabelle died instantly . . ."

"I don't care about them! I wanted Flanders dead. Now, tell me—where is he? Did a dead body just crawl away into the mountains?"

"No. He was dead, I tell you."

"Did you check him to be certain?"

"Raoul, Flanders was cloaked in blood. If he wasn't dead he crawled off somewhere to die. Believe me, he is dead."

Raoul wasn't easily pacified by Diego's comment. "And if he isn't?"

Diego smiled a bit too bravely for a man who was facing a human devil. "Then he will be soon."

"Bah! Your promises and brave talk leave me cold." Raoul threw himself into the chair behind his desk. "You and those idiots you hired must scour the countryside. I want Daniel's body found. Do you understand?"

"*Sí*," Diego said and shook as the hard glittering eye impaled him.

Raoul waved him away. "Get out of my sight."

After Diego left, Raoul wondered if nothing would go the way he planned. Of course Lianne was his wife and a pleasure in bed, but she didn't love him. He thought once she knew Daniel Flanders was dead, she'd begin to care for him in the way he knew she could if she let herself. She had mentioned Isabelle's death in passing when she arrived home from the opera yesterday. But she hadn't spoken about Daniel, and she must have known he had accompanied the woman. Somehow Lianne had made her face a blank. He hadn't a clue as to her thoughts.

But if Daniel Flanders were still alive, he'd soon be dead.

Later in the week, the mutilated body of a young man, apparently of the same height and weight as Daniel, was found by a shepherd in the mountains, not far from where the murders had occurred. Lianne was so overcome with grief that she wasn't even shocked when Raoul offered to claim the body and bury it. She only knew as she stood over the black coffin at the cemetery that the man she loved was dead. The father of her child was dead. She could barely speak, barely think. Otherwise, she'd have wondered why Raoul was suddenly so solicitous.

"*Querida,* you must stop mourning so hard," Raoul chastised her days later.

Lianne lay in bed, unable to summon the energy to get up though it was well past noon. She had even stopped performing, her grief was so great.

"I don't feel well." She offered Raoul a lame excuse.

He stood at the foot of the bed, hands clasped behind him. "I think I know what will get you up and about, my dove."

She looked at him, uncaring.

"Would you like for me to send for your daughter?"

"Désirée?" She mouthed the name in disbelief.

"Have you more than one child?" Raoul grinned. "You'd do that for me?"

"*Sí,* and much more, Lianne. Anything you wish is yours."

Coming to sit beside her, he took her hand, then tenderly kissed her lips. "Don't you know how much I love you?"

She was beginning to and this surprised her. She knew she had his passion, that he was in love with her, but she had no idea he loved her so deeply.

"I can't believe you'd send for her," she remarked, not able to answer him. She was afraid he'd ask her if she loved him, and at that moment she couldn't tell him she didn't and never would. She wanted her child with her!

"A child should be with its mother. I'll write to Dera and request the child be sent immediately." He grew quiet, then continued. "I shall inform her about Daniel."

"*Merci,* Raoul," she said, her voice breaking.

He kissed her again before he left the bedroom.

She watched the closed door, unable to believe she'd soon have her child with her. Daniel's child. She hoped Désirée still resembled him. At least there was a living, breathing reminder of him.

Suddenly life seemed brighter. She rose from the bed and rang for Josephine. Daniel might be dead, but he'd always live in her heart, even if he had humiliated her. She had loved him, would always love him. The child was the bond which connected her to him in life and in death. But she must start to live again. Soon her child would be with her, and she had much to do before Désirée arrived.

Carmen sat in the *sala* of the luxuriously furnished house of Diego Gonzalez. She couldn't think of it as hers though they had been married for almost three months. She watched him from the corner of her eye while she counted the stitches of the sampler in her lap. He sat cross-legged on the tiled floor with a kitten on his knee, stroking the poor creature so roughly that Carmen breathed a sigh of relief when the animal managed to wiggle free of his hold and scamper onto the patio into the darkness.

Diego was rough with animals and people. She'd

attest to that. He had a mean, sadistic streak. More than once she'd endured a slight beating when she didn't please him, and it seemed as the marriage wore on, she pleased him less and less.

His monkey face grinned when she looked directly at him at one point, and Carmen shivered. Holy Mother, she thought to herself, protect me. She knew that look.

"You're the picture of domestic bliss," he told her.

Her hand shook as she pushed the needle through the fabric. *"Gracias,"* she said.

Diego laughed loudly and sounded like a hyena. "Such a quiet girl you are, Carmen. Have you any thoughts in your head? If so, I should like to hear them."

She had plenty of thoughts, but most of them concerned how much she'd like to be a young and not so grieving widow. She hated Diego; and she hated her father for forcing her to marry such a detestable man.

"I think only about making a good home."

Diego stood up. His shirt was opened at the neck to reveal a stubble of dark hair. He had rolled up his sleeves because the night was warm. He clenched his hands which were covered in the same dark brown as his chest. Those hands! How she hated them!

"What about making babies?"

Carmen's mouth trembled. "We've been married a short time, Diego." He hadn't touched her in a few weeks, not since the death of his ex-mistress, Isabelle Hidalgo. For some reason he'd been preoccupied, and she wondered if he'd possessed true feelings for the woman. But lately he was gayer, happier than she'd ever seen him.

"The time has come to make children, Carmen. Your father would be very pleased."

"And of course you must please my father!" she snapped without thinking.

His little eyes narrowed to slits. "*Sí*. He gave you to me as my bride, and though I didn't want you, you serve a purpose and must do my bidding."

Diego pulled her from the sofa, wrenching her arm in the process. "Go to the bedroom and prepare yourself for me. Now!"

She didn't want to. In fact Carmen never wanted to feel his hairy hands upon her again. She hated the smell of him, the filthy things he did to her when they were in bed, but worst of all, she despised the pain he inflicted on her. He never cared for her, and she felt the marriage act was only to punish women. The image of her mother came to her mind. Perhaps she had endured Raoul's touch without complaint and maybe even enjoyed it a little since she had loved her husband, but Carmen didn't love hers. She wouldn't allow Diego to abuse her again.

"You'll hurt me. I shall tell my father if you bruise me again."

"Stupid girl! Your father detests the sight of you. He won't protect you from me. You think I've hurt you before, just wait and see what awaits you this night."

Diego pulled her protesting body from the *sala,* down the hall to the bedroom. He threw her headlong into the room and locked the door. He took the knife he carried inside his boot and laid it on the credenza, then undressed.

"Take off your clothes, Carmen!" he ordered.

"I won't."

"*Madre de Dios,* you will!"

He rushed toward her and grabbed her around the waist. He tore at her gown, ripping it down below her hips.

"Your body is nothing special. I've seen middle-aged whores with better bodies, and they know how to please a man. You're a plump little hen with the personality of a stone. I want you only to make a child to seal my fate with your father's wealth. Now, if I were married to your stepmother, that is a different story. She has a body to drive a man mad with desire. Your body only drives one mad.''

"I hate you!'' she screamed and kicked at his shin, hurling herself away from him.

Diego stopped for a moment, puzzled and surprised. "Ah, I think I have a wildcat here. I like when you're upset, Carmen. You make me want you more.''

As he advanced toward her, Carmen knew once he got her again, he'd beat her into submission. But she vowed she wouldn't lie like a lump of clay while he pleasured himself. No, she wouldn't let him touch her again. Into her mind's eye popped the image of Felix, the *lepero*. She didn't know why but suddenly she felt very brave.

The gleam of Diego's knife caught her eye. Just before Diego reached her, she dodged him and made a dash for the credenza. She picked up the knife and held it in front of her.

"Touch me, and I'll pierce your black heart, Diego.''

He seemed amused, totally unaware she intended to use it if necessary. But he decided that once he got hold of her, she'd pay for her misbehavior though it did excite him. He'd never seen Carmen with a flushed face, her hair loose around her shoulders. He wanted her and he'd have her.

He grinned and decided to use the oldest trick imaginable. A look of horror then appeared on his face.

"A rat! Carmen, a rat!'' He pointed to the spot at her feet, and without realizing it, her gaze strayed. Diego bounded and wrapped his arms around her body. "Now I've got you!''

However, he had forgotten that though Carmen lowered her arm for a moment, she still held the knife.

When he picked her up, her hand reached around his back and she dug the blade into the sinew and muscle.

They fell to the floor. Diego's eyes glazed over. Blood spilled from his mouth. She knew she had killed him.

Chapter 43

"I'm not concerned about the scandal," Lianne said and held a sobbing Carmen against her breast. "For once, Raoul, think about your daughter and not your own interests."

"She killed her husband for God's sake!" he shouted above Carmen's sudden wailing. "Diego wasn't perfect, but I could count upon him."

"For what?" Lianne snapped. "To do your dirty work? That was all he was good for. He tried to rape her, tried to rape his own wife. He got what he deserved."

Raoul threw up his hands in disgust. "Thank God the only servant at the house was half-blind and too old to see what Carmen had done. I shall arrange it so the authorities will think Diego was killed by an intruder and Carmen found his body soon after he was knifed. In the week we shall leave for Pachuca until the wagging tongues die down." Raoul left the *sala,* a look of total aggravation on his face.

Lianne stroked Carmen's hair. "You'll be all right, Carmencita. You did the only thing you could have done under the circumstances."

Lianne's soothing tone of voice calmed Carmen. She looked at Lianne, and her dark eyes resembled those of a small, hurt puppy. "I shouldn't have killed Diego. He was my husband. But he hurt me so much when he touched me. He was cruel.'' She grew quiet for a moment then said, ''I am glad he will no longer hurt me.''

"So am I," Lianne said.

True to Raoul's word, the authorities judged Diego's death to be murder by an intruder. Within the week the bags were packed and loaded on a coach for the trip to Pachuca. Lianne, Raoul and Carmen rode in a separate coach while Josephine rode in the one with the valises.

Lianne didn't think she'd be glad to leave Mexico City, but she was. There were too many memories of Daniel, and she grew very upset when they neared the spot on the road where she knew Daniel and Isabelle had been murdered by banditti.

Raoul glanced her way, and she discerned a mixture of compassion and jealousy in his eye. However, he took her hand and squeezed it.

"Soon your daughter shall be with you," he said.

She nodded but was unable to manage a smile though the thought of having her child with her filled her with great joy.

When Lianne spotted the XiXi Mountains she knew Pachuca lay not far beyond. As they passed the foot of the mountain, curiously shaped rocks of immense size known as the Peñas Cargadas caught her attention. Some people picnicked there, laughing in the afternoon sun despite their bedraggled attire. A young woman with long dark hair in a braid which hung down her back danced to and fro. Her short red skirt whipped around long, tanned legs.

Lianne watched the woman's movements in fascination and realized that she danced for only one man. The man her attention was riveted on stood a distance away from the other men who clustered around her, clapping their hands in appreciation of her dancing. He leaned against a rock with his muscular arms folded across his chest and lazily surveyed her.

Lianne could see his clothes were old but clean. His face was covered in dark hair, but she couldn't see higher than his nose because the sombrero he wore obscured her vision, casting a shadow over the upper portion of his face.

As the carriage drew in front of the group, the man looked up. From the window she noticed he stiffened perceptibly. Though she couldn't see his eyes, she felt his gaze upon her, and she knew he wasn't looking at her in friendship.

An odd sensation overtook her, and for a brief moment, her breath caught in her throat. The man seemed so familiar.

From beside her, she heard Raoul's contemptuous voice. "Peasants! Have they nothing better to do than dance and sing in the hot sun?" But she didn't withdraw her gaze, and though she didn't turn to look back when the carriage had passed, she knew the man watched her.

During the next few days, they settled into a routine. Upon waking in the morning, Raoul left for the mine and didn't return until noon. After a late lunch, siesta time approached. Raoul insisted Lianne join him in the bedroom for activities other than sleeping. She knew he loved her to distraction, that he adored her. This knowledge gave her power. So one afternoon just before Raoul drifted off to sleep, she kissed his mouth.

"Raoul?"

"Hmm?"

"Am I mistress of your hacienda, truly your wife?"

"*Sí,*" he answered sleepily.

"Then everyone must obey me?"

"*Sí.*"

"Even the men in the mines?"

"Uh . . . huh."

She watched him for some minutes as his breathing grew steady.

"Raoul."

No answer. He was asleep.

Smiling to herself, she slipped from under his arm and dressed in a gaily decorated peasant's blouse and violet skirt. She pulled on her sandals and quietly left the darkened room to face the brilliant sunshine of the afternoon through the patio doors.

She left the house to wander along the terrace which sloped to a ravine. Bright feathered ducks and wild geese swam and flew above the river which flowed through the property of Raoul de Lovis. Viaducts and chimney stacks were seen not far from the house as she walked to the amalgamation court.

Mules harnessed in teams were driven back and forth across the court. This was where the ore which had been taken from the mine and sprinkled with water until it became a muddy paste was laid out. Then salt, mercury and copper sulfate were used as preservatives. The mules were used, as were barefoot workmen, to stir the mixture. When the mercury was added, the mixture became lead-colored, but the process took hours of sloshing with bare feet and hooves.

The overseer was directing this scenario when Lianne approached. He smiled and inclined his head. "Good afternoon, Dona Lianne."

"Good afternoon, Raphael. I have a small favor to ask of you."

"Anything, Dona Lianne."

Lianne shot him a brilliant smile. "I should like to visit the mine."

"I must ask Don Raoul," the man replied.

"Are you going to go against a direct request, Raphael? I don't think my husband would be pleased if you refuse me."

"The mines are unsafe for such a lady as yourself."

"I'll take my chances. I wish you to accompany me."

She drew herself to her full height, and squared her shoulders. She must appear authoritative and apparently she looked the part. Raphael nodded and escorted her to a gently sloping shaft in the hillside which led to a flight of large stairs.

Lianne had only been to the mine once and knew it was the largest in Mexico. Torches hung upon the walls, and she had no difficulty finding her way as she followed after Raphael.

Much of the manual labor was performed by Indains known as *tenateros*. They were half-naked and carried heavy bags upon their slim shoulders. She was aware that these men watched her out of the corners of their eyes. They wore hats like inverted cones with tallow candles set into the center so they could see while they worked.

Suddenly Raphael stopped. "Dona Lianne, do you wish a tour of the mine?"

"No, I would like to see a young man who was sent here some months ago. His name is Felix."

Raphael looked curiously at her. *"Sí,* I know Felix."

"Take me to him then."

"As you wish." Raphael turned and Lianne followed him into a sloping cavern. Everywhere men watched her, and she felt embarrassed and wondered how Raoul would take her little jaunt into his silver mine. But she didn't care. She could wrap him around her fingers. For the moment she must find Felix.

When they stopped, Lianne saw a group of men filling sacks. Immediately she picked out Felix but noticed one difference. While he was dressed as scantily as the Indians, he was the only one chained to the wall. Evidently Raoul didn't want Felix to escape.

At her approach Felix looked up, focusing his eyes as if unable to believe he saw her.

"Señora Lianne!"

"Hello, Felix," she said softly. "I've come to free you." She turned to Raphael. "Unchain him."

"Señora, I cannot."

"Can't or won't?" she asked.

"Both. Don Raoul will be very displeased. I don't wish to be in trouble."

Raphael seemed like a good sort of person to her, and she was sorry to put him such a postion, but she was determined to free Felix from the mine.

"I personally will take responsibility for this, Raphael. Unchain him. Now."

Her tone left no doubt that she intended to be obeyed. Reluctantly Raphael unlocked the long chain from around Felix's waist.

"Gracias, amigo," she told Raphael and motioned to Felix to follow her.

When they were outside, and the brilliant sun splashed her hair with fire, she laughed.

"That was easier than I expected."

Felix squinted and adjusted his eyes to the sunshine. "Don Raoul will beat both of us."

"No, he won't. After we find you a change of clothes, you're free to leave."

"I have nowhere to go, señora."

"Then stay here with me. You may drive my carriage again. I promise you that Raoul won't lay a hand upon you."

"How can you be so certain, señora?"

"Because, my dear Felix," she said and grinned, "I know his weakness."

And she did. When she returned to the bedroom, she told Raoul what she had done. As she expected he ranted and raved, but she wrapped her arms around him and pushed her breasts against him.

"Will you deny me this favor, Raoul? Just an hour ago you told me I was mistress here and must be obeyed."

"Lianne . . ."

She kissed him with long, languid kisses, and when he stripped off her clothes, she knew she had won.

* * *

"Do you see a carriage yet?" Lianne asked Carmen who waited by the front window.

"Not yet," Carmen replied. "How often are you going to ask me? Only five minutes ago I said I saw nothing."

Lianne hurried to the window as she had at least forty times in the last hour. She peered into the gathering gloom of evening. The peaks of the Sierra Madre Oriental mountain range in the distance had already dissolved into a purple haze. Lianne grew agitated. Suppose Maria didn't arrive this evening? She'd go mad. The thought that she might not hold her Désirée in her arms today made her pace the floor of the *sala*. But she stopped suddenly as a thought struck her.

Turning to Carmen, she put her hands to her face. "What if the carriage was attacked by banditti? I've heard reports lately that some coaches have been stopped and the victims robbed. What if . . ." She couldn't say the words. The memory of what had happened to Daniel was still too painful though the incident had occurred almost four months earlier. Raoul had sent his personal coach to meet Maria and Désirée in Mexico City, and he had even sent three of his brawniest men on the hacienda to accompany them to Pachuca. Perhaps Raoul should have taken time off from the mine to meet Maria and the child himself instead of leaving the job to others. Lianne knew he was very busy with hacienda matters now, but if something happened to her baby, she'd never forgive him. He had assured her that Désirée and her nurse would arrive safely. Still an ice-cold shiver ran down Lianne's back.

"Don't think such a thing," Carmen warned and crossed herself.

At that moment Felix burst into the *sala*. "Señora Lianne, the coach is coming up the road!"

Instead of rushing to the window, Lianne took

Felix's word and ran into the foyer, pulled open the front door and flew into a small courtyard at the front of the house. Pushing open the iron gates, she was on the road in time to see the coach emerge from the encroaching darkness.

When the horses halted in front of her, the carriage door opened and out stepped Maria with one of the men's hands to guide her.

Lianne threw her arms around the portly woman. Maria's eyes filled with tears as did Lianne's.

"I never thought to see you again," Lianne cried in joy.

"Such a long time," Maria said and sobbed.

The two women parted when a small voice inside the carriage said, "Maria."

Instantly Lianne looked away from the woman. Her eyes took in the tiny person who stood in the doorway of the coach. She gasped. This child couldn't be Désirée. She wasn't the little toddler any longer, but a small person, almost three years old. And the most exquisite little girl Lianne had ever laid eyes upon. Her face was small, her features perfect. Except for the dark hair coloring and the eyes which were an ocean gray, Désirée resembled her mother.

Désirée's small chin quivered, and she seemed about to cry. "Maria, I want to go home."

Lianne approached her with hope in her heart. She smiled at her daughter and said softly, "Désirée, I'm your mother. Come to Mama, baby. I want to hold you."

She reached out for the child, but Désirée let out a huge piercing scream. "Maria! Maria!" Throwing herself headlong into Maria's comforting arms, she buried her exquisite little face in Maria's shoulder.

Reality trampled the hope within Lianne's breast. "She doesn't remember me," she said to Maria, her voice breaking.

Maria patted the small back. "I half expected

this, Lianne. She has known only me and Dera for so long. Give her time to come to know you again.''

"But I wished to hold her . . .'' Lianne's arms ached. Instead of reaching for the child, she patted her silky dark hair. "I'm your mama, Désirée. You must remember me.''

"Let's settle her in,'' Maria suggested softly.

Lianne nodded and led the way into the house.

That night she tiptoed into the room which she had set up for Désirée, next to hers and Raoul's. She watched her sleeping child and touched the tiny hand which rested on the pillow.

In her whole life she'd never seen a more beautiful little girl. And the child was hers. But not hers. She hadn't expected Désirée not to remember her. She should have known the child wouldn't recognize her. After all she had been a little over a year old when she left. However, as Lianne gazed at the life she and Daniel had made, she didn't blame Désirée. She blamed Raoul for this new blow to her existence. His obsession had cost her more than she could have imagined.

"I'll never forgive him,'' she whispered. "He has taken everything from me. Even the love of my own daughter.''

When she left the nursery and walked into her bedroom to lie in Raoul's arms, she knew that one day she'd even the score with Raoul. And when she did, he'd be very sorry he had ever desired her.

Chapter 44

Carmen watched Lianne as she walked in the garden with Désirée, their hands entwined. The child had been with them for two weeks, and there seemed no hope that the little girl would ever take to Lianne as a child to its mother. However, today there appeared to be the first glimmer of acceptance of Lianne by Désirée.

For the past hour Lianne had snug French songs to Désirée and Carmen thought she'd go insane as Désirée insisted Lianne sing them over and over again. Still Lianne had an abundance of patience which Carmen admired. She didn't think she'd be so calm with a child, but then perhaps she was still a spoiled child herself in many ways.

She missed her own mother very much. Elena had been her comfort, her mainstay. Now she had no one. Lianne tried and she was very grateful to her and had grown to care for her. However, Lianne couldn't take her mother's place.

Then there was Diego. Funny, she thought to herself, I don't even think very much about him. It was almost as if he had never existed, but he had. The bruises may have healed upon her flesh, but the pain within her soul hadn't. Diego had been an animal.

"Señora Gonzalez."

She turned to find Felix standing behind her. His head blocked the morning sun, and he smiled broadly at her. For the first time she noticed that Felix was no longer thin, but had filled out very nicely. His shoulders were broader, his arms muscular, apparently from the hard work in the mine. Carmen blushed as the thought of a naked Felix came to mind. To cover up her own embarrassment, she said rather harshly, "What is it?"

"You wished me to remind you when it was eleven o'clock, señora. You wanted to ride before lunch."

Carmen looked toward the garden where Lianne entertained her child, then at the book beside her on the terrace chair. She really was a little bored and would welcome the ride, but the sun was hot.

"I don't know, Felix. I burn easily."

"Forget the sun. You must live life while you can."

That made a great deal of sense to her. She remembered her mother. Elena had always done what was proper, avoided risk. And what had happened to her? She had died suddenly. Carmen didn't want to die until she had lived a bit, and the marriage to Diego had been like an early death. But she was alive!

"*Gracias,* Felix. I shall ride today."

"*Bueno,* señora. May I accompany you? I've heard there are banditti in the hills."

"You would protect me?" She asked this in a joking way, but her heart soared when he answered.

"With my life."

She knew he meant this. No one had ever said such a thing to her in her life. She didn't know how to reply to this and couldn't look him in the eyes. "I'll change and meet you at the stables," she said and hurried into the house.

Within half an hour Carmen's red roan cantered beside Felix who rode on a chestnut mare. They trotted past the mine then toward the distant hillside. Small golden marigolds peeked through the lush green grass of the countryside, and Carmen breathed deeply of the

sweet smelling air. She realized she hadn't felt such
peace since before her mother died and thought it
strange she should feel this way with Felix who, after
all, was a *lepero*. However, she was coming to think of
him more as a person worthy of her company. She
found herself liking him because he rode in companionable silence.

While the horses grazed, Carmen joined Felix
who sat on the grass.

"I remember one other time we did this," she
said, surprising herself.

Felix grinned. *"Sí.* The day I carried you from the
carriage so you'd not muddy your gown. If I
remember it was an especially ugly, black dress."

Her mouth trembled. "I was mourning my
mother."

"I'm sorry. I had forgotten."

Carmen controlled herself, and she gave him a
bright smile. "No harm done." After a few seconds,
she sobered. "So much has happened since then."

"Sí."

"Was it very awful for you in the mines?" she
asked him but knew she shouldn't have when she
noticed his back stiffen.

"Sí."

"I'm sorry my father sent you there. It was wrong
of him. Lianne told me she said you wished to stay
here after she took you from the mines. Why? Don't
you wish your freedom, Felix?"

Felix looked at her, his eyes met hers. "I am free,
señora. I'm not a slave. I chose to stay here."

"I think you stayed because of Lianne. Are you in
love with her? I mean you risked your life to help her
escape my father." Carmen sounded haughty though
she didn't wish to. For some reason she disliked
thinking that Felix might be in love with her stepmother.

"Is that what you think, señora?"

"*Sí,* I do. You're in love with my father's wife."

His eyes measured her for a moment, then Felix stood up. "I am in Dona Lianne's employ. I need not make an explanation to you."

Felix's tone was so cold she chilled in the warm afternoon. She rose also, and in a huff she mounted her horse without help. Felix was impossible, she found herself thinking when she was later in her room, changing from her riding outfit. She hadn't even summoned Josephine to aid her. Thrashing about her wardrobe, she pulled out a bright red gown, embroidered with golden roses on the bodice and sleeves.

She recalled Felix's comment about the dress she had worn that day months ago—the dress he said was so ugly. Well, this gown was quite beautiful and as she dressed in it, she refused to admit to herself that she wanted to show Felix she could look nice, even pretty.

During her marriage to Diego, she purposely dressed in black and claimed it was to honor her poor mother. But now, she wished to prove a point to the *lepero,* as she called Felix in her mind.

When she finished and surveyed herself in the mirror, she gave a tiny smile. She looked quite nice, she decided. Her hair was ebony black and she took a rose from a vase, trimmed it, and placed it behind her ear. The bright red and gold of the dress livened her pale complexion and amber sparks danced within her dark eyes.

Twirling before the mirror, Carmen giggled. She stopped, dizzy and excited.

"Just let that *lepero* call me ugly now!" she cried in delight to her reflection.

Someone watched her. Lianne knew eyes were upon her but the garden was empty of everyone save herself and Désirée who slept in a ball beside her on the bench. She looked down at her child and smiled. Their play that morning had worn them both out, and Lianne was glad to see Maria padding through the arched doors to retrieve her charge.

Désirée mumbled but leaned limply against Maria's ample bosom when she was picked up and carried into the house to the nursery. Lianne smiled to herself to realize how well the morning had progressed. She felt certain that her daughter would accept her once again. They had played games, sung songs, and Désirée had even reached for Lianne's hand. But Lianne was content to wait for her child's love.

Getting up, she walked among the brilliant blooms and gently touched the blossoms. Raoul hadn't returned from the mines as yet, and she knew he had a great deal of paper work on his desk. She hoped he'd be late today. She didn't relish an afternoon tryst with him. He had given her her daughter back, and in his own formal, aloof way, was kind to the child. However, she doubted if she'd ever feel much genuine warmth for him. He had taken too much from her to be forgiven.

The glaring sun gleamed on the peach-colored peasant's blouse and skirt she wore. Perspiration gathered on her brow and between her breasts but evaporated as a chill coursed up her spine. Glancing around the garden, she still saw no one but knew someone watched her. As her gaze careened across the terrace to the mountains, she started. Someone did watch her! She had an unencumbered view of a man wearing a sombrero astride a horse.

Though he was a distance away, she recognized him as the man at the foot of the mountains who had watched the young girl dance for him—the man who had watched the de Lovis carriage with such interest the day Lianne arrived in Pachuca.

"What is he doing watching me like this?" Lianne asked herself. Annoyance etched itself upon her face, but uneasiness invaded her. She felt violated by his gaze upon her. However, she didn't move away or shield her face. She straightened and glared at him until she saw him nudge the horse along the sloping incline of the mountain. When he disappeared, she let out a long relieved sigh.

"Carmen doesn't show the proper respect for Diego. I shall talk with her about this. What will people think? She is barely two months widowed, and she wears clothes so bright it appears she never cared for him."

"Well, she didn't," Lianne told Raoul and continued brushing her hair. "I see no reason why she must pretend she cared about him. Diego was monstrous to her."

Raoul's eye flickered over the lush picture Lianne made as she sat before the dressing table, trailing the brush through the thick auburn tresses. The sheer nightdress did little to cover her lush curves. Desire grew within him. Never in his life had he been unable to quench his passion for a woman. Never had a woman lay in his arms and responded to him as Lianne did. But she didn't love him, and he knew this. He didn't know a woman could take part in sexual love and feel nothing for the man involved. Apparently they could, and he was learning quite a bit about women from her.

He discovered Lianne had a healthy appetite for lovemaking, and though this discovery pleased him, it disturbed him. What would he do if another man caught her eye? That was highly probable since she made no bones that she didn't love him, so he couldn't count on her faithfulness. Sending for her child had helped matters between them. She no longer looked at him in scorn or hatred. Though he had no inkling, what she felt, she was truly Dona Lianne, his wife, the woman he wished to bear his children. He knew he had ensnared her, yet he wondered how tight the trap would hold. No matter how she felt about him, he must keep her.

Raoul cleared his throat. "Lianne, I think it's time you bore me a child."

He watched her hand stop in mid-air. He even saw the whitening of her knuckles around the silver brush.

"I hadn't thought about having a child, Raoul. Désirée occupies my thoughts and my time."

"Don't you wish to bear me an heir, *querida*?" His tone was smooth but tense.

"Of course," Lianne replied and continued brushing her hair.

"*Bueno.* However, I wonder if you mean your words."

"I do, but I haven't gotten pregnant since the miscarriage . . . Perhaps I'll never have any other children."

"*Sí*, Lianne. You'll have mine."

He rose from his reclining position on the bed and made his intentions clear. He wanted a son by her and would get one.

Felix finished polishing the silver harnesses which graced the necks of Raoul's stallions. The hour grew late, past midnight, he thought. Weariness overcame him, and he knew he'd soon have to retire. Señora Carmen was an early riser and would invade the peaceful stables early for her morning ride. He'd have to accompany her, because the threat of banditti grew worse.

He put the harnesses on a table and stopped when a slight noise caught his attention. Looking around the stable, lit only by a candle, he saw nothing.

"Probably mice," he said aloud. After a few seconds, his thoughts drifted back to Carmen, and without realizing it, he smiled. In the past few weeks, she had been much nicer to him and he admitted he thought she was very pretty lately. She no longer dressed in black or somber colors, but she resembled a peacock in brilliant blues and reds. Even her hair was prettier now that she wore it down, cascading around her shoulders in dark waves.

The mental image of her pleased him, but he attempted to resist it. Carmen was the daughter of Raoul de Lovis, the man who had raped his sister and caused the deaths of his parents. He must never forget that. The feelings he possessed for Carmen had to be quelled, because he couldn't allow himself to care for her in any way. She was a grand lady, and he figured that soon Raoul would find her another husband to replace Diego. Someone whom Raoul would approve. No, he had to fight his feelings for Carmen Fortuna de Lovis Gonzalez. But that presented a problem, because each time she was near him, he wanted to kiss her. He wondered at her reaction if he ever did, and sweat broke out upon his brow. She'd probably swat him as if he were a fly and hurl nasty invectives at him. Still, he liked to think about kissing her and hoped she'd never learn that she was the reason he had stayed on the hacienda after Lianne took him from the mines.

A shuffling noise caught his attention, ending all thoughts about Carmen. Felix knew he wasn't alone.

"Who is there?" he called out. "Show yourself!" He grabbed for the knife which was hidden inside his boot.

Felix waited for some seconds and held the knife tightly in his hand. The candle sputtered as a draft whipped through the stable, encasing the room in darkness.

Every nerve in Felix's body grew taut. Used to the mine's dimness, his eyes quickly adjusted to the darkness. Someone was in the room with him. He could feel the other person nearby, hear his breathing.

"Who are you?" Felix asked. What do you want here?"

Despite the control Felix attempted over his body,

he jumped when the disembodied voice sounded in the darkness.

"I think Raoul de Lovis owes you a debt," the gravelly voice said. "I am here to see that you are paid."

Chapter 45

It was eight months to the day since Daniel's death when Lianne readied for the drive into Pachuca. She didn't wish to go to the fiesta in honor of the new viceroy, Don Felix Berenguer de Marquina, but Raoul had insisted though she claimed ill health.

As Josephine helped her into a lavender gown, cut low with small sleeves that revealed a good portion of porcelain shoulders and arms, Josephine grinned.

"It's a good thing the waist on this gown is high, Dona Lianne."

Lianne barely breathed as she turned and faced the woman who grinned as if she were somehow responsible for the condition in which Lianne found herself.

"If you dare tell Don Raoul that I am pregnant, I shall dismiss you immediately."

Josephine backed away, hurt showing on her face.

"You have to tell him soon. He'll be able to see you're carrying a child. Don Raoul is very observant."

How well Lianne knew that fact, but she hadn't wanted to admit to herself that she was pregnant again. However, there was no denying the truth now and she realized that she belonged to Raoul in all ways.

Once their child was born, a bond would be forged which couldn't be broken.

"I will break the news to him in my own good time, Josephine," Lianne said and purposely kept her tone on a stern, businesslike level. The woman always thought she was more than an employee, and this rankled Lianne because she disliked Josephine and didn't trust her. "Now finish my hair. I'm sure my husband is waiting for me."

In silence Josephine finished the upsweep; tiny red-gold curls framed Lianne's perfectly shaped face. When Lianne joined Raoul and Carmen in the *sala* later, Lianne noted how very pretty Carmen looked in a dress of brilliant gold silk, threaded with silver.

The sparkling Mexican sky shone above the carriage as it wound its way toward Pachuca. Since coming to the hacienda, Lianne hadn't left it to go into the town. She had no reason to leave her daughter who now regarded Lianne as her mother. The two were inseparable. Lianne worried, as the carriage sped along, that the child would wake during the night and cry for her. She knew Maria was there and would take good care of her, but the maternal instinct within Lianne was strong. But for the child she carried, Raoul's child, she felt nothing.

"What is wrong, *querida*? You're tired?"

Lianne nodded but said, "I will be fine."

Raoul stroked his moustache in contemplation and took in her ivory complexion which appeared paler than usual and the catlike eyes that appeared sleepy. Then his gaze wandered to her waist, and he smiled.

"Lianne, are you pregnant?"

She started, and Carmen squealed.

"Are you having a baby?" Carmen asked.

What was the use? She may as well get it over with. "I'm having a child."

"How wonderful!" Carmen gushed and surprised Lianne with her delight.

Taking Lianne's hand, Raoul placed a tender kiss in the palm. "I'm a very happy and fortunate man, *querida.*"

Lianne offered him a tremulous smile. She should be happy, but she wasn't. She didn't want Raoul's child, and she wasn't certain why. When she realized she was pregnant that first time with his baby, she had been ready to accept it, after a while, out of loneliness. But she couldn't forget that that child had been the reason for her marriage to Raoul and had destroyed her happiness with Daniel. However, Daniel was now gone but this new baby seemed to open old wounds.

"I'm glad you're pleased," Lianne said.

His face told her he was more than pleased. Why can't he be a different type of man? Lianne wondered and knew she could never love this baby's father, not like she had loved Daniel.

Daniel. His face rose unbidden before her eyes in the dark coach, almost as if she could see him clearly before her. A sob rose within her, and she grew afraid she'd give vent to her feelings when suddenly the carriage lurched forward.

The sound of gunfire rent the air.

"Madre de Dios!" Carmen said and glanced out of the window. "Banditti, Papa!"

Loud voices surrounded them, echoing in the still night air.

Lianne grabbed Raoul's arm, and he motioned for her to remain quiet. Two armed guards rode in the front seat of the coach with Felix as the driver, but from the swarm of dark figures outside, she doubted they'd be much help. "What the hell?" Raoul rasped, and Lianne immediately saw what was wrong. The guards had climbed down from their perch and were handing over their rifles to the bandits.

The carriage door was thrown open and a gravelly voice asked them to step out.

Raoul went first, followed by Lianne and Carmen, who shook like a wildflower in the wind.

"Ah, Don Raoul, how good of you to accommodate us."

Lianne's gaze slid to the gravel-voiced man who
surveyed them on horseback. The moon was high and
bright. She recognized the man who now spoke as the
man with the sombrero whom she had seen on two
different occasions. Even now he wore his hat, slung
low over his eyes, and she barely made out the black
beard which covered his face. A gray poncho was
thrown across his broad shoulders.

"What is it you want?" Raoul asked. "Money? I
have very little with me, so robbing me will not fill
your pockets."

The man laughed and turned to his compadres.
"Don Raoul thinks we want money."

The others laughed and jostled each other with an
elbow. Lianne could tell Raoul was furious instead of
frightened, but he appeared quite calm despite their
precarious circumstances.

"Then what is it you want, *bastardo*?"

"Ah, Don Raoul, you're becoming impatient.
That is something you must beware of." The bearded
man stroked his chin. "There are ten guns pointed at
you, and some of my men are quite eager to do away
with you. You see, many of their relatives have
suffered at your hands in the mine. So, please, keep
your tongue inside your head, otherwise, you might
find it lying upon the ground."

"Your motley crew doesn't scare me. Now what
are your terms? What do you want?" Raoul asked
again.

The man's voice was a low growl when he spoke.
"Haven't you guessed by now?"

Lianne felt Raoul's hand tighten around her
wrist.

"No!" he cried. "I shall kill you first!"

"*Amigo,* your brave talk does nothing for me."
The man motioned to two of his men, and they

grabbed Raoul's arms and held him at bay though he kicked at them.

"Papa!" Carmen cried, as another man came forward, grabed her by the waist and lifted her to his horse.

"Carmen!" Raoul's face paled visibly, but grew whiter when a man lifted Lianne from her feet and handed her struggling, and squealing to the bearded man on the horse.

"Raoul!"

"Lianne!"

Raoul screamed her name over and over as the bearded man positioned her in front of him. "If you harm her, I'll kill you. I swear I will!"

"Ah, señor, you wound me." His raspy voice fanned Lianne's ear. "This is a form of justice for us. We take your two most valuable possessions—your daughter and your wife." His hand caressed Lianne's breasts. "I've heard your wife is very beautiful, now I shall find this out for myself."

"Bastardo!"

"Escort Don Raoul to his hacienda," the man commanded the two men who held Raoul. Then his head lifted to the carriage. "Ready, Felix?"

"Sí."

To Lianne's astonishment, Felix jumped from the coach and hopped onto a horse. She discerned pure pleasure on his face and suddenly she knew that Felix had led them into a trap, that the armed men had also been part of it, because even now they were riding to the mountains.

Turning his horse around, the bearded man followed in the same direction. Raoul's voice, calling her name, was lost beneath the din of galloping hoofs.

Chapter 46

The pathway grew narrower as the horses slowly trotted along the mountain's ledge. The group of bandits laughed and talked among themselves, now seeming confident that no one heard them or would follow them.

Despite her fear, she rested her drooping head against her captor's chest. She didn't know where they were headed or what would happen once they got there. This man and his whole group could rape her and Carmen, then dispose of their bodies. No one would ever find them. With each step the horse took, she felt herself being torn from civilization and Raoul. She detested her husband, but at this moment, she prayed to God he'd find them.

After a while the sound of other voices, raised in song, drifted toward her. She lifted her head, and through the blackness of the night, she saw torches lighting the scene ahead of them.

Soon the horses climbed higher and they entered the torchlit area. Men, and a woman, dressed in ponchos and sombreros surrounded them, and some whooped in delight when Carmen and Lianne came into view.

"Where are we? Who are these people?" Lianne asked the man who sat behind her, her fear vanishing and curiosity taking its place.

"You ask too many questions, *chica,*" he growled.

"And I will ask many more," she told him.

Though she didn't see his face, she sensed he smiled.

When the man stopped the horse, people swarmed around him, congratulating him on a job well done. Lianne noticed Felix was among these people, and she wondered how he could have participated in such a thing, but she had to remember that Felix wanted Raoul punished. However, she hadn't expected he'd use her and Carmen to do it.

The girl Lianne remembered from the rock, the day she arrived in Pachuca, approached them. Her dark eyes darted over Lianne in a look of utter hatred and contempt. Her long braid swung forward, resting on her shoulder.

"So you have captured the wife of Raoul de Lovis, El Lince."

"With Felix's help," the man said, and his hold tightened around Lianne's waist until she thought she'd be unable to catch a breath.

The girl's vicious gaze swept across Lianne's face, then to the thin gown she wore. Her hand shot out and pulled at the bodice of the gown, ripping the fabric until nothing but Lianne's chemise stood between her and the cool night air.

"How dare you, you filthy thing!" Lianne cried and attempted to cover herself with her shawl.

A knife appeared in the girl's hand. "I should like to cut out this she-cat's tongue," she said to the man she called El Lince.

He laughed in his gravelly way. "Theresa, you may get your chance soon enough, but for tonight, I must see to our guests' comfort."

"Comfort!" Theresa spat upon the ground. "This devil woman and De Lovis's spawn should sleep on the ground with the snakes. A woman who'd marry such a man deserves no better."

"Be that as it may, but I'm weary now and wish to rest."

Concern flooded Theresa's face. "Are you all right? You don't feel ill again?"

El Lince shook his head. "I am well. Don't fear for me."

He started to move past her with Lianne held tight against him, but Theresa's hand shot out and stilled him. "Will you come sleep beside me tonight?"

"An irresistible invitation," he said and winked at her.

Theresa's face expressed hope, but as they passed her, Lianne felt her hate-filled eyes boring through her back. Did the silly female think she had designs on the man? Was that why the girl seemed to hate her so? She'd never done anything to one of these people, but whatever suffering Raoul had brought upon them was now her and Carmen's nightmare.

The entrance to a cave loomed ahead. El Lince pushed her into its torchlit confines. Lianne saw that cooking pots had been set up, pallets and blankets rested against the walls. She realized this was the bandits' hideout. Dear God, she thought, Raoul will never find us here.

Grabbing her arm, El Lince propelled her further into the cave, away from the living quarters of the others until they entered a tiny section like a small chamber, lit by a lone candle on a rock. A pallet lay on the earthen floor, and Lianne noticed that the blankets looked clean. He motioned for her to sit.

"Suppose I don't want to sit," she said and turned to face her captor.

"Then don't," he replied in that menacing, gravelly way of his, "but you better do what I say. I take no disobedience from any of my people, especially not from the *puta* of Raoul de Lovis."

Color suffused Lianne's face, and she sputtered before she could get out a sound. "You know I'm his wife!"

She could feel him surveying her from under his sombrero. "I know that very well," he said, and she swore she heard jealousy in his voice.

"You can't keep me here, El Lince." She knew that meant the lynx and wondered why the man had such a name. Perhaps he wished to keep his identity secret.

"Do you intend to escape?"

"*Sí.* Every prisoner has a duty to escape."

"Well," he said and passed a hand over his beard, "I should hate to see a bullet enter your lovely body, or worse, one of my men may decide to take liberties with you before your death. You see, Dona Lianne, you don't realize that my people wish to be free of your husband's control. Many of their loved ones died from brutal beatings in the mines. Some of these people were Indians, some Mexican. But all have one thing in common—they hate your husband, and that hatred includes you and his daughter."

"Where is my stepdaughter?" Lianne asked.

"She is hidden somewhere else in the cave. I don't wish you to be with her. Together, you both might try and escape. Alone you won't, because the one left behind will suffer."

"You and your nasty group are monsters! But my husband will find us, and when he does, he'll devise such tortures for all of you that whatever happened to those men in the mine will seem like nothing."

"I'm sure he will, Dona Lianne. Now, if you don't mind, I'll be on my way."

"To sleep with your Theresa?" Lianne snapped, though a part of her envied the girl. El Lince made a handsome figure of a man, and even if she couldn't see all of his face, she knew he was probably very handsome. But he was a criminal, a *bandito,* she told herself.

"Jealous, *chica*?"

"You're a filthy man!" she cried and turned away.

She heard his footsteps as they left the chamber

and his muffled comments to someone nearby. She scampered to the doorway and, peering out, she saw two dangerous-looking men on either side of the door with rifles.

"Señora?" one of them said and pointed the gun at her.

Lianne withdrew into the confines of the chamber and sat upon the pallet. She pulled the blanket around her, and when the urge came to cry, she didn't. She had to be strong.

Lianne woke with a start when fingers touched her shoulder. Before her stood Felix with a cup of warm tea in his hand.

"I thought you would like this, señora," he said and placed it beside her on the floor.

"I'd like to wring your neck!" Lianne snapped at him, her eyes raking over him.

"Forgive me, but I understand how you feel."

"Do you?" she asked and rose from the pallet. She shook out the creases of her gown and pulled the torn bodice together before wrapping her shawl securely around her.

"*Sí.* Your husband carted me off to the mines like a cow to market. He beat me unmercifully before he sent me, then when I arrived there, I was beaten again. To make me strong, Raphael said. But I knew I was beaten because Raoul de Lovis wished it. I understand very well your rage, Dona Lianne. You must believe I wouldn't have agreed to this except for . . ."

"Yes?"

Felix shuffled his feet. "Never mind. Just know that you and Carmen won't be harmed. El Lince would never allow that."

"You seem to be quite taken with El Lince. Who is he? What does he really want with us? Money? Tell him he can have all he wants. I'll see he's paid handsomely for our safe return to Pachuca."

"I don't think it's money he wants, Dona Lianne. El Lince has a debt to repay Raoul de Lovis."

Lianne sighed her exasperation. "It appears that everyone detests my husband, but I refuse to be made a pawn in El Lince's game. I shall escape from here, Felix, and when I do I'll make certain that you, El Lince, and all of his cohorts suffer for this. When Raoul finds your merry group, he'll send every last one of you straight to hell."

"He is the devil and can do it," came El Lince's gravelly voice from the entranceway.

Lianne spun around. Her hair looked as fiery as she felt as she stood in the candle glow. El Lince motioned to Felix to leave, but when they were alone she walked up to the man and spat in his face.

"I admit Raoul de Lovis is a devil, but you're one also, señor. And I'm not afraid of you. After living with one for so long, I have no fear of either of you."

Lianne didn't know what the man's reaction would be, and she braced herself for the onslaught she felt sure would follow. However, El Lince only took the banadana wrapped around his neck and wiped the spot on his cheek. This was when she saw the jagged scar on his throat. She realized that the man had been injured and not that long ago.

Though the sombrero obscured his eyes, she felt them upon her face. Calmly he retied the scarf around his neck.

"Am I so repulsive to you, chica?" His tone was husky and she realized he was defensive about the injury. Compassion welled within her, and she wasn't certain why. Evidently the cut had injured the vocal cords, and that was why he sounded like a wounded mountain cat. Like a lynx!

Lianne didn't wish her captor to see he had touched a soft spot in her. After all, she quickly told herself, he was a kidnapper.

"I find everything about you repulsive."

He laughed. "Then I won't bother you with my company, but I hope you will accept a gift."

"What sort of gift?" Lianne eyed him suspiciously when he went to the opening and came back inside with a white peasant blouse, a pair of breeches and sandals, plus a blue and orange poncho.

"Your dress is torn, and you'll need these for later."

"Later? What do you mean for later?"

"You ask too many questions. Just change, Dona Lianne."

"Whose clothes are these?"

"If you must know, the blouse and sandals are Theresa's. The pants and poncho are mine."

Lianne glared. "I suppose Theresa gave me these things out of the goodness of her heart. Or did you leave the wench nothing to wear?"

"Dona Lianne," he said and grinned. "You seem quite interested in my relationship with Theresa. Jealous, in fact. I'm a gentleman and refuse to talk about her. However, I will say that Theresa looks wonderful without clothes."

"I'd like to slit your throat!" Lianne screamed, then stopped short when she realized what she had said.

"I'm sorry about that, but someone already beat you to it." El Lince turned and went through the opening. Lianne didn't even bother to look outside. She knew the guards were still there.

Carmen beat her fists against Felix's chest, knocking the cup from his hand.

"Filthy *lepero*! How could you do this to us? I thought you were our friend. Didn't Lianne save you from the mine, didn't you like me a little?"

He grabbed at her fists and held them tight. He did like her, he liked her a great deal, and that was the problem. If he could only harden his heart toward Carmen, then he'd be able to seek revenge on Raoul de Lovis with a clear conscience. But he knew El Lince didn't wish harm to her or to Lianne. He wondered briefly if he should have become involved at all. The last time he helped someone he wound up beaten and sent into the mine. If Raoul found him, he knew that his next punishment would be much worse than the mine.

But he couldn't tell Carmen he cared about her. She'd never believe him.

"No harm shall come to you. I promise."

"The promise of a *lepero* is nothing." Carmen pulled away. "Leave me alone. I don't wish to see your face!"

"I brought you some clothes," he said, ignoring her. "They're for the journey."

"What journey?"

"Further away from here. We ride north tomorrow."

"I don't understand," Carmen said. "If we are to leave here, then how will my father find us? What of the ransom?"

Felix shook his head. "There is no ransom."

"But I thought . . ."

"I've said too much already. Just remember that you won't be harmed." Then he was gone.

None of it made any sense to Lianne. El Lince hadn't bothered to inform her where they were going, but she knew it was northward. But why? If he wanted Raoul to pay a ransom, why was he purposely riding away from the safety of his hideout?

She didn't question him, because she felt certain he wouldn't tell her. She did feel better seeing that Carmen was all right and sharing a horse with Felix. The girl had a look of distaste on her face, and Lianne wondered if it was because she disliked the pants she was forced to wear, or if she wished to hide her feelings for Felix. Either way, Lianne didn't blame her. She felt the same dislike. Especially for the man who sat behind her, his tanned and scarred hands on the reins.

The image of Daniel's hands flashed through her

mind. His hands had looked very much like this man's, only they weren't scarred or rough to the touch. And she knew El Lince had rough hands. She remembered how they felt when he caressed her breast in front of Raoul. But her eyes misted thinking of Daniel, and without realizing it, she sighed his name.

"What did you say?" the gruff voice asked, and she felt him stiffen behind her.

"Nothing that concerns you."

"That's where you are wrong, Dona Lianne. While you're in my care, your every breath, every thought, every smile concerns me."

"Then return me and my stepdaughter to my husband."

"Ah, you wound me with your haste to leave us. Haven't I been a good host to you, seen to your needs?"

She leaned back and would almost have seen his eyes staring at her, except he lowered the brim of the sombrero.

"Don't you ever take that thing off?" she asked, instead of the stinging retort she had intended.

"*Sí*. When I make love."

"I should have guessed!"

"Since you're so eager to see me without my sombrero, perhaps I will oblige you one night. Hmmm?"

This time Lianne stiffened and turned her attention to the mountainous incline ahead.

"I'd rather die than have someone like you touch me," she said.

"But you allow your husband, a murderer, to make love to you. Why not me?"

His arms tightened, and she felt squeezed between them, almost as if he were purposely trying to torment her for sleeping with her own husband.

"How do you know Raoul is a murderer?" she asked and caught a breath.

"Because," he breathed into her ear, "he ordered

Theresa's husband killed."

"I didn't know that." Now she knew why Theresa disliked her.

"Si, and many others have gone into the mine, never to return. Your husband has quite a force of men on his hacienda. But his men won't help him now. We ride high into the mountains to lure him away from familiar territory."

Now she understood the reason for the journey. Raoul's men would tire, but Lianne knew Raoul wouldn't. He would find her and Carmen if he died in the process. Lianne wondered if it would make a difference to El Lince to tell him she carried a child. Perhaps he'd forget his revenge and return her to the hacienda unharmed. But she changed her mind. If he realized she carried the child of Raoul de Lovis, he might make things more unpleasant for her.

"Is Theresa the main reason you seek to harm my husband?"

"Ah, I hear jealousy in your voice again, Dona Lianne. What would your husband say if he knew how often you question me about Theresa?"

They had been speaking Spanish, but at that moment, Lianne responded in English, a language she felt sure he didn't understand. "Go to hell, you arrogant pig!"

"Como?"

She said nothing else, and when she thought she'd go insane if they didn't stop to rest, El Lince called a halt to his party of twenty riders.

"We'll make camp here for the night," he told her.

Here was a picturesque spot on the side of a mountain which overlooked a deep ravine, lush with vegetation and interlaced with the deep purple hue of orchids. For a moment Lianne forgot she was a prisoner as she stood under the magnificent evening sky which touched the valley. However, Theresa quickly brought her back to reality.

"Here," she said and tossed Lianne a well-worn blanket.

"Gracias." Lianne inclined her head in the girl's direction.

"El Lince told me to see you are comfortable until he returns from scouting the area, so I have. Now find a spot for yourself to sleep, but remember, *puta,* I will keep an eye on you, as will every person here."

Lianne considered her for a moment before speaking. "I find it strange that you call me such a name when you're the only woman in their midst. Carmen and I are prisoners, but you belong. I doubt if you sleep alone, Theresa, and I wonder how many of these men you've pleasured during the long nights."

Theresa's dark eyes boiled. "I sleep with no man but El Lince. I'm his woman! Don't forget that, *puta.*"

"I'm not a whore, Theresa. I'm lawfully married to Raoul de Lovis. I see no ring on your finger."

Lianne began to move aside, but Theresa stopped her with a strong grip on Lianne's wrist. "El Lince is mine. I nursed him back to health. If not for me, he'd be dead, and he knows it. He owes me a great deal. In time I expect to become his wife, though Domingo has eyes for me also."

Theresa's honesty startled Lianne, but she seemed to care for El Lince. However, Lianne was more interested in the man. "What was wrong with him? I noticed he is scarred."

"You do not know. El Lince has not told you?" she asked in disbelief.

"Told me what?"

"That your husband is responsible for his injuries. El Lince was nearly killed on the orders of Raoul de Lovis. I cannot believe he didn't tell you . . ."

Lianne shrugged as if the information was of little importance to her, but suddenly she was afraid. No wonder El Lince hated Raoul, and that hatred extended to her and Carmen. Oh, he had been nice enough, but how long would it be before his anger erupted and he harmed them?

"Help me with the cooking," Theresa ordered Lianne brusquely. "You make the coffee," she told Carmen.

While they performed their appointed chores, Lianne whispered to Carmen when Theresa was out of earshot. "We have to escape."

"*Sí*," Carmen said through clenched teeth. "When?"

"I don't know yet. They keep us apart at night, but it must be tonight. Watch me carefully. Somehow we will sneak away from here."

"I'm afraid, Lianne."

Lianne gave her what she hoped was a confident smile. "We'll make it."

Later that evening when the sky was completely black, El Lince hadn't returned. The others settled down under their blankets, their bellies full. Soon snores reverberated through the quiet night.

Lianne lay under her blanket. Carmen was about thirty feet from her. Their only problem was Felix who sat on a rock above them. Every so often when one of them moved, he cast a wary eye below him. He clutched a rifle in his hand, but Lianne wondered if he'd really use it. She had no doubt he hated Raoul, but did he hate her so much, Carmen so much, that he'd actually shoot them? Lianne didn't think so.

She decided the time was now. She'd put Felix to the test.

Sitting up, she looked around. The campfire dimmed, and everyone was asleep. Even Theresa snored softly. Felix's attention happened to be diverted for a moment by the roar of a mountain lion, and he didn't see her slither from under her blanket over to where Carmen lay. But Carmen was ready.

With a speed which surprised Lianne, Carmen crawled away from the firelight into the darkness with

Lianne following. The ground was hard and dotted with bramble bushes which tore at their clothes but neither of them cared. Once they were a distance away, they'd run all night if they had to. Their sense of freedom grew as they crawled farther without detection. Finally, Lianne stopped and listened.

The night was silent. No gunfire disturbed the stillness, and no voices were raised in alarm. No one knew they were gone. Felix might, but he evidently didn't know which direction they took.

"We did it, Carmen!" Lianne said, excitement in her voice. "We can stand now."

"I can't believe no one has followed us," Carmen whispered worriedly and rose along with Lianne. "Felix watched us closely."

"Perhaps he isn't as good a watchdog as El Lince thought. Now let's go."

"But where, Lianne? Can you see to follow the trail we took this afternoon? We're three days from Pachuca."

Lianne barely discerned her hand in front of her face, but the inky blackness wouldn't deter her. She took Carmen's hand. "Follow me," she said.

Carmen stalled. "Let's wait until daylight."

"No. They'll find us then. Our hope is to travel at night and find a cave to rest in during the day. We mustn't be found, Carmen. El Lince detests Raoul, and I think he may kill us."

"Felix wouldn't allow that," Carmen told her.

"*Sí*. Felix hates him for the death of his sister and his parents. Believe me, Felix isn't our friend."

"I think he is."

Carmen's defense of Felix puzzled Lianne, but she didn't have time to dwell upon it. They had to get far away by morning. If only she knew which direction to go in. The sky was so dark, there were no stars tonight. She dragged Carmen behind her, and they crept down the side of a ravine, then across flat ground until they discovered a hillside. Up they plodded, nearly falling and tumbling down again, but they persevered until they reached the top.

Carmen was out of breath. "That was some climb!"

"We made it though," Lianne said and sat down on the ground. "By morning, we'll be far away from El Lince and his men."

"Ah, *chica,* I thought you liked me."

The unmistakable gravel voice pierced the darkness. Lianne and Carmen both stood and held onto one another. His horse snorted and nudged at them. Then they heard another horse nearby and Felix's voice.

"I should have been more wary of them, El Lince. I'm sorry."

"Don't worry, Felix. I knew they wouldn't get far."

"And how did you know that, El Lince?" Lianne asked and straightened her spine. She might be frightened, but she refused to let this menacing man know it.

He laughed and coming forward, he lifted her from the ground and set her before him on his horse while Felix did the same with Carmen.

"The campsite wasn't picked by accident. I knew the ravine below us formed a circle. That if you tried to escape, which you did, you'd not be able to find your way at night. You'd wander until you came up the side of the mountain. All you did was make a 360 degree turn."

"All that energy wasted," Carmen said and gulped back tears.

"Not so," replied El Lince whose hand rested intimately upon Lianne's thigh. "I see now that you both need better watching. Felix, you shall take charge of Carmen, and I will look after the wife of Raoul de Lovis."

True fear shot through Lianne. His voice held a warning which she couldn't ignore. With El Lince watching her every move, she'd be unable to escape.

When they reached camp, some of the men stirred, but Theresa was awake.

"How did this happen?" she asked.

"Go to sleep, Theresa," El Lince told her.

"Sleep beside me," she begged.

"I must guard our guest."

"*Puta!*" Theresa said and spat at Lianne before retreating to her blanket.

El Lince laughed and helped Lianne off of the horse.

"Don't laugh at her," she scolded him. "She loves you."

"Theresa doesn't know who she loves. One day, she wants me, the next she's hot for Domingo or one of the other men."

When her feet touched the ground, her hands rested against the rough poncho which covered his chest. In the darkness his features were obliterated, and she smelled his musky scent, could feel the rapid beating of his heart beneath the cloth. His breath caressed her face, and he was so close she thought for an instant that his lips brushed her hair.

Suddenly he jerked her arm and walked her to a spot away from the others where a natural ledge was formed above the ravine and separated them from the rest by a wall of bramble bush. He threw a blanket upon the ground and ordered her to lie down, then he joined her and covered them with another blanket.

"You intend to sleep beside me?" she asked.

"Of course."

"I won't try and escape again."

"I know you won't, because I'll be aware of every move you make, Dona Lianne."

It seemed the situation was settled, but Lianne wasn't. She lay unmoving beside him, fearful that he'd touch her, take liberties with her. Would this nightmare ever end? Would Raoul never find them? she wondered.

The absurdity of it all struck her. She actually

prayed for Raoul to find them. The man she hated more than anyone on earth, even more than El Lince, was to be her salvation. If not for Raoul, she'd be married to Daniel now, and Daniel would be alive. She'd not be lying next to a *bandito*, a man probably no better than her husband.

"Can't you sleep, *chica*?" his voice asked later.

At the moment she was thinking of Désirée. "I hope my little girl is all right. I miss her."

El Lince's breathing stilled, then he extinguished a sigh. "I had a daughter once."

"What happened to her?" she asked.

"Her mother was unfaithful and took her away."

"I'm sorry."

"You should be," he growled. "Go to sleep, Dona Lianne. I'm not here to spill my guts to you."

Lianne trembled. What had she said to deserve such a strange response. She didn't know this man, or his unfaithful wife, woman, whatever the case may be. And she didn't care. She only wanted to return to Raoul's hacienda.

She hadn't realized she slept until she woke feeling cozy and warm. However, she instantly realized that she lay within El Lince's arms, her back against his chest and that his mouth was against her neck, and his hand was under her blouse!

Part of her rebelled and she almost pulled away, but at that moment his hand began an upward exploration from her ribcage to the round fullness of her right breast. Her breathing almost ceased when his warm hand cupped its heaviness. The other part of her quieted while his thumb tenderly flicked the nipple until it stood hard and firm. She knew she should stop this, but the wonderful sensations building within her wouldn't allow her to.

Then she felt his mouth at the nape of her neck, kissing the flesh. What should she do? Should she let him know she was awake? Perhaps he'd stop, but she didn't want him to stop. And this thought horrified her.

She felt his fingers burn a pathway from her right to her left breast, massaging it in the same sensual way. Then his hand snaked downward, past her ribcage, and stopped at the waist cord which held up the breeches. But the pants belonged to him and were large around her so that they rested low upon her hips. He didn't have to undo the cord as his hand made its way beneath the material and moved over her abdomen to its destination.

She muffled her groan when his fingers touched the spot between her thighs. Liquid fire coursed through her, threatening to singe her flesh. She didn't know why she allowed him to touch her, to give her the ultimate pleasure a man could give to a woman, but when his fingers slid inside her and worked their magic, the pleasure built until she thought she'd go mad.

Her breathing grew rapid each time his fingers moved in and out, and without realizing it, she writhed and arched against them. For the first time since she had loved Daniel, she felt herself dissolving, melting, floating in a sea of desire. Raoul was a good lover, but she felt he only loved to please himself. This man, this bandit, was acutally pleasuring her, and when her body could stand the torment no longer, it exploded.

She knew he felt the ripple of pleasure which washed over her when he pulled her against him. "You liked that, *chica*," he growled into her ear.

She had more than liked it. She had loved it, but she wouldn't admit it to him and was unable to look at him, but he twisted her body so she saw the outline of his face, and the fact that he didn't wear the sombrero wasn't lost on her. Still it was took dark to see his features clearly.

He kissed her mouth with tiny kisses and sucked at her lips. Lianne groaned and he laughed when he heard her.

"*Sí*, you like a man's hands upon you, and I think you'd like more of me, but not today, *chica*. It's nearly dawn, and we must move on. However, soon I'll take you and have you writhing beneath me like the *puta* you really are."

Hot waves of humiliation mingled with embarrassment within her. How dare he say such a thing to her! Did he enjoy tormenting her, taking her over the brink of sanity only to insult her? But she couldn't deny she had felt desire for him and if he had continued, she'd have made love to him. What was wrong with her? Why did she want this man, this man of all men? Why must he be the one to touch her heart?

She sat up. "Don't come near me again," she told him in a shaky voice.

Even in the darkness she imagined he grinned. "I will, Lianne, and when I do you'll welcome me with open arms . . . and legs." He laughed aloud and tousled her hair as if she were a plaything for his amusement. He got up and left her side.

Lianne watched his outline in the approaching dawn and saw he had replaced the sombrero. She had to get away from El Lince. She was pregnant with Raoul's child, and knew that if he approached her again, she wouldn't resist. What's wrong with me? she asked herself that morning as they continued their journey and wondered if she really was a whore as El Lince had said.

Chapter 47

"I don't understand you, Felix." Carmen eyed Felix with contempt as she served him a plate of beans the next evening. "I've never hurt you. My father, he is a different matter, but Lianne has also been more than kind to you. If not for her, you'd still be in the mine."

"I'm pleased that you see Dona Lianne for the special person she is," he said and shoved a spoonful of beans into his mouth.

Carmen sat beside him and positioned the plate on her lap. "She helped me when I needed help. Did you know that I killed Diego Gonzalez?"

Felix stopped eating and held the spoon aloft. Carmen saw by the look of shock and surprise on his face that he didn't know how Diego died.

"I only knew your husband was dead, killed by an intruder."

Carmen laughed. "Father arranged everything. That's the official story, but I stabbed Diego. He tried . . . to rape me. Diego wasn't a considerate lover and often he beat me, but I never ran to Lianne for help, though she had sworn she'd help me. But this time I didn't beg for Diego's mercy. I thought of you, Felix, and knew you were strong. Your strength gave me courage."

"I see." Felix continued eating as if she had just told him the sky was blue. Didn't he care that she had murdered her husband, or did he feel it was justice that she suffer as his family had suffered at the hands of her father?

"Do you think I am a bad person?" she asked him, not quite certain why his opinion of her mattered.

"What I think shouldn't matter to you, Carmen."

She timidly reached out and touched his arm. "But it does," she said softly.

Half expecting him to take her hand, she was surprised when he stood up and barely looked at her. "I must tend to the horses," he said and left her.

Carmen gulped back a sob. "Stupid *lepero*," she whispered.

The rest of El Lince's group milled about the campfire. Some finished eating and others huddled beneath the blankets for the night. Lianne felt an unrest in the air, though she couldn't explain why. A few of the men looked at her with hard, cold eyes as they had done on many occasions, but this night she sensed something more in their eyes. A sensation of dread overcame her when one of the men known as Domingo came forward from a small circle of men with Theresa by his side. The two of them stopped before El Lince who finished mopping his plate with a piece of stale bread.

"We want to speak to you," Theresa said to El Lince, ignoring Lianne's presence.

"Quiet!" Domingo ordered. "I am the man here. I will talk."

Theresa grew silent, but her eyes glowed bright. Lianne felt strangely ill. Once before she had seen a woman look like that. She recalled Paulette Dubois' eyes had glittered their hatred for her the night she arranged for Daniel to be in the summerhouse. The night Victor had turned away from her as her friend. Now Theresa seemed to have stirred Domingo and the others, and Lianne knew their vicious looks were for her.

"What do you want?" El Lince asked.

"How long must we travel before we face Raoul de Lovis?" Domingo placed his hands on his hips and appeared forbidding, but the man's stance didn't bother El Lince.

"We've come to the end of the trip. No more running."

"This is where you will face de Lovis? Here on this mountain?"

"*Sí*. We're at the top. De Lovis will be at the bottom and unable to reach us. There's one path to the bottom. When his men come up, we pick them off one at a time."

"How do you know he will even come this way?" Domingo asked.

El Lince smiled. "I've left a trail a child could follow. Never fear, *amigo*, de Lovis will come."

"Hmmph!" Theresa scoffed. "Just what will happen to *her* after de Lovis is dead? I don't think you will rid yourself of this one."

"You ask too many questions, Theresa, and the answers don't concern you." El Lince practically growled at her, and Theresa jumped.

"I see now that I was right to be wary of her." Theresa inclined her head towards Lianne. "You want her, El Lince, and that is not good for my people. Your heart has grown soft, otherwise, this *puta* would have been made to suffer for her husband's crimes."

"Theresa is right," Domingo said and the men who gathered around them nodded their heads in agreement.

"What do you wish me to do with Dona Lianne? The choice is yours," El Lince told them. His cold smile struck fear in Lianne's breast.

"Our custom has always been to whip the *putas*. This one deserves such a punishment," Theresa insisted. "And if you do not do this, El Lince, we'll know you are not our true leader, and I will wish to heaven I had let you die that day on the road."

"Ah, Theresa, your suspicions disturb me, but since that is the custom among you, then so be it. At dawn, Dona Lianne shall pay for her sins."

The men nodded in silent agreement and wandered away to sleep, but Theresa smiled in triumph at Lianne before joining Domingo under his blanket.

"So I am to suffer because I married Raoul de Lovis." Lianne faced El Lince. She wished she could see his whole face, but the sombrero obscured it from her.

"Aren't you afraid?" he asked.

"Yes." Her whisper was low and strained, and her hands trembled.

"Do you trust me, Lianne?"

She didn't believe he asked her such an absurd question, but she realized she did trust him. "Yes."

"Then be watchful and on your guard. Ask me no questions, but know that I'll protect you."

Later that night, El Lince tapped her shoulder and rose from the blanket beside her. She stood with him and they quietly made their way through the maze of sleeping men. Lianne caught a glimpse of Theresa enfolded in Domingo's arms, but no one noticed them leave the campsite and head down the mountain path. At the bottom, Lianne discovered El Lince's horse waited, and Felix and Carmen were already mounted on his.

"Where are we going?" Lianne asked him when they rode through the starry night.

He sighed and his breath ruffled the auburn wisps of her hair. "To find your husband, *chica*. We ride toward Raoul de Lovis."

Lianne thought El Lince must wish to die. She couldn't believe she heard him correctly, but there was no doubt, they traveled in the same direction they had come.

"I imagine your husband is about a day's ride

from us," he said at one point. Soft pink light streaked the violet sky and bathed the landscape in the same hues.

Lianne rested her head against his hard chest, unable to comprehend the man. Why was he returning her to her husband?

El Lince read her mind before she asked the question aloud. "I must face de Lovis as an equal. I was wrong to kidnap you and Carmen. I allowed my pain to interfere with rational thought. Evidently you wished to be his wife and willingly gave yourself to him. I can't blame you for all of it."

"I don't understand what you're talking about."

"Don't worry. If you're lucky you never will."

When the sun blazed down upon them, El Lince and Felix stopped the horses by a cave at the foot of a mountain whose entrance had been covered with bramble bush. After Felix removed the brush, he led Carmen and the horse into the dark depths with El Lince's horse and its riders following.

"Only we know the cave is here," El Lince informed Lianne. "We'll rest here until evening. Then we'll start toward Pachuca."

Lianne didn't know if she wanted to return to Pachuca and Raoul, but she knew she had to. She had her daughter there and carried another child. There was no other alternative.

"I can't wait for a bath," Lianne said and meant it. It had been five days since she'd bathed.

"Me too," agreed Carmen.

Felix grinned. "Shall I tell them?" he asked El Lince. El Lince nodded.

"There is an underground pool in the cave. You may both bathe there."

"Really!" squealed Carmen. "Take me there right now. I demand it!"

"First we build a fire," El Lince said. "Then you ladies may bathe."

After a fire was made by Felix and El Lince,

everyone settled down for a few minutes by its warming flames. The cave's walls were illuminated by the soft glow. Lianne relaxed against the wall and thought the situation she found herself in strange. Here she sat in companionable silence with her kidnappers and wasn't in the least frightened. El Lince had saved her from the sting of the whip and had forfeited his position with the *banditos*. But why?

"I do wish to bathe," Carmen said and scratched at her neck.

El Lince turned to Lianne. "Do you want to bathe now?"

Lianne liked the feeling of cozy warmth which had invaded her body. She shook her head, and El Lince told Felix to take a torch and escort Carmen to the pool.

When they departed, Lianne said, "I think they might like to be alone."

"Ah, you're playing cupid." El Lince smiled.

"Carmen deserves some happiness, even if only for a few hours. Her life with her husband was horrible. I think the only reason she doesn't feel guilty over his death is because Diego deserved to die."

"Carmen killed him, didn't she?"

"Yes, she stabbed him when he tried to rape her."

"I owe Carmen my thanks. If she hadn't killed him, I would have."

"You knew Diego?"

He nodded. The sombrero obscured his eyes. "Very well."

He said nothing else, but from his biting tone, she decided it was a good thing Diego had died at Carmen's hands rather than El Lince's.

Lianne moved closer to the fire and made a futile attempt to see beneath his sombrero. "It's aggravating to speak to someone I can't see clearly. I wish you'd allow me to see your face."

"For your own safety, it's best you don't, Dona Lianne."

"How formal you are! The other night you weren't so cold."

"You made me lose my head."

She recalled the feel of his hands upon her and her response. She found herself blushing. "Do you lose your head often, El Lince? Theresa was one of your conquests, too."

"I admit she was, but I needed Theresa. She was a good friend to me, but I never loved her. I loved only one woman, and she betrayed me."

"I'm sorry," Lianne said, "but your past has nothing to do with me."

His silence gave her cause to feel that she was somehow responsible for whatever pain he carried inside him. She resented feeling this way, but she did owe him her thanks for saving her from the whip and thought perhaps he might not be as menacing as he seemed.

"I'm grateful to you for protecting me. I know you've ostracized yourself from your people for my sake. Why did you do it?"

His head turned in her direction. "Don't think I did it out of a sense of nobility. I only hate to see such beautiful flesh scarred."

She shrank at the venom in his voice and retreated to her place against the wall. He had certainly told her!

"You can turn around now," Carmen told Felix when she finished stepping into the breeches and pulling her poncho over her head. The water had chilled her but revitalized her. She shook her wet head. "I feel so clean now."

Felix turned around, having had to face in the opposite direction while Carmen bathed. But she didn't know that he had sneaked a look at her as the water lapped over her. In the torchlight she had seemed like a beautiful, voluptuous water nymph to him, and rage washed over him to think of the way Diego Gonzalez had abused her. But no longer. The man was dead, and Felix suddenly wished to make up for any pain she had suffered.

Carmen moved forward and laughed up into his face. "Whatever is wrong with you, Felix? You look so odd."

He wondered if she was able to see the desire on his face for her, read his thoughts. He wished she could. Things would be so much easier, but he knew Carmen was basically still innocent and had never tasted passion for a man. *Madre de Dios!* he thought to himself. I love her!

Unable to resist, he took her hand. The moment he touched her he knew he wanted her, that he'd never love anyone else. And when he bent and kissed her gently on the lips, he knew he must marry her and make her his own. Never mind that she was the daughter of Raoul de Lovis. He loved her. He did!

"Felix," she said breathlessly. "Why did you kiss me?"

Should he tell her and risk being called a *lepero* in that haughty voice of hers? "Carmen, I . . . love you." There, he had said it.

"I love you, too," she said. "I've loved you since that day you carried me across the mud puddle."

Felix didn't believe his ears, but there was no doubt she loved him when she threw her arms around him and pressed her lush body against his, kissing him with a passion which equaled his own. "Love me now, Felix. Please," she begged between drugging kisses.

He groaned her name but put her from him. "No."

"You love me, don't you?"

"*Sí*, more than my life, but will you marry me, Carmen? I want you as my wife, and I fear I'm not good enough for you."

"Silly *lepero*." She laughed her delight. "I'll marry you and live on the streets with you."

"I'll be a good husband to you, Carmen. I swear this on my mother's grave."

"Then make love to me. Now."

Her pleading nearly pushed him over the edge. He wanted to love her then and there, but he resisted. Carmen deserved to be his wife when he loved her, and he hoped he might erase the ugliness of Diego's memory when he made her his.

"Carmen, when I make you my wife, it will be in all ways, but I want the experience to be beautiful for you. I want our love to blossom in a special place, a place filled with flowers and sunshine. When I love you, my ring shall be on your finger. Then I'll know you are truly my wife. I have relatives in Vera Cruz. We can make a life there."

"That sounds wonderful," Carmen said. "I love you, Felix. But what about El Lince? How will we escape from him?"

"El Lince is my friend and yours, also. He'll let me leave with you today. I think it's time you knew all about the man who calls himself El Lince."

Chapter 48

Lianne couldn't believe Carmen and Felix were gone. She stared in disbelief at the cave entrance an hour later, unable to grasp the fact that El Lince had allowed them to leave. She remembered Carmen's hug and parting words to her, whispered in her ear, "El Lince isn't what he seems to be. He had been badly hurt. Remember that when you learn the truth. He'll need you."

At the moment Lianne didn't care what El Lince needed, she yearned to be free of him, but she felt his gaze upon her though he pretended to be occupied with wolfing down a piece of bread he had taken from his saddlebag.

"Your supper's waiting," he said and nodded toward her bread.

She turned gleaming green eyes upon him. "That's not food fit for a pig!"

"It's the best I could do," he said.

Lianne shivered though the fire still blazed. She envied Carmen her freedom, but it seemed that El Lince wasn't about to free her. Did he really intend to return her to Raoul, or was he playing a perverted game with her? She shivered again and El Lince noticed.

He got up and went to the bag which hung over his horse and took out a small silver flask. "Here." He threw it to her, and it landed in her lap. "Drink some of this. It will warm you."

"What is it?"

"Whiskey, of course."

"Of course," she said, as if she were somehow supposed to know he preferred it. Lianne opened the flask and drank the warming brew. She coughed, unable to catch her breath.

"You never could get the taste for it," he said.

When she finished her coughing spell, she eyed him. "How do you know that I dislike whiskey?"

"I don't." He practically growled at her and finished eating his bread.

Lianne, however, began to get used to the whiskey and she swallowed a bit more than she had intended. After a while, she didn't feel cold any more, but she was unaware that her face was becomingly flushed or that her voice was rather thick when she spoke.

"You're a strange man," she said to El Lince.

He didn't say anything to her, but she hadn't expected him to. She suddenly felt talkative and lonely for her child, for Daniel. What was there about this man that made her feel familiar? At the moment she didn't bother to question it, she only wanted the chance to say what had been in her heart for so long.

"I loved someone once, too," she told him. "But Raoul snatched me away from him. Then when I thought I might find happiness, the man I loved was killed . . . by banditti." She involuntarily sneered.

"What parted you and the man you loved?" he asked and startled her with his question.

"My husband." Lianne sighed and rested her head against the wall of the cave. "He arranged it so that Daniel would think I didn't love him. I did love him, and tried to tell him Raoul drugged me, but he wouldn't listen to me. So . . ." She heaved another sigh. "I lost him."

El Lince retreated into silence again, then he said, "Your Daniel was very stupid."

"No, only human."

Lianne felt sleepy, and she closed her eyes. Before long she slept. When she opened her eyes again, it was nearly daylight. Small streaks of sunlight poured into the cave's opening not covered by the brush. She looked around but didn't see El Lince. Standing up, she moved to the opening, pushing brush aside, and looked out. She still didn't see him.

The thought struck her that this was the perfect time to make her escape. His horse was only feet from her. She could ride away and return to the hacienda. He'd never be able to catch her, but for a reason she never knew, she turned back into the depths of the cave and picked up the torch Felix had used the day before. She put it into the fire until it glowed brightly and she made her way deeper into the cave's dark confines.

From a short distance away, she heard the slight rush of water. Walking toward the sound, she halted when she saw El Lince's naked body immersed in the sparkling water. Another torch was attached to the wall, and she wondered why he hadn't bothered to inquire if she wished to bathe. From where she stood, she observed him without his knowing it. On the ground beside the clear water his clothes and his sombrero were in a pile. Now she would see if he was as handsome as she thought.

Inching closer but hidden behind a rock, she saw the broadness of his back, the sleek wetness of his dark hair against his neck. But she gave a quiet gasp to see a long scar which ran in a diagonal direction from his right shoulder blade to the waist. Was this another wound inflicted by one of Raoul's henchmen? Had Diego done this? That would account for his hatred of both men. She wondered this in silence as she watched him.

When El Lince turned toward the torchlight and faced in her direction, she saw other scars on his broad chest. Though dark chest hair covered them, the scars could be clearly seen. Pity filled her, and she almost decided to leave him in peace when she stopped short.

Lianne blinked. El Lince had light-colored eyes. Why would a Mexican bandit have eyes that gleamed like gray crystal? Her heart began to beat faster. She had known only one man with ocean gray eyes, only one man who could make her pulses race, her body feel like jelly. But he's dead! she screamed to herself. However, at that moment, she realized he wasn't. Daniel bathed in the pool. He was alive!

Why has he done this to me? she asked herself. However, she knew it was done out of pain. Carmen must have known the truth when she left and told her in the only way she could. Had she, herself, suspected El Lince was Daniel the whole time? Is that why she had melted when he touched her, why she hadn't fled when she had the chance?

She wondered if he had forgiven her for acting like a whore in Raoul's arms in San Augustin de las Cuevas. He had said "your Daniel was very stupid." Did that mean he now understood she had never stopped loving him? She must know the truth.

Stepping from behind the rock, she slowly walked to the side of the pool. Daniel looked up but seeing her, he turned his face away.

"You didn't tell me you were going to bathe," she said.

"Sorry, but you were asleep."

The gruffness of his voice shook her for an instant. Daniel had had such a warm voice, and now it was gone because of Raoul. But she still loved Daniel, and nothing mattered to her at the moment but that he see she loved him.

Lianne laid the torch against the wall and pulled off her poncho. This was followed by the peasant blouse, her sandals and then the pants. When Daniel heard the soft splash in the pool, he turned.

He watched her, and for the moment, he had apparently forgotten she could see his full face. She moved her hands in the waist-deep water, then sensuously entangled them in the mat of hair on his chest. Her mouth began a slow deliberate trail of kisses along one of the scars.

"What are you doing?" he rasped.

"I'm seducing you, El Lince."

"You really are a whore!" He grabbed a handful of auburn hair but didn't push her away. "You had a chance to escape, I gave it to you; but since you didn't run, I'll give you what you're begging for, Dona Lianne."

"I know," she said weakly and her body melted when his lips claimed hers in a kiss so hard and filled with fire, she drooped against him.

Lianne moaned when his mouth moved from her lips to the sensitive cord along her neck, then lower until his mouth suckled at her breasts. She threaded her fingers through the darkness of his hair.

"You like this, *chica*?" he asked.

"Yes, yes," she moaned.

"Then I'll give you more."

Not realizing what he was doing, Lianne gasped when he lifted her from her feet and carried her to a blanket which lay on the ground. The pool's surface was almost even with the ground, and after he laid her on the blanket, he stayed in the water. Pulling her toward him, her calves dangled in the cool depths while he opened her legs. She felt his lips moving along her knees, then up her inner thighs until she felt his tongue lap at the inner core of her.

Lianne moaned and writhed, almost pulling from him, but he held her hips in place while he pleasured her. Tiny sparks ignited within her, threatening to explode, and when she would have, he lifted her head from her softness.

"Whose whore are you?" he growled. "Who do you belong to?"

"I'm yours!" she gasped.

He moved out of the water and positioning

himself on his knees, he slipped into her and then pulled her up so that she sat upon his lap as he worked his sensuous magic over her body. Within the glow of the torches, they rode the crest of desire, and when his love spilled into her, she clawed at his back as she found her own ecstasy.

"Daniel! Daniel! I love you so!" she cried.

"You knew it was me."

"Yes. Oh, Daniel, why have you done this?"

"Because I saw you making love to Raoul and heard you say you loved him."

"But I told you what happened. Can you forgive me."

"Do you love him, Lianne?"

She sighed and kissed his mouth. "I love only you, Daniel. Forever. I nearly died when I thought you had been killed."

"Raoul's orders, Diego's handiwork. I was ill for months afterward. Theresa found me and nursed me to health."

"I'm grateful to her," Lianne said. "But a body was found."

"I don't know about that. Apparently Diego hadn't done his job well and didn't wish Raoul to know. So, he must have killed someone else. I wish I had had the chance to kill Diego. But I will kill Raoul. I swear it!"

Lianne still sat on his lap and held onto him, afraid he'd leave her. "What will you do about me? I don't want to return to Raoul. I love you, Daniel. We can be together now."

In the light she saw Daniel's eyes gleamed. "Yes, Lianne, we can be together now. But I have to face Raoul to free you from him. I owe him a great deal and I wish to repay him."

"I want only you," she whispered and kissed him.

The click of rifles broke the silence and startled them. *"Querida,* how good to see you, and Daniel." Raoul stood in front of them, his men lined up behind him. "I hate to break up this amorous coupling, but I fear I must."

Striding forward, Raoul pulled Lianne's naked body from Daniel's and threw the blanket at her. "Cover yourself!" he ordered, but before she could pull the blanket around her, his men encircled Daniel.

He turned toward Daniel. "Take a long look at my beautiful wife," he told him. "This is the last time you'll see or sample her flesh. Lianne is mine, and I intend to keep her as mine. But you've committed the worst sin, Daniel. You coupled with my pregnant wife, so your suffering shall be greater than anything you can imagine."

Raoul pulled the blanket around her and picked her up. She screamed as he carried her from the cave.

Chapter 49

"I want to see Désirée!" Lianne demanded.

"You're insane if you think I will bring your bastard to you after this. If I choose to keep you locked in here until Doomsday, I will!" Raoul eyed Lianne in contempt. He was forbidding as he stood in the center of their bedroom with whip in hand. The ruffled white shirt and black breeches and boots only enhanced the diabolical image. Lianne had never seen him this enraged before, but she had no fear he'd hurt her. She carried his child, and he wanted the child more than anything. However, she hadn't bargained on being tied to the bed like a trussed hen, but she knew he was taking no chances she'd escape him. She also knew his wrath wouldn't touch her as long as she was pregnant, but Daniel wouldn't be so lucky. Even now she wondered if Raoul had killed him yet.

Almost as if he read her thoughts, he peered down at her. "Are you concerned about your paramour?"

"You know I am. Where is he? What have you done to Daniel?"

"Nothing, but he shall suffer the punishment he deserves. I once wished to be rid of him, and would have succeeded if stupid Diego hadn't botched things, but now I shall enjoy watching Daniel Flanders die a long, painful death. And you will witness his last hours, Lianne."

"No!"

"Sí, and if you cry out, he'll suffer more."

He cracked the whip on the bedpost as if to give credence to his words. "I love you, Lianne. God only knows why, but I do. You've put me through more hell than any woman I've ever had, but I'll gladly accept what fate offers me to keep you."

"Oh, Raoul," she said bitingly, "you've never loved anyone but yourself. You want me because I never wanted you. I know how you treat the women you love, the ones you desire. I heard all about Inez, the shoemaker's daughter. Didn't you know she was Felix's sister? Perhaps Felix will return and take his vengeance out upon you. And then Elena. Poor Elena, the mother of your daughter. I know you poisoned her. Think how Carmen will feel if she learns you killed her mother, wonder what she might do to you. And then me, Raoul. Remember what you've taken from me, the pain you've caused me. You may love me, but I'm the one you should fear."

He shook his head. "No, *querida.* When Daniel is dead, you'll love me, desire me."

"I only desire to see you burn in hell."

His hand tightened on the whip, but he smiled coldly. "Daniel will be dead before the day is over, Lianne." He turned and went to the door. "Josephine, come here!"

Within seconds, Josephine arrived. "Prepare Dona Lianne for the execution of her lover. "Raoul left the room.

Josephine looked stricken to find Lianne nude and tied to the bed. "What has he done?" she cried.

"Raoul's insane," Lianne said calmly. "I must get away from here. I have to help Daniel."

"That won't do any good. Already the men prepare the amalgamation court for the execution."

"What do they plan to do with him?" Raoul hadn't discussed the details with her.

Josephine shivered. "A horrible death, Dona

Lianne. Monsieur Flanders is to be laid upon the ore mixture, his hands and legs tied to stakes. Then the mules are to . . . to . . ." Her voice faltered.

Lianne had seen the teams of mules drive back and forth over the mixture to smooth it out many times. "Only Raoul could think of something so horrible. I must escape. Please help me."

The woman shook her head. "I can't. There's nothing to be done but dress as Don Raoul requested."

"You're a spineless woman," Lianne snapped.

"I know, but I watched my husband die at the hands of a man very much like your husband, and I don't wish to suffer like that."

Josephine took a bright pink dress from the wardrobe. "Don Raoul requested you dress festively."

Lianne considered knocking Josephine down when Josephine untied her bonds, but she resisted because she heard Raoul outside the bedroom. Instead she dressed and allowed the woman to fix her hair, then Raoul entered the room again, a smile on his face.

"You're beautiful, *querida*." He gave her his arm. "Our afternoon enjoyment is waiting on the amalgamation court." They breezed from the room as if they were to attend an opera in Mexico City, but Lianne wondered how she'd find a way to help Daniel. However, when she saw Daniel tied like an animal in the muddy paste on the court, she knew she'd be unable to help him at all. Raoul's men surrounded him with drawn rifles, and the team of mules Raoul intended to use to trample Daniel to death waited.

"If you sob or scream one word to him, his suffering will be greater. Understand?" Raoul said.

Lianne nodded, too overcome to say anything. The man she loved lay like a statue, his bronzed body covered in ragged breeches and baking in the afternoon sun. Was this how it was to end for them?

Raoul pulled her alongside him, and they stopped on the side of the patio. Raphael, the mine overseer, came forward. A worried frown creased his forehead.

"Don Raoul, are you sure about this? The men feel like murderers."

"No one disobeys Raoul de Lovis! Get on with it!"

"*Sí, sí.*" Raphael shook his head and walked towards the man who controlled the team.

Lianne kept her gaze on Daniel, and he watched her from his ocean gray eyes. She saw love in their depths, a love which would defeat Raoul, even in death, and words weren't necessary to convey that love.

"It won't be long now," Raoul said.

She didn't look at Raoul, only at Daniel. Suddenly she felt a slight tremor. Was she trembling so badly she imagined her feet moved? But Raoul was absorbed by the spectacle of Daniel as he waited to die.

Raoul nodded to Raphael to move the team, but the man who controlled the mules shook his head.

"What's wrong?" Raoul called.

"Alberto refuses to take part in this, Don Raoul!" Raphael called back.

Raoul ordered Alberto to come forward, and when the man stood in front of him with a defiant expression on his face, Raoul took his knife from his belt and stabbed the man in the heart.

Lianne screamed and would have fainted, but Raoul held her up with his other arm. "Take this insolent dog away!"

Some men gathered and silently removed the dead man, but their faces were filled with hatred. Lianne wondered why none of them could see Raoul was insane. Was she the only one?

"Raphael, you take charge of the mules!" Raoul ordered.

It was evident Raphael didn't wish to do this, but he also didn't want to die. So, he took the harnesses in his hand and urged the mules forward. At first, the animals balked. "What is the matter with them?" Raoul screamed.

Raphael said he didn't know, but after a few seconds, the mules crept closer to Daniel.

"Ah, *querida,* take a last look at your lover's body. Now it is intact, but in another few hours there will be very little of him left."

"Beware of me, Raoul," Lianne said, her voice breaking, "because I shall kill you."

"An empty threat, Lianne," he said, appearing unconcerned.

As Raphael continued on his course, Lianne cringed. She sensed Daniel's fear, and the tears streamed freely down her face. She loved him so much, and he suffered this fate because he loved her. When the mules were inches away from Daniel's legs, she turned her head away and heaved a sob.

Raoul took her chin and roughly pulled her face toward the scene before her. "Watch him suffer, Lianne! Watch and remember!"

Lianne felt weak, sick, as if she were dying inside.

Without warning the sound of gunfire splintered the air. Everyone turned toward the mountains, the direction the shots came from. Lianne held her breath to see a group of men on horseback, riding fast, and shouting, "Surrender de Lovis! Surrender!"

She recognized the group as the bandits who followed El Lince, and leading them was Felix!

Raoul shouted to his men, "Fire upon them!"

But Lianne knew this was her chance. She screamed to the men, "Fight with them against Raoul de Lovis. Free your family, your friends, from the mine!"

A cheer went up in the courtyard, and the men rushed forward to open the gates for Felix and his group. But before Lianne grasped the implications of this, Raoul pulled her behind a shed. He picked her up and ran fast toward the ravine alongside the mine.

"Let me go!" she railed at him.

"Never! You're mine, Lianne!"

Raoul ran faster than she ever thought it possible
for a man to run. They rounded the viaduct, then went
up the hillside to an area filled with trees and foliage.
Her hair caught on a branch, but Raoul continued,
unaware of Lianne's agonizing screams as a curl was
ripped away.

She cried from pain, from fear, from hate, when
he finally stopped before a large tree. To her astonishment Raoul pulled on a branch and the tree opened.
They stepped into a dark crevice, and he set her down
and dragged her along the dimly lit passageways.

"Where are we?" she asked and thought he had
wrenched her arm from its socket he pulled so hard.

"In the mine, but no one will find us here,
querida. This is a passage beneath the mine itself. I
thought this might happen one day, so I prepared
well."

She understood what he meant when they stepped
into a small room, complete with bed, wash basin, a
change of clothes for him and her.

"We can't stay here forever. What about food?"
she asked.

"I'll take care of that. There is a tunnel which
leads to the kitchen. I can sneak in and out at night.
We'll stay here until the rabble have departed."

"Raoul, you're insane!"

"Insane over you." He tenderly touched her
cheek. "Daniel may live, Lianne, but he'll never have
you. When all is clear, I'll take you away from here.
We'll return to Spain, or perhaps go to Brazil. But
you're my wife and the mother of my child. I don't
intend to give you up."

A sudden earth tremor caused her to stumble and
fall beside the bed. Raoul held his ground and helped
her up.

"A slight earth tremor. Nothing to worry about."

"Raoul, we must get out of here!"

"We stay!"

From the corner of her eye, Lianne spotted a large candlestick. When another tremor rumbled beneath them, she purposely fell toward the stick and picked it up. Its heaviness weighed her down, but Raoul had fallen also, and lifting it she hit the side of his head.

Blood spewed from his temple, and he groaned. Without looking where she headed, Lianne ran out of the small room and down the torchlit corridors. She didn't know where she ran, and no idea where the corridors led. She felt herself running upward and realized she must be entering the heart of the mine.

No one was working, not a soul was in sight. She noticed the heavy bags the Indians carried on their shoulders lay abandoned on the ground, as if they had been dropped in haste. But where was the passageway which led to the stairs and fresh air. She knew she had to get out of there if what she thought might happen came to pass. She didn't want to die in an earthquake, and she prayed harder than she had ever prayed in her life. She had to find her way out and get to the hacienda and her child. The house had been built to withstand earthquakes, but she knew that if one struck while she was in the mine, she'd perish.

She ran to what she thought was an opening, but before he neared it, an arm reached out and grabbed her.

"No!" she screamed.

"Lianne, it's Daniel!"

She quieted and looked into the face of the man she loved. Sobbing overcame her and she clung to him. "Take me from here, please!"

"Where's Raoul?" he asked.

"Forget about him. I hit him on the head. I only want to get Désirée and leave."

"Not until I even the score with de Lovis."

"*Sí*, Daniel," came Raoul's voice from behind him. "But the score will be settled in my favor."

Raoul staggered forward in the torchlight. Blood

dripped from his temple, and his glittering dark eye impaled them. Lianne jumped back and pulled at Daniel but he didn't budge.

"No matter how you die, Raoul, you deserve worse. But even if you kill me, you'll never escape from here. Felix knows about your secret tunnel, and the men will soon swarm into it and drag you away."

Raoul's diabolical laugh echoed over them. "No one touches Raoul de Lovis. He is invincible!"

Raoul grabbed for the knife in his boot and would have thrown it at Daniel, but Daniel was faster and warded it off with the butt of the rifle he carried.

Aiming the gun at Raoul, he fired. Raoul laughed again. "I told you de Lovis is invincible."

He advanced then, and Lianne thought he hadn't been hurt, but blood covered his white shirt like a red blanket. Still he moved forward, a terrified look in his eye.

"Lianne. Lianne. I'm dying," he said and collapsed by her feet.

"Leave him," Daniel growled when she bent down.

"I can't," she said.

She gazed into Raoul's face. He smiled at her, and though she could see death on his countenance, the smile was warm and rich. A part of her wondered about the man he could have become if he had only allowed real love to touch him and not manipulated the people he wished to possess.

He clutched her hand. "*Querida,* my Lianne, you do care about me. I know you do." His breathing grew ragged. "Take care of my son, raise him to be a decent man . . . unlike his father."

"How do you know I'll have a son?" she asked.

He smiled weakly. "Raoul de Lovis gets whatever he wants." A spasm of bloody coughing seized him. She cradled his head in her lap, not caring that he stained her pink gown with his blood.

He sighed. "Tell . . . tell Carmen . . . I love her."

This request brought tears to Lianne's eyes. If only he had told Carmen this before.

Lianne felt the earth tremble. "Go," Raoul said. "Take your Daniel and leave before the mine caves in."

Lianne shook her head. "We'll take you with us."

"No. Go. You were right, *querida*. I should have been wary of you. I die from love."

"Raoul . . ."

"Go." His voice was a whisper. "Take her, Daniel."

Daniel helped her up, but she bent down again and kissed Raoul. "I'll take care of our son. I promise." Then Daniel whisked her from the mine just as a large trembling shook the earth.

They barely made it up the long flight of stairs leading outside, but inside the mine Raoul knew when the ceiling collapsed. After that, he knew nothing.

Chapter 50

Some small buildings on the hacienda were damaged, but the main house was left intact with only minor breakage of objects inside.

Lianne ran into the house and held Désirée in an iron-tight grasp, unable to believe that they were free to leave with Daniel. Felix joined them in the house, Carmen at his side. When Lianne told Carmen what Raoul had said before he died, Carmen wept.

"I loved him, too, but he was a strange man, a hard man to care for. Sometimes he was very evil," Carmen said.

Lianne agreed but resisted about telling her that Raoul had ordered Elena's death. She felt it better the girl remember him with some affection. "I believe he wanted to die, Carmen."

"What will you do now?" Carmen asked Lianne.

"I'll return to Louisiana," Lianne said, but wondered if Daniel still wanted her. He stood apart from her and Carmen. He wore the ragged pants and seemed quite ominous and strangely silent.

She stood up and walked over to him. "Do you still want me?" she asked, unaware that Carmen and Felix had discreetly left the room. "I intend to have Raoul's baby."

"I know."

"You didn't answer my question. Do you still want me?"

She trembled so hard, he couldn't help but notice. Daniel enfolded her in his arms and kissed her lips with such warmth and tenderness that she started to cry.

"What's wrong now?" he asked in the gruff voice she didn't mind any longer.

"You do want me, Daniel!" She threw her arms around him.

"Never doubt that, my sweet."

Daniel and Lianne married in Mexico City a few days later. Then they started for Green Meadows with Maria and Désirée. Josephine had been sent packing without references, and Lianne didn't care what happened to her. Felix and Carmen remained on the hacienda, because Lianne had turned all her inheritance as Raoul's widow over to Carmen. She knew that with Felix, as Carmen's husband and new owner of the mine, the people would be content.

When they arrived at Green Meadows, Dera's happiness and love overwhelmed them. "I knew from the moment you arrived here," Dera told Lianne, "that you and Daniel were destined to be together. I'm so very happy."

Lianne was happy for Dera, also, because no sooner had they settled in, than Paul and Allison with the twins and their little girl showed up on the doorstep. But that wasn't the last surprise. Doctor Markham put in an appearance, and he and Dera announced they would soon be married and move to Williamsburg.

"Seems like you'll be the mistress here," Daniel said to Lianne when they stood on the porch that evening and listened to the gentle lapping of the river.

"And you'll be the official master," she said and smiled at him. "Aren't you happy your mother is marrying again?"

"Yes, I am, but my father was part of her life for

so long. He still seems to be in this house. I imagine I even hear his voice at times.'' He grinned. ''I used to sound a little like him once.''

''I like how you sound now, how you look, how you feel.''

Daniel pulled Lianne into his arms. ''I love you, Lianne Flannery.''

''Flannery? That's a surprise.''

''I'm surprised too, but I think it's time I buried my animosity toward my father, the past. I don't feel the need to bury my troubles in a bottle any longer, not since finding you again. Daniel Flannery is a happy man.''

At that second, the child growing within Lianne kicked, and Daniel felt it as he held her in his arms. ''The baby's a fiesty little boy,'' she said.

''Yes,'' he agreed and tilted her chin. Daniel loved her and would love this child. Though it wasn't his own, he had told her that the child was part of her, and now part of him. ''But how can you be certain it's a boy?'' he asked her.

''Because Raoul de Lovis always gets what he wants.''

''No,'' Daniel said. ''He doesn't.''

When his lips sought hers and claimed them, binding her to him in loving ecstasy, she knew he was right.

FOR THE FINEST
IN CONTEMPORARY
WOMEN'S FICTION,
FOLLOW LEISURE'S LEAD

2310-5	**PATTERNS**	$3.95 US, $4.50 Can
2304-0	**VENTURES**	$3.50 US, $3.95 Can
2291-5	**GIVERS AND TAKERS**	$3.25 US, $3.75 Can
2279-6	**MARGUERITE TANNER**	3.50 US, 3.95 Can
2268-0	**OPTIONS**	$3.75 US, $4.50 Can
2257-5	**TO LOVE A STRANGER**	$3.75 US, $4.50 Can
2250-8	**FRAGMENTS**	$3.25
2249-4	**THE LOVING SEASON**	$3.50
2230-3	**A PROMISE BROKEN**	$3.25
2227-3	**THE HEART FORGIVES**	$3.75 US, $4.50 Can
2217-6	**THE GLITTER GAME**	$3.75 US, $4.50 Can
2207-9	**PARTINGS**	$3.50 US, $4.25 Can
2196-x	**THE LOVE ARENA**	$3.75 US, $4.50 Can
2155-2	**TOMORROW AND FOREVER**	$2.75
2143-9	**AMERICAN BEAUTY**	$3.50 US, $3.95 Can

Make the Most of Your Leisure Time
with
LEISURE BOOKS

Please send me the following titles:

Quantity	Book Number	Price
_____	_____	_____
_____	_____	_____
_____	_____	_____
_____	_____	_____
_____	_____	_____

If out of stock on any of the above titles, please send me the alternate title(s) listed below:

_____	_____	_____
_____	_____	_____
_____	_____	_____
_____	_____	_____

Postage & Handling _____

Total Enclosed $_____

☐ Please send me a free catalog.

NAME _____
(please print)

ADDRESS _____

CITY _____ STATE _____ ZIP_____

Please include $1.00 shipping and handling for the first book ordered and 25¢ for each book thereafter in the same order. All orders are shipped within approximately 4 weeks via postal service book rate. PAYMENT MUST ACCOMPANY ALL ORDERS.*

*Canadian orders must be paid in US dollars payable through a New York banking facility.

Mail coupon to: **Dorchester Publishing Co., Inc.
6 East 39 Street, Suite 900
New York, NY 10016
Att: ORDER DEPT.**